D0275621

A Bitter Legacy

By Lynda Page and available from Headline

Evie
Annie
Josie
Peggie
And One For Luck
Just By Chance
At The Toss Of A Sixpence
Any Old Iron
Now Or Never
In For A Penny
All Or Nothing
A Cut Above
Out With The Old
Against The Odds
No Going Back
Whatever It Takes
A Lucky Break
For What It's Worth
Onwards And Upwards
The Sooner The Better
A Mother's Sin
Time For A Change
No Way Out
Secrets To Keep
A Bitter Legacy

Lynda
PAGE

A Bitter Legacy

headline

Copyright © 2010 Lynda Page

The right of Lynda Page to be identified as the Author of
the Work has been asserted by her in accordance with the
Copyright, Designs and Patents Act 1988.

First published in 2010 by
HEADLINE PUBLISHING GROUP

1

Apart from any use permitted under UK copyright law, this
publication may only be reproduced, stored, or transmitted, in any
form, or by any means, with prior permission in writing of the
publishers or, in the case of reprographic production, in accordance with
the terms of licences issued by the Copyright Licensing Agency.

All characters in this publication are fictitious and any resemblance
to real persons, living or dead, is purely coincidental.

Cataloguing in Publication Data is available from the British Library

ISBN 978 0 7553 4906 7

Typeset in StempelGaramond by Palimpsest Book Production Limited,
Falkirk, Stirlingshire

Printed and bound in Great Britain by
Clays Ltd, St Ives plc

Headline's policy is to use papers that are natural, renewable and
recyclable products and made from wood grown in sustainable forests.
The logging and manufacturing processes are expected to conform to the
environmental regulations of the country of origin.

HEADLINE PUBLISHING GROUP
An Hachette UK Company
338 Euston Road
London NW1 3BH

www.headline.co.uk
www.hachette.co.uk

For The Godfathers
Matthew Wright and Gavin Eyres

If friends were bought in shops, I would bankrupt
myself to buy you both.

With all my love
Lynda

PORTSMOUTH CITY COUNCIL	
C800432863	
HJ	10-Sep-2010
AF	£19.99
9780755349067	

CHAPTER ONE

1961

In the dank, pitch-black cupboard under the stairs, Camella Rogers fought to slow her breathing, calm the pounding of her heart, stop herself from shaking, terrified that the slightest sound would alert her assailant to her whereabouts. She froze rigid as a frenzied voice bellowed: 'I know you're here! Now I'm not in the mood for games . . . show yourself before I get *really* angry. Then you'll be sorry, believe me!'

The crash of a dining-chair being overturned followed, to underline the seriousness of the threat.

Cam hadn't yet recovered from their last altercation; still wasn't sure which had hurt her most: the physical pain she had suffered or the emotional wound inflicted by the person who should be the closest to her in the world. As if in reminder, a sharp stabbing pain pierced her temple, which showed the dark purple and yellowing bruise of a recent blow from a fist. Cam gave a violent shudder, not relishing the thought of a repeat performance, possibly more ferocious than the last. She feared it would come, though, if she didn't succumb to the demand being made of her. But then, how could she when she hadn't got what was being sought from her?

She heard the pounding of footsteps descending the stairs, a door opening, then steps crossing the room above. Her assailant was in Cam's bedroom. A thud overhead. Cam knew it was from knees hitting the wooden floor. She was being looked for under her bed. Then there was the sound of her wardrobe door opening, and moments later a bang as it was angrily slammed shut. The footsteps

1

pounded out of her room, down the short corridor and into the bedroom next-door. More muffled sounds of searching and murmurs of displeasure reached her hiding place.

Cam's fear mounted. On hearing the back gate open, suspecting who was arriving through it, her survival instincts had kicked in. Without further thought she had hidden herself, in the hope of avoiding a confrontation until she'd had more time to come up with a way to satisfy them. But there were only a few places in a two-bedroomed terrace house where a person could hide themselves, and it was just a matter of time before she was discovered.

The footsteps were coming back down the stairs now. Cam stiffened, holding her breath to freeze herself completely still. The footsteps stopped. For a moment all was quiet. The next thing she knew the door of the cupboard was yanked open, daylight flooded in, and for a moment she was blinded. Then her eyes became accustomed to the glare and she found herself staring into the furious eyes of her granddaughter.

CHAPTER TWO

Cam sought frantically for a way to defuse this explosive situation. The only thing she could think of was to look mortally relieved to see her granddaughter and say to her, 'Oh, thank goodness you found me, dear. I was beginning to think I'd be stuck in this dreadful place for hours. The door shut behind me after I came in . . . must have been the wind . . . I couldn't get it open again. I shall have to ask Brian to have a look at it. I was looking for . . . er . . . rags to use for dusters. There's an old sheet in here somewhere that'll do the job.'

Belinda Rogers, her slight figure dressed beatnik-style in fitted black Capri pants ending at the calf, green shirt with sleeves turned back to just before her elbows, a spotted scarf knotted around her neck and flat black pumps on her feet, shot a disparaging glance at the handbag her grandmother was clutching tightly to her chest.

'And you needed your handbag with you to look for an old sheet?' she replied, a sneer twisting her plain, narrow face beneath a mop of curly red hair which she had tried to tame into an elfin cut.

Cam looked blankly down at the offending article for a moment before lifting her gaze back to Belinda, saying, 'Oh, I didn't realise I'd picked it up. Must be getting dottled in my old age.'

A look of impatience on her face, the girl snapped, 'Just cut it out, I don't want to be in the same room as you any longer than I have to be. Now hand over what I came for! Then I can be out of here and never have anything to do with you again.'

Cam flinched at the look of pure loathing in her granddaughter's eyes. If only she could persuade Belinda to listen to her version of

3

events, maybe she could make the girl realise that what she'd been told was nothing but wicked lies. Cam was convinced it had shocked Lindy so badly it had caused this sudden character change in her. But the girl was in no mood to listen to anything she had to say at the moment, and the way matters stood between them she would never be.

Not wanting to incite any further violence against her, Cam stretched her cramped legs then crawled reluctantly out of the cupboard where she had hidden amidst a collection of household paraphernalia amassed over her forty-nine years. She straightened herself slowly while her granddaughter, who only a couple of days ago would have given her own life to save her grandmother's, stared at her coldly. She stuck out her hand, an expectant expression on her face.

An ashen-faced Cam gulped and, taking a deep breath, began nervously, 'Look, Lindy . . .'

'I'm not your Lindy,' Belinda hurled back at her. 'Since I found out the truth about you, you're no longer my grandmother. No longer anything to me, in fact. It sickens me to think I'm even related to you. Now, give me my savings book before I rip this house apart.'

Before Cam could stop her, she'd grabbed the handbag and tipped it up, quickly scanning the contents on the floor. Not seeing what she was desperately seeking, she fixed her eyes on her grandmother. 'I'll give you one more chance,' she threatened.

Cam stuttered, 'I wasn't lying, Lind— Belinda. I just can't find it.' She'd said the same thing when Lindy had turned up yesterday to demand her savings book and Cam had felt it was pointless trying to explain her suspicions as to who actually had the book. In the mood Lindy was currently in, she wouldn't believe her. 'I've looked high and low for it, honestly I have, but I just can't find it. I put it somewhere safe and can't remember where, that's all. It will come back to me, though. Please, just give me a bit more time,' she pleaded.

Lindy spat, 'How many places in this poky little hole can you hide something? You've been lying to me all my life and you're still lying to me now, even though I've found you out. You know where that book is, you just don't want to give it to me!' She shook her clenched fist at Cam and frenziedly shouted, 'I want my savings book. You've no right to be keeping what's mine from me.'

Cam cried, 'Please, just give me a bit more time . . . I'll find the book, I promise I will.' Though why she was promising that she didn't know. It wasn't possible, she knew that.

Just then there was a knock on the back door. It opened and a voice called out, 'Is everything all right, Cam? What's all the screaming and shouting about?'

Both women jumped and spun around to see their worried-looking neighbour appearing through the door from the kitchen. She was a sparrow-like woman, wearing a pale blue Crimplene shirt-waister dress, protected by a faded floral wraparound apron. Her sparse mousy hair was wrapped around a dozen or so pink rollers. She had a pair of old, oversized slippers on her feet that slip-slopped as she walked.

It was Lindy who quickly explained to the new arrival, 'Nan got stuck in the cupboard under the stairs. You must have heard her screaming and shouting, trying to attract someone's attention. She dropped her handbag and spilled everything out of it as she was getting out.'

June Brindle chuckled at Cam. 'Daft 'a'porth you are! Well, now I know no one's being murdered, I'll be back off to ready meself for bingo tonight. And that's what you should be doing, Cam, getting ready for tonight . . . not messing around getting yerself locked in cupboards. I'll meet you out the front as usual at seven.'

Cam knew that as soon as June disappeared Lindy's assault on her would resume, and couldn't face it. She grabbed her neigh-bour's arm. 'Stay and have a cuppa,' she urged her. 'You've time to have a cuppa with me, June . . . help me get over the shock of being stuck in that dark hole, thinking I'd be there all night.' Knowing her neighbour had a weakness for her Victoria sponge cake, Cam added by way of bribery, 'I've a slice of jam sponge to go with it.' Then she addressed Lindy. 'Would you like a cuppa and slice of cake too, dear?'

Lindy glared at her darkly, then pulled her grandmother out of earshot of their neighbour and whispered, 'You can *have* the money. You know how long it took me to save up that thirty quid . . . how many odd jobs for neighbours I did, and always saving half of my pocket money like you kept encouraging me to do. Now I know why!

I wasn't building a nest egg for myself, was I? It was for *you*. Well, I hope it brings you nothing but misery.'

As Lindy walked past June on her way to the front door she planted a smile on her face and said to her, ''Bye, Mrs Brindle. Hope you're lucky at the bingo tonight.'

June's small grey eyes sparkled and her sharp nose twitched. 'So do I, ducky. There's an accumulator jackpot of twenty quid and hopefully it's got my name on it . . . or yer gran's. Either way it doesn't matter as we always share any winnings among us. I'm really hankering after going to Butlin's Holiday Camp in Skeggy this summer. Joe ain't keen, reckons we can't afford it, but my share of the winnings would cover it nicely and he won't have any argument against that. See you soon then, love,' she said, giving Lindy a little wave as the girl went out of the front door.

'Such a lovely girl, your Lindy,' said June, munching greedily on a generous slice of cake a short while later. The two women were sitting opposite each other at Cam's well-scrubbed kitchen table. 'Never given you a minute's trouble, has she? She didn't look that happy to me, though, when she went off just now.'

June was looking at Cam, expecting her to say why. But Cam wasn't listening to her, too deeply immersed in her own worrying thoughts. Lindy had led her to believe just now that she wasn't coming back. How then would Cam ever have the chance to make her see that it wasn't her grandmother who had acted so cruelly towards her but the person who had told her such wicked lies?

Getting no response from her friend, June eyed her and said, 'You haven't listened to a word I've said. What's up, gel?' Getting no response, she urged, 'Cam?'

'Eh?' She looked at her friend blankly for a moment, before mentally shaking herself. 'Sorry, June. That . . . er . . . spell in the cupboard has rather shaken me up.'

Spotting the inflamed bruise on her friend's temple, June said, 'You gave your head a right knock when you was in there. You need to put some witch hazel on that.'

Cam smiled wanly at her. 'Thanks, I will.'

Having finished her cake, June drained the dregs from her cup.

'Thanks for the cake, love, it was delicious as always.' An excited spark glinted in her eyes. 'I'm off to finish getting ready. Just my hair to brush out and then a bit of lippy. You get a move on, too. We don't want to be late and risk not getting a decent seat.' She scraped back her chair and stood up. 'If you're ready before I am, come round. I've a drop of sherry left over from me grandson's Christening last Sunday.'

As much as she looked forward to her night at the bingo with Ann, June and the other women they met there, tonight Cam definitely wasn't in the mood to go out socialising, not with all she had on her mind. But then, neither was she in a position to turn her back on an opportunity of acquiring a substantial amount of money. What were the odds of her winning the top prize? Or any of the prizes for that matter? Pretty low, in her opinion. She had been going weekly to bingo for about five years now and had only won one line worth five shillings, which she had shared between them. And there was the entrance fee to consider. Only a few shillings but that money would go some way to paying Lindy back. 'I really don't feel up to going tonight, June. I've a terrible headache brewing,' she said.

June look downcast. 'Ahhh, Cam,' she moaned. 'We all have such a laugh. It won't be the same if you're not there. I've a really good feeling on me that we're in for a win tonight. Have a couple of aspirin and a glass of sherry round mine before we go. That'll soon sort you out.'

It was clear to Cam how disappointed June was that she wouldn't be part of tonight's jollifications, not to mention how her best friend Ann would take her no-show. Regardless, she just could not summon the energy to put on a brave face. 'No, really, I'm not up to it. It's bed for me tonight.'

June gave her a sharp look. Her neighbour, usually so full of get up and go, looked completely drained of life, as if she had lost everything she treasured. It must be some headache she was suffering, to make her look like she'd welcome death as a blessed relief. 'Well, I must admit, you don't look that great, but then neither would I if I'd locked meself in a cupboard and banged my head as hard as you must have to get that bruise.' She sighed. 'Bed is probably the best place for yer. I'll give your regards to the other gels. Hope yer feeling better tomorrow.'

It wasn't until June had shut the door behind her that Cam dropped her guard. Shoulders sagging in despair, she allowed the miserable, desolate tears she had been holding back to roll like a river down her face and splash on the table beneath.

How had it come to this? she screamed inside her mind. That her beloved granddaughter actually believed her to be a thief and a liar and had acted so viciously towards her . . . and there was nothing Cam could do to change that state of affairs. She had suffered much heartache in her life but none to compare with the emotional devastation she was suffering now.

She could blame the person whose vileness had corrupted her granddaughter's mind against her; could blame herself for the decisions she had made in the past that had turned out to be serious errors of judgement. But only one person was ultimately responsible – and he was faceless and nameless to her, and would forever remain so. His mindless actions had caused utter devastation, not only for Cam herself but for two other people he would never even know existed.

She wondered if he ever gave that night a thought; suffered any remorse over what he'd done; had any idea that his selfishness was to wreak such havoc on the life of the young girl he'd chosen as his victim.

Cam had managed to lock the memories of that night away in the back of her mind, barely thinking of them in her fierce desire to put it behind her. But tonight, her fragile emotions left her with no strength to fight the memories. Despite herself, her thoughts flew back to the events that had led her to this sorry situation . . .

CHAPTER THREE

1930

It was a dark, dank evening, the heavily laden sky threatening to overspill, but eighteen-year-old Cam did not notice. Neither was she bothered that she had left her umbrella behind in her lodgings, and risked a soaking. Humming a popular tune to herself, she hurried down the unlit towpath by the canal, desperate not to be late.

'Full of the joys of spring' went nowhere near describing her mood. She was absolutely elated! Adrian Chapin had finally asked her out on a date. That was where she was headed now, to meet him as arranged at eight o'clock in front of the Clock Tower in the centre of town. She'd so wanted to look her best and had fussed and fretted over her few decent items of clothing, trying everything on several times in several different combinations until she had settled on a pretty pink Peter Pan-collared blouse and an ivory A-line skirt. By the time she had applied her makeup and done her hair, Cam found she was running late and wouldn't get to the bus stop in time. Not wanting to leave Adrian standing waiting for her, she decided to walk, taking the short cut to town along the canal path.

Being the attractive young woman she was, this wasn't Cam's first date, but it was the first one that she thought might lead to better things. She and Adrian both worked for the GPO: Cam as a telephonist, Adrian in the accounts department. To his work colleagues he might appear the old-fashioned sort, judging by his sober clothes and serious appearance behind his horn-rimmed spectacles, but Cam had learned a bit about him in their encounters at work. Over a two-year period they had progressed from a brief

9

exchange of smiles while passing in corridors, to saying hello, and sometimes finding themselves at the same table in the canteen. As they had become on more familiar terms, they'd started to confide in each other. Cam realised Adrian's serious façade was something he displayed at work because he wanted to get on. Outside work he liked to do fun things and was a snazzy dresser.

For quite a while she had thought her interest in him was one-sided, but then his delight upon seeing her whenever their paths crossed became unmistakable. She instinctively knew it was just a matter of time before he plucked up the courage to ask her out. At long last he had done so, yesterday, just as they were leaving the canteen to return to their respective work stations. Pulling her out of earshot of the rest of their colleagues, Adrian had asked her if she fancied going with him to the pictures the following night. Cam had wanted to jump for joy but, thankfully, had managed a sedate 'Yes, I'd like that', and arrangements to meet had been made.

Anyone observing the confident-looking young woman hurrying on her way down the towpath that night would have assumed she came from a stable, loving background. But they would have been wrong. An only child, Cam was three years old when her father had been killed in the early years of the Great War. Her mother died only a year afterwards, from blood poisoning resulting from an untreated cut suffered while she worked as a sock turner in a hosiery factory. With no other relatives to care for her, Cam was taken under the wing of the local council. It wasn't until she was much older, and was able to understand the ways of the world, that Cam had realised she had been lucky in what happened to her next. The couple who ran the children's home, Albert and Rachael Cummings, were strict but fair. Unlike many other wardens of children's homes, they did their best to make the lives of their forty charges as comfortable and happy as possible. The children fortunate enough to be placed under the Cummings' care were taught by them that they might have lost their parents, one way or another, and have to be raised by strangers, but that didn't mean they weren't as good as any other children; just as capable of achieving whatever they set their mind on.

On leaving school it was time for the children to make their own way in the world. They were helped by the Cummings to obtain lodgings and jobs for themselves. The majority of the girls went to work in local factories, either at a machine or on a production line, but that idea didn't appeal to Cam. Office work did. It was usually considered out of their league by the orphanage girls, but in an endeavour to do her best for Cam, Rachael Cummings went out of her way to beg a favour from a friend whose daughter was a supervisor with the GPO. She could at least get Cam an interview with them, for the post of trainee telephonist, then the rest was up to her. Primed on how to act and what to say, and herself determined to get the job, Cam made a good impression on her interviewers. After several days of nail-biting, she received a letter confirming her success. She started her new job the following Monday, and at the same time moved into lodgings.

Her room was in a three-storey Victorian terrace house in the Fosse Road Central district of town, a once prosperous area that had over the last decade or so fallen into decline. It was small but clean, if not over-comfortable as the furniture and soft furnishings were old and worn. Her landlady was a prim elderly woman and Cam didn't need to be told that she would be keeping a beady eye on her new lodger, making sure she adhered to all the house rules or else she'd be out.

Three years later, at the age of eighteen, Cam had impressed her employers enough for them to promote her to senior telephonist level. The extra wage this brought with it meant she could afford to rent a place of her own. She had managed to get on well enough with her landlady, by making sure she never broke any of her strict house rules, but she was now holding down a responsible job and shouldn't be having to request permission from her landlady to stay out later than nine or give a reason why she wanted to invite her friends in for a chat. A small one-bedroomed flat, where the landlord did not live on the premises, would suit her nicely and she was on the lookout for one.

As Cam made her way to meet Adrian, her future looked bright and promising. Little did she know that in only a matter of seconds it was all going to be cruelly ripped from her.

When the blow came she was glancing at her watch, pleased to note that at her present pace she would reach her destination with minutes to spare. A heavy thump on the back of her head stunned her for a second. It felt as if the world had suddenly stood still. Then the pain hit her. Stars danced before her eyes. Everything suddenly went black.

CHAPTER FOUR

Cam's whole body hurt, every muscle, every fibre of it. Her head was pounding as if someone was systematically hitting her skull from inside with a sledge hammer. Hard, sharp things were sticking into her sides and back. She felt terribly cold and wet. In the distance she could hear the intermittent barking of a dog, then something wet was licking her face. She forced her eyes open. It took her a second or two to focus her vision and then she froze in terror to see a pair of brown eyes looking directly into hers. It took her a moment to realise the eyes belonged to a dog. Next thing she knew an elderly, shabby-looking man was bending over her, his face wreathed in concern. He was asking her if she was all right . . .

She couldn't be or she wouldn't hurt so much. Cam knew something had happened to her. But what? And where was she? 'Have I been run over?' she uttered, as that was the only thing she could think of.

'Not unless it was by a barge. You're by the canal. In the undergrowth off the towpath,' the old man told her in a cracked voice. 'D'yer think anything is broken, ducky?' he enquired.

Cam ached so much she wasn't sure. But what was she doing down by the canal? Then a memory returned to her. She'd been on her way to meet Adrian. He'd be waiting for her now, wondering where she was, maybe thinking she wasn't coming! She tried to struggle up while blurting out, 'What time is it? I'm going to be late . . . I must get off.' But the struggle to sit up was too much for her and despite herself she collapsed back, giving out a sharp cry of pain.

'I don't think yer going anywhere at the moment, lovey,' the old man told her. 'You've had a hell of a bad fall . . . must have to be in the state you're in now. Tripped somehow on a protruding stone in the towpath, but I'm not sure how you came to be such a distance into the undergrowth. In yer dazed state you must have crawled here, that's all I can think.'

Of all the questions rushing around Cam's mind, all that was paramount was the concern that Adrian would be waiting for her, thinking she wasn't coming. 'What time is it?' she urged.

'Oh, well, I left home just after eight fifteen to take Rover on his walk so it must be getting on for eight thirty by now. Let me try and help yer sit up?'

She'd been lying unconscious for over half an hour! Had she blacked out? Adrian would have assumed she hadn't bothered to turn up, and she'd waited so long for him to ask her out . . . Miserable fat tears welled in Cam's eyes. 'He'll think I've stood him up,' she wailed.

'I take it yer mean yer boyfriend? Well, I'm sure the lad will understand when he finds out you met with an accident on the way. Let's try and sit you up and assess what damage you've caused yerself.'

With difficulty, Cam did her best to ease herself upright enough for him to slip his arm underneath her. While she clung on to him they managed to get her into a sitting position. She felt dizzy and sick.

The old man looked at her searchingly. Despite the darkness of the night, he could see she was in a sorry state. There was dried blood around the scratches on her face where branches and twigs must have caught her. Her stockings were ripped and her clothes sopping wet from the deluge of rain they'd had a while earlier, and caked in mud. 'D'yer think yer've broken anything?' he enquired.

One at a time Cam gingerly moved her arms and legs. Nothing appeared to be broken, thank God, just badly aching and sore. And her head was still pounding like mad, especially the back of it. Suddenly a memory stirred and she raised her hand. She felt a good-sized lump which was very tender to her light touch. She proclaimed, 'I didn't have an accident. I was hit on the back of the head.'

'What . . . yer mean you were attacked?'

All thoughts of Adrian were temporarily swept aside as the full impact of what had happened to her flooded in. Cam began to shake as the shock hit her. Why would someone attack her? For what reason? 'My handbag? Where's my handbag?' she cried.

The man took a look around. In the gloomy darkness it was difficult for him to see anything. Then he saw a shadowy shape moving about nearby. He peered hard at it. It was his dog, sniffing at something in a dense patch of weeds and nettles. Rover had found the handbag. The old man retrieved it, getting stung by nettles in the process, and returned with the bag. 'This it?' he asked, giving it to her.

Cam took it from him and opened it up. Quickly examining the contents, she said in dismay, 'My purse is empty.'

'Was yer carrying much?'

'About three shillings.' Enough for her to have offered to pay her way and catch the bus home.

The man's face was screwed up in anger. 'I can't believe someone was so desperate they'd stoop to attacking a pretty young woman for just a few shillings. I suppose, though, yer lucky he didn't hit you harder and kill yer. What was yer thinking, walking alone down here at this time of night?'

It was stupid to have done so, but at the time she had been so intent on getting to town Cam hadn't paused to think about it.

'Did yer get a look at whoever did this to yer?' he asked her then.

She thought for a moment and shook her head. 'I don't remember seeing anyone, all the time I was on the path.'

'Bloody coward was obviously hiding in the undergrowth, waiting for someone to come along. He obviously hit you and dragged you away so he could rifle through your possessions unobserved. Let's hope the police catch the bugger and put him away for a very long time. Stop him doing what he has to you to anyone else.'

Cam vehemently hoped so too. Then it struck her that she'd be wasting her time even reporting the attack and robbery to the police when she could give them absolutely nothing to go on by way of a description.

The old boy was saying to her, 'Anyway, best get off the wet ground else yer'll catch yer death. And yer need to get out of those wet clothes too. Reckon you can stand up?'

Cam looked unsure but said, 'I'll try.'

She reached up to grab the gnarled hand he was offering her, wondering if the frail-looking old man had the strength in him to help her up. In a most undignified manner, between them they finally managed to get her on her feet. Now that she was upright she was able to assess her condition better. Apart from her head, she was very sore under her arms, obviously from her attacker grabbing her and dragging her off the path and into the undergrowth. From the waist down she felt as if she'd been wrung through the mangle. Her hips felt particularly battered and bruised, and so did the tops of her legs, the damage to them obviously being done as she had been dragged across jutting stones and sharp branches and twigs.

'I only live a short walk away. Come home with me and let me missus tek a look at yer,' her rescuer offered. 'Yer look like you could do with a hot cuppa.'

Cam managed to give him a wan smile. 'Thanks, but I don't live that far away myself.'

'Well, least I can do is see you home safely.'

Apart from her painful injuries, Cam was feeling very stupid for taking the route she had, and also very angry at the nameless, faceless person who had prevented her from making that much longed for date with Adrian. And what he must be thinking of her! Surely, though, he would sympathise when she explained to him what had prevented her from turning up, and would arrange another occasion. She would see him in the canteen at break or lunchtime tomorrow. Now, though, she just wanted to get home, strip off her sodden clothes, tend to her injuries and curl up under the covers of her bed.

'I do appreciate your offer but I just want to get home. Thank you so much for coming to my assistance,' she said.

'It's Rover yer want to thank, gel, for finding you in the first place. Come to think of it, where is that dratted dog? ROVER!' he bellowed. When no bark was heard and no dog appeared, he said,

'Looks like he's gone home ahead of me. Let me at least see you as far as where the street lights start.'

A few minutes later, having again thanked the old man for his help, Cam left him and painfully hobbled her way home.

In order not to alert her landlady to her return, and risk her coming out of her rooms with questions and unlooked for advice, Cam deftly let herself in at the front door, closed it quietly behind her and crept up the stairs to her second-floor room at the back.

In the flickering light from the gas mantle she eased herself out of her clothes, dismayed to see that her good coat was ripped past repair at the back. Her skirt too was ruined. Anger dominated her emotions now. Not only had she been robbed of her money, what little of it she'd had, but she had also been left with the cost of replacing her clothes. Regardless, she didn't want to wear them again anyway and be constantly reminded of this night. Ripping off the rest of her attire, Cam grabbed an old carrier bag she had been keeping for rubbish and squashed every item she had been wearing into it, put on her housecoat and took the bag downstairs and out to the dustbin at the back.

When she was in her room once more, she poured ice-cold water from the jug on the washstand into the bowl, fetched a bottle of witch hazel from her cupboard and also a clean flannel. Taking off her housecoat, she examined herself. She had no full-length mirror but, using a hand mirror, looked at her backside. From what she could see it was covered in bruises, and the backs of her legs were heavily scratched and grazed. There were bruises around the tops of both arms as well. The front of her legs seemed to have escaped any damage, but somehow jutting stones, branches or twigs must have caught the inside of her thighs as she was yanked along. Bruises were ripening there, and there was a trail of dried blood down the inside of her right leg which must have come from a cut somewhere. There were also several scratches on her face. Thankfully, none of the scratches or cuts she had sustained looked to be deep enough to cause lasting scars. One thing was for certain, though, she would never again travel down any route at night that wasn't well lit. She had learned a painful lesson.

It took her a good while to dab witch hazel on all the bruises and abrasions that she was able to reach, which afterwards stung. As soon as she was finished, Cam put on her nightdress and climbed into bed, but sleep was a long time coming. Every time she closed her eyes she saw a face that was featureless, apart from an evil grinning mouth, smiling tauntingly before her.

CHAPTER FIVE

Cam woke the next morning feeling stiff and sore, still in shock from the attack, still extremely upset that her date with Adrian had been denied her. But she was determined to go to work, not only because she couldn't afford to lose a day's pay but also to explain to him why she'd let him down and hope they could make new arrangements.

A pair of thick woollen stockings concealed the injuries to the backs of her legs, and the scratches on the sides of her face were hidden by her fashionable curved bob. Outwardly there were no signs of her ordeal.

The army of telephonists the GPO employed took their breaks in rotation so that the switchboards were never left without enough staff manning them. The other departments had set times for their breaks. Consequently, Cam's breaks and Adrian's didn't always coincide; it could be several days before they did. Today, though, they coincided.

As soon as Adrian arrived and spotted Cam, to her dismay he made it very clear he didn't want to have anything to do with her. He blatantly steered his companions to a table well away from where she was sitting with two of her fellow telephonists. At that moment Cam was thankful she hadn't shared her euphoria at being asked out by him with her colleagues, not sure whether Adrian himself would want their date becoming common knowledge, and so was now spared the embarrassment of his obvious ignoring of her. She knew why he felt aggrieved, but was determined to put him right on that and hope he'd rearrange their date. So as soon as she saw him take his leave, earlier than the rest of his colleagues, Cam excused herself from her companions and went after him. As Adrian marched off down the corridor, he blatantly ignored her call for him to wait. But, not to be deterred, despite its being against company rules for her to run in the corridor, Cam did so. She caught him up and grabbed hold of his arm, pulling him to a halt.

Adrian spun round to face her, shrugging himself free from her grip and glaring at her darkly. Before she could say a word, he was hissing angrily at her: 'You've made me look a right charlie! It was humiliating enough, standing there waiting for someone and them not coming . . . not even having the courtesy to send an explanation either. But all my work friends knew how much I liked you. They've been badgering me for ages to ask you out. Do you know how much courage it took me, thinking a pretty girl like you would never ever consider me?' For a brief second the dark glare left his face to be replaced by a hurt expression. 'When you agreed to go out with me, I was over the moon.' Then his eyes hardened again. 'Of course, the first thing all my friends asked me this morning was how last night went. Now I'm the butt of their jokes. Thank you very much for that! If you don't mind . . .'

Cam blurted out, 'Oh, please listen to me, Adrian! I never turned up because I was attacked and robbed on my way to meet you.'

He stared at her, stupefied, having trouble taking in her words. 'You were attacked?' he uttered. 'Oh, I just thought you'd found something better to do with your evening than spend it with me.' Then his face darkened again. 'I hope the bobbies caught the blighter and he'll be made to pay for what he did to you.' Then, full of concern now, he asked, 'Are you all right? Did he hurt you? You say you were robbed . . . did he get away with much?'

A warm glow rushed through Cam at this show of concern for her. 'I only had a few shillings on me, and suffered no lasting damage, thank goodness.' She shifted awkwardly on her feet and said coyly, 'I'm just glad I've managed to put you right as to why I didn't turn up last night.'

He smiled down at her. 'I'm glad you have, too. I can't tell you how disappointed I was when you never came. What about tonight, if you're not doing anything?'

'I'm not,' Cam interjected. Then blushed red at her own show of eagerness and blustered, 'I mean, I'm not doing anything special.'

He laughed. 'Well, you are now. Same time, same place?'

Smiling, she nodded. But she'd make sure she was ready in plenty of time tonight so as to be able to catch the bus.

Cam had a circle of friends whom she'd met through work, and one, Ann Boardman, with whom she'd grown up in the children's home. Their friendship had continued after they had both left to make their own way in the world. Ann was the only person Cam felt she could confide in on a personal level. She was a plump, homely-looking girl, six months older than Cam, who had been found abandoned while barely days old. The closest she had to family were the couple who'd cared for her in the home. Now she worked as an overlocker in Pex hosiery factory on West Bridge and was courting strong with a lad called Brian, an apprentice mechanic in a small backstreet garage. Ann had a tendency to speak her mind before she considered the consequences. The two women met every Saturday afternoon for a wander around the town and, if they'd money to spare, enjoyed a cup of tea and a cake.

Four months after the attack the girls were sitting opposite each other in the British Homes Stores cafe.

'You gonna eat that bun or are you waiting for it to go stale?' Ann asked after watching her friend absentmindedly pushing it around her plate for the last five minutes while Ann herself had been demolishing the two she'd bought herself and drinking her tea.

Cam stared at her blankly for a moment before responding, 'I fancied it when I bought it, but somehow I don't now. I've been doing that a lot recently with all sorts of food.' She pushed her plate towards her friend. 'You can have it, if you like.'

Ann snatched up the cake. 'I do like! Iced buns are my favourite.' Taking a bite, she looked at her friend searchingly. 'You're not your usual chatty self. Nothing wrong between you and Adrian, is there?'

'No, nothing at all,' Cam assured her, eyes dreamy. 'I think he's the one I'm going to spend the rest of my life with, Ann. We get on so well together. I'm positive he feels the same about me.'

'Well, wouldn't it just be something if we were all planning our weddings together? So, if it's nothing to do with Adrian, what is wrong with you then?'

Cam pulled a face and gave a shrug. 'The only way I can describe how I feel is "out of sorts".'

Ann pulled a face then. 'What sort of out of sorts?'

Cam took a glance around to make sure no other diners were eavesdropping on their conversation and, lowering her voice, said, 'Oh, just very bloated . . . if someone stuck a pin in me, I'd go whizzing off like a burst balloon. If I bloat out much more I shall definitely not be able to get my skirts done up. I'm having a job as it is. And my chest hurts. Lately, I feel so tired all the time too. I must be about to have a monthly. Although, as you know, I don't have them every month. Sometimes I can go two or three months between, and when it does come it's really heavy and painful. Then I get them regular for a bit, then they go irregular again. I'm going through an irregular time, I suppose. I don't keep a check but it's got to be getting on for three months at least since I had my last one.'

Ann gave her an envious look. 'I wish I was like that. As you know, I suffer terribly every twenty-six days on the dot. For a good two days, I feel like my insides are being mangled. Men don't know how lucky they are, not to have to go through what we women do. But my monthlies never make me go off certain foods . . . if anything I want to eat more, especially cake and chocolate. Oh, that reminds me, my landlady has asked me to get her a chunk of slab cake from the Home and Colonial. Don't let me forget, will you?'

Cam scoffed, 'As if you're likely to, when it comes to buying cake you know your landlady is going to ask you to share with her.' Then she added wistfully, 'You are lucky with Mrs Middleton.'

'Yes, I am,' Ann readily agreed. 'She's like a mum to me. And her family treat me as one of them. How's your escape plan from Attila the Hun progressing, by the way? Seen any suitable flats since I saw you last week?'

Cam sighed. 'I don't seem to have the energy to look at the moment.'

'What about a really hot bath? That might help bring your monthly on,' Ann suggested.

Cam tutted. 'Miss Peters makes me feel grateful she allows me a bath once a week, with just enough water to cover the bottom. That's one of the many things I'm really looking forward to when I get my own place . . . not having to cart the tin bath up three flights of stairs to my room each week, then the pan of hot water, then the bucket of cold, then carting it all back down again when I've finished.'

'I don't know why you cart the dirty water down and don't just open the window and chuck it out. Bit of luck, the old trout will be standing underneath it! Just because you rent a room from her, doesn't mean she can dictate how you live your life. Anyway, hopefully soon you'll find a flat that suits and be able to do what the hell you like, without her beady eyes on you all the time. Oh, talking of time, I can't stay in town as long as I normally do. I want to get home and make a start on my new dress. Mrs M is going to have the table cleared so we can cut it out before tea, ready to start sewing up tomorrow.'

'Have you any idea what material you fancy for your new dress?'

'I've seen exactly what I fancy, in Marshall and Snelgrove's. I was early for meeting you so had a gander around their fabric department meantime. What I don't fancy is the cost! Well, I can't afford their prices, can I? I've just got to hope there's something similar on the market at a fraction of what Marshall's are asking.'

'Oh, and I need some stockings while we're there,' said Cam as they both gathered their belongings and took their leave.

Two weeks later Cam's period still hadn't arrived and she was really starting to worry. Its lateness wasn't what was concerning her, as after all they came irregularly anyway, but the debilitating effects were really causing her bother. Her bloated stomach was starting to protrude noticeably, and she was only just able to get her skirts done up. Her breasts had swollen at least a size bigger and were bursting over the top of her brassiere. The constant tiredness was beginning to get her down, too, and some foods that she had previously devoured with relish she now couldn't face. She had been to the chemist and purchased a remedy that promised on the label to ease water retention, but it hadn't worked for her. Well, that wasn't exactly true; she was going to the toilet far more than she normally did, but it hadn't diminished her bloating at all. If anything it was getting worse.

Cam couldn't ask her prim landlady for advice on such a personal problem. Miss Peters pulled a disapproving face whenever the topic of their stilted conversations at the meal table became any more risqué than what the weather was like. The girls Cam was friendly with at work would discuss everyday events in their lives, would even go so far as divulging that they had let their boyfriends kiss them, but nothing more intimate than that. So except for Ann, whose only advice had been for Cam to have a hot bath, she had no one she could confide in about her problem. All she could do was hope that her period came soon and put an end to her suffering.

Her day had been no more arduous than usual. As senior telephonist she now supervised fifteen other members of staff, running backwards and forwards, dealing with any problems they had with difficult customers, stepping in when posts had to be left for various reasons. Previously Cam would have been looking forward to using her free time to its fullest. She had plenty of things to occupy her that evening: library books to return before they became overdue; a friend from work who belonged to a women's group that was meeting that night and had asked her to go along with a view to joining; washing a few smalls; a programme she was keen to listen to on the radio. But somehow she felt as if all the energy had been drained from her and she was left with only enough to strip off her clothes and climb into bed. Her landlady, though, would not be pleased if she did not appear for dinner and clear her plate.

Miss Peters, a tall, spindly, sharp-featured woman, her iron-grey hair scraped back into a tight bun at the back of her head, was deeply resentful that her widowed father had gambled away most of her inheritance. She'd then been left with no choice after his death but to sell off all the family furniture and jewellery, and had finally been reduced to opening her house to a lodger in order to eke out what bit of money she had left, praying that it saw her out. She was frugal by nature and did not believe in big meals. Regardless, she was a good cook, albeit plain, and what she placed before Cam was always tasty, if rarely enough to find her leaving Miss Peters' table feeling full and satisfied.

That night, as she stared down at the small piece of liver, spoonful of fried onions and scoop of mashed potato that was put before her, Cam couldn't help noticing that Miss Peters was watching her closely.

'Something wrong with your meal, Miss Rogers?'

Cam shot a look at her landlady. 'Oh, er . . . no, not at all, Miss Peters,' she insisted. 'It looks delicious. It's just . . . for some reason . . . I'm not very hungry tonight, that's all.'

The elderly woman laid down her knife and fork and stared at her fixedly. 'Is there something you have to tell me, Miss Rogers?'

Cam eyed her, bemused. 'Such as what, Miss Peters?'

She gave a snort of irritation and snapped, 'Please do not insult my intelligence. I may not have married but that doesn't mean I am not fully conversant with the workings of the female body. The way yours is rounding out recently . . . your difficulty in eating certain foods when previously you have readily tucked into them . . . your general tiredness of late when normally you have always been so full of energy. You are expecting a baby, Miss Rogers! It's my opinion that you are at least three months pregnant . . . maybe four.'

Cam was staring at her in total shock.

'I am so disappointed in you, Miss Rogers,' her landlady was continuing in a disapproving tone. 'I had always thought you a very respectable girl. Mrs Cummings spoke so highly of you when she came to see me about considering you for a lodger. I would never have allowed you over my doorstep had I known you were not trustworthy. It's obvious you don't even have the decency to admit to your condition. I will not have others believe that I condone your sinful actions. I cannot allow you to live in my house any longer. I expect you to vacate your room by the end of the week.'

Cam erupted, 'Miss Peters, I can assure you that I'm *not* pregnant. I've never been with a man in that way.'

Annoyed, the other woman snapped, 'I did ask you not to insult my intelligence. You obviously *have* been with a man "in that way". Kindly leave my table. I will not share it with a . . . a harlot.' She wagged a bony finger at Cam. 'That's what you are – a harlot! For the rest of your time here you'll take your meals in your room. Now, please go.'

Her tone was so final that Cam had no choice but to do as she'd been told.

Up in her room she sat on her bed, outraged that her landlady could accuse her of being pregnant, branding her a loose woman when she most definitely was not. Time was going to show Miss Peters that she was wrong in her assumption, but it wasn't on Cam's side. Miss Peters had told her to vacate her room by Friday. Part of her was frightened about not being able to secure new lodgings before then and having to pay much more for a hotel room meantime, eating into the money she had been painstakingly saving towards furnishing her new flat when she got it, but the other part of her was glad that Miss Peters herself had given her the push she needed to break free from her over-strict regime. Now was the obvious time for Cam to get herself a flat but, should she find one that was suitable for her, references would need to be taken up by the landlord, and that could take a couple of weeks.

That was going to be her priority, though, getting herself a flat, but in the meantime the only option open to her was to find new lodgings. Usually people advertised their spare rooms in shop windows. There was no time like the present. Without further ado she grabbed her bag and, as it was a warm summer evening, set off without a coat.

Cam was gratified to spot three rooms being advertised in the window of the local corner shop. She was by no means a snob, and would take what she could get, but two of them were in streets in a very rough part of the area. The other was in a street where residents took better care of their properties, and the men weren't all of the opinion that they hadn't had a good Saturday night unless they had ended up incapacitated by drink and had a good fight.

A short time later, a homely-looking woman answered Cam's knock on the door of her three-bedroomed terrace house. She was wiping fat floury hands on the bottom of her wraparound apron and the smell of fresh bread baking wafted out from behind her. Cam had noted that the nets on the windows were dolly-blue white. The woman gave Cam a warm smile of greeting and asked, 'Yes, love?'

Her instincts told her that this woman would prove to be the kind of landlady Ann had. One who provided her lodgers with warm, clean accommodation and good nourishing food, but did not feel that just because they were living under her roof it gave her the right to dictate how they should live their lives. 'I've come about the room. It hasn't gone?' added Cam worriedly.

The woman was giving her the once over meanwhile. 'No, it's still vacant.' Then she fixed Cam's eyes with hers and said, 'But I don't tek pregnant women, and especially an unmarried one. You ain't married, are yer? You ain't wearing a ring.'

Cam couldn't believe it! For the second time that night she was being accused of being pregnant. 'I can assure you, I'm not expecting a baby,' she said with conviction.

The woman snorted in disgust. 'Don't tek me for an idiot, me duck. Besides the fact I've had four kids of me own, I know a pregnant woman when I see one. You're at least three . . .' her eyes flashed down to Cam's belly, then back to her face '. . . could be four months gone, in my opinion. Now, if yer don't mind, I've bread that needs teking out of the oven.'

With that she stepped back inside and shut the door.

Cam stared at it for several long moments, her mind in a whirl. Like Miss Peters, this potential landlady had mistaken the cause of the bloating Cam was suffering. Would other potential landladies too deny her accommodation after assuming the same thing when they looked at her, not giving her chance to explain their mistake? Panic reared within her. She'd find herself homeless unless she found a way to prove she was not the sort of girl people were accusing her of being. The only way to prove she wasn't would be to wait for time to pass and no baby to appear. Time she hadn't got.

A wave of hopelessness filled her. What on earth was she going to do? Then suddenly an idea sprang to mind. Of course, Ann would vouch for her! Wednesday was one of her nights for meeting Brian, but Cam had no doubt that in the circumstances her friend would get a message to him informing him she would be late. She could come with Cam to revisit this potential landlady and soon put her right on her mistake, then she would change her mind about letting Cam lodge with her. As long as, that was, she could get to Ann's own lodgings before she left to meet Brian. They were on the other side of town, two bus rides away. Cam took a hurried glance at her watch. It was six thirty. Ann usually left her lodgings around seven thirty to meet Brian at eight. Provided the buses were running on time, Cam should manage to get there with a little time to spare.

Spinning on her heel, she rushed off to the bus stop.

The buses were for a change running to time. It was 7.15 when Cam arrived at Ann's lodgings, out of breath as she'd run from the bus stop.

She had just raised her hand to rap on the door when it burst open and her friend Ann, about to charge out, stopped dead in her tracks to gawp in surprise on seeing Cam standing there. 'What a shock you gave me!' she declared. Then, with a grin, 'But a nice shock.' It struck her that Cam knew this was a night she usually saw Brian, so it was obvious this wasn't just a friendly visit. She worriedly demanded, 'What's wrong?'

Cam began, 'I'm so sorry to bother you on the night you see Brian, only I need your help with a problem I have. I don't really want to tell you about it here in the street . . .'

'If you have a problem you need my help with, it doesn't matter what night it is,' responded Ann with conviction. She led Cam down a short, dimly lit corridor into the back room. Once they were there she demanded, 'What do you need my help with, then?'

Cam was so consumed by her need to divulge all to her friend that she did not notice her landlady sitting knitting in the chair by the fire.

'Well, you know about my problem with my monthly curse? It still hasn't shown and it's really getting me down. But anyway . . . when I got home tonight, Miss Peters accused me of being pregnant! She wouldn't listen to my explanation of why I'm swollen out and has given me my notice. Said she wasn't having a . . . oh, Ann, she called me a harlot! Said she wasn't having a harlot like me living under her roof, and wants me out by Friday.

'Well, I wasted no time looking for new lodgings. I fancied the sound of one place being advertised and went round to enquire after it. The woman whose room it was told me it was still vacant but that she didn't take pregnant women. She looked at me so . . .' Tears sprang to Cam's eyes then. 'She made me feel so dirty – and she'd no right to as I'm not about to become an unmarried mother. Will you come with me, Ann, and make her believe that I'm not expecting? I'm so worried I'm going to end up on the streets otherwise because they all think I am.'

Another voice spoke up then. 'I have to say, I can't blame yer landlady or that other woman for their mistake, love. I must admit, you do indeed look about four months gone.'

Cam and her friend both glanced across at Ann's landlady, who sat staring back at them. For a moment the only sound in the room was the rhythmic clicking of her knitting needles.

Not Mrs Middleton too! Cam was getting mortally fed up now of being accused of being something she wasn't. 'It's my very late monthly that's swelling me out like I am, Mrs Middleton,' she snapped.

Matter-of-factly she replied, 'And I've had a few of them in me time, ducky. Was over two months late once, and terrified I was expecting again. Thankfully I wasn't ... and never was so glad to have it finally come. Five kiddies all under the age of ten was enough for me to cope with. I've a couple of friends who suffered very irregular curses. One never had it from one year to the next ... doctor told her she'd more than likely not have children as her women's bits were obviously not working properly. But he was wrong 'cos she eventually went on to have eight! But when she wasn't in the family way, her haphazard monthlies – or yearlies sometimes, I should say – never made her swell out to look like she was four months pregnant. Not like you look.'

She paused for a moment while she concentrated on picking up a dropped stitch and then continued, 'I know yer a good gel, Camella. I've had Ann living with me long enough to be sure that she wouldn't be friends with you if you didn't share the same moral outlook. But ... well ... three women sharing the same opinion about you. The chance of one being mistaken is high, but three?' She eyed Cam thoughtfully for a moment before she asked, 'Excuse me for being personal, love, but have yer noticed if yer nipples and the areas around 'em have got darker recently?'

Cam reddened in acute embarrassment and Ann shot her landlady a look as though to say, What sort of question is that to be asking my friend?

'There is a good reason I'm wanting to know, so have they?' Ethel Middleton urged her.

Cam responded awkwardly, 'Well, as a matter of fact, they have. I thought every woman's did when they got to my age.'

Ethel eyed her gravely. 'No, love, it's one of the definite signs of being in the family way. It's no late curse yer suffering. I do hope for your sake that the father of yer baby will do right by yer.'

Cam snapped at her, 'I've only been seeing my boyfriend for four months and he has never so much as touched me anywhere inappropriate, Mrs Middleton. I don't know much . . . well, hardly anything . . . about that kind of thing, but I do know that you have to have done things with a man to fall pregnant. I've never been with a man in that way and don't intend to until I get married. I must have gone darker around . . . those places . . . because . . . well, I just have. So you see, you, Miss Peters and the other woman are wrong about me.'

She turned to address Ann, ask her again if she would go and correct the potential landlady in her mistake and hope that she would change her mind about letting Cam have her room, but was stopped in her tracks by the look of pure horror on her friend's homely face.

'Ann, what's wrong?' Cam urged her.

'Well, it's just that a thought suddenly struck me when you said you'd never been with a man. What if you didn't *know* you'd been with a man, Cam?'

Cam stared at her, bemused. 'What? But of course I would know if I'd been with a man.'

'But that night you were knocked out and robbed . . .'

'You were knocked out and robbed?' Ethel erupted, aghast. 'You poor child. Did the police catch the rotter?' she demanded.

Cam shook her head. 'I didn't see who it was so couldn't give them a description. I thought it would be a waste of time reporting it, so I never. I just wanted to forget it. Anyway, why are you bringing all this up, Ann?'

'Well . . . while you were unconscious, you don't think . . . well . . . that the man did more to you than rob you, do you?'

Cam flashed her a strange look. 'Such as?' Then the penny dropped and she turned ashen. Her mind flew back to that night. She'd been in a hurry, excited, not really noticing anything about her on the deserted towpath. Then, suddenly, feeling that tremendous blow to the back of her head, and opening her eyes to find a dog licking her face, and the old man peering at her, and finding out she'd been unconscious for nearly thirty minutes. She remembered feeling dreadfully sore and achey afterwards, suffering cuts, grazes and bruising, especially to her lower half. Her coat and skirt had been ruined, and because she'd wanted no reminder of that night, she had ripped off every stitch of clothing she had been wearing and immediately thrown it away.

Now things were striking her that she hadn't noticed at the time, in her traumatised state. Cam couldn't recall taking off her knickers and pushing them into the carrier, to throw away along with the rest of her clothes. Was that because she hadn't had them on? Were they lying in the undergrowth where her attacker had discarded them? And there had been that trail of dried blood running down the inside of her thigh . . .

As the horrible truth of all that had happened to her that night finally dawned, Cam clasped her hand to her mouth and slowly backed towards a dining-chair, sinking down on it. Her terrified eyes were fixed on Ann as she uttered, 'You think my attacker not only robbed me but . . . but . . .'

Ann said the words for her that she could not. 'Raped you too.' Tears of distress for her friend sprang to her own eyes as she stared at Cam in mortification.

In her chair by the fire, Ethel had been struck speechless by this revelation and didn't even notice she had dropped several stitches when her knitting needles had fallen out of her hands with the shock. To her, a young girl getting herself pregnant because she'd let a man persuade her into having sex with him was one thing; but to become pregnant in the way this young girl was saying she had . . . to have had a cowardly specimen of a man render her unconscious then not only rob her but carry off her precious virginity too, and, worst of all, leave her carrying his child! He had taken from her the whole of the promising future Ethel knew through Ann that this young woman had been building for herself. If she knew who he was, Ethel would have had no hesitation at that moment in grabbing her carving knife, seeking him out and personally castrating him. He deserved no less in her eyes.

Laying aside her knitting, she quietly rose and went off into the kitchen to make a cup of tea, wishing she had something stronger to offer Cam. She could do with something stronger herself after learning what she had!

Cam and Ann were staring blindly at each other, both trying to comprehend this terrible state of affairs and its dire consequences. For several long minutes the only sounds in the house were those of Ethel making tea in the kitchen.

Finally Cam got to her feet and said quietly to Ann, 'You're going to be very late for meeting Brian. If you hurry he might not be too cross with you.'

Ann looked at her, stunned. 'Forget about Brian. We need to talk about . . .'

Cam held up a hand to stop her. 'I can't talk about this at the moment. I can't even take it in, let alone try and take any decision on what I'm going to do. Don't let this evening be ruined for both of us. Go and enjoy yourself with Brian.'

Ann gawped at her. 'Are you mad? You're my best friend. How can I enjoy myself, knowing you have this hanging over your head? We need to work out what you're going to do. And, whatever you decide, I'm going to be there for you every step of the way, like I know you would be for me if I were in your position.'

Cam swallowed back a lump in her throat. 'I know that, Ann, but at the moment I just need to be by myself. To try and get my thoughts around all this. It's not fair on Brian to leave him waiting for you. I'll come and see you tomorrow. Hopefully I'll be thinking more clearly and, with your help, I'll decide what to do then.' She looked at her friend imploringly. 'You won't tell Brian about this, will you? I couldn't bear people thinking I'm the kind of woman Miss Peters said I am.' Then miserable tears filled her eyes and rolled down her desolate face. 'They will though, won't they, me being unmarried?'

With that she spun on her heel and fled.

CHAPTER SIX

Cam walked aimlessly, her thoughts haphazard, as she fought to accept her true condition. That she was in fact pregnant with the child of a man who had raped her, a man she couldn't even put a face to. Not only that, but in two days she would be homeless too. And how long was she going to be able to conceal her condition from her employers ... after that she'd be out of a job, with no means of supporting herself. She had no family to turn to, not even distant. Her only close friend was living in lodgings herself, so couldn't offer Cam a roof over her head while she tried to fathom out what she was going to do. And what about Adrian? She loved him so much. Had harboured such high hopes that he was the one for her, and had no reason to believe he didn't view her in the same way. How was he going to react to this news?

A loud squeaking noise broke into her thoughts and Cam stopped walking to see what it was. Coming towards her she saw a young woman in her late-teens, pushing a dilapidated old coach pram. Cam stood aside and watched the woman pass her. She was shoddily dressed, shoes down-at-heel, and her young face held a desolate, given-up-on-life look. In the dirty pram, a grubby thin cover over it, lay a listless, undernourished-looking infant.

As Cam watched the woman trudge off down the street, a vision rose up before her. She saw herself as that young woman a year from now, her own life as deprived and hopeless as hers appeared to be. The vision terrified Cam. That was not the kind of life ... existence ... she wanted to have for herself. She wanted a good man by her side, a home fit to raise a family in, and when children came along, for them to be wanted and with enough money coming in for her to care for them properly. Cam made her mind up there and then: she couldn't have this child. Couldn't live the life of a single mother, or subject a child to the kind of life suffered by the infant in that pram.

She glanced down at her belly and placed her hand on the small mound beginning to develop there. A sudden feeling of revulsion swirled within her. This child was not conceived from a loving union, or even a consenting one. It had been conceived through its father's selfish desire to sate his lust. The woman whom he'd chosen to satisfy himself with could have been anyone; she had just happened to be in the wrong place, at the wrong time. How, in the circumstances, could Cam ever love this child, having no feeling towards it but resentment for ruining her life?

She felt a sudden desperate need to be rid of it. Had it been possible she would have ripped it from her, there and then. But she would be rid of it as soon as she possibly could. She would have it aborted. She had no idea how she'd go about achieving that or how much it would cost, but hopefully the money she had been saving to furnish her flat with would be enough. People were only suspecting she was pregnant at the moment, it not having been confirmed by a medical professional. If she solved the problem now, no one would be any the wiser.

Anger swelled within her then, fury against the unknown man who had bought her to this situation: that she was being forced to resort to end a life, the guilt of which she would have to live with for the rest of her own. Tears of distress filled her eyes then tumbled down her face. Just as quickly the anger she'd felt faded, to be replaced by a mood of utter despair. It wasn't fair that she was in this position! Thrusting a hand into her skirt pocket, she pulled out a handkerchief to wipe her face dry.

She jumped when a voice unexpectedly asked her, 'You all right, love?'

She found herself looking into the rheumy eyes of a shabby old woman walking a mangy-looking dog. 'Er . . . I'm fine, thank you,' Cam lied.

The old dear eyed her knowingly. 'If he's meking yer so miserable, ducky, then he ain't worth it. Plenty more fish in the sea for a pretty thing like you.'

With that she went on her way.

Cam looked after her. If only her problem were as simple. She gave a deep sigh. Feeling sorry for herself wasn't going to get her life back on track. She needed to find someone who would know how to go about solving her problem. Someone she could trust to keep this personal knowledge of her to themselves. Trouble was, except for Ann she didn't know of anyone who filled those criteria. Like herself, Ann wouldn't have a clue how to go about something like this.

Her mind thrashed about for a way out of her predicament. Who could help her? She was just about to concede defeat when it suddenly struck her that she did have someone to turn to and couldn't understand why she hadn't come to mind before. The woman who had promised to do her best for Cam from the moment she had landed in her care at the age of four, and had never failed in that promise: Rachael Cummings. And Cam, knowing her routine as well as she did, realised that now was a good time to go and see her.

She took a look around her, trying to fathom just where she was, and was greatly surprised when she realised she was in the actual street where Rachael Cummings resided. It was as if her subconscious had brought her here.

The instant Rachael opened the door and saw who her visitor was a beam of delight split her face. 'Well, bless my soul, how wonderful to see you, Camella. I was just thinking of you and Ann . . . well, all the children we've had the privilege of caring for over the years. I was wondering how you were all getting on in the big wide world; now you can tell me yourself. We're leaving the home, you see. Well, retiring . . . we're both coming up for seventy. Mr Cummings reaches that grand old age next week, in fact, and the authorities think it's time for a younger couple to take over. In truth, they're right. Looking after forty or so children is for a couple with younger bones than ours. How we were going to manage moneywise was a worry, but thankfully my sister has done well for herself and has a guest house on the East Coast. She has offered us live-in jobs. I'm going to do the cooking and Mr Cummings will do all the odd jobs.'

A tear sparkled in her eye. It was in a sad tone of voice that she continued, 'It won't be easy for us, leaving this place behind, but, well, age creeps up on everyone, doesn't it?' Her face brightened then as she added, 'Anyway, come on in, love, come on in.'

She stood aside to allow Cam entry into the imposing hall of the children's home. As Rachael led her down the familiar shabby corridor towards the back of the huge house, showing signs of all the wear and tear caused by the young residents who had come and gone over the last few decades, she was saying, 'I've just got all the younger kiddies into bed and the older ones are in the sitting-room entertaining themselves, so we've the kitchen to ourselves for a while. Mr Cummings has gone off to a British Legion meeting. He'll be sorry he's missed you.'

Although Cam would have dearly liked to have seen the kindly man who had done his best to be a surrogate father to her during the time she was in the Cummings' care, she was relieved to have Rachael to herself in view of the delicate reason she had come here.

Cam sat down at the huge well-worn pine table while Rachael busied herself at the other end of the kitchen, mashing a pot of tea. For a moment Cam was transported back to her childhood when she'd sat at this table, squashed in amongst all the other children of varying ages, being served plain but very appetising meals by Rachael and the cook. Now and again Mr Cummings would chide one or other of the children for bad manners or boisterous behaviour, while always encouraging them all to talk to each other about how their individual days had gone. It wasn't until after she had left the Cummings' care to make her own way in the world that Cam had realised how lucky she had been to find a refuge here.

Placing the tray of tea on the table, Rachael sat down opposite Cam and started to pass a cup over to her. As she did so, for the first time she caught a proper view of her visitor's face, and what she saw made her own cloud over with worry. 'Oh, it's not a social call after all, is it? I was so pleased to see you, I didn't notice you'd been crying.' Pushing the cup of tea in front of Cam, she said, 'You're in some sort of trouble, aren't you? You need my help, don't you, love? I'll do whatever I can for you. So what's ailing you?'

Cam's heart swelled with deep affection for the woman before her. Outwardly she seemed the sort it would be hard to feel affection for – more the sort to be terrified of, especially for children.

She was rake-thin, with sparse greying hair pulled tight into a bun at the base of her scrawny neck. With a pointed chin and a long, sharp-ended nose, she had a witch-like appearance. But looks, in Rachael's case, were deceiving. She was at heart a warm, compassionate woman. Countless fearful children had been comforted by the embrace of her sinewy arms, Cam included. Rachael was never too busy or tired if one of her charges was in need of attention.

Tongue-tied, Cam stared at her. How did she broach such a subject?

Rachael leaned over and patted her hand. 'It's all right, love. Now I've had a good look at you, I can see for myself why you're here.' She stared sadly at the girl for a moment before giving a heavy sigh. 'Well, you aren't the first this has happened to and you won't be the last, love. I take it the father doesn't want to know?'

Tears welled in Cam's eyes as she uttered, 'I don't know who the father is.'

A look of shock crossed Rachael's face at this. 'Well, you never was the flighty sort, Camella, so unless you've changed drastically since you left here, are you telling me you were taken advantage of against your wishes?'

Cam shuddered and nodded. Wringing her hands, head bowed, she told Rachael everything.

'I don't want this baby,' she finished. 'How can I love it? How can I feel anything for it but hatred . . . revulsion . . . after how it came to be inside me?' Her face contorted in sheer panic 'I want it out of me! Please, can you help me find someone to do that for me? Please, please,' she begged.

Rachael sat impassively while she listened to Cam's terrible story unfold. Inside her emotions were raging against the faceless man whose selfishness had resulted in such terrible consequences for his innocent victim. And this story was sounding rather similar to that of another young girl she had known . . . Whatever decision Camella made regarding the child she was carrying, whether she kept it or let it go, her life, like that other young girl's, would never be the same again.

Face grave, she leaned over and grabbed Cam's hand, squeezing it hard. 'My dear, after what you've told me, I can understand completely why you want to be rid of the child you're carrying, but do you know anything about abortion . . . what it entails, Camella?'

Snivelling, the girl shook her head. 'Not how it's done, no, I don't, but I know it's what women have to do to get rid of a baby they don't want. I don't care what it involves! I don't want this baby, and I'll do whatever it takes to get rid of it.'

Rachael sighed heavily again, then leaned back in her chair, folded her arms and looked stolidly at Cam. 'Well, I think there are a few things you need to know before you decide on anything you may deeply regret later. More women die in terrible agony than survive having an abortion. It's illegal so the only way you can get a doctor to perform one is if he'll take a hefty backhander . . . hundreds of pounds . . . and you have to be in the know even to know such a person. Working-class folk don't have that kind of money so it's a backstreet woman for the likes of us.

'She usually does her work on her kitchen table. Causes the baby to come away by using a knitting needle or crochet hook . . . sometimes a hat pin or any other sharp metal instrument she prefers. You just have to hope, Camella, that the woman you've chosen sterilises the equipment she uses or there's a serious risk of blood poisoning or some other nasty, life-threatening illness. Then she sends you on your way, her job done. Sometimes the baby comes away easily, with not much discomfort, followed by a very heavy period. You are very lucky indeed if this is the case because usually the pain of the body rejecting the baby is indescribable and it can go on for days.' She paused to let the information she had just imparted sink in before quietly asking. 'Still want an abortion, Camella?'

She nodded vehemently. 'I can put up with a few days of pain if it means that monster's baby is not inside me any longer.'

With worry in her eyes, Rachael looked hard at Cam for several long moments before taking a deep breath and telling her, 'I knew a young girl once who found herself in the same position as you are. She, though, at least knew who the father of the baby was. They had been courting since they'd been fourteen, loved each other deeply and wanted to spend the rest of their lives together. To find that she was pregnant came as a shock to them both, but they were overjoyed. Trouble was, they were only sixteen and couldn't keep the baby without their parents' help until they were old enough to get married and him earning enough to get them a place of their own.

'Both sets of parents were set against the idea. The pair of them were hardly out of nappies themselves, they argued, and had no idea how hard it was to raise a child at any age let alone their young one. Despite all their pleading and begging, the couple's parents decided it was in their children's best interests that the girl should have an abortion. Both mothers accompanied her to a woman who had been recommended to them.'

She paused again, long enough to take a deep breath. 'I've told you how it's done, Camella, so I won't go through that again, but the girl I'm telling you about wasn't one of the fortunate few who get away with just a severe stomach ache for a few hours, followed by a heavy period. They'd only just managed to get her back home before the horrendous pain began. Within a short while she was delirious with agony and haemorrhaging. The doctor was called and immediately had her whipped into hospital. Thankfully the staff there managed to save her life . . . only just, mind, it was touch and go for a number of days . . . but in order to do so they had to perform a hysterectomy. That's the medical term for taking out all her women's bits, Camella.'

Cam was staring at her in horror. 'Oh, my God!' she uttered. 'That poor girl wasn't able to have any more children?'

Rachael sadly shook her head. 'Not of her own she didn't. She was lucky in that her young man stood by her. They mourned together, and came to terms with what had happened and what the future held for them then. They had both wanted a large family and, of course, that was never going to be. Then it came to them that just because they were never going to have their own children to love, didn't mean there weren't other children who wouldn't benefit from their care. When they were old enough, the young couple got married and have since spent their lives giving all the love they would have bestowed on their own children to others who, for varying reasons, have no parents of their own to love them.'

Cam stared at her for a moment, wondering which children she was referring to. Then it hit her. Orphan children like she herself had been! The girl in Rachael's story was in fact herself, and the young man Mr Cummings.

If Rachael had guessed that Cam had realised she was indeed talking about herself, she did not show it but asked, 'Still want to go ahead and have an abortion, and take all the risks it involves, Camella?'

After hearing what she had, Cam's mind had been thrown into a turmoil. She stared back wildly, not replying.

'Or there's always the other route . . .'

'Oh, what's that?'

'Trying to get your own body to reject the baby by making yourself ill. You can take large doses of washing powder in gin while sitting in a boiling hot bath. Or Beecham's Powders in castor oil. There are plenty of other concoctions equally as nasty I can tell you about. Of course, none of them is guaranteed actually to make the baby come away, just to make you very sick, and there's also a chance the baby could be born deformed in some way through the harm caused it by trying to abort it.'

Rachael leaned over and grabbed Cam's hand again, squeezing it tightly. 'When you were brought to me as a little girl, I vowed to do my best by you. That promise I made hasn't changed just because you've left our care. That's what I'm trying to do now, Camella . . . do my best for you by giving you the full facts about what you're contemplating, before you do anything you might live to regret.'

Fresh tears filled Cam's eyes. 'I don't want to risk dying in horrible agony. I don't want to risk not being able to have children in the future . . . I might meet a nice man, mightn't I, and him want to marry me and me be the mother of his children? But I don't want this child, Mrs Cummings, I really don't. Oh, what am I going to do?' she wailed.

Rachael gently told her, 'There is another way, dear.'

Wild but hopeful eyes were fixed on hers. 'There is?'

'You could have the child and . . .'

Before Rachael could say another word, Cam erupted, 'What? No, I can't! I told you I . . .'

'Hear me out, please, Camella?' Rachael cut her short. 'You could have the baby and then, if you really are of the same mind when it's born, you could have it adopted. There are many decent people who cannot have children of their own and would give it a good home.

Then you can get on with your own life ... meet that nice man you've just told me about, settle down and have a child ... children ... many of them. But this time with the man you've chosen to have them with. I know you're angry with this baby, Camella, and I perfectly understand why you are, but remember, it is as innocent in all this as you are.'

Cam stared absently down at the small mound of her belly and placed one hand on it. A shred of feeling for the child developing within her stirred. She hadn't changed her mind, she still didn't want it, didn't feel she could overlook the way it had been conceived or ever be a mother to it, but Rachael had terrified the life out of her with those stories. It seemed to Cam she had no choice but to let it carry on growing inside her. The feeling she was experiencing towards the child was one of pity. Cam herself knew her own mother had loved her; had left her baby to be cared for by others through no fault of her own. This child would go through life knowing its mother hadn't loved it but had freely handed it over to be cared for by others. Hopefully, though, the people who raised it would make up for the love and affection Cam herself was unable to give it. She raised her head and looked at Rachael, a determined jut to her chin. 'If I know this baby has brought some joy to a couple who can't have any of their own, then at least I'll feel some good has come out of the terrible way it was conceived.'

Rachael heaved a sigh of relief. 'When it's born, you might change your mind and want to keep it.'

Cam vehemently shook her head. 'I won't. Just the thought of carrying it until it's ready to be born ...' She gave a shudder. 'Well, I want to get it over with and then forget about it all.'

Rachael felt that Cam was coping with enough just now without being made aware that for even the most hardened women, which Cam was not, try as she might, only total amnesia about this episode in her life would ever make her forget it.

CHAPTER SEVEN

Lying exhausted on the bed, bloodied sheets still around her, Cam stared up at the stern-faced nun addressing her, feeling stupefied. 'I . . . don't understand. What do you mean, the adoptive parents have changed their mind about the baby?'

Sister Teresa snapped impatiently, 'They don't want it, it's as simple as that.'

'But why? I mean, I've been told since you first found them for my baby that they couldn't wait for it to be born and take it home. Have everything prepared for it. Even chose a name for it.'

'They didn't take to it. The poor woman is beside herself. She had a horde of people coming tonight to welcome the child into the family, and now that will have to be postponed until another one comes along for them.' She gave Cam a scathing look. 'Of course, there'll never be a shortage of babies for adoption with girls like you so free with their favours.'

Eyes wide in bewilderment, mouth opening and closing, Cam was unable to believe that, after months of planning to surrender her baby, the prospective parents had had a sudden change of mind. It didn't make sense to her. 'Well . . . if they have changed their minds, surely you've another couple who'd want the baby?'

The nun brusquely barked, 'We've a list of desperate couples, but people want pretty, angelic-looking children. Yours is the sort only a mother could love. Finding a couple desperate enough to take on your child could be time-consuming, and we haven't the facilities to care for it meantime. You are its mother, it's up to you to see to it. What you decide to do with it after you leave here is up to you. Now, I did ask you to get yourself cleaned up and back to your room. After a few hours' rest, as yours was a straightforward birth with no complications, you can leave. Hurry with your ablutions, the child will want feeding shortly.'

A pain-wracked scream rent the air then, heralding the need of another, and before Cam could stop her the nun had left the room.

In utter shock from this turn of events, Cam ran a hand through her sweat-soaked hair. This was not how it was supposed to be. She had been instructed when she had first arrived at the home that her baby would be taken straight from her after its birth and given to its new parents. Only hours later she would be free to go on her way and get on with her life.

After her decision to carry the child to term then give it up for adoption, on Rachael's advice Cam had managed, by wearing looser clothes and a girdle, to keep her condition secret from her employers and others around, including Adrian. She knew she should end her relationship with him but each time they met she couldn't bring herself to say anything because once the deed was done, the love of her life would be gone forever. But the time for splitting up was drawing closer, as was the time for leaving her coveted job. For another month, at least, she had been able to save as much as she could to put alongside her other few pounds of savings, to fund a new beginning after the birth.

Unusually for someone who found it difficult to keep her opinions to herself, Ann had never openly voiced to Cam what she herself would do should she find herself in Cam's position, but had instead showed her friend her full support in her decision to have the baby adopted. She had pleaded with her own landlady who had eventually agreed to allow Cam to share Ann's room until it was time for her to go into the home. For a price, of course.

In the hope that the GPO might take her back when the child had been born, Cam had concocted the story that she wasn't after all quite the orphan she had thought herself to be as an elderly maiden aunt on her father's side, after years of trying, had finally tracked her down. She was terminally ill in Scotland and Cam was the only person who could care for her. Hence the reason why she was asking temporarily to leave their employ. To her relief, her boss had told Cam on the day she left that should a suitable post be vacant after her stint of caring for her aunt was over, then he would readily consider her for it.

Her weeks spent in the home waiting for the ordeal of the birth to be over were not at all restful. The home itself was a four-storey, rambling, austere, red-brick structure, originally built for a wealthy factory owner but bought by the Church and now run using charitable donations. The nuns supported fallen women throughout their pregnancy and placed those babies who were unwanted with adoptive parents. The home's rules were rigid and had to be adhered to or girls would find themselves ousted, the only other place open to the likes of them the workhouse. They all rose at six in the morning, and before breakfast ablutions had to be carried out, chamber pots emptied and beds made. The six former bedrooms had been converted into a series of cell-like cubicles, devoid of heating and each containing only a bed and a chest of drawers. Prayers were to be attended on Sundays, whether you were a believer or not.

Breakfast at eight consisted of a bowl of lumpy porridge and cup of weak tea. Lunch was usually thin soup and a slice of bread at one o'clock. Dinner consisted of some sort of watery stew: fibrous meat that had to be hunted for on the plate, boiled potatoes, and whatever vegetables were in season in the garden.

Each girl was expected to work hard for the privilege of being granted a place in the home and was assigned daily tasks. As if carrying their developing child were not tiring enough, the additional work was back-breaking. Some women were set to cleaning duties on their hands and knees, scrubbing floors; others laboured in the kitchen preparing meals and then cleaning up afterwards; still more in the laundry or the garden. Woe betide anyone who complained one iota or refused an allotted task. The only girls exempt from work were those who had been declared at risk by a doctor.

Many of the girls Cam was incarcerated with for the duration were the sort who liked to cause trouble, to relieve their boredom. She'd managed to steer clear of any involvement so hadn't had to endure the many punishments the nuns dished out, like extra work duties or being sent to sit alone with a pile of sewing until lights out at eight. Keeping what was hers from more unscrupulous types took some cunning. Cam quickly learned, after losing a precious bar of soap and two pairs of knickers, to double check upon leaving her room that she had securely locked the door, and never to leave her handbag unattended. She had had the foresight only to bring a little money in with her, keeping the rest to fund her future with after she left the home.

There were, though, a couple of girls with whom Cam had forged friendships; women who, like herself, respected other people and their property. She would spend what leisure time she had with them. One girl she got on well with was called Iris Tower. She was twenty-one, a couple of years older than Cam. Her story was typical of many of the other girls in the home, insomuch as the father of her baby had encouraged her to let him have his way with her by promising her she would not suffer by it – and then turned his back on her when she announced she was expecting. Iris, though, couldn't bear the thought of giving up her child and, although she had no idea how she was going to manage as her family had disowned her, was determined to keep it. Cam couldn't bring herself to inform even the nuns the truth of how she had become pregnant so, as far as everyone in the home was concerned, her story was the same as the likes of Iris. Her friend's baby was due around the same time as Cam's.

The nuns allowed the girls no visitors and, not wanting her condition to be spotted by anyone who knew her in her need to put this all behind her after the birth, Cam had elected not to go out on the weekly shopping trip they were permitted. She had kept in contact with Ann via letters.

Not a deceitful person by nature, Cam felt guilty for the lies she was having to tell to cover her tracks, but comforted herself with the argument that they were necessary to protect her reputation when she rejoined society after her confinement. The lie she had told Adrian, and his response to it, would leave her feeling guilty forever, though. She knew by his whole attitude towards her that he was as fond of her as she was of him, seeing a joint future for them. But regardless of what he felt for her, she could not expect him to welcome the fact that she was expecting another man's child, no matter how it was conceived, or to wait for her and resume their relationship after it was born.

He would never have guessed the emotional pain Cam was in when she matter-of-factly told him, while they sat together having a cup of coffee in a cafe before a proposed visit to the cinema, that she didn't want to see him any more. He wasn't the one for her. The hurt, bewilderment, devastation of her announcement, plainly written on his face, broke her heart. How she calmly got up and walked away from the love of her life she would never know. Adrian was never far from her thoughts, though, and she wondered continually if her feelings for him would lessen with the passing of time.

Remembering Rachael's words, that the baby she was carrying was as innocent as she herself was in all this, Cam tried her hardest not to resent it for ruining her life, but instead centre all her anger on its faceless father. At low moments, though, when she was alone in the dark in her cell-like room, when she thought of the life that could have been hers, she could not help but bear a grudge against the child and was willing the time to come when she would be relieved of it.

Apart from general tiredness, Cam's pregnancy had proceeded without mishap. The developing baby became lively, especially towards the end, and gave her many sleepless nights. But at long last, just after two on a bitterly cold February morning, she awoke from a fitful sleep to find her nightclothes and bedding soaking wet. Her waters had broken.

All the nuns assigned by their order to run the mother and baby home seemed to have been specially hand-picked for their lack of any compassion or understanding towards the girls they cared for. The nun on duty that night was a hatchet-faced old crone who, regardless of how each woman in the home had come to be pregnant, was of the opinion that they were all the lowest of the low, and treated them as such. If she could make their labour a more arduous experience than it already was, then she would go out of her way to do so. Despite Cam's pains making it difficult for her to walk, after being summoned by the shouts of another girl, Sister Agnes did not offer to assist Cam but brusquely led her down two flights of stairs, then through a series of draughty corridors at the back of the rambling house, to where the three labour rooms were situated. Nor did she help Cam get herself up on the bed where she would spend her labour. There was a small fire burning in the grate, which barely look the chill from the room, and apart from her nightdress and a thin cotton cover over her, there was nothing else to keep her warm. During her twelve-hour labour she was only checked on twice, and casually told to ring the bell to summon the duty nun when she felt the urge to push.

By the time she did feel the urge, Cam was so exhausted from the excruciating pain she was enduring that she barely had the strength to reach over and ring it. It took an hour of pushing before the baby finally made its appearance. Cam was so weak by this time that she wasn't aware of the child crying, or of the nun who had delivered it giving it a clean before swaddling it in a blanket and leaving the room with it, ordering Cam to clean herself up and get herself back to her own room.

She hadn't realised that she had fallen asleep until she was unceremoniously roused by Sister Teresa, giving her a hard shake then matter-of-factly informing her that the baby's adoption had fallen through and care of it was reverting back to Cam.

She sank back on the bed as a feeling of sheer doom enveloped her. She felt like a caged animal with no means of escape. Was it not bad enough that for nine months she had carried the child then gone through the excruciating ordeal of giving birth to it? Now she was being told the parents who had been lined up to adopt it had mysteriously changed their minds.

Despite her exhaustion, Cam's brain began to whirl. She hadn't planned to care for this baby, had nothing prepared, not even a stitch of clothing for it. But she didn't want to care for it, had no inclination whatsoever even to try.

And just what had the nun meant when she had said that Cam's baby was the sort that only a mother could love?

Then the nun's barked orders came back to her. She'd been told to clean herself up. She had enough on her plate without facing the penalty for disobeying orders. With an effort Cam managed to get herself off the bed and, despite worrying that her legs would collapse beneath her from the dizziness she was experiencing, stripped off her bloodied nightgown and wiped herself down as best she could, using the icy water in the jug and bowl, and a bar of hard yellow carbolic soap.

She then put on the clean nightdress and dressing gown she had brought down with her along with a pair of knickers and a thick wadding pad. She had just got herself back to the bed and, in great relief, sunk her weary body on to the edge of it, when the door opened and Sister Teresa returned. She carried a bundle in her arms.

She came straight to Cam and thrust the bundle at her, saying, 'I'll escort you back to your room. Come along.'

Cam could hardly keep up with the nun as she was marched back down the maze of corridors, up two flights of stairs and into her room. She was informed that she would be expected to have her belongings packed and be ready to depart the home at six o'clock that evening so that the next occupant could take up residence.

Sheer panic reared within Cam at being left alone with her baby. She felt absolutely no attachment to it and had never even handled one before, so had no idea what to do. What was she supposed to feed it with? She'd been given no bottle with milk in it. Putting the bundle carefully on her bed, she rushed to the door and caught Sister Teresa just as she was about to descend the stairs.

'Sister, how do I feed the baby?' Cam called to her.

Sister Teresa turned her head and shot her a look that said, *How stupid are you?* 'For goodness' sake, don't you know what Nature intended your breasts for? Put the child to a nipple and the rest comes naturally.'

With that she disappeared down the stairs.

Cam returned to her room, shutting the door behind her, and went across to the bed to stare down at the swaddled baby. Sister Teresa had wrapped it so snugly in the blanket that its face couldn't be viewed from where she stood. This was Cam's baby, had grown inside her, and she'd endured horrendous hours of painful labour giving birth to it. But she felt nothing towards it whatsoever. Was she a monster for not feeling any motherly impulse for her own child? All she felt was frightened and begrudging because now she was left with its care when what she really wanted was to close this demeaning chapter of her life.

The baby began to stir then whimper. Panic surged within her. The very thought of putting the child to her breast totally repelled her, but if she did not then it would starve to death. She had no choice.

49

Cam leaned over and gingerly unfolded the edges of the blanket from the child's face. Her immediate reaction was one of shock. The infant's face resembled an old apple: all wizened. It had a large dome-shaped forehead that appeared to fill half the face, the closed eyes were sunken, and the rest of the features narrowed to a pointed chin. There were tufts, here and there, of carrot-red hair sprouting from the top of the head. The skin was pale, almost translucent, veins prominent on the sides of the forehead.

Cam now understood what Sister Teresa had meant when she had said that this baby was the sort only a mother could love. There was nothing endearing about its face at all.

The baby's mouth opened then to let out a shriek. Its loudness seemed impossible from such a tiny human being. And the shrieking continued, growing in volume. The sound of the cry was like metal scraping glass. It hurt Cam's ears.

To still the noise, she automatically picked up the baby, sitting down on the bed with it, holding it away from her, mouthing, 'Shooosh, baby, shoosh.'

Her actions did not quell the child's screeching. It was obviously hungry and wouldn't let up until its hunger pangs had been satisfied.

Gulping hard, to try and push down the nausea that was rising from her stomach, Cam pulled down the front of her nightdress to expose a breast and reluctantly drew the screaming baby towards her so that its lips just touched her nipple. The baby immediately clamped on to it, like a seasoned veteran at feeding, and sucked hard. It seemed to Cam an age before the child was satisfied and released its hold on her. But then, immediately, it began to scream again. It took her a few seconds to realise that the breast the child had been on was no longer producing what it wanted. She reluctantly placed it against her other breast and once again it immediately clamped hold of it and sucked hard. It seemed an age again before it had had its fill and released its hold, whereupon it immediately fell asleep. Both her breasts were now painfully throbbing, the nipples sore. The whole experience had proved revolting to Cam. She never wished to do it again.

As she made to put the child back down on the bed, its eyes

suddenly opened and appeared to fix on hers. Cam shuddered violently. Surely she must be mistaking the look it was giving her? But she knew a look of pure hatred when she saw it, and it was visible in her baby's eyes.

Suddenly the door opened and Sister Teresa entered. Seeing Cam's exposed breasts and the baby in her arms, she said, 'Good, you've fed the child. Get some rest now and be ready to leave at six.'

Fear enveloped her then and hysterically Cam blurted out: 'But I can't take it with me, I just can't! It hates me . . . it does. Look at the way it's looking at me.'

Sister Teresa shot her a look of disdain. 'Don't be so ridiculous. Babies can't even see properly until they're six weeks old.' She went over to the chest and put a small pile of items on top of it. 'In light of the circumstances, the fact that you were not expecting to take your baby with you when you left, I've found a couple of nightdresses for it, along with a blanket and a couple of nappies to tide you over.'

A panic-stricken Cam stared after the nun as she left the room.

CHAPTER EIGHT

The park bench offered Cam no protection from the bitter weather. Not that she was aware of it or at all concerned. The way she was feeling at the moment, death would come as a blessed relief, discharging her from her huge burden of what to do with this child she had only a few hours before given birth to.

She had nowhere to take the baby while she decided what to do next. The room she had hoped to share with Ann while she found herself new lodgings and a job was only small, with hardly space for them both let alone a baby too, and it had taken much persuasion on Ann's part to get her landlady to agree to just Cam staying. It was highly unlikely she would agree to take the baby as well, even for a night or two. The landlady had once commented in Cam's presence that, over the years spent raising her own nine children, she'd had a bellyful of screaming kids, running her ragged and giving her sleepless nights. She meant her remaining time to be peaceful, so any visiting grandchildren had better respect that or it would be straight back to their parents.

The sound of footsteps alerted Cam to the approach of a young woman. She was dressed smartly for an evening out, and as she passed by flashed Cam a haughty look. It then struck her what a dreadful sight she must be. Her once fashionable bob, having grown out during her incarceration in the fallen women's home, was now hanging down lank and greasy; her old coat stretched over her still-swollen belly, a loose, unbecoming maternity dress visible underneath. The bundle in her arms was obviously a newborn infant; the brown suitcase by her feet was clearly all she possessed in the world.

Several months ago she would have been that woman passing by

53

on her way to a social engagement, and would probably have dismissed the sort of figure she herself cut now as the type who was free with her favours. A slut. But Cam wasn't that kind of woman, couldn't bear people looking at her as though she was the lowest of the low. To stop it happening again she needed to resolve her problem. But one thing this encounter with the stuck-up woman had taught her was that never again would she judge a person by their looks.

Her thoughts returned to her own situation as she glanced down at the child in her arms. Thankfully it was still sleeping, satisfied for the time being. As Cam had tried to rest before her departure it had been on her mind to slip out of the home without the baby, but the nuns had obviously anticipated that she might have that thought and had monitored her departure from her room to the main gates, securely locking every door behind her, so that solution had been denied her. Another struck her then. She could abandon the child on this bench she was sitting on. Leave whoever discovered the baby the problem of what to do with it. But the park would be closing shortly. What if its discovery wasn't made before then and it was left out in this bitter weather all night? Although she had no maternal feelings for it, Cam didn't wish it dead.

She shivered as a gust of freezing wind swirled about her. She really ought to find shelter for the night. Ann was keeping her savings book for her but Cam still had enough on her person, that she had managed to keep safe from the light-fingered sort in the home, for a cheap bed and breakfast. Hopefully they wouldn't have rules prohibiting a baby. And, before morning, she'd decide what to do about the child.

She made to rise, then stopped as the obvious solution struck her like a thunderbolt. The sheer exhaustion of the birth had prevented her from thinking of it before. She would put the child in the care of a children's home. The Cummings would take good care of it, just like they had done of her. And the council authorities periodically brought couples to the home who were looking for children to adopt, in most cases babies. Hopefully a couple would see beyond this child's unattractiveness and want it for their own. Either way, she could happily start to rebuild her life, knowing the child was being cared for.

The children's home was housed in the same type of four-storey villa as the fallen women's home, and looked equally neglected with its peeling doors and window frames, and leaking guttering. Mr Cummings had always done his best to keep it looking respectable and had Cam not been so consumed by her need to be rid of her unwanted child, she would have been most surprised to find the house so dilapidated and the usually well-kept garden overgrown.

She stole up the front path and made her way around the side of the house, to the back door where she proposed to leave the child on the step. She knew from past experience that at this time of night either Rachael or the cook would be in the kitchen, tidying after the evening meal and preparing the bedtime drinks for the younger children. With a shriek like her child was capable of making, its discovery would not be in doubt when it woke. As Cam crept on she prayed it did not wake now and its cries alert everybody before she had deposited it and made her get away.

As she had expected, lights from the kitchen were blazing through the two large sash windows, illuminating the wide terraced area that ran across the back of the house, separating it from the garden. Cam just managed to spot a collection of battered toys before she fell over them, and made a hurried detour. Again, had she not been consumed by more important matters, it would have struck her that Mr Cummings had always kept all the toys in good condition. As she ducked under the kitchen windows she was relieved to hear a voice coming from within the house. Someone was angry by the sound of it, but Cam hadn't time to stop and discover why. She needed to deposit the child then make her get away before she herself was discovered and brought to book. She dreaded to think what the punishment was for being caught abandoning your own child.

With the baby deposited safely on the doorstep, Cam made to leave . . . but something within her pulled her back. The child would not be able to understand but, regardless, she felt it deserved an explanation of why its mother was doing what she was. In a whisper she told it: 'You weren't supposed to be born. You were forced on me, you see. That's why I can't be a mother to you. Mr and Mrs Cummings are good people, they'll look after you. I've done right by you, giving you to them.' She paused for a moment before she added, 'Goodbye.'

Cam turned away and hurriedly began to retrace her steps. She was just ducking under the second of the two large windows when, from inside, a cry of pain rang out and stopped her in her tracks. Automatically she glanced through the window to see what and who had caused it.

Around the large pine table sat several children, of ages ranging from about four to twelve. Before them each was a plate full of what appeared to Cam to be an unappetising porridge-like substance. All the children were looking either worried or terrified, each with a submissive stoop to their shoulders. One child was openly sobbing, rubbing the side of his head. Stomping around the table, holding a thin cane in one hand and slapping the end of it into her other palm, was an obese woman, almost as wide as she was tall. Her rotund face was wreathed in an ugly scowl and she was shouting so loudly now that Cam could clearly hear every word.

'You're all ungrateful little bastards! How dare yer say my food tastes 'orrible? You should be thankful you're getting fed. Grateful yer've got a roof over yer heads and people looking after yer, when yer own parents couldn't be bothered. Now get yer dinner down yer necks before I ram it down yer meself – and give yer a taste of this after.' She waved the cane menacingly at them.

The kitchen door opened then and a short wiry man entered. He didn't look at all happy to see the children still sitting at the table and barked, 'What're these tykes still doing here? Yer know I like to eat me dinner in peace.'

The fat woman was busy opening the oven door and taking out a plate on which was piled a very appetising wedge of pie, succulent meat and gravy oozing out of it, along with potatoes and vegetables. Going over to place it at the head of the table, she said, 'None of the little beggars is leaving this table 'til every plate is cleared. I ain't having the authorities dismissing us from our jobs 'cos any of the kids have malnutrition.'

He snapped back at her, 'If they ain't eating it, they can't be hungry, can they?' Then addressed the children. 'Bed . . . the lot of yer. But be warned, yer'll get what yer've left for yer breakfast. Now scoot before I let Mrs Briggs loose on yer for a good whipping!'

All the children frantically scraped back their chairs and made a run for the door, disappearing through it.

Mr Briggs had a sneer of satisfaction on his weaselly face as he made his way round the table to sit down and start tucking into his meal. Armed with her own plate of food, Mrs Briggs wedged her bulk on a chair next to her husband and began greedily tucking in also. Dribbles of gravy ran down her chin.

The kitchen door opened again and Cam saw a thin, pale-looking girl of about fourteen enter.

Mrs Briggs shouted at her, 'What have I told yer about disturbing me and Mr Briggs when we're eating?'

The girl visibly trembled, and stuttered, 'Oh, I'm . . . I'm so . . . so sorry, Mrs Briggs. I thought you'd both finished. It won't happen again.' She began to back out.

'Mek sure it don't,' Mrs Briggs bellowed warningly back. 'Well, yer might tell me what yer wanted, being as you've already disturbed us.'

'Just to let you know, I've got all the younger ones in bed.'

Shoving a laden forkful of food into her mouth, Mrs Briggs responded, 'Good. There's a bag of mending that needs doing in the cupboard under the stairs, yer can get cracking on that. Tell Esme to get started on the pile of ironing in the laundry room, and Sara to come in here in fifteen minutes to get this kitchen cleared up. Danny and Michael are to fill the coal buckets and get the water in for the morning. Not having you lot lazing around while there's work to be done. Now get out!'

As soon as the girl had departed, Mr Briggs grumbled, 'Bloody kids. Nothing but a nuisance. They should all be strangled at birth.'

'Yeah, well, they get on my nerves as much as they do yours but without this lot we wouldn't have such cushy jobs or a roof over our heads.'

'Huh, yeah, I suppose. Good idea of yours to dismiss the char and get the kids to cover the work she did so we could pocket her wage, eh?'

Mrs Briggs laughed. 'And the cook too, with me doing all the cooking. Those Cummings people before us must have been mad to feed them kids same as they ate 'emselves. And with the other savings we're meking, by the time we come to leave here we should be able to live handsomely.'

Cam couldn't believe what she was hearing or seeing. These people were dreadful. Who were they? And where were the Cummings? Then a memory stirred of the night she had come to seek Rachael's help, and of her saying that she and Mr Cummings were retiring. Only Cam herself had been so consumed by her own problem at the time she had not properly taken on board what she was being told. These people must be the Cummings' replacements. How lucky she had been to have been placed with kind people, not these two cruel, selfish individuals now running the home.

Cam jumped and glanced across at the child on the doorstep as it gave a small whimper. Was it just stirring in its sleep or waking up? At any minute it might start to wail, alerting those two dreadful people to its presence, and they'd come rushing out to investigate the noise. She'd better go, before she was discovered. Then Cam's conscience started to nag at her. She stared blindly over at the infant, her sense of right and wrong battling against her all-consuming need to close the door on this dreadful episode in her life. In truth, there was no contest. Cam might not have any maternal feelings for the child, but she knew she couldn't knowingly subject it to the sort of existence the children inside this house led, and merrily get on with her own life, sleeping soundly in her bed at night.

The baby stirred again and gave out another whimper. From inside the house Cam heard Mrs Briggs say, 'What was that noise?' To which Mr Briggs responded, 'I never heard 'ote.' They soon would, though, when the child started to howl with that loud, high-pitched squeal it had. Dashing over to the doorstep, she scooped up the bundle and fled back to the street, only stopping long enough to collect her abandoned suitcase from inside the gate.

An hour later Cam sighed wearily as the third landlady of a bed and breakfast establishment shut the door in her face, after telling her that a baby wasn't welcome since it would disturb the sleep of her other guests.

Thankfully the child had settled into a sleep again, but it was now getting on for nine o'clock, nearly four hours since it had last been fed, and from the scant information Sister Teresa had imparted to her before she had left, babies were fed every four hours – in some cases even more frequently, should the child prove a hungry one. And not only was she risking the baby's health by being out in this bitter weather, but her own as well. If a cheap bed and breakfast desperate for trade wouldn't take them both in, a hotel wasn't likely to for the same reason. Besides, she hadn't enough money to afford a hotel room. But they needed some sort of shelter for the night.

Bone weary, with hardly the energy now to put one foot in front of the other, her arms aching terribly from holding the baby in one and virtually dragging the heavy suitcase along in the other, Cam was walking aimlessly, all her thoughts concentrated on the problem of finding some sort of shelter for the night. Then, through the gloom of the dark evening, her eyes fixed on a door hanging open before her. She saw that it was a side door, leading into a disused warehouse. Most of its windows were broken, the entrance to the door choked with clumps of nettles and other weeds as was the rest of the alley around it.

Cam suddenly likened herself to Joseph and Mary, so desperate for shelter they had to settle for a stable. No such luxury for her, though. It seemed she was being given no choice but to accept the refuge of this crumbling building.

Inside the door, her legs throbbing where nettles had stung them, she put down the suitcase and stared into the gloomy cavernous space before her. It felt eerie, as if she was standing at the entrance to a deep dark cave. After accustoming her eyes, she saw with dismay that the building's final inhabitants seemed to have stripped the place bare, or else what had been left behind by them had been pilfered by locals. Just rubble from the crumbling walls and debris from the disintegrating ceiling above littered the concrete floor. Careful to avoid the rubble, Cam slowly ventured further inside, looking around her as she did so. She gave a heavy sigh. At least Mary and Joseph had warm straw to sleep on in the stable and a manger in which to put their child. There didn't seem anything she could use by way of protection from the cold in here. She had thought the fallen women's home to be austere and uninviting, but in comparison to this accommodation she was being forced to accept, it had been a palace.

Above the screech of the icy wind whipping through the broken windows and chinks in the walls where the masonry was disintegrating, another sound alerted her. A skittering noise. She shuddered violently, her heart beginning to race. It appeared that the place wasn't entirely deserted after all. Rats resided here. The child stirred in her aching arms, then its mouth opened to emit a howl, immediately growing in intensity, seeming to reverberate off the walls and hit her full force. It obviously wanted feeding, and right now. If anything would keep the rats away, this noise would.

It opened its eyes then, and although Sister Teresa had told her babies could not focus their vision until they were at least six weeks old, Cam knew she was not imagining the look of pure hatred it gave her. She shuddered and dragged her own eyes away from it, hurriedly looking around for a place to settle herself while she satisfied its hunger again, though the thought still filled her with absolute revulsion. Out of the gloom to the right of her, just next to the door she had come in by, she could make out an integral structure with an unbroken window and door at the front of it. A small office. It had probably been used by the goods inwards clerk when the place had been thriving. The door leading into it was shut. Hopefully that meant no rats inside.

Picking up her suitcase, the howling child now beginning to squirm angrily in the crook of her arm, Cam made her way over to the small room. Putting the case down, she turned the knob and gave the door a push. Thankfully it wasn't locked, but the door appeared to be stuck. She turned the knob again and, with what little strength she had left, pushed her shoulder against it. It opened far enough for a fearful Cam to step in. She was relieved to note that her entry into the room had resulted in no skittering of rats. The space was barely five foot square and completely empty, like the rest of the building, but at least she wasn't going to spend the night frightened to sleep in case rats attacked, and with the door shut it was semi-sheltered from the icy wind that was whipping around the rest of the building.

She squatted uncomfortably on the hard, cold concrete floor.

With her breasts painfully throbbing, all the time trying to force away feelings of revulsion, Cam fed the child. It seemed to take an age to satisfy its hunger, but finally it did and fell asleep again. Cam was ravenously hungry herself, only having had a slice of sparingly buttered toast and cup of weak tea by way of sustenance since she'd given birth.

She straightened her clothes and slumped back exhaustedly against the unyielding wall. She felt as if life itself had been drained from her. She was having difficulty supporting the child in her arm. Sleep was just about to overtake her when she jolted awake. If she was unconscious, the child could easily slip from her grasp, land on the hard floor and be injured. Would it be safer in her lap? But that wasn't the answer either as, should she move in her own sleep, it could slip and again end up on the hard floor. Then a simple solution struck her. With one hand she pulled the suitcase to her and opened it up, then nestled the swaddled child on top of her items of clothing. Finally she huddled back against the wall again. At least she could rest herself now, knowing the child was comfortable.

As her eyes drooped shut, a feeling of utter hopelessness consumed Cam. Her visions of rebuilding a once promising future had been replaced by an endless black void. She had never felt so alone in all her life, so trapped by a situation that her bewildered mind could see no escape from. Maybe she would see things more clearly in the morning, she thought, trying to be positive. Then, just as sleep rendered her unconscious, a face swam before her. Ann. If ever she'd needed her friend it was now. Ann might have an idea how to resolve her problem. If memory served her right, it was Sunday tomorrow. Ann usually saw Brian in the afternoon, but she would be in in the morning, getting herself organised for work the next day. Remembering that she wasn't quite alone in the world brought a glimmer of comfort to Cam. Then sleep took her into oblivion.

CHAPTER NINE

Ann's homely face reflected a mixture of shock and great delight on finding Cam at the other side of the door when she answered her summons just before nine the next morning. The infant had woken Cam three times during the night, demanding to be fed, but thankfully had immediately gone back to sleep as soon as it was satisfied. She was still sore and fatigued from the effects of giving birth, and added to that was stiffness from sleeping on the uncomfortable warehouse floor.

Ann blurted out excitedly, 'Oh, Cam, Cam! How wonderful to see you. I haven't been able to get you out my mind these past couple of weeks, knowing it was your due time. Well, it's obviously all over as you're here now. I'm so glad to see you. I've got some wonderful news for you . . .'

She made to launch herself on Cam and give her a bear hug of welcome, then stopped short, fixing her eyes on the bundle in the crook of her friend's arm. In utter disbelief Ann exclaimed, 'Is that what I think it is? Oh, so you kept the baby? Couldn't bear the thought of giving it away after all?'

Worrying questions then blasted through her mind. Where did Cam propose to live? How was she going to pay her way with a baby in tow? And with her own maternal instincts running riot, she desperately wanted a peek at the child. It was then that she saw how truly wretched her friend looked. Not just tired from what she had just been through, giving birth to a baby, but like she'd got the whole weight of the world on her shoulders. Ann knew her friend well and there was something dreadfully wrong with her. 'What's going on, Cam?' she demanded.

'I do need to talk to you. I really need your help.' Cam's bottom lip started to tremble and she couldn't stop the tears then. They flooded down her face as she sobbed, 'I don't know what to do.'

Ann grabbed her arm and pulled Cam inside, ordering her, 'Go into the back room and settle the baby while I mash you a strong cup of tea. Mrs M is out, gone to morning service, then on to dinner at her eldest daughter's, so we have the place to ourselves.'

A short while later, thankfully with the child still sleeping and placed securely in the seat of an armchair, both women were sitting together at the gate-legged dining-table, armed with cups of strong sweet tea. Cam's tasted like nectar to her, the first decent cup she'd had since she had gone into the home several months ago. It was a joke amongst the girls there that, after mashing a pot for themselves, the nuns would dry out the leaves and use them for the young mothers' brew. Dishwater had more colour than the tea those nuns served.

Ann laid a reassuring hand on Cam's arm. 'Obviously the enormity of what you've taken on hasn't sunk in, love. So . . . it's not going to be easy bringing up a baby on your own, bloody hard in fact, but I'll help you as much as I can. And it'll all be worth it, watching the child grow up instead of not knowing how it's faring . . . whether strangers are treating it right.'

Cam miserably shook her head. 'But that's just it, Ann. I don't want to raise the baby. I never changed my mind about having it adopted. The nuns gave me no choice but to take it with me when I left. The parents they'd lined up for it decided they didn't want it.'

Ann's look of confusion changed to one of astonishment. 'What do you mean, they didn't want it? I mean, I should imagine that to go down the adoption route you'd be desperate for a baby. It's not like buying a dress from a catalogue and then deciding when it arrives you don't like it and sending it back. What reason did they give for refusing to take it? Oh . . . is it not right? I mean, is it . . . deformed in some way? Is that why they didn't want it? Oh, the poor little mite.'

'The reason they didn't want it is not because it's deformed. It's because . . . well . . . you see . . . it's not exactly . . . well, the sort of baby you take to.'

'What do you mean?' Before Cam could try and explain further,

Ann had jumped up and gone over to where the child lay. Carefully she eased away the covers and instantly she saw its face, never one to think before she spoke her mind, exclaimed in mortification: 'Oh! Oh, dear me, gel, Mother Nature certainly missed this one out when she was dishing out the looks. Poor little thing. It doesn't resemble you at all, does it? Must take after its father . . . so I dread to think what *he* looks like.' She turned to glance over at Cam sympathetically. 'Look on the bright side, gel. They do say that ugly ducklings can turn into beautiful swans. So let's hope this happens in this little mite's case, eh?' Then she asked, 'Is it a boy or a girl?'

Cam was so consumed with her own worries that Ann's blunt comments on the child's looks were lost on her. She stared blankly over at her friend. 'I don't know. I didn't ask. I was so . . . so . . . well, you can imagine how I was feeling, to be told I had to take responsibility for it when that was the last thing I was thinking of.'

'That's very understandable,' Ann commiserated. 'But didn't you see when you changed its nappy?'

Cam gawped at her. 'Oh! It was so distressing for me, having to feed it, I completely forgot that needed doing.' She looked worried. 'But I don't know how to change a nappy, Ann. The nuns did show the girls who were keeping their babies how to bath and change them, using a doll, but I wasn't keeping mine so I wasn't shown anything.'

'Good job I know, then, having watched my landlady with her grandchildren over the years I've been lodging here. Have you a clean nappy and I'll show you?'

'Sister Teresa gave me a few bits of clothing to help me out. About the only nice thing they did for me the whole time I was there. I thought nuns were supposed to be kind and compassionate, but the ones in the home were as cold and unsympathetic as they come. They treated all us women like we were the lowest form of life because we'd gone against God's rules and given ourselves to a man, not controlled ourselves until we were married. No matter how we girls came to be unmarried mothers, we didn't deserve to be treated like scum. Hopefully there's a nappy amongst the pile of baby clothes in my suitcase. But can't it wait until it wakes up for its next feed? I'm afraid it'll start crying.'

'All babies cry, Cam.'

I doubt very much if it's as loudly and gratingly as this one does, Cam thought. Besides, she didn't want to have any more to do with the child than she had to. 'No, please leave it,' she urged. 'It'll wake up soon enough.'

Ann eased the blanket over the sleeping infant and made her way back to sit down at the table. 'You'll make a marvellous mother, Cam. It's not going to be easy, I won't deny it, but other women do it and you can too.'

Cam looked at her for a moment then began to cry again, big fat miserable tears. 'I'm not natural, Ann,' she blubbered. 'There's something dreadfully wrong with me.'

Ann grabbed her hand and squeezed it hard. 'There's n'ote wrong with you, and I know you better than anyone.'

'But there is, Ann. I'm a monster. I'm a wicked woman. I have to be when I don't . . .' her voice trailed off for a moment before she blurted out '. . . have any motherly feelings for my baby. When I feed it, I feel sick to my stomach. It repels me. I don't want it, Ann. I don't want to be its mother. I want my own life back, without this baby in it. All it does is keep reminding me of what that man did to me.'

Ann's own thoughts were raging. She would like a large family herself when the time was right, and for wonderful Brian to be the father. She couldn't imagine not loving any of her children and knew she would strive her hardest to be the best mother she could to them. But then Cam didn't even know the father of this child, let alone have a relationship with him, and had certainly not wanted it after what he had done to her. She had been in love with another man at the time, had harboured high hopes that he was the one she'd spend her life with, and because of this child's father's attack on her, had been given no choice but to walk away from the man she loved, all her hopes and dreams of a future with him shattered. Was it surprising she didn't have any maternal feelings for her child?

Ann was shaken out of her thoughts by Cam telling her, 'When I was in the home, all I did was will the day to come when I'd be rid of it from my body. It shouldn't have been there . . . I never asked for it to be . . . its vile father gave me no choice. How I despise

66

that man for what he did to me! Can you imagine what it's like, Ann, to hate someone so much you wish them dead yet not be able even to put a face to them?'

Ann couldn't. She just shook her head.

Cam continued, 'When I was in labour it was the most painful thing you can imagine . . . it felt like I was splitting in two. I was so frightened, left on my own for most of it, but all I could think of was that, when it was over, I could finally put this nightmare behind me. I'd do right by the child, give it to people who were desperate to be parents, who would love it and give it a good life, and then I could get on with mine.' She paused long enough to blow her streaming nose. 'After I was told the adoption wasn't going to happen, and that as the child was mine it was up to me to take responsibility for it, whether I wanted to or not, I was in total shock and horror at the thought. I had never for a minute considered that would happen, and I wasn't prepared. It was on my mind to make a run for it as soon as I'd regained some of my strength, but the nuns aren't stupid. They watched me like hawks, to make sure I took the baby with me.'

Then she described her fruitless visit to the children's home, and what she had discovered about the heartless pair who'd taken over from the Cummings. Her sense of desolation when she realised she'd have to take the child away with her.

'But what kind of woman am I, who doesn't have any feelings other than resentment for her own child? A cold, heartless one, that's what. And there's another thing. I know you're going to think I'm stupid, but it hates me. I know babies can't see properly until they're a few weeks old but this one looks at me with such hatred. If looks could kill, I'd be dead, believe me.'

Ann said to her with conviction, 'You're no more cold and heartless than I am, Cam. If you were, you'd have left the baby on a park bench or that doorstep, turned and walked away, and never given it another thought. As for it hating you . . . that's just your imagination running riot because you feel guilty about not having any motherly feelings yet. Look, we need to concentrate on where you go from here.'

Ann had always felt that no matter what hardships a mother was facing, what personal crises, a child belonged with its mother and mothers who did abandon their children were downright selfish. She'd been abandoned herself at only a few days old, with just the clothes on her back, in a dirty old pram left outside a shop. She knew nothing of her parents or why she'd been deserted by them, and knew what it felt like to grow up feeling unwanted by the very people who are supposed to want you the most, especially the mother who'd grown you inside her. But now, actually witnessing for herself Cam's situation, seeing how utterly distressed she was by having the responsibility of raising a child she'd conceived in the worst possible circumstances, she was left wondering if she'd perhaps been too harsh in judging all mothers who abandoned their children as heartless.

She told Cam, 'I'm glad you didn't abandon the baby as I don't fancy visiting you in jail. The nuns in the home would only have to see its photograph in the newspapers and they'd immediately be contacting the police and giving them your name. Well, the baby is very memorable, isn't it?'

Cam looked at Ann, dumbstruck. In her desperation to be rid of the child that fact hadn't registered with her. Now her head drooped so far forward that her forehead touched the table. Cradling her arms around it, desolate tears flowed and she blubbered, 'I've got to keep the baby, haven't I, Ann? Whether I want to or not, I'll have to be a mother to it. I've got enough money to get us a place for a few weeks . . . that's provided I can find someone to take us both, that is . . . but after that . . . Well, there's only one place I know we can go. Oh, I can't bear the thought of living in there! I've heard it's so awful. Oh, Ann, I wish I was dead.'

Ann looked at her blankly for a moment, wondering where she meant. Then it hit her. The workhouse! Her own thoughts raged. It wasn't right that Cam and her baby should land up in such a hell-hole when the situation she was in was none of her making and neither was the fact that she had no family to turn to. There must be another alternative, there just had to be. Then she realised it wasn't true that Cam had no one to turn to. She had, and had come to that person for help. Ann herself. But what could she do? She hadn't a place of her own so couldn't offer Cam a roof over her head. Then the obvious solution came to her. Oh, but it would mean making a huge sacrifice that would pain her very much . . . Ann wrestled with her conscience.

But, when it came down to it, there was no battle to fight. Cam was her friend. How could she justify withholding a possible escape route? Before she suggested her own resolution to the problem, though, there was something she needed to do.

She realised Cam was getting up. 'Where are you going?' Ann demanded.

'I've got to try and find us somewhere to stay. I can't bear the thought of sleeping in that warehouse again tonight, but if I can't find anyone to take us both then I'll have no choice.'

Ann grabbed her arm and pulled her back down. 'You're not going anywhere. It's bitter cold outside and you look done in. You need a good sleep. You'll be thinking clearer then and things might not look so bad.' She knew that was just an effort to make Cam feel better when in truth matters couldn't be any worse. Hopefully, though, when she learned what Ann herself had planned, she would see a way out of her dire situation.

Ann told her, 'I've just remembered . . . Mrs Middleton asked me to do an errand for her and she won't be pleased if I haven't when she gets home. While I'm out, take yourself and the baby up to my room. Hopefully it'll sleep for a while yet so you can get some sleep yourself. Put it in the suitcase like you did last night in the warehouse. It won't hurt to leave changing the nappy until I get back.'

Cam had no energy, no fight left in her to do anything other than what her friend was ordering her. 'Thank you, Ann,' she sighed tiredly. As she rose to pick up the baby and make her way to Ann's room, a memory stirred. 'Oh, didn't you say you'd some news to tell me when I first arrived? I could do with some good news for a change. What is it then?'

'Oh, er . . . do you know, I can't remember what it was now. Couldn't have been that good if I've forgotten what it was, could it?'

Cam looked disappointed. 'Oh, I was hoping you were going to tell me Brian was going to make an honest woman of you and I would have a wedding to look forward to.'

Ann responded matter-of-factly, 'No such luck, I'm afraid. He has never mentioned marriage to me. Anyway, I'm in no hurry. I'm happy being single for a good while yet.' She was putting on her coat now and collecting her handbag. 'I'll try not to be too long.'

CHAPTER TEN

Brian had already told Ann the previous evening what he was going to be up to that Sunday morning: repairing a hole in the roof of the dusty old cobweb-filled shed where spades, hoes, rakes and other gardening tools jostled for space with all manner of other gardening paraphernalia collected over the years the allotment had been in his family. Brian would inherit it one day, as his father had from his father, and hoped to have a son to pass on to himself.

A pleasant-faced, stockily built nineteen year old with a shock of thick black hair, Brian Williams was dressed in shabby work overalls over an old jacket, a worn pair of flannel trousers, shirt and hand-knitted sleeveless V-neck. He was up a rickety home-made ladder, tacking a piece of asphalt over a hole in the roof, when Ann arrived. He was concentrating on getting the job done as quickly as he could as he didn't like heights and wasn't aware of Ann's arrival until she called up to him, 'Can I have a word, Brian?'

He stopped what he was doing to look down at her tentatively, thinking the ground seemed an awfully long way away but would only take a second or so to reach should he lose his balance. His fear of heights, though, was swept away by delight at the unexpected appearance of the love of his life. Then he frowned, bothered. It looked to him like Ann had come out in a rush. Her hair was not tidily brushed as usual, and the skirt and blouse she was wearing were old ones she wore around the house when tackling chores. Her coat was her work one. Ann, like the majority of the population, usually made it a rule that Sundays were the one day of the week when you made every effort to look your best when going out. So what had brought her here, seeking him out, in such a rush

71

that she hadn't followed her usual custom? Regardless, she could be wearing an old sack and she'd still look stunning to him.

Despite the fact he had several nails in his mouth he managed to make himself sound coherent when he responded, 'Hello, beautiful. What brings you here? Not that it's not a nice surprise but you're usually tackling your ironing or whatever it is you get up to at this time of a Sunday morning.' Then his face became worried. 'No one has died, have they? Oh, have I done something to upset you?'

She called back, 'Not unless you've found someone else you love more than me.'

He grinned cheekily. 'Now where am I going to find another woman who matches up to you?'

'Well, that's it, you're not. I'm Miss Perfect, me . . . well, perfect for you at any rate. Anyway, I haven't time for bantering about. I need to talk to you.'

'Oh, what about?'

Ann wasn't at all looking forward to saying what she had to say. In irritation she snapped, 'If you think I'm shouting what I have to say to you for all to hear then you're mistaken. Come down so I can talk to you face to face.'

Wondering why it couldn't wait until she came round to his parents' house later this afternoon for tea, Brian took the nails from his mouth, balanced the old hammer he was using on the shed roof, then carefully negotiated the rungs, jumping down the last two to stand facing her.

Before he could say anything, she was asking him, 'Is there somewhere private we can talk? And I need to get out of this cold . . . I'm freezing.'

'Private? Oh! Well, me dad's shed is about as private as it gets around here. Dad is over at Wilfred Carter's allotment, helping him spread his manure as Wilf's hurt his back. Between you and me, I know Dad is hoping there'll be some 'oss muck spare that Wilf will give to him.'

But Ann wasn't listening to what she perceived to be trivial chit-chat compared to what she had to talk to him about. She was already pushing the rotting door open to get inside the shed.

With both of them sitting in old moth-eaten deckchairs, Ann was worriedly wringing her hands, trying to think of the best way to word what she was about to say, while Brian was staring at her anxiously, his mind working overtime.

He couldn't stand the suspense any longer and urged, 'Just spill it then, love, will you? You're making me a nervous wreck, wondering what you've got to tell me.'

Ann took a deep breath. Here goes, she thought. 'There's no easy way of saying this, but . . . well . . .' Then she just couldn't bring herself to tell him what she had to as she knew it was going to hurt him so much, and blurted, 'I can't come for tea this afternoon.'

'Oh! But you always come for tea on a Sunday . . . well, since we got serious you have. Mam's expecting you. And why couldn't you have told me this outside? Why did you need to tell me in private?'

'Well . . . I knew you'd be hurt.' She then inwardly scolded herself for only putting off the inevitable. Just tell him what you have to and get it over with, she ordered herself. She took another deep breath. 'That's not all I have to tell you.'

'Oh!'

She took another huge breath and, wringing her hands tightly, blustered, 'I can't marry you, Brian . . . well, not for a while anyway. I need to move in with Cam and support her until she can cope on her own.'

His face fell in shock, his mind whirling madly at such an unexpected announcement. Ann had been thrilled beyond his dreams when he had proposed to her several weeks ago, though he agreed to her request that they should keep their news to themselves until Cam had returned, as Ann wanted her dearest friend to be the first to know. They were both young admittedly, in truth couldn't afford to marry or for him to keep her since he still had two years to go to complete his apprenticeship as a mechanic with a local garage. But his mother and father, he knew without a doubt, were very happy with his choice and would have agreed to the young couple living with them until they could afford a place of their own. Ann's wages would have paid their keep and with what was left, combined with his apprentice's pay they would have been able to have a night out now and again, and put some past for saving. Since then Ann had said only that she couldn't wait for Cam to come back so they could announce to the world their commitment to each other, so this coming out of the blue had knocked him for six.

He exclaimed, 'Eh? But why? I'm glad Cam's back as I know how much you've missed her . . . I like her myself and missed her too . . . but for someone like her, with her experience at the GPO, it won't take long to get a job and someone is always looking for a lodger.' His face filled with hurt. 'I know Cam's your best friend but I'm the man you're going to marry and spend the rest of your life with. Shouldn't I come first with you?'

Ann looked guilty. 'Yes, you're right, you should, but on this occasion I need to put Cam first. She's much more than my best friend, Brian. I love her as much as I would a sister. I owe her such a lot.'

'Owe her? Money, you mean?'

'No, not money, Brian. If it hadn't been for the likes of Cam befriending me when I so desperately needed one, I dread to think what kind of childhood I would have had, being bullied the way I was. You know I was raised in an orphanage but I've never told you just how miserable a time I was having there before Cam came to join us.' Her eyes glazed over as she remembered their first meeting. 'She was four and still in shock from losing her mother so wouldn't speak to anyone. I was fat as a child and painfully shy. I found it really hard to make friends. Some of the other kids picked on me, would play nasty tricks, make my life hell every chance they got. Always behind the Cummings' back, though, as those kids were well aware they wouldn't stand for bullying in any way and they'd be punished for what they were doing to me.

'The day Cam arrived at the home, Mrs Cummings introduced her to us kids who weren't at school yet. I remember Cam was clinging to Mrs Cummings' skirt, looking really terrified, and it took a lot of persuading for her to sit with us at the table. She wouldn't join in with what we were doing . . . drawing, I think . . . but just sat there staring into space. I didn't take much notice of her because as far as I was concerned she was just another potential bully to join the ones who plagued the life out of me. After dinner that evening, I was playing quite happily by myself in a corner of the playroom with a doll. Suddenly it was being yanked out of my hands and I was being slapped around the head by Betty Willetts. She was telling me that if I wanted to play with anything out of the toy box in future, I was to ask her for permission.

'Betty was three years older than me and a big-built girl. I wasn't the only one she picked on, and we were all smaller and younger than she was. She would demand we save our snacks for her and give her any sweets we were lucky enough to get – or risk retribution from her fist. I'd had a taste of that fist. She once gave me a hefty punch in the ribs for refusing to give her my night-time biscuit. I couldn't breathe properly for a week after so I never refused again. Anyway, she slapped me really hard and made me cry, which Betty and her group of cronies thought hilarious. They started teasing me mercilessly for being a cry baby until finally they got tired and went off to torment someone else.

'Then I realised someone was sitting beside me, clutching my hand. It was Cam. The first words she ever said to me were, "Don't let the beggars get the better of you. Me Mam told me that when a girl down our street used to chase me so she could pull my pigtails. She was jealous as she'd had to have her hair shaved off 'cos she'd got nits. *'Keep letting her away with it and it'll only get worse,'* Mam told me. *'So next time you see Letty Neville making a beeline for you, don't run, stand and face her. And if she tugs your hair, you give her a taste of her own medicine and she won't bother you again.'* I did what Mam said, but I never tugged her hair as she hadn't got any. Instead I gave her a hard kick with me steel toe-capped boots, and Mam was right. She never came near me again."

'Cam must have seen that the thought of standing up to Betty filled me with horror because she said, "Don't worry, next time that big girl and her silly friends start on you, I'll be with you and we'll stand up to 'em together."

'We never stood up to them together, though. Next time Betty Willetts made to bully me, I chickened out, stood and wet myself in the corner, but you should have seen the bruise Cam's steel toe-capped boots gave her! And how surprised she was to hear that Cam would do it again if she and her cronies didn't leave me alone. They never came near me again with Cam as my bodyguard. My life improved drastically from that day on. Cam and I became inseparable. Having my own friend at long last, and a popular girl like her, gave me the confidence I needed to come out of my shell. Cam told me that having me to look out for, and as her friend to share things with, helped her get over her mother's death.'

Brian's own family had been living on the breadline while he was growing up, their finances only improving when he and his two brothers had started work and were able to contribute. He'd never known as a kid what it was like to have a new pair of trousers or shoes, had lost count of the time the better off kids in the area teased him for having his arse hanging out of his pass-me-down short trousers, and in respect of material possessions he hadn't fared any better than Ann had in the home. Unlike her, though, he'd had a very loving mother and father, tucking him into bed at night, sponging his brow when he was sick, nurturing and encouraging him at every possible turn. He couldn't imagine what it must have been like . . . was still like, in fact, for Ann . . . not to have a loving family's support. Well, he couldn't make up for Ann's past, but he could make sure she never lacked a warm loving family around her at all times in future, he decided.

He said to her, 'I'm sure if you explained to Cam that we are getting . . .'

To his shock, Ann blurted out, 'Cam mustn't know about our plans to get married else she'll never go along with mine about her sharing with me. She'll think she's coming between us.'

'But she *is* coming between us if you are putting her before me, Ann,' he said, hurt. 'Or are you having doubts about me and this is your way of letting me down gently?'

She vehemently assured him, 'No, you daft sod. I couldn't be more sure about you. I love you more than life itself and can't wait to be your wife, but I'm going to have to be patient as I have to see Cam through this bad time first.' She took a deep breath. 'Brian, I'm going to tell you what happened to her. It's something only me and Mrs Middleton know, so I'm swearing you to secrecy. Mrs Middleton only knows about it because Cam didn't know she was there when she told me . . .'

Brian was looking worried, wondering just what Ann was about to tell him. 'You know I won't breathe a word. Will you please put me out of my misery as to why you need to move in with Cam instead of marrying me?'

Ann took another deep breath. 'You know I told you Cam had gone away to look after a sick relative who suddenly materialised out of the blue? Well, that wasn't exactly the truth. I didn't like lying to you but I did it to shield her. She did go away, but it wasn't to care for a relative . . . there never was a long-lost relative. Cam went away to have a baby.'

He was visibly shaken by this revelation. 'What! Cam had a baby? Well, blow me down. But I didn't think her the type to . . . well, not wait until she was married. And her and Adrian hadn't been courting that long for them to be . . . er . . . you know. He didn't seem the type to me not to honour his responsibilities, so why . . .'

Ann cut in, 'Adrian wasn't the father, Brian. We don't know his actual identity.' She reminded him of when Cam was attacked the year before. How it had seemed that, apart from a few cuts and bruises, she'd suffered no lasting ill effects. 'Only it turned out that she wasn't fine after all, Brian. When she'd been knocked unconscious, her attacker not only stole off her, he also had his way with her. It's him who's . . .'

'Oh, God, do you mean she was raped?' he exclaimed.

She snapped, 'You're butting in again. It's hard enough me telling you this personal stuff about Cam. But, yes, she was raped. And I was going to say, before you interrupted me, that it's the bastard who took advantage of her who's the father.' Ann didn't think that Brian needed to know that Cam was so distraught on discovering she was pregnant by her attacker that she'd contemplated abortion. 'I don't know the right words to describe how devastated she was, Brian. That's why she finished with Adrian. She couldn't expect him to court her when she was carrying a baby by the man who'd raped her. It broke her heart to have Adrian believe he wasn't special to her, that she saw no future for them, when the opposite was in fact the truth.'

Brian was sadly shaking his head. He was appalled that any man could take what he wanted from a woman without her consent, let alone a lovely woman like Cam who'd had a good future ahead of her. Now that lay in ruins through one man's cowardly attack on her.

He was not a man who considered violence a way to solve any problem, but in this case, if he ever happened to discover the man's identity, then he wouldn't be responsible for his actions. The man definitely would not be able to rape a woman again after Brian had finished with him. He made to express his feelings to Ann then changed his mind for fear she would scold him for interrupting her again.

Ann told him the story of how Cam had come to find herself responsible for her unwanted child.

'Poor Cam. I can't imagine what she's been going through,' he sighed.

'Nor can I,' said Ann. Her face puckered up in anger. 'The nuns left her for the most part on her own while she was in labour. She must have been terrified. If I'd known, I'd have barged my way in and been with her throughout . . . and I'd have liked to see those nuns try and shift me.' She frowned. 'If I don't help her get on her feet then there's only one place she can go with the baby and that's the workhouse. While I have breath in my body, I will not stand by and let her do that. Cam's lost her strength of mind at the moment. Just like she was strong for me when we were children, I need to be strong for her now until she gets her strength of mind back and can cope on her own. I know without doubt she'd do the same for me. I haven't told her my plan yet as I felt it only right to tell you first.'

'But what if she won't accept your charity?'

'Cam's in no position to refuse. Anyway, by the time I've finished, she'll believe she's doing me a huge favour by moving in with me.'

'But keeping the two of you and the baby on your wage, Ann? Well . . .'

She cut in. 'Yes, it'll be a struggle, Brian, I'm under no illusion about that. We'll be lucky to afford bread and scrape some nights for dinner, but going hungry has got to be better than life in the work-house. Once you're in a place like that, it's the devil's own job to claw your way out of it. Hopefully, Cam will be able to get some sort of outwork that she can do when the baby's asleep to help money-wise, but she needs to come to terms with being a mother first so I can't bank on that for . . . well, a few weeks at least.'

Brian was looking bothered. 'How long do you think it'll take before Cam will be able to manage on her own then? I mean, how long have I to wait before our marriage plans are back on track again?'

Ann gave a disdainful tut. 'You men ask the daftest questions. How do I know? That's like asking how long it will take someone to get over the death of someone very dear to them. Some people get over it very quickly, others take years.'

'Years!' he exclaimed.

'I'm just giving you an example. At the moment Cam can't see the wood for the trees, sees the workhouse as her only option, but hopefully having me there for her will make her realise she can find a better life. It might not be the one she had planned for herself, but at least it's a better one than she can see at the moment.' She paused and looked at him levelly before saying, 'I have to do this, Brian. What sort of friend would I be if I turned my back on her? But ... well ... I'll understand if you won't wait for me while I see this through.'

He gave a grunt. 'Seems I've got no choice but to wait for you. I love you, don't I?'

Tears sprang to Ann's eyes. 'Oh, Brian,' she said. 'Hopefully you won't have to wait too long.'

CHAPTER ELEVEN

Fired up with enthusiasm to get her plan off the ground, on her way back to her lodgings Ann visited every corner shop in the area to study the cards in the windows. If anyone was offering accommodation this was where she would find it advertised. She hoped it wouldn't take long to secure somewhere as the sooner she was helping Cam sort out her life, the sooner she herself could become Brian's wife.

Ann was now at the last shop and her hopes of finding anywhere for them to live had completely evaporated. All manner of accommodation was being offered but only a handful of places were in her price range. These were two or three rooms upstairs in someone else's houses, not really suitable for their needs, but that hardly mattered as all of them were stipulating no children were welcome. Ann thought of expanding her search to other areas but where she already lived was primarily populated by low-paid, working-class people like herself, and the quality of the housing and the rents asked reflected that. If she couldn't afford anything around here, she wouldn't be able to anywhere. A dreadful feeling of foreboding was creeping through her. As matters stood, it seemed her one and only chance of stopping her friend from ending up in the work-house was not going to work out. Though how she was going to carry on with her own life, living comfortably with Ethel Middleton and planning her wedding to Brian, knowing what kind of existence the workhouse would be subjecting Cam and her baby to, Ann had no idea.

She was just about to turn and make her way home, debating whether to tell Cam of her scheme so that at least her friend knew she had tried to do something for her, when out of the corner of her eye she spotted a card lying askew on top of a display of packets of soap powder. It had obviously come unstuck from the window and fallen down.

Despite being of the opinion that she was wasting her time, Ann tilted her head and ran her eyes over it. It read: *Vacant. One-bedroomed upstairs flat.* She nearly stopped there, sure it would be out of her price range like all the other vacant one-bedroomed flats she had seen on offer that morning. Despite herself, though, she carried on reading. What she saw next made her stare at the words dumbfounded. Surely her eyes were deceiving her! But they weren't. The rent being asked for the flat was definitely six shillings and sixpence a week.

From what Ann had observed this morning the average rent for a one-bedroomed flat, in a street where the residents took pride in their homes and looked out for one other, was eight shillings a week. She herself paid six shillings and sixpence for her lodgings in one small room, albeit including her meals. And there was nothing on the card to state that the owner would not accept children. She couldn't understand why it was so cheap. Well, it just had to be that the owner was far more interested in getting decent tenants who would look after the place than he was in the money that could be made from it.

It was Sunday today and it would be very remiss of her to be disturbing anyone on their day of rest. She would go and view the flat straight after work tomorrow evening. Then a worrying thought struck her. What if someone beat her to it while she was at work? A flat within her price range might never come up again. Ann made up her mind. Sunday or not, she was going to go round and enquire after it. She wasn't exactly dressed to make a good impression on a prospective landlord, but should she take the time to go back home and dress more respectably, then again, someone else might beat her to it.

Without further ado, she kicked up her heels and headed off.

Ann was confused when she arrived at a neat-looking terrace house and not, as she had expected, two maisonettes on ground and first floor. Then she realised that, of course, this was obviously where

82

the landlord's rent collector must live. The landlord himself more than likely lived in the type of house, in the type of area, Ann herself could only dream of living in. After she'd knocked on the door it was opened to her by a harassed-looking, middle-aged woman, who was wiping her hands on the bottom of her stained apron. Ann had obviously disturbed her while she was preparing Sunday dinner. She looked enquiringly at the caller.

In an apologetic tone Ann said to her, 'I'm sorry to bother you but I've come about the flat advertised in Frear's shop window.'

The woman said, 'Oh, it's my husband you want. I'll warn you, he ain't gonna be very happy about having his day of rest disturbed.' She went back inside, shutting the door behind her.

Several moments later it was opened again by a small wiry man of about fifty who was pulling his braces over his shoulders. His wife was right, he didn't look at all happy about having his peace disrupted. 'Wife sez yer've come about the one-bed flat?'

Ann eagerly responded, 'I do apologise for not being properly dressed but, yes, I have. For me and my friend and her...'

'Lady, I don't care what you wear or who the hell lives in the flat as long as the rent's paid promptly. But I'll remind you it's Sunday today and I don't work on a Sunday. Come back tomorrow about six. I'll show yer the flat then.'

'Oh, but I'm worried it'll be gone by then. I do appreciate it's a Sunday but couldn't you just...'

He cut in sharply, 'Got cloth ears, have yer? I've already said, I don't work on a Sunday. If yer that keen on it, be here at nine tomorrow morning and I'll tek yer to view it then.'

'Oh, but I'll be at work.'

'Well, then, six tomorrow night. And if the flat's gone, it's just too bad.'

He made to step back inside and shut the door. Fearful she would lose the flat to someone else, Ann blurted, 'I'll take it! You will let me have it, won't you?'

He looked at her in surprise for a moment, then said, 'You good for the rent?'

'Oh, yes. I work at Pex Hosiery... have done since I left school. I'm sure I can get a reference if you need one.'

He scratched the back of his neck. 'You look honest enough to me, so I'll tek yer word for it. Be warned, mind, no rent when I come to collect and I won't accept excuses. It's immediate eviction. Well, seeing as you've saved me the time of teking yer to see the flat, I'll make a concession and break my rule about not working on a Sunday. I'll sort out the rent book for yer and get yer the keys. You can move in whenever you like.'

Ann exclaimed in delight, 'Really? Oh, that's wonderful. Thank you so much.' That meant Cam wouldn't have to traipse the streets looking for someone to take her and the baby tonight, and possibly end up again in the derelict warehouse.

He went back inside and, a moment later, returned holding a new rent book and pen. Having asked Ann's name and completed the rest of the details, he handed it to her, saying, 'That'll be two pounds, six shillings and sixpence.'

Ann gasped. 'How much?'

'The six and six is for the week's rent in advance, and two pounds is for all the stuff that comes with the flat.'

Oh, the flat came fully equipped? This was getting better and better. They hadn't got any furniture or even the most basic of household equipment between them and Ann had reckoned on managing without until they could buy what they needed. But the problem was that although she could manage the rent money, out of her last week's wage, she hadn't got the two pounds for all the stuff that came with the flat. Having still a few months to go before she was considered fully trained – despite the fact that she completed her work as quickly and professionally as the best machinists in the factory – Ann was on training pay and had never had any spare to set aside. Cam's job had paid far more than hers and Ann knew she had been saving up to equip her own flat before she had discovered she was pregnant. Upon departing for the home to await the birth of her baby, Cam had entrusted her PO book to Ann's safekeeping, but out of respect she had never looked in it to see how much was there. She just had to hope that her friend did indeed have the two pounds.

She told the rent collector, 'I can pay the rent money now but I'll have to give you the rest for all the other stuff tomorrow. It has to be drawn out of the Post Office.' She prayed he would accept that.

'I'll be in at seven. Make sure you bring it then or yer out – and yer won't get a refund on the rent yer've paid. I collect the rents in that street on a Friday night round about eight.'

Ann handed him the six shillings and sixpence and he handed her a set of keys and the rent book. Without another word to her, he went back inside and shut the door.

He definitely wasn't the sort of friendly rent collector who called on Mrs Middleton each week, and would stop for a cup of tea if he had time. Still, it didn't matter how offhand he was; what did was that she had secured Cam and her baby a roof over their heads, and herself the ability to help her friend rebuild her life.

Ann couldn't wait to tell her the good news!

CHAPTER TWELVE

Ann found Cam fast asleep on the sofa, the baby in the suitcase asleep too, and despite how desperate she was to impart her good news, she felt it would be so cruel to wake them. It was apparent that Cam had fed the child during her absence as the buttons on her blouse were only partway done up. She'd obviously fallen asleep before she had finished doing them up. It distressed Ann to see that, even in sleep, the strain Cam was under was very apparent on her face. Well, hopefully that would lift when Ann had told her the news.

She tiptoed back into the kitchen, pulling the door to behind her, and put on the kettle. It suddenly struck her that Cam probably hadn't eaten since she'd left the home the previous evening. She felt guilty for not thinking of that and offering her something when she had turned up earlier that morning. Well, she could make up for it by having a hot meal ready for her friend when she woke up.

Cam would have slept until the baby woke her for its next feed had Ann not dropped the colander on the kitchen floor when she reached up to unhook it. She wanted to drain the potatoes she'd par-boiled, ready to toss in hot fat and roast in the oven to accompany the chicken leg Mrs Middleton had left her, knowing she was going out for dinner herself. There was not enough meat on the chicken leg for the two of them. Cam would get it, Ann disguising the fact that she had no meat on her own plate. Her friend needed to have her strength built back up after having the baby.

The clang of the colander hitting the floor had Cam sitting bolt upright, looking around in a daze, wondering just where she was. Ann, worried that her clumsiness would have awoken her friend, popped her head around the door to check and looked dismayed to see that it had. 'Oh, I'm sorry I woke you, Cam. Clumsy clot, I am, dropping the colander on the floor. Did the baby let you sleep all the time I've been gone?'

Cam gave a weary shake of her head. 'It started howling to be fed only moments after you left. It seemed to take ages this time to have its fill.' She gently touched both breasts, wincing at the tenderness of her nipples where the child had tightly clamped its gums on to them.

'Well, try and get a bit more rest while I finish off cooking us dinner.'

Cam was ravenous but her need to find accommodation for her and the baby was far more important. She shook her head. 'I really haven't time for sleeping any more. I need to find us somewhere to stay tonight.' She gave a heavy sigh. 'Ann, pray I find somewhere that'll take me and the baby. I can't bear the thought of staying in that warehouse again.'

Ann gave a secretive smile. 'I don't need to pray for anything of the sort. I've such good news to tell you! Well, I hope you'll think it good news . . . I'm sure you will. Look, let me just put the spuds in to roast and pour you a cuppa, then we can sit down and I'll tell you.'

A short while later Cam was staring at Ann in utterly incredulity. 'You seriously want me and the baby to move in with you?'

Ann vigorously nodded. 'I've already told you, I was going to ask you if you would consider sharing when you came home. The baby doesn't change that. It's been good living with Mrs Middleton, but I'm ready to get my own place now. There's no one else I'd rather share with than you. You'd be doing me a big favour if you said yes. Just think of it, Cam. Deciding what we want for dinner and not having to eat what's dished up to us, whether we fancy it or not. Not having to put up with the landlady's family visiting, and having to make up an excuse to go to our room or out 'cos they're driving us mad. We can have such fun, making the place homely with our own things and not having to look at someone else's hideous knick-knacks. And it'll be fun for me, too, helping you look after the baby. And I could give you plenty more reasons for us moving in together.

'I didn't mention anything about this when you first got here with the baby, and told me your experiences trying to get a room last night, because I thought it best to find out if I could find us somewhere that'd take us first, before I put it to you.'

Cam was having trouble swallowing for the lump that was constricting her throat. Ann's proposition was the answer to her accommodation problem. She would have liked nothing more than to allow a tide of relief to flood through her that this burden had been lifted from her, but Ann had not thought her proposition through properly. There was at least one glaring problem that Cam could see that wouldn't have presented itself to Ann. Not to point it out to her wouldn't be fair; Cam wouldn't be Ann's best friend if she didn't.

'Oh, Ann, us sharing a place and having you to help me with the baby . . . well, it's the answer to my prayers. But there's something you don't seem to have thought of or you wouldn't be suggesting what you have. I can pay my share at the moment out of my savings, but once that's gone — and there won't be much left after I've got the baby the basics of what it needs — I won't be able to pay my way until I at least stop breast feeding and can get a minder who doesn't charge the earth so I can go out to work.'

'I had thought about that,' Ann told her. 'It's not going to be easy, we'll have to watch every penny, but my wages will cover us. We'll *make* them do . . . until you're in a position to look for work. Maybe there's some outwork you could do at home while the baby's sleeping? I could ask at my place to see if any is going. You might not earn much but every bit will help. In the meantime, you could take care of the housework and cooking as your contribution.'

Cam eyed her with deep affection. 'You have thought about this all, haven't you?' She gave a deep sigh. 'Oh, Ann, I really want to take you up on your offer, you don't know how much I do, but . . .'

'But what?'

'Have you thought what people are going to think of you for sharing a place with an unmarried mother? What about Brian and his family? What will they think?'

'I don't give a damn what people think,' Ann replied firmly. 'It's you I'm worried for, people thinking you're a loose woman when that couldn't be further from the truth.' She lapsed into silence for a moment before saying to Cam, 'There's no real reason why anyone should know you aren't married, is there? I mean, when someone tells us they're married, we don't ask to see their marriage certificate for proof, do we? They tell us they're married and we accept that. So, Cam, from now on you're not an unmarried mother, you're a widow. Mrs Rogers, not Miss. If anyone asks, you lost your husband not long after you got married and found out you were pregnant. He had a terrible accident . . . He . . . er . . .' A vision of Brian doing his balancing act on the ladder earlier that morning sprang to mind. 'He died after falling off a ladder when he was fixing a hole in a roof. Be best for the baby, too, people thinking its dad's dead and it's legitimate. It won't get taunted rotten when it goes to school by other kids that way, will it? You remember how we were taunted by the kids with parents when we went to school?'

Cam could, only too well; could still feel the pain and hurt of being ridiculed for having no parents, through no fault of her own.

To Cam's bemusement Ann jumped up from her chair then and dashed over to the mantle over the fire, lifting up a cheap pottery vase. She brought it back to the table where she tipped it up, allowing the contents to spill out. Amongst the several sewing needles, hooks and eyes, a couple of farthings and some balls of fluff, were three brass curtain rings. Ann picked one up and held it out to Cam, saying to her, 'Your wedding ring. These three curtain rings have been in here for as long as I've been lodging, so I doubt Mrs M will miss one.'

Cam took it and placed it on the third finger of her left hand, then held out her hand to look at it. 'In the right light, you could mistake it for gold, couldn't you? This simple curtain ring changes everything, doesn't it? When people see me wearing it they'll automatically think I'm married.'

'Now that's all settled, you've no excuse not to move in with me, have you?'

Cam shook her head.

Ann was telling her, 'We can move into the flat today as it comes fully equipped. So no more traipsing streets looking for a place to stay or derelict warehouses for you. No more worry about landing in the workhouse either.'

To Ann's joy she saw the look of desolation fade from Cam's eyes to be replaced by one of hope. Cam herself felt a great weight lift from her shoulders and a flood of relief wash through her.

'What's the flat like?' she eagerly asked Ann.

'Well, I haven't actually seen it.' She explained why. 'So we'll both see it for the first time together.' Then she remembered the money for all the stuff that came with the flat. 'We're so fortunate that we haven't got to buy anything for the flat as everything comes with it, but we do still have to pay for it.'

'How much?'

'Well, it's cheap really considering we don't have to buy anything and can move in straight away. Two pounds. That means my half would be a pound only I haven't got a pound, Cam. I used all I had to pay the rent. I was hoping you'd have it in your savings and then I could pay you back my half when I can . . . it might be in dribs and drabs, though.' She eyed Cam worriedly. 'You do have it, don't you, or we lose the flat?'

Thankfully she had. It had taken her four years to amass £9.16s.6d. in her Post Office savings account. Now that money was going to have to be used to buy things she had never anticipated needing: like a crib for the child, bedding, and baby clothes. After paying out the two pounds, she hoped that the remainder would stretch to getting the basics the baby needed, plus keep her paying her way until such time as she could find work. Hopefully Ann would come up trumps with some outwork she could fit in around caring for the baby.

Over in the suitcase the baby stirred. Ann flashed a glance over at it then looked back at Cam, asking, 'Did you attempt to change its nappy while I was out? If you did, what is it then . . . a boy or girl? And it needs a name, Cam. You can't keep calling it *it*.'

Cam looked across at the child. When it had woken only moments after Ann had left, demanding to be fed by letting out its ear-piercing, high-pitched squeal, she had not forgotten that it was well overdue for a nappy change. Wanting the least possible contact with it, she had sat on the sofa, holding it away from her and trying not to look while she fed it. As soon as it was satisfied, she had put it back into the suitcase and then immediately fallen asleep herself, but not before praying that she'd wake to find her maternal feelings for her own child had somehow miraculously stirred, even just a little, so she wouldn't feel such revulsion when she had to handle it. But they hadn't, not even a little. Cam still resented the child's presence in her life and all she had been forced to give up for it; couldn't bear to think it was part of her, her own blood flowing around its veins, that it could show traits of hers come time, features and characteristics.

But how she was acting towards her child wasn't fair. It was a human being after all. She wouldn't treat a helpless animal in such a cold, callous way. To thrive and grow it needed more than feeding and its nappy changing; it needed to be properly handled, with care and attention, held close in her arms, made to feel it was loved . . . all the things that adoptive parents would have done for it but that now she was expected to do. Somehow she had to find a way to bring herself to look after the baby as it should be cared for. She wished she knew how, though.

Cam didn't realise that Ann was watching her closely; hadn't noticed her friend witness her recoil at the thought of the physical contact she'd need to make in order to change the child's nappy. She knew Cam was struggling with her conscience for her lack of maternal feelings, and wished she herself could wave a magic wand that would awaken her friend's love for the child instead of her hostility. Suddenly an idea began to take shape in Ann's mind. It might sound ridiculous to Cam, but then it just might work well enough to help her attend to the child's basic needs. And, come time, maybe her maternal feelings for it would start to emerge.

Ann laid a hand on Cam's arm and gently said to her, 'I know you're still having trouble warming to the baby, but I have an idea that might help. It might sound a bit daft to you . . .'

'I'm willing to give anything a try, Ann,' Cam eagerly interjected. 'I can't go on like this . . . it's not fair to it. I'm not surprised it looks at me like it does. Young as it is, it must know how I feel about it.'

Ann said with conviction, 'I'm sure the baby doesn't look at you in the way you think it does. As for my idea . . . well, how about you pretending to yourself that you're caring for it on behalf of someone else? Like its own mother has had to go away for a while and you're just looking after it meantime. People who adopt learn to love other people's children like they are their own, don't they?'

Cam stared thoughtfully at Ann. Her idea was far-fetched but regardless it was worth a try. She told her, 'I could pretend I've a sister and I'm the baby's auntie.'

Ann smiled. 'And I'm its other auntie, giving you a hand. Well, I think we aunties need to change your sister's baby's nappy. If I fold it for you and talk you through it, do you want to give it a try?'

For the first time since her return, Ann saw Cam smile.

A short while later they both held their breath as the still-sleeping child's nappy was unpinned and removed, and its gender was finally revealed.

'Oh, you . . . your sister has a little girl,' said Ann, while thinking to herself that during her absence the child's looks hadn't improved any. It was still just as ugly, and she wasn't a robust baby at all, quite small and puny in fact.

I've got a daughter, Cam was thinking. She searched her feelings, hoping to find there a spark of warmth for the child now she knew its gender, but still there was nothing but resentment. It was strange, though, but her resentment towards it wasn't quite so fierce since she had begun to make herself believe she was only caring for the child on behalf of a fictitious sister.

'What about Constance?' Ann said to her. 'Very grand-sounding.'

'Pardon?'

'For its name.'

Cam looked at her blankly. She hadn't thought of a name for her child, it hadn't entered her head. Her brows knotted in thought. She had always intended to name any girl child she had after her mother: Edith. Such a regal and strong-sounding name, and she had a vague memory that her mother had been named after her own grandmother, so it was a family name. She herself had been named after her paternal grandmother, Camella. But it didn't seem right to follow family tradition when this child shouldn't have been born to her in the first place. Cam shook her head. 'I think I . . . my sister . . . would like something more . . . pretty-sounding than Constance.'

'Mmmm,' mouthed Ann, as usual not thinking before she spoke.

'Yes, it needs something about it to be pretty.' She lapsed into thought for a moment, exploring other names that she thought were pretty-sounding. 'Oh, what about Rosemary? Rose for short?'

Having come up with nothing she liked better herself, Cam mulled this over for a moment then nodded. 'Yes, that's pretty. Just Rose, though. I . . . my sister would like that.'

Ann smiled. 'That's settled then.' She addressed the sleeping child. 'Hello, Rose. I hope you're happy with your name.'

The child opened its eyes and looked directly at her for several seconds before they drifted shut again. Ann gave a violent shudder. She knew what Cam meant now and she hadn't been exaggerating. If looks could kill . . .

Both women jumped then as the sound of the back door opening and shutting reached their ears. Mrs Middleton had returned. She was much earlier than she had told Ann she'd be. And the dinner wasn't quite done yet so Cam hadn't been fed. Ann knew that she wouldn't mind the fact that Cam was here, but she wouldn't take kindly to a baby that could, as babies did, cry at any time and grate on her nerves, especially on her day of rest.

Ethel was calling out, 'Ann, you there, ducky? Can yer come and help me get me boots off? Me back's gone and I can't bend down to unzip 'em.'

Ann had turned pale. She was not looking forward to telling her landlady she was leaving, and that very afternoon too. Ethel had often told her that she was the best lodger she had ever had and wasn't going to be happy at the prospect of taking in another who might not fit in so well as Ann had done.

Cam sensed what she was thinking. 'I'd better make myself scarce and leave you to break your news to Mrs M.'

Ann hated the thought of asking Cam to wait for her out in the open in this cold weather but as it was Sunday there was nowhere open so had no alternative but to tell her, 'Go out the front and I'll meet you on the street corner as soon as I can. I'll try not to keep you waiting too long.'

It was just under an hour later when Ann joined Cam who was perched on a low wall, waiting. Ann was laden down with her heavy suitcase of belongings and a brown carrier bag.

'Was Mrs M very upset when you told her you were leaving?' Cam asked, easing herself off the wall, mindful not to disturb Rose who was sleeping in her aching arms. She was so cold her bones felt as if they were made of stone.

Ann nodded as she rested the heavy case on the ground. 'She wasn't in the best of moods. Her daughter's three children all have bad colds. They weren't allowed out and drove her daft, running rampage around the house. They gave her a bad headache . . . that's why she came back early. As you can imagine, my news just made her day.'

To protect Cam she had told Ethel that Cam had after all decided to keep her baby and needed help getting on her feet, so that was why Ann was moving in with her. And, as luck would have it, a flat they could afford was available for them to move into with immediate effect.

'She had a tear in her eye when I first told her, but she appreciated it was time for me to move on. Her good humour was restored a bit when I told her I hadn't had time to eat the dinner I'd cooked as I was late for meeting you. She'd left her daughter's before they'd dished up the dinner. She was very thoughtful, though. While I was doing my packing she made us up some cheese sandwiches as she knew no shops would be open for us to get any food and didn't like the thought of us going hungry until tomorrow. She's given us a bit of tea, sugar, half a pint of milk, a knob of margarine, and the rest of the loaf she made the sandwiches from for toast for tomorrow's breakfast.'

'That was very nice of her,' said Cam, her mouth salivating at the thought of the cheese sandwiches. It was getting on for eighteen hours since she'd last eaten and she was beginning to feel faint with hunger. 'We'll have to have Mrs M round for tea once we're settled.'

'Yes, we will. Oh, no, in my rush not to keep you waiting longer than I had to, I forgot to give her our new address. Oh, never mind, I'll pop in after work one night and give it her then. I must tell Brian too. I'll do that during my dinner break tomorrow.' A mischievous smile curved her lips. 'It'll be nice for me and Brian to be able to sit on a sofa together without having Mrs M watching our every move from her armchair. And not having to check all the time with her if it's all right for him to come round.'

'Whenever you want some time alone with Brian, I will always make myself scarce,' Cam told her.

Ann smiled at her. 'I know you would, but the flat will be your home as much as it is mine. I wouldn't dream of asking you to make yourself scarce in your own home.' She gave a giggle. 'Anyway, sneaking a kiss and a cuddle on your own sofa wouldn't be as exciting or feel as naughty as when you do it as soon as the likes of Brian's parents' or Mrs M's backs are turned.' Her face filled with excitement. 'Come on, let's hurry. I can't wait to see the flat.'

'Neither can I,' replied Cam. 'Where is it?'

Ann stared at her blankly for a moment. 'Oh, that's a point, I don't know.' She opened her handbag and fished around in it for the rent book. Finding it, she pulled it out, shut the handbag and opened up the book to look at the address the landlord's agent had written in it. 'Sun Street. Number fifty-seven.'

'Sun Street. It sounds nice,' said Cam.

'It does,' agreed Ann. 'I've no idea where it is, though.'

'No, neither have I.'

A man was heading towards them, tugging along a reluctant mongrel dog who obviously hadn't wanted to leave a warm fireside for a walk with its master in the cold.

'Excuse me.' Ann waylaid the man as he made to pass them. 'Could you direct us to Sun Street, please?'

The man looked at them both strangely for a moment before he asked, 'You sure that's where yer want to go?'

Meanwhile Cam was distracted by the mangy-looking dog that was sniffing around her shoes.

'I'm positive,' Ann told the man. 'Me and my friend are moving into a flat there.'

He shot them an even stranger look before launching into a lengthy list of directions. When he had finished, he gave the dog's lead a hard tug and went on his way.

'Did you see the look that man gave us when I told him where we wanted to go?' Ann asked Cam.

She shook her head. 'I wasn't taking any notice. His dog was a bit too keen on my shoes and I was worried it was either going to bite my ankle or wee up my leg. What kind of look did he give us?'

'Sort of peculiar.'

'Oh! Well, maybe he thinks the likes of us not good enough to live on Sun Street.'

'Me and you are good enough to live on any street,' Ann snapped. 'Cheek of the man, if that's what he was thinking.'

CHAPTER THIRTEEN

The directions took them through a warren of backstreets that became increasingly more neglected the further on they journeyed. It felt to both women as if they were entering a thick dense jungle, only instead of trees and vegetation it was the encroaching buildings that were preventing any light from penetrating. Following the man's directions was proving quite difficult for them as several street names were missing, just marks on walls where once they had been, so the girls just had to hope that the turns they took were the right ones.

The sign on the street they were walking down now was missing, and the street itself was squalid to say the least. It was actually a dead end at the bottom, blocked off by the back end of a factory or warehouse – it was hard to determine which, but it looked disused as all the windows in the building were broken and large gaps in the roof exposed rotting beams where tiles had fallen off. The hotch-potch of antiquated dwellings around it, most of which had been built early in the last century, were soot-grimed from the years they had stood in the drifts of black smoke belching from the surrounding factory chimneys. The streets were much narrower here than the ones they had left behind. Several of the dwellings they passed seemed to be listing dangerously, clinging together like a stack of cards about to topple any moment, but it was apparent people were still residing in them. The glass in several of the gas lamps was either cracked or broken from stones being thrown at them. The cobbles on the pavement were buckled, making walking along difficult. They constantly had to be vigilant not to trip on protruding ones, and in the road there were more potholes than cobbles, which were all filled with muddy water. Rotting rubbish filled the gutters, intermittent piles of dog excrement soiled the pavement, grimy nets hung at unwashed windows and doorsteps looked as if they hadn't been scrubbed for decades. Lines strung across the street held threadbare dingy washing. The only greenery growing in this street was weeds.

Despite the bitter weather, a group of raggedly dressed children were playing football with a tin can. Several slovenly, hard-faced women lounged against front door frames, most with handmade cigarettes dangling from the corner of their mouths. They stopped their gossiping with each other to look suspiciously at the two strangers as they passed by.

They seemed to have been walking for such a long time. Cam, already low on energy before they had set off, was now struggling to put one foot in front of the other. The baby felt like a tonne weight in the aching crook of her arm, the suitcase as if it was filled with house bricks. She knew she was bleeding heavily and urgently needed to change her wadding before an embarrassing situation resulted.

Ann came to a stop, saying, 'This looks like a dead end to me. According to the man's instructions this should be Sun Street... God forbid!'

Cam looked pale. 'It can't be much further, can it? Only the baby is due to wake for another feed any time.'

Ann pulled a perplexed expression. 'We're obviously in completely the wrong area. That man has either given us the wrong directions or we've taken a wrong turn somewhere.' She stole a furtive glance over at the fierce women on their doorsteps, still looking over at them suspiciously. She didn't fancy approaching them for directions. She made to ask Cam if she would do the deed when she spotted a threadbare old woman shuffling towards them. 'We'll ask this old dear how we get out of this God forsaken place and hope she knows how we find Sun Street from here.'

As the woman came up to them, Ann said to her, 'Excuse me, but we seem to have got ourselves lost. We're looking for Sun Street. You don't happen to know how we can get there from here, do you?'

A pair of old eyes looked at them warily for a moment before she replied, 'This *is* Sun Street. Whoever named it was having a joke.

We never seem to see the sunshine here, even in the height of summer.' She noticed their cases and added, 'You must be the new tenants for the vacant flat just a bit further down? Last tenants just upped and left last week, leaving most of their stuff behind. Where they went to no one seems to know, but wherever it is it's got to be a damned sight better than here.' She eyed them both with deep sympathy. 'Welcome to Hell.'

With that she went on her way.

Desperate to free her aching arms from their load, and to rest a weary body still recovering its strength after giving birth, Cam was also very worried Rose might start howling for a feed at any minute. She was facing the prospect of doing it out in the open if they didn't reach their destination very soon. The fact they had arrived somewhere so grim wasn't registering with her at the moment.

Ann, though, was frozen in horror. How stupid she had been, to take the tenancy on a flat she hadn't even seen. What had she brought Cam, the baby and herself to? Judging by the street, she didn't need to guess what condition the flat would be in. Definitely not the cosy image she had built up in her mind! No wonder the rent being asked was cheap compared to others. She should have realised at the time, but in her urgent need to find Cam and herself a place to live, all sense and reason had left her. No wonder the man they had asked directions from had given them the look he had. He had obviously known what this area was like and couldn't believe they were voluntarily coming to live here. And that crook of a landlord had had the damned cheek to charge them for the stuff the last tenants had left behind! They had no choice but to pay it, though, or he'd revoke their tenancy. Ann hoped that the last tenants had left nice stuff and that all the pots and pans were cleaned before they scarpered off.

She felt an overwhelming urge to turn about and rush back to the lighter, airier streets only a mile away, where no litter was allowed to fall and the residents took pride in their homes and didn't stare at strangers as if deciding whether or not they were worth robbing. She could always beg Ethel Middleton to take her back into her comfortable home . . .

But that would mean abandoning Cam and her baby. Ann couldn't do that. Whether she liked it or not, until they could afford something better, this hell-hole was where she was going to be living.

She was very aware that to voice these feelings to Cam would make her start to question just why Ann had suggested sharing, and wasn't about to let her know she was only doing it for Cam's benefit. Taking a deep breath, Ann heaved up her suitcase and said airily, 'Well, only a few yards to go now. Come on.'

Cam was mortally relieved to hear it.

An overwhelming smell of damp and general decay hit them as soon as they stepped over the threshold into a dark forbidding hallway where large chunks of plaster had fallen off in places, exposing the rotting lattice framework beneath. The black and while tiles on the floor were nearly all cracked or broken and sticky under their feet, it being apparent they hadn't been washed for God knew how long. Cobwebs hung thickly from every corner of the cracked and damp-marked ceiling, and around the gas mantles.

There was a door to the right of them. There was nothing on it to indicate whether this was the entrance to the downstairs or the upstairs flat. At the other end of the corridor, to their left, was another door and it didn't look as though there was any indication on that either. There was a door at the end of the corridor with stained glass in it which must lead into the back yard.

Ann looked at Cam, her intention being to ask her which door she thought they should try. But Cam was in no fit state to make any decisions. She was exhausted, about to drop, and Ann needed to get her seated before she collapsed.

Ann shuddered then. She sensed she was being watched. Her head shot around to look at the door to the right of her. It was open a crack, and a rheumy eye was peering out at her.

She smiled politely. 'Hello. We're your new . . .'

Before Ann had chance to say any more the eye withdrew and the door opened just enough to reveal a dirty witch-like old crone, dressed from head to toe in threadbare black. She looked at least a hundred to nineteen-year-old Ann. A foul stench oozed out from behind her. It made Ann's stomach churn. In an age-cracked voice, the woman barked, 'I knows who yer are. Yer the new lot for upstairs. Well, I'll tell you the same as I told all the other tenants before yer. I keeps meself to meself so don't bother coming a-knocking for cups of sugar or a spoon of tea when yer've run out, 'cos yer'll get n'ote from me.'

With that, she slammed shut her door.

Ann was left gawping. Not a friendly neighbour then, she thought. At least she now knew which door to take.

Relieving Cam of her suitcase and letting her follow behind, Ann struggled up with both cases, arriving on a small landing with another door facing her. Dropping the cases, she unlocked that door and went inside.

Ann took a look around. The room she had entered was in a worse state than she had expected. It was about twenty foot long by twelve wide. One half was set out as a kitchen, the other as a living area. In the kitchen end the window had a tattered-looking paper blind pulled halfway down. Ann guessed it looked out on to the yard. Under it was a heavily stained and cracked pot sink with one large dull brass tap, albeit it was mostly green through lack of cleaning, and a warped wooden draining board. There was one large cupboard for storage and one low one. Both were empty. The low one held two gas rings. A battered, blackened saucepan sat on one of them. It was going to be very difficult cooking meals for them both on just two gas rings. Both cupboards showed the signs of years of wear. On the wall above the low one were three empty shelves. In the middle of the kitchen area stood a rickety gate-legged table with two old chairs pushed underneath it, the stuffing on their seats coming out in places. The floor covering was a piece of black-and-white checkered linoleum that was holey and threadbare in parts.

The living area held a shabby and uncomfortable-looking dark brown horsehair sofa and two matching wing-back chairs, all set around an old-fashioned, cast-iron fireplace, with an oven on the side that was desperately in need of blackleading. On the wall opposite the fireplace stood a huge Victorian relic of a dresser. Ann had never seen anything quite so ugly but it would serve its purpose for storing things in.

All the white-washed walls were dingy with age and, as in the hallway, plaster had fallen off in places to expose the rotting lathes underneath. Black soot rings discoloured the areas above the gas mantles. The previous tenants had left piles of rubbish all over, which was beginning to decay. Ann shuddered when she spotted three dead mice on the floor in the kitchen and another body sticking out from beneath the sofa. All the windows in the flat had rotting and warped window frames, newspaper stuffed in the gaps in an attempt to stop the wind howling though, and several of the panes were cracked.

Ann noticed another door at the side of the Victorian dresser and deduced it must lead into the bedroom. She went to investigate. It held a rusting iron bed frame with a suspect-looking flock mattress on it; a washstand with one of its legs broken and held up by a house brick; an old chest of drawers. The decor and window frames were in the same depressing state as the rest of the flat. It was also freezing cold in here, almost as cold as it was outside.

Back in the living area, Ann picked up the one moth-eaten cushion off the sofa and gave it a pat. A cloud of dust flew out. She gave an angry sigh. No wonder the last tenants had left all this stuff behind. All it was fit for was throwing on a bonfire and burning. And she had been stupid enough to agree to pay two pounds for it! She had to admire the agent's way of making himself some money, though, albeit at their expense. Judging from what she had observed up to now, people in this street were poorer than church mice, so she did wonder why the last tenants had absconded leaving just about everything they couldn't carry behind. In a hurry, obviously. And how naive of her to have assumed that his use of the word 'furnishings' meant the flat was equipped with all, or at least the basics, they'd need: such as pots and pans, crockery, sheets and blankets for the bed. Money for those things would have to be found. She just had to hope that Cam had enough for now. Ann would pay her share as and when she could.

She shut her eyes and tried to envision how the place would look after being cleared of the last tenants' rubbish and the dead mice; the holes in the walls patched; a fire burning in the grate and the mantles on low, a few personal bits and pieces of hers and Cam's dotted about after they'd scrubbed the place top to bottom. She opened her eyes again, issuing a heavy sigh. There was more chance of making Brian's dad's old shed homely than there ever was this place.

She suddenly realised that Cam was very quiet. In fact, she hadn't seen her since stepping into the flat to take a look around. Cam had been following behind coming up the stairs. Where was she? Her mind racing, Ann dashed over to the door leading to the stairs and then stopped short. Cam was perched on the top step, her head resting against the wall, Rose still fast asleep in the crook of her arm.

Cam flashed her a wan smile and in a laboured voice said, 'I just had to sit down for a few minutes.'

Ann leaned down and slipped her arm around her. 'Let me help you up. You can have a rest while I make you a cuppa. Er . . . before you go into the flat, I feel I should warn you that . . .'

Cam held up one hand. 'I don't care what the flat is like. I'm just so grateful you wanted a place of your own and asked me to share with you.'

Ann had no doubt that Cam genuinely meant that, but whether she'd still be of the same mind when she wasn't so tired and was able properly to take in her new surroundings remained to be seen.

She had just worked out how to turn on the gas rings, having first asked Cam for threepence to put in the gas meter, when an horrendous, ear-piecing squeal made her nearly jump out of her skin. Ann spun around, proclaiming, 'Good Lord, what on earth is that?'

Above the commotion, Cam shouted to her, 'It's the baby waking up for her feed.'

Ann gawped in astonishment. It seemed impossible for such a scrawny little thing to make such a racket. She just hoped that Rose didn't cry very often!

CHAPTER FOURTEEN

Cam stood in the middle of the living area, her dressing gown on over her clothes in an effort to ward off the cold, and stared around her. The only words she could find to describe the flat were 'absolutely atrocious'. A fire burning brightly in the grate would have done a little to help the ambience of the place, but they had no fuel. She could just about remember the house she had lived in with her widowed mother before she had died. She had struggled to keep them both on her paltry laundry assistant's wage, and they'd lived in a two up, two down terrace house which had been so damp that mildew had grown in the cracks in the walls, and a continuous battle was fought to keep bugs and rodents at bay. The children's home, too, had been a cold and draughty mausoleum and that also had its problems with vermin, but both places were palaces compared to this dwelling. In fact, the whole building, the street, the surrounding streets, needed condemning as totally unfit for human habitation. And as for the furniture . . . it certainly wasn't worth at all the money they were being made to hand over for it.

As she stood looking around, it was extremely difficult for Cam to understand why her friend was so desperate to leave her comfortable lodgings with Ethel Middleton for a place of her own that she'd reduce herself to living in such a dump as this. But, thankfully, she had been. If not, Cam herself and Rose would be in a place that was worse . . . if that were possible. Cam vowed she would do her best to help Ann make the flat as homely as they could, which wasn't going to be an easy task as it was doubtful they'd have any funds to spare for luxuries.

There was so much to do just to get it in a liveable state that she didn't know where to begin. Ann had made an attempt yesterday afternoon by clearing away most of the rubbish the last tenants had left behind, along with the dead mice and finding a few more, but she hadn't been able to sweep the floors as they hadn't a brush. She had burned some of the rubbish in the grate, which had afforded them both a temporary bit of heat. Cam had felt so guilty for not being able to give her a hand. Her brain had been willing but her body just would not let her.

After Ann had helped her on to the sofa, she'd hardly been able to muster the energy to feed the baby and drink the most welcome cup of tea that Ann had made her along with her share of the cheese sandwiches Mrs Middleton had kindly made them. Ann had had to brew the tea in the blackened, battered saucepan after boiling the water up in it, and then they both drank their share from it as it was the only receptacle they had until they could manage to buy some crockery. Cam had then drifted in and out of sleep as Ann had laboured on. She could barely even remember going to bed.

She certainly remembered being woken by Rose twice during the night for a feed; there was no way even the deepest of sleepers could have failed to be woken by the frenzied screaming the child made. Both times had Ann sitting bolt upright, proclaiming, '*What the . . . Oh, it's the baby*,' before flopping back down again. Having no sheets or blankets, their coats and dressing gowns had been all they'd had to keep them warm, but the protection they had offered had not been enough to ward off the bitter night air, even when they'd cuddled into each other. Adding to their difficulties were the noises filtering through from outside: of other screaming children, adults bawling at one another, barking dogs and screeching cats.

Cam had been half awake, feeding Rose in an armchair at just after six that morning, when Ann had come through dressed for work, the restless night very evident in her whole demeanour. As she made her way into the kitchen area to put the saucepan of water on the gas ring to boil, she said through a yawn, 'Morning. I can see by looking at you, that you slept as well as I did.'

Cam looked apologetically at her. 'I'm so sorry Rose kept waking you up. It'd probably be better if I slept on the sofa until she starts sleeping through.'

'It was only twice, Cam. She sleeps well really, considering some wake up several times during the night. Mrs M said one of her grand-kids doesn't sleep at all! Anyway, Rose has got some holler on her. I'd still hear her. Let's hope she grows out of that. I wouldn't let you sleep on that sofa anyway, it's not even comfortable to sit on.

'I didn't get much sleep because I was so bloody cold. I have no idea how Eskimos sleep in igloos! We need to get some blankets. And there was that racket coming from outside . . . I don't know how anyone sleeps in this street with all that going on.'

The water in the saucepan began to boil and she turned off the gas underneath and put a spoon of tea leaves in. While it brewed she continued, 'You really need to take it easy for the next few days, recoup your strength, but if you could find the energy, could you go to the Post Office and get the money out to pay that crook of an agent for the furniture, in case his threat to have us evicted isn't a bluff? We also need enough to buy some fuel and food and at least a couple of blankets and some crockery. After I've been to the agent's, I'll make a visit to the merchant to get him to deliver us a bag of coal. Hopefully Brian might know how we can get hold of some wood to eke that out, then I'll visit a pawnbroker . . . there's got to be one close to here . . . and when I get back, I'll make us some dinner. As for my share of the money, you know I'll pay it to you . . .'

Cam cut in, 'Ann, you're my best friend. What's mine is yours. I'm just so glad I did save what I have otherwise . . . I just hope we can stretch it out to cover what we and the baby need. But don't forget to ask if any outwork is going at your place, please.'

Despite their need for money, Ann had no intention of asking about outwork for Cam this soon . . . maybe in a week or so, once she had got more used to being a mother. Regardless, she assured Cam she would.

As much as Cam wanted to obey her friend's instructions and take it easy today, she felt it wasn't at all fair that Ann should graft all day and then come home to an evening of more hard graft. The least Cam felt she could do was push herself to get the shopping done, a fire burning in the grate and a meal ready for Ann when she came home, even if she had no energy left to do anything more than that today.

Rose was due her next feed about ten o'clock. It was now seven thirty, so that would give her two and a half hours to get what she needed to do done, then be back to the flat to feed the child again. She looked down at the baby, nestled snugly in the suitcase on the sofa. Cam inwardly searched herself for any new spark of motherly feeling for the child. There was still nothing. But Ann's suggestion of pretending she was only the baby's carer, not its mother, was helping her enormously. She did not feel so vengeful towards Rose when she needed to attend to her, and treated her with more gentleness. Her thoughts returned to the tasks she needed to tackle today. A cradle for Rose she could manage without for the time being as the child was comfortable enough in the suitcase, but Cam did know that she couldn't manage without a pram. She had no idea what even a second-hand one would cost her but hoped it wasn't going to make too much of a dent in her savings, leaving her less to buy the other items they couldn't manage without.

Cam had never had so much money in her purse before, never felt so rich, but in truth was as poor as a church mouse. Every penny she had on her would be needed, and there was no way for her to earn any more at present. She had drawn out £7. After she'd put aside the furniture money, that left her £5 to buy what she needed today, and then stretch to cover her share of their living expenses. Cam judged it would last her four, maybe five weeks. She hoped Ann hadn't forgotten to enquire about outwork.

Now that she was better able to take in her surroundings than she had been yesterday, stepping out into Sun Street and seeing the poverty around her had come as a shock. Once again she questioned Ann's desperate desire for a place of her own. She obviously had her reasons, but damned if Cam could think what they were. There had been no one around to ask directions from, so with one end of the street blocked she went in the other direction. She had a vague memory that they had entered the street yesterday from the left and couldn't remember passing a parade of shops on their way. Cam turned right and hadn't gone far when she spotted a woman carrying a shopping basket, and decided to follow her.

It was with surprise that, within five minutes, entering from a jitty, she found herself in a busy thoroughfare and realised this was the bottom end of Wharf Street, where the very poorest in the area lived. Pawnbrokers and junk shops were doing a thriving trade, and butchers sold more horse – or as the locals called it 'old nag' meat – than beef or chicken as it was far cheaper. The pubs here sold only the weakest of beer. At the other end of Wharf Street pawnbrokers and second-hand shops still did a good trade but stocked far better quality stuff, commanding higher prices, and the housing was far superior, the residents considering themselves a cut above.

The first two pawn shops that Cam stepped inside had her beating a hasty retreat as the places had smelled so revolting she couldn't imagine the state of the bedding and clothing they traded in. The third she entered wasn't so bad, or the place itself so dark and dingy, so she made her way to the counter. The elderly man behind it was wearing a shabby army greatcoat that swamped his thin hunched body, a thick woollen scarf wrapped around his neck, grey moth-eaten fingerless gloves over his claw-like hands. He had long straggly grey hair resting on his shoulders, and a beard that left only his hooked nose and shrewd beady eyes visible.

Within minutes of Cam asking him if he had a pram, he had taken her into the back, moved aside a pile of items and was showing her a green Silver Cross coach pram. The paintwork was very scratched and the bodywork, from the side she could see it, had a couple of dents in it, the chrome mostly pitted and rusting and the interior engrained with dirt. It needed a good scrub and the lining was ripped in places. There were cobwebs hanging inside the hood and a good layer of dust over it too. It was apparent that the pram had been here for a very long time. Cam wished there was somewhere she could put Rose down so that she could examine it more closely for any further defects before she began to haggle with the pawnbroker over the price, but there wasn't.

Hitching the child more comfortably in her arms, she asked, 'How much do you want for it?'

She did not miss the spark that lit the pawnbroker's eye. He rubbed his hands together, then ran one hand over the hood. 'Very good quality, this pram. It belonged . . .'

Cam had no time for playing games. She had too much to do and the morning was wearing on. She needed to be back in the flat before Rose started howling to be fed. 'To lots of people, judging by the state it's in,' she cut in. 'I'd just like to know how much you want for it?'

The man sucked in his cheeks, making a great display of appraising the pram. It was several long moments before he finally replied, 'Best I can do is twenty-five bob.'

He was expecting almost a week's wage for that dilapidated old thing! Did he think she was made of money? Then it twigged with Cam. His keen eye for a profit had noted the quality of her coat . . . albeit she couldn't get it done up at the moment and it had been second-hand when she had bought it . . . but it was far superior to what his other customers would wear around here, from what she had seen of their threadbare state. Judging by this, he'd obviously decided he could get a bit more profit out of Cam than he would his regulars. Yesterday she would not have had the mental capacity to realise this or the energy to haggle. She was still well below par, but not enough to let this man fleece her.

'Oh, well, if that's your best price then I'll go and see what the other pawnies around here can do for me. Pity, given the rest of the things I need . . . crockery, cutlery, pans . . .'

The gleam in his eye when he learned that there was more of a profit to be made than just on the pram did not escape Cam. She knew her words had had the desired effect. She turned and began to weave her way back to the door. As expected, he called after her, 'Let's not be hasty. Come back and we'll talk about it.'

She turned to look at him. 'That pram would have to be a lot less than twenty-five shillings for me even to consider buying it.'

He heaved a sigh. 'Does no one realise I have to feed my family? Eighteen shillings . . . I can't go lower than that.'

She was back by the pram now and appraising it. The body of it was so big Cam could fit at least four babies of Rose's size in it, but the baby was going to grow so it would do her for all the time she'd need the use of a pram. It would take a lot of effort to clean away the years of grime from it, and even then it would still be a battered old pram that she was always going to be embarrassed to be seen pushing. But the days of her putting pride above necessity were over for Cam while Rose prohibited her from earning. She still felt that eighteen shillings was too much, though. 'Fifteen shillings. That's all I can afford. If you're not willing to accept that I'll be on my way.'

The look she was giving the pawnbroker left him in no doubt she was telling the truth. He slowly hissed out his breath, holding his hands up in mock surrender. 'You've other things you need, you said?'

'Have we settled on a price for the pram?'

He heaved another huge sigh. 'All right, all right. It breaks my heart . . . and my wife'll break my neck when I tell her I have no money for her today! Fifteen shillings it is. Now, you mentioned you needed crockery and cutlery. I have several beautiful bone china services and silver cutlery sets to show you.'

Cam hid a smile. 'I just need two of everything – and everyday stuff, not bone china and Sheffield plate.'

The gleam in his eyes vanished.

An hour later, having wiped out the pram as much as she could using a grey piece of rag the pawnbroker had lent her, with Rose lying snugly sideways under the hood and the rest of the pram piled high with purchases, Cam struggled to negotiate her way out of the shop. She was pleased with herself for getting everything they needed, with enough left over to buy their basic food requirements and a bag of coal. The coal merchant was her next port of call.

The middle-aged merchant, his back permanently stooped from years spent humping heavy sacks, looked at Cam as though she was stupid when she asked if a bag of coal could be delivered to Sun Street. He responded while still heaving filled sacks on to a cart. 'Don't deliver down there, ducky. Few streets round about neither. As soon as me back was turned, horse, cart and load would disappear, never to be seen again.'

'Oh! So how do I get a bag of fuel, if you won't deliver it?'

Again he looked at her as though she was stupid. 'That's your problem, love. If you don't tek it now, though, I won't be back from me round 'til after six. Now, d'yer mind, I have to get on.'

The thought of having to do without any heat in the freezing flat for another night did not appeal. Neither did the thought of having to come back here in the dark and cold of the evening. Cam's eyes fell on the pram. She didn't like the thought of this either but there was no other option for her but to unload it, hope she could make enough room in the belly of it for the coal, replace the padded board Rose lay on, and then reload all her other purchases securely.

The coalman had long since left her to it, to begin his deliveries. His wife was keeping her beady eye on Cam all the time, to make sure she didn't take any more than she had paid for. Finally Cam hauled the laden pram out of the merchant's and back into the street. She'd only made room for a quarter-bag of coal, but that was better than none. Now all that was left on her list was groceries.

With no room in the pram for even so much as a thimble, the four brown carrier bags of shopping were cutting into Cam's wrists as she heaved the pram back to Sun Street, hoping her rapidly flagging energy would hold out. As she made her way down the street, despite the cold, damp, overcast weather, she saw that several women had gathered around a doorway. They stopped their gossiping to stare over at her. Several children, obviously truanting from school, stopped playing their gutter game to watch her too. Cam couldn't understand what they were finding so interesting about her, but their scrutiny was most unnerving and she couldn't get away fast enough.

Having negotiated the cumbersome pram inside the door of the house and into the passage, she parked it beside the door leading upstairs to their flat. Rose was still sleeping so Cam took the bags of shopping up first then came back to collect her, placing her in her makeshift cradle and hoping she would stay asleep long enough for Cam to unload the pram of its cargo. Maybe even enough time for her to make a fire and start warming this place up.

Hurrying back down the stairs, she turned into the passage and stopped short, her mouth falling open, eyes bulging in shock, on not seeing what she was expecting to. The pram and its contents were not there. The passage was empty.

She stood frozen in utter bewilderment, her thoughts turning somersaults. She wasn't losing her mind; she *had* left the pram there, piled with her purchases. So where on earth was it? It couldn't have rolled outside into the yard as the door to that was locked. Her mind sought again for an answer to the pram's whereabouts. Then the only solution to its disappearance hit her. Someone had stolen it! Sheer panic reared up in her. Her heart began to thump painfully and her mind screamed: Please don't let this be true! There was no more money to replace what was in that pram or the pram itself. Cam shot across to the outer door and burst out into the street. It was completely devoid of human life. The gossiping women and playing children had disappeared. Only an emaciated, mangy-looking dog lay shivering by a gas lamp, looking sorry for itself, and rubbish fluttered in the cold wind.

Either all or one of those women were behind the stealing of the pram and its contents, Cam knew that without a doubt. She had only herself to blame, though, for giving them the opportunity by not thinking of locking the outer door after her when she came in. But she could not challenge those she felt responsible. She had no proof to support her claim. Then a thought struck her. Had their downstairs neighbour happened to see anything? Dashing back inside, Cam hammered on the door. She seemed to wait for an age before it finally opened just a crack and she saw an eye peering out at her.

'I'm so sorry to bother you. I live upstairs . . .'

To Cam's surprise, the eye disappeared and the door opened just enough for the old crone to poke out her wizened face. She barked at Cam, 'Like I told the other gel, I likes to keep meself to meself. I don't care what yer want. Now bugger off!'

With that she withdrew her head and slammed shut the door, causing a chunk of plaster to fall off the passage wall.

Cam stood there for a moment, staring at the closed door in shock Well, at least their neighbour wasn't going to be the type who would constantly be asking them to run errands for her, or popping up to their flat unannounced seeking company.

Cam dashed back into the street, looking this way and that, not knowing what she was hoping for as deep down she knew she had seen the last of the pram and its contents. She was so upset, so furious, she had to fight with herself not to collapse in a heap and beat her fists against the cobbles. With no means of replacing the stolen items, they couldn't function. This meant Ann would have no choice but to hope Mrs Middleton had not taken anyone else in to replace her as yet, and Cam herself would take Rose to the one place that filled her with overwhelming dread.

From upstairs, Rose's demands to be fed reached her ears. Shoulders slumped in defeat, Cam went to her. She cried the whole time the baby fed and, huddled on the sofa, dressing gown pulled around her, was still crying miserably when Ann arrived home from work several hours later.

After nine hours spent over her machine, fighting to keep herself awake after her restless night, Ann had been hoping that on her way back from the Post Office Cam would have arranged with the coalman to make a delivery and she'd arrive to find a blazing fire and a welcoming cup of tea to enjoy before she went out again to attend to her errands. So it was with a sense of shock that she walked in the door to find the air in the flat colder than it felt outside, an air of neglect about the place, and apparently no one at home until the sounds of Cam's sobbing reached her. Face wreathed in worry, Ann ran over to the sofa and squatted down to take her friend's shaking hand, demanding, 'What on earth is the matter?'

She was so consumed in her misery, Cam hadn't heard Ann come in. She jumped in shock as a hand grasped hers. It took her a moment to realise this was Ann. Immediately she threw herself on her, blubbering, 'Everything is gone . . . What are we going to do, Ann . . . what are we going to do?'

Her face puckered up in bewilderment. 'I don't understand what you're on about. We haven't got anything until I go and get it.'

'But we had,' Cam stuttered, and told Ann everything between sobs.

'At first I thought my mind was playing tricks on me when I found the pram gone. I ran outside and the street was absolutely deserted, apart from a dog. If only that dog could talk . . . Then I thought our neighbour in the downstairs flat might have seen something, so I knocked to ask but all I got was an eye peering at me through a crack in the door. Then I was told to bugger off and the door was shut on me.'

That was Ann's introduction to their neighbour too. But she had more important matters to worry about than their unwelcoming neighbour.

She fell back on her haunches, scraping a hand through her hair. There were things they could manage without until more money was found to buy them, but others they just had to have, such as blankets and coal. Another night without proper warmth could see them both risking pneumonia, and there was no telling how having no heat in the flat would affect the baby.

Ann shut her eyes as a wave of fury erupted within her against the thieves. No matter how desperate for money they had been, had it not occurred to them that, to have moved into such a street as this, the people they were stealing off were as deprived as they themselves? Their selfish actions had put paid to Ann's aim of keeping Cam and her baby out of the workhouse. She opened her eyes and fixed them on her friend. She was consumed in misery again, head buried in the crook of her arm, the rise and fall of her shoulders telling Ann that she was crying, obviously dreading what fate awaited her and her baby now. Ann felt guilty that no such fate awaited her. She could still find a warm house and a comfortable bed, either via Ethel Middleton or Brian's mother. She desperately wanted to put her friend's mind at rest that this was just a temporary setback they could overcome, but in fact it was a major catastrophe they had absolutely no means of resolving.

She gave a shudder. It was so damned cold in here. Maybe she could find something in the yard – an old crate or such like – that she could make a fire with, to at least afford them a bit of warmth while they had their . . . well, it would feel like their last supper. At least the thieves hadn't got away with the food along with every-thing else.

She had just stood up when the door burst open and Brian stood framed in the entrance. He had obviously received the note informing him of her new address that she had delivered to his mother's house that lunchtime. Ann knew instantly by the look on his face exactly what he thought of his future wife's new place of abode and of her living here. Before he could voice his opinion, though, she had dashed over to join him and grabbed his arm, dragging him over to the kitchen area, out of earshot of Cam. Because she was unable to take out her anger and frustration on those responsible for bringing such devastation on them, she took it out on him.

'You don't need to tell me what you think of this place . . . I can see by your face. Well, I'm sorry if my moving in here is causing you embarrassment. I know you don't want others to find out your girlfriend is living in such a hell-hole. But I'm not embarrassed! It's a place for Cam and the baby to live, and that's all that matters. If you can find us something better at the same rent as we pay for this we'll happily move in. Anyway, as it turns out your embarrassment is going to be short-lived. We can't stay here now because some kind soul helped themselves to all the stuff Cam went out and got for us this morning. We can't do without what they took, and we've no money to replace any of it, so that means that after all this Cam and the baby are going to end up . . .'

Ann's voice trailed off. She was too distressed to speak the words. Instead she told him, 'I was just about to go down to the yard and see if there's something I can make a fire with, to take the chill off the air while we have something to eat before we pack up to leave. Well, we can't stay here another night, not without blankets.' She then waited for Brian to make an offer to see to that for her, but he was just standing there, looking at her vacantly. Her frustration and anger at the situation spilled over then and she lashed out at him: 'Oh, why don't you just go home? You're neither use nor ornament here.' She then scowled at him darkly, her next statement pronounced in an icy tone: 'I'm not so sure I want to be marrying a man who acts like the village idiot in a crisis.'

With that she spun on her heels, snatched up the set of house keys and stormed off.

The yard was dark and shadowy, the only light there a weak one emitted by the gas lamp in the jitty. Ann was familiar with the yard, having ventured into it several times since moving in so as to use the privy. After witnessing the dire state of the flat, she hadn't expected the outside convenience to be in anywhere near the condition her ex-landlady had kept hers, but even so hadn't expected it to be quite so stomach-churning.

She was mindful that the yard itself was cluttered with all manner of unwanted items left behind by past occupants of the flats, which could prove hazardous if she wasn't careful where she stepped. She was also very conscious that it was probable rats were nesting in the mounds of rotting rubbish piled around, and didn't wish to encounter any of them.

As she began tentatively to make a search for anything suitable to build a fire with, her anger towards Brian mounted. Maybe he wasn't the man she'd thought he was . . . not offering to take this task off her hands but instead just standing there with that idiotic look on his face, when he knew that her dearest friend's life couldn't get any worse and Ann really needed to be with her to offer what support she could. Her face puckered in thought. In all the time she had known him, he'd never not jumped to her assistance before tonight. So why hadn't he? But then, she hadn't given him a chance to say hello, let alone anything else, but had verbally attacked him for what she'd assumed he'd been going to say. If he had stopped her expressing her opinion in the way she had him, she would certainly have put him in his place. A surge of remorse filled Ann. On reflection, why should Brian have offered his help when she had belittled him that way? And in front of Cam, though it was doubtful she would have been paying any attention considering what else she had on her mind. She would apologise to Brian as soon as she returned upstairs.

Against a din of babies screaming, children bickering, adults arguing, dogs barking, cats screeching, dustbin lids crashing, back doors banging, Ann carried on with her search for something to make a fire with. Finally, hidden behind an antiquated, rusting lawn-mower, she came across a few logs – enough to give them some heat for a couple of hours – and some sticks to use for kindling. She silently thanked the person who had left them there.

Back in the flat, she deposited the logs and sticks on the hearth, then frowned. Cam and the baby were still as she had left them but there was no sign at all of Brian. Ann's heart began to hammer; a painful knot twisted in her stomach. Had he taken her at her word and ended their relationship? She couldn't blame him if so. She had been so nasty to him. But hadn't he realised that she had just been taking her hurt and frustration for her friend's dire plight out on him? An urge to chase after him, explain herself to him, beg him to forgive her, ran through her. But addressing her own problems would have to wait. She could not bring herself to abandon Cam as her friend was in no fit state to be left on her own.

Feeling utterly helpless, Ann put the pan of water to boil on a gas ring, then set about making a fire. A while later the heat it threw out helped to warm their bodies but did little to thaw the chill in both women's hearts. The cheese sandwiches Ann had put together sat untouched, despite their both being hungry, each of them far too consumed by their own misery to eat. Cam was contemplating what life was going to be like for her in the workhouse; Ann what her life was going to be with her best friend in the workhouse and the possibility of being without Brian too.

Time was marching on. Albeit neither of them had spoken openly of the fact that they had no choice but to vacate the flat, both of them were aware they would have to make a move soon. Ann was surprised that the furious agent hadn't been round and turfed them both out by now, due to the fact she had broken her promise to pay over the two pounds for the furniture by seven this evening. It was now getting on for nine. Although she had enough on her plate to contend with, part of her wished he would show up as it would afford her some pleasure at least to see his expression when she told the odious man it was not going to happen. Cam needed every penny of what little she had left of her savings.

Ann's eyes then fell on the child, asleep in the suitcase by the side of the sofa. The poor thing hadn't had a good start in life. No idea who its father was, and a mother fighting to quash her resentment of it for ruining her life. And there was no getting away from it: the child was ugly. What kind of future could it hope to have, being raised in the workhouse? Rising above her pity for the baby, though, was a feeling of guilty relief that she herself would not have to endure its ear-splitting howls much longer.

Huddled on the sofa, through the black mist of desolation swirling in her mind, her subconscious told Cam that sitting here wallowing in misery was achieving nothing but only delaying the inevitable. Rose was due another feed in just over an hour and she didn't at all fancy having to do it down a dark alley in this bitter weather. Also, she didn't know whether the workhouse doors shut at a certain time of night. It didn't seem fair to Cam that in fact she still had the means to pay to keep them out of the workhouse for a week or two, but finding a landlady willing to take in a baby was an impossibility. But then, she supposed that knowing she wasn't quite destitute might afford her some comfort in the dark days that lay ahead of her. In future, should a chance of escape come her way, then that small sum left in her Post Office account could be a Godsend. Ann would keep her savings book safe for her.

'Once I'm in there, do you think I'll be allowed out to meet you?' she asked her friend.

Ann didn't have any idea of the rules and regulations of the workhouse so couldn't answer Cam's question. She was vehemently praying that life inside the Dickensian place was not as bad as she had heard.

The fire had almost died out. There were no logs left to replenish it and both women knew that they couldn't justify delaying their departure any longer.

It was Cam who made the first move, saying quietly, 'I'd best get my things together.'

Ann sighed heavily, 'Yes, me too.'

The door burst open for the second time that night and Brian loomed in the doorway, saying in annoyance, 'Didn't you hear me shouting from the passageway? Well, on second thoughts, maybe you couldn't hear me over all the din the neighbours around here seem to make. Anyway, give me the house keys, quick, so I can lock the front door. I don't want the same thing that happened this morning to happen again.' He spotted the keys on the ledge of the big dresser where Ann had put them on coming in from the yard. Snatching them up, he disappeared again.

Brian's behaviour was very confusing to Cam and she looked to Ann for an answer. Ann's feelings were in turmoil. She was as confused as Cam, but also overjoyed to see him. Her need to put matters right between them rose above everything else. Jumping up, she chased after him.

Turning into the passage at the bottom of the stairs, Ann stopped short, her jaw dropping, eyes wide with shock at the sight that met her. Parked by the wall to the side of the hall was a dilapidated coach pram, overspilling with all manner of household items. She was staring at it in such disbelief she did not see Brian making his way back down the passage towards her after locking the front door.

He was saying to her in a warning tone, 'Haven't the pair of you learned anything after what happened this morning? You must make sure you lock the front door after you every time you come in, or the types around here will have the clothes off your backs while you're wearing them and have them sold and be spending the proceeds before you even know it.'

Ann wasn't listening, her eyes still fixed on the pram and its contents. 'How did you get our stuff back? I mean, how did you know who'd taken it? How did you get them to . . .'

'Oh, this isn't the stuff you had stolen this morning,' he told her.

Face wreathed in bewilderment, she looked at him. 'Well, where has it come from then?'

'That's where I've been . . . getting it all. Me mam donated what she could spare . . . don't worry, I didn't tell her about Cam being an unmarried mother, just that you'd a friend with a new baby who'd had all her stuff stolen and no money to replace it. Well, she went and ransacked her cupboards for what she could spare and then popped round to see her neighbour. The rest of the neighbours heard then and all gave what they could spare. I haggled for a few things over at the pawn. Oh, and I got the pram off Vi Lambert. It's been rotting in her yard for as long as I can remember so I went and asked her if she'd part with it. I told her why, thinking it might jog her conscience a little, but the miserable old bugger still wanted five bob for it.' Brian smiled proudly. 'I got her down to half a crown in the end. We'll give it a good scrub and I can bash out the dents in the sides. It'll be like new.'

That was an exaggeration, to say the least. The pram was in such bad condition Ann very much doubted even a scrappy would be willing to take it for nothing. But with some work on it, it would at least be useable and far better than nothing. A sudden rush of emotion flooded her. With tears filling her eyes, she threw her arms around Brian, hugging him and blubbering, 'Oh, Brian, you are the most wonderful man!'

He kissed the top of her head. 'Well, you've obviously realised that I ain't happy about you living here, Ann, but I appreciate that this place is the best you can afford while helping your friend. I just wish I was out of my apprenticeship and earning more money. Then we could have got a place and Cam could have lived with us until she was able to manage by herself. Anyway, I couldn't stand by and do n'ote when I heard that all your stuff had got pinched and you had no money to replace it. I know this stuff ain't up to much – Mam said she was about to chuck the sheets out, they're so thread-bare – but it'll all do until you can get better, won't it?'

Ann lifted her head and smiled at him. Her voice was choked with emotion when she said, 'It'll all do the job just fine, Brian. I don't know how to thank you, or your mam and her neighbours. This means Cam won't end up in the workhouse now.' Then she cried urgently, 'I must tell her!' Releasing her hold on Brian, she went to the door leading to the flat upstairs and shouted, 'Cam, come down here . . . quick!'

She shouted back, 'I'm just about to wrap Rose up for our journey.'

'Leave that and come down. Now,' Ann commanded.

Seconds later footsteps pounded down the stairs and a bewildered Cam arrived to join them in the passage. She looked worried. 'What's the matter?' It was then that she noticed the pram and its load and in shock proclaimed, 'Oh, my God, our stuff's been returned. But how . . . Oh, but this isn't what I bought this morning so where has it . . .'

'Brian got it all for us,' Ann butted in.

'Well, my mam and her neighbours donated most of it,' Brian informed her, being a modest man and not wanting to take all the glory.

Cam's eyes were darting wildly. 'But this means . . . it means . . .'

'That we can stay here now,' Ann cried, jumping up and down, clapping her hands.

The defeated sag of Cam's shoulders was seen to lift, her worry lines to ease. With tears of gratitude in her eyes, she threw herself on Brian, hugging him fiercely. 'Oh, thank you! Thank you so much for what you've done.'

He was getting embarrassed by all the gratitude that was being shown him when to his mind all he'd done was what anyone would have in the circumstances. He peeled Cam off him, saying, 'Let's start getting this lot upstairs. Oh, there're a few lumps of coal in the belly of the pram . . . enough for a couple of fires. Me mam sent it to help you out. That's the first thing I'll do, get one going for you.'

Cam was on her way up the stairs, her arms laden with several blankets and a spare set of patched bed linen, along with two worn towels. Taking the opportunity of getting Brian on his own for a few moments, with her face wreathed in remorse, Ann laid a hand on his arm and said, 'I am so sorry, I truly am, Brian. You know I didn't mean it, don't you?'

He was trying to move stuff so he could get at the coal while not breaking the few pieces of everyday pots, albeit every one of them sporting either a chip or a crack or both. 'Forgive you for what?' he asked her, bemused.

'For what I said to you.'

He stopped what he was doing to look at her, puzzled. 'What was it you said to me – and when?'

Ann opened her mouth to tell him, then quickly snapped it shut. She knew Brian well enough to realise that if he was asking her this then he really didn't have a clue what she was talking about. At the time he'd obviously been lost in his own thoughts about how he could help them replace the stuff they'd had stolen. She inwardly heaved a great sigh of relief. What she had said, and the tone of voice she had used, could have caused an irreconcilable rift in their relationship. She had been lucky it hadn't. This really ought to teach her to think before she spoke in future. Her mind sought for an answer to fob him off with, and while she was doing that another thought struck her. Looking at him quizzically, Ann asked, 'Just where did you get the money to buy that pram off Old Mother Lambert, and for the stuff you got at the pawn?'

Brian was thrown for a moment by her unexpected question. He shifted uncomfortably on his feet. 'Oh, well . . . you see . . . when I was telling you I was helping me mam out more as she was feeling the pinch because Dad's hours have been cut . . . well, I wasn't exactly being truthful. I mean, I didn't lie about me dad's hours going down due to the recession starting to bite . . . I just hope my job and yours won't be affected . . . but Mam hasn't asked me to stump up any more yet. No, I've been saving to buy you an engagement ring . . . not an expensive one, of course, but something nice. It was that money I used.' He eyed her worriedly. 'You're not angry with me, are you?'

Ann exclaimed, aghast, 'Oh, Brian, how could you think I'd be angry with you for saving my friend from the workhouse instead of putting a ring on my finger? You daft 'a'porth,' she scolded him, slapping him playfully on the arm. Then she cocked an eyebrow at him before adding, 'But that doesn't mean I'm not angry with you for missing that film I wanted to see at the pictures the other week, with James Cagney and Jean Harlow in it. You were lying to me that you had no money when really you had but were squirrelling it away.' She giggled at the look on his face. 'Come on, let's find this coal so you can make us a decent fire.'

CHAPTER FIFTEEN

With her face screwed up in despair, Cam gave a groan as she clamped her hands over her ears. She was desperately trying to complete an order of outwork that was being collected the next afternoon: snipping the tag ends off socks, pairing them up, and banding them into dozens, then grosses. For someone of her intelligence, the work was monotonous and laborious, and the bags of work she'd still to do were piled underneath the window in the living-room. It seemed, though, that Rose was hell-bent on not giving her the peace to get on and complete the task. If the order wasn't ready on time, Cam could lose the much-coveted job that Ann had secured for her.

In truth, the wage she was paid for the long hours she put in was pitifully low, a ha'penny for each completed twelve dozen, but the money Cam contributed towards the housekeeping made the difference between their being able to afford bones to make soup with, a filling of cheese or potted meat in their sandwiches instead of just margarine, and more fuel for the fire. If she lost this job there was no telling if she'd ever secure another that she could do at home. Work was drying up everywhere as the recession bit deeper. Men were being laid off in their thousands, their protests often ending in mob violence which achieved nothing. If the orders weren't there then the factory owners couldn't afford to pay them for idling about, and as matters stood there didn't seem to be any positive signs of matters improving. If anything they were getting worse. Queues at the soup kitchens were growing longer each day.

Through hard work on both women's part the flat was now as clean as it was possible to get it, although no amount of scrubbing or rearranging the shabby furniture would disguise the fact that it was in truth unfit for human beings to live in. Their budget had prohibited them from buying any homely bits and pieces, but regardless, it was far more welcoming than Cam imagined the workhouse would be. Ann assured her that, no matter what the place was like, she preferred being in control of her own life than having it governed by a landlady, no matter how nice she was or comfortable her home.

The landlord's agent hadn't been at all amused by the fact that Ann had broken her promise to hand over the money for the furnishings on their first day and had stormed around the next morning, demanding it at once or they could get out. According to him, there were plenty eager to take their place. He hadn't been mollified by the excuse he was given, either, snatching the money and warning Cam that the rent had better be ready for him to collect next Friday evening as no excuses for non-payment would be accepted.

Life was a struggle for them, managing on as little money as they were, and the locals still looked on the new arrivals like interlopers even nine months later. They had both been very angry and upset over the theft and the fact that the culprit had got away Scot-free, but regardless were determined not to put themselves in a vulnerable position and be stolen from again, adhering strictly to Brian's advice about locking the front entrance behind them on every arrival and departure. Despite the locals' attitude, the two young women had tried to ingratiate themselves by smiling and voicing a greeting whenever they passed by, but it seemed that to be accepted here you had to have several generations of local residence behind you and to have been born in these streets. But for the time being this was all they could afford, and both of them were adamant no mean-minded neighbours were going to make them leave until they were ready. And they both felt sure that not all the residents were the type you daren't turn your back on; that sprinkled amongst them must be sorts like themselves, decent and law-abiding, who had just landed up in these parts by misfortune.

The protective cover of her hands over her ears was doing nothing to lessen the noise Rose was making so Cam dropped them and tried mentally to block it out while she continued with her work. There was nothing physically wrong with the child. She wasn't hungry, her nappy wasn't wet or dirty, and she wasn't suffering from wind or a temperature, indicating she was sickening for something. She might be cold, though, her hysterical thrashing having removed the covers from her. Cam had already been through three times since she had put her down at seven thirty to cover her back up, only for her to kick them off again immediately.

For the first two months of her life Rose had caused few problems, had slept for the majority of the time and was very content during the short intervals she was awake . . . as long as she was fed the instant she demanded to be, or else all hell was let loose. But now, at nine months, she had developed into a very demanding child. Nothing ever seemed to please her. She only had one mood: disagreeable. From the moment she awoke in the morning until she went to sleep at night, she grizzled and moaned and at least twice a day, for no apparent reason, would throw an hysterical tantrum, only calming down when her energy was spent. She did not like being held, didn't respond to being played with, didn't content herself with her own company. Most babies started to smile at about six weeks old, but Cam had never seen Rose's lips formed into anything but a scowl. And she still glared at her mother in the same intense way that she had done since birth, making Cam shudder to think what lay behind it.

No matter how ridiculous it seemed, looking back now, Cam could only conclude that for the first weeks of her life Rose had been lulling her into a false sense of security while she built her own strength up for the disruption she was going to cause.

Cam was mortally grateful that Ann was out of the flat through work and seeing Brian more than she was in, or she feared that her friend wouldn't want to continue their living arrangement, unable to put up with such a cantankerous child. How Cam hoped this behaviour was just a phase Rose would eventually grow out of!

Her cries grew louder, filling the entire flat and drowning out the noises filtering in from outside. Cam was surprised their miserable neighbour downstairs didn't complain. She must be deaf for this now not to be bothering her. But it was bothering Cam, preventing her from concentrating on her work, and it appeared that no matter how tired Rose was, she was not going to give in to sleep until all her energies were spent. There was no telling how long it would be before that happened. Maybe a walk in the pram might send her off to sleep. It had done the trick in the past.

But at the thought, Cam gave a heavy sigh as her eyes fell on the fire. It wasn't a roaring one as they couldn't afford to be so indulgent but it was warm enough to take the chill off the air. Since Brian had done a makeshift job of covering up the holes in the walls and the newspaper stuffed in the warped windows had been renewed, most of the heat now remained in the room. The weather had turned unusually cold for mid-September and tonight was dark, with a chilly north wind blowing which she would need to wrap up against. But it wasn't the thought of leaving the warmth of the fire or the chilly weather outside that was making Cam reluctant to venture out so much as what she could encounter, a lone woman, in these badly lit streets. Whenever she had had no choice but to resort to getting Rose to sleep this way before, it had still been light and she had felt relatively safe. The aftermath of the last time she had ventured out in the dark was still very fresh in her mind. She lapsed into thought for a moment, debating what to do, then gave herself a mental shake, telling herself not to be so pathetic. She couldn't spend the rest of her life only going out in daylight hours, for fear of what might happen. As long as she didn't stray down unlit paths and kept vigilant, she'd be fine.

Getting herself ready, she then went into the bedroom to collect the screaming, flailing child. For a moment she stood and looked down at her in the old cot she had managed to barter for at the pawnbroker's when Rose had outgrown the suitcase. There was no sign yet of the ugly little duckling transforming into a beautiful swan, but she was still only nine months old and there was plenty of time for that yet. She appeared much the same as she had when born, only bigger . . . still a skinny little thing with translucent skin, large forehead tapering down to a pointed chin, her carrot-red hair still sprouting freely and forming corkscrew curls now.

Having convinced herself that she was this child's surrogate mother on behalf of a fictitious sister had enabled Cam to care for Rose the way she felt any child entrusted to her safekeeping should be. Stopping breast feeding had come as a great relief to her; not having to endure cracked, sore nipples any longer, the heaviness of milk-swollen breasts or the embarrassment of them constantly leaking into the front of her blouse or dress, was a big step forward. She was still having difficulty feeling any actual love for her daughter, though, even the love of an aunt for a niece. With the best will in the world, Rose's permanent sour temperament, along with her odd looks and that way she had of glaring, made her a very difficult child to warm to. The strongest feeling Cam had for her was still that of pity for how she'd come about – that her mother had no bond with her; that as matters stood she had been dealt a cruel blow when good looks were being dished out by Mother Nature – but in a strange way the pity she felt had evolved into a form of protective ness. Cam wanted to shield her from the nasty-minded cruelty that was likely to come her way should her personality and looks not improve as she grew older. When Cam was young herself, she and Ann along with the children they'd lived with had suffered their fair share of cruel taunts from other kids, some from narrow-minded parents even, for their parentless status. Cam knew how horrible it felt to be considered different. She might not have the feelings for Rose that a mother should, but she did not like the thought of any child being ridiculed or ostracised because they weren't considered pretty or lacked a parent.

She leaned over the cot and scooped up the hysterical child, holding her tightly so she didn't drop her as Rose thrashed about. With a struggle, Cam wrapped her up warmly, then took her downstairs to the passage where she kept the battered antiquated coach pram, now minus the dents in its sides courtesy of Brian and scrubbed as clean as it could be. Cam put her baby inside. Making sure she'd locked the outside door, she turned into the street and started to make her way down it, Rose still screaming and squirming as though in agonising pain.

The street seemed deserted and was badly lit through several gas lamps being broken. They had been for a good while, the council obviously considering repairs in these dilapidated streets not to be a priority. The lamps that were working cast long shadows and created dark patches where the light didn't reach. The fact the sky was overcast, with no moonlight, didn't help. Cam hurried along, knowing she wouldn't feel so vulnerable in streets that were better lit.

The motion of the pram was thankfully starting to have a soothing effect on Rose. Her howls were reducing in their intensity and her flailing had lessened. Hopefully she was finally tiring. Now she was out of the backstreets and in the better lit thoroughfare of Wharf Street, Cam started to relax and find she was actually enjoying her outing, albeit there was the constant nagging at the back of her mind that she really should be back home, working hard to finish her order. The longer she was out, the less sleep she would get since she'd have to work into the small hours of the morning to make up for lost time. She hadn't realised she had walked so far until she stopped, recognising that she had reached Belgrave Gate. Rose had been quiet for a while but Cam dare not stop to peek at her, just in case she was still awake and it started her off again. Hopefully she was asleep, and by the time she got back home would be in a deep one so Cam could transport her from the pram back to her cot without her waking up, and then have some peace to get on with her work.

She made to turn the pram around and retrace her steps when the sound of laughter coming from across the road made her look over. A woman and a man had just arrived at the booking office of the Palace Theatre. It was apparent they'd been running. With his profile to Cam, the man fumbled in his inside jacket pocket for his wallet to pay for the tickets. The woman was playfully urging him to hurry up. She was very attractive and smartly dressed, but it was the man who was holding all of Cam's attention. He reminded her so much of Adrian. His height; the style of his clothes; the way he wore his Homburg hat at a slightly jaunty angle on the side of his head; the way a lock of hair flopped over his forehead; the style of spectacles he wore. Over his jacket the man was wearing a trenchcoat, the same style Adrian had worn.

Cam had spent countless hours in her tiny cell-like room, while she waited for the birth of her baby, mourning the loss of the love of her life. It had taken her many hours of miserable crying before finally she had realised that dwelling on what might have been was only prolonging her agony. With a great effort she had managed to put

Adrian's memory to the recesses of her mind. When it was triggered by the snatch of a song or a reminder of a film they had seen together, she had learned the trick of swiftly switching her thoughts to something else, anything, it didn't matter how trivial, and concentrating on that until the difficult reminder had passed. Now, seeing Adrian's likeness was bringing the sharp pain of his loss back to stab her again. All she could see in her mind's eye was the pain and bewilderment on his handsome face when she had told him it was over between them, lying about the real reason.

Having paid for the tickets, she watched the man slip his arm around the woman's waist and lean in towards her to whisper something in her ear. Cam felt her heart ripping in two. That was the way Adrian used to hold her. Then, as he turned to escort the woman inside the theatre, Cam caught a glimpse of his face full on and her breath caught in her throat. The man across the road wasn't just the image of Adrian. He *was* Adrian.

Deep in her heart she had always known a man like him would meet someone else, but actually to have this confirmed, see what the woman looked like and how happy they appeared together, was unbearable for Cam.

Tears of distress blurred her eyes. She wiped them away with the back of her hand. Despite herself, she looked across the road to catch one more glimpse of him but he had disappeared inside the theatre with his companion. Cam felt an urge to rush across the road and breathe in the air that he had just breathed so as to feel close to him one last time. She actually made to do that, then pulled herself up short. What good would it do, apart from make her look stupid in front of the box office clerk? She should be glad for Adrian that he had found happiness with someone else after the hurt and dejection he must have suffered after she had ended their relationship. Thankfully they moved in completely different circles now and the chances of her happening on him again just by chance, as she had done tonight, had to be very remote.

Taking several deep breaths and with her heart weighing like lead inside her, Cam turned around the pram and set off back home.

Despite trying with all her might to put the episode behind her, arriving back in the dire surroundings of Sun Street after being reminded what her life could have been like, only served to deepen her depression. She had barely ventured a few yards down the street when she felt a presence by her side and jerked round her head to find a man leering at her. He was tall and thin with lank, greasy hair and a sallow, pock-marked complexion. His clothes were threadbare, and a strong smell of body odour, cigarettes and beer, amongst other nauseating stenches, was seeping off him. It was apparent he was drunk by the way he was swaying, almost falling into her and stumbling over his own feet.

Cam quickened her pace to get away from him but the man grabbed her arm, gripping it tightly, forcing her to a halt.

'What's all the rush?' he slurred. With his free hand, he pulled a half-empty bottle of beer from his pocket and brandished it in front of her. 'Why don't yer ditch the kid and have a drink wi' me? We could find somewhere to mek ourselves comfy and have some fun. I know a place we could go.' The way he looked at her and licked his lips left her in no doubt what he meant by this.

Icy beads of sweat began to form on Cam's brow, a cold chill to run up her spine. She flashed a glance up and down the street but apart from themselves there was no sign of any other human being she could call upon for help. She did her best to wrench free her arm, but without success. 'Let me go. I need to get home!' she cried at him.

He smirked at her. 'Not to yer old man, 'cos I know you ain't got one. Made it my business to find out all about you newcomers. Yer friend's got a fella, ain't she? Thick-set bloke, comes round quite a bit . . . not that I'm bothered as I ain't interested in 'er. She's too tubby for my tastes. I like 'em nice and slim, like you, with a good pair of breasts. I bet you ain't had a bit of how's yer father since you had the nipper. Yer must be gagging for a bit by now. So go on, lose the kid and I'll show yer what yer've been missing.'

Cam was outraged that this man knew what he did about her and by his unkind words about Ann. But even worse was the fact this filthy-bodied and -minded individual could think she would be even remotely interested in anything he had to offer her. At the same time, though, she was very aware that she needed to be careful just how she refused his offer. He could take offence in the inebriated state he was in, and she didn't like the thought of how he could retaliate.

As she sought the best way to deal with this, she heard the sound of a door opening behind her and a female voice declaring, '*There* you are! I thought you wasn't coming. Kettle's on.'

Cam turned her head to see a shabbily dressed girl of around her own age, smiling at her. She frowned, bewildered. The girl was addressing her as if they were old friends yet Cam had never met her before. Obviously she was being mistaken for someone else, but she was relieved by the intervention.

The girl was now standing beside Cam and speaking to the man. 'Hello, Mr Hinge. How good of you to see my friend safely back. Never know who you could meet on a dark night like this. Well, I expect you're needing to get home to your wife and kids. We won't keep you. Thanks again for being so gentlemanly.'

Swaying dangerously, Bert Hinge shot her a murderous look, then, mumbling inaudibly under his breath, he stumbled off across the road.

The girl turned to Cam and advised her, 'Get yourself a hammer.'

Cam's face looked mystified. 'A hammer! Whatever for?'

'To protect yourself with whenever you go out in these streets after dark. I never go out on a night without mine. Well, actually, I don't go out at night now, but that's beside the point. There's people around these parts that'd have the shoes off your feet and be away before you'd even noticed.'

'Oh, I don't need to be told that,' Cam responded, a hint of anger in her voice. 'Only it was far more than just my shoes . . . the baby's pram and what it was loaded with at the time. I'd just used the last of my money to buy it all. We'd hardly been living here twenty-four hours. I'd only turned my back for two minutes. Me and Ann never arrive home now without locking the front door securely as soon as we come in. Ann's boyfriend, Brian, has cemented broken glass along the top of the back wall, to stop people climbing over, and there's barbed wire along the top of the gate, just in case anyone tries to get in the back way.'

'Well, you can't be too careful. But get yourself a hammer and make sure you carry it with you if you go out at night again while it's dark, then you'll stop the likes of Hinge in his tracks just by showing him you'd defend yourself should he try 'ote. There's one or two like him around here who think all women are fair game when they fancy a bit of the other. It's their poor wives I pity. Having said that, I'm not really surprised some men stray from home with the banshee sort they have there.'

She gave Cam a broad smile before continuing, 'Anyway, there are some nice people in these streets. Mrs Jones, a couple of doors down, would do anything for anybody if she could, and so would her husband. Mrs Knox comes across as hard-faced, but when you get to know her she's a nice woman really. Then there's me and me mam ...' Her face clouded over with concern. 'Oh, thinking of me mam, I'm getting a bit worried about her. She's late home. She does for a woman on Humberstone Road, amongst others, and sometimes has to stay late to clear up after Madam's had guests for dinner. But Mam never mentioned she'd been asked to stay late tonight. That's what I was doing, looking out for her, when I happened to see Bert Hinge accosting you and thought I'd better stick me two penn'orth in before things turned ugly.'

'And I can't thank you enough that you decided to,' Cam responded in all sincerity. 'That Hinge man didn't seem to be in the mood to accept no for an answer. Anyway, I'm sure your mam will be home soon. She probably forgot to tell you she had to work late tonight,' she tried to reassure the girl.

She flashed a smile. 'It won't be the first time.'

Cam said to her, 'Well, thank you again for coming to my rescue. I'll take your advice and get something to defend myself with if I go out in the dark again.'

'It's better to be safe than sorry.' Cam made to set off then, but the young woman stopped her by saying, 'Would you like to come in for a cuppa?'

Cam really felt she should go home and get cracking on her work, but she had taken a liking to her saviour and felt the least she could do was share a cup of tea with this woman who had rescued her from a potentially dangerous situation. And she'd lived in this street for nine months and wasn't on friendly terms with anyone so it would be nice to be, especially someone of her own age. Rose had not stirred since Cam had stopped pushing the pram. She must be asleep or she'd certainly have let them know that she wasn't. Just to make sure, Cam tentatively poked her head inside the pram and eased back the blanket obscuring Rose's face. She was sound asleep. She looked at the young woman and smiled. 'A cuppa would be most welcome.'

'Come on then, I'll give you a hand getting the pram inside. I'm Ivy, by the way . . . Ivy Bishop.'

The two-hundred-year-old weaver's cottage Cam was taken into consisted of one room downstairs and one up, the latter accessed by a rickety, steep staircase. The dingy distempered walls were crumbling, patches of black mould abundant despite evidence that the cottage's occupants were labouring to keep it at bay. The frames of the tiny mullioned windows were flaking, rotting wood visible beneath. The floor was of cracked, cold flagstones. The only heat came from the small fire in a tiny antiquated range on the back wall. On a stand by the back door stood a huge enamel jug and bowl to hold water collected from the communal pump outside. The few pieces of furniture were antiquated and heavily worn, but regardless the dwelling was clean and, as far as Cam could tell, bug-free, the only smell permeating the air that of damp and decay, which the inhabitants could do nothing about.

'Is your husband a sailor or someone who works away?' Ivy asked Cam as she poured boiling water into the pot from a blackened kettle that had been hanging by a hook over the fire.

Cam was sitting on an uncomfortable chair with a wobbly leg at the old kitchen table. Her mind had been on the fact that she hadn't believed people could live in worse conditions than she and Ann did. Seeing this place, she knew now she was wrong as these people certainly did. She realised Ivy was saying something to her and, looking at her vacantly, said, 'I'm sorry?'

'I was asking if your husband works away? Well, it's just that you're wearing a wedding ring but I've not seen anyone but you and another young woman coming and going from your flat . . . oh, except for the stocky man I've seen the other woman going off with. I assume he's her boyfriend? Not that I'm nosey,' Ivy added worriedly. 'Well,

I don't mean to be, I just happen to look out of the window now and again and see things.'

Thank heavens she did, Cam thought, or she dreaded to think how she herself would have got out of that situation earlier. She looked down at her hands, unable to meet Ivy's eye when she told her lie. 'My husband is dead. We'd not long been married. I'd just found out I was expecting. It's very upsetting for me to talk about it so . . .'

Her face wreathed in pity and understanding, Ivy came over to the table and grasped Cam's hands, cutting her short with, 'I fully understand that you don't want to talk about it . . . bring all the pain of that awful time back.' Her voice had lowered to barely a whisper, her face was puckering in sorrow. 'My husband died too, only weeks after we'd got married . . . the same as you. I'd just found out I was expecting so, you see, I do understand how you're feeling.'

She released Cam's hands and sank down on the chair beside hers, eyes glinting. In a tear-choked voice she told Cam, 'We hadn't planned to have a baby so soon after we got married, it just happened. I was scared to death. Felt I wasn't ready to be a mother and was worried about how we'd manage as Cyril didn't earn that much, but he was over the moon. He told me that Mother Nature obviously thought I was ready to be a mother and that he knew I'd make a wonderful one. He said we'd manage moneywise; said he'd stop smoking his baccy and having his couple of pints on a Friday night after work if it came to it. I stopped being scared then. Thought I'd nothing to fear, having a wonderful man like Cyril beside me. I started to look forward to our first baby arriving. We planned to have as many as we could afford to raise properly.'

Ivy paused for a moment to wipe another tear from her cheek before continuing. 'It was a stupid accident that killed my Cyril. He was helping a neighbour replace some rotting wood in an upstairs window. His foot slipped on a rung of the ladder, and he fell off it and smashed his head on the cobbles. He died instantly, so the doctor said. I never even got a chance to say goodbye to him. He never got to see his son.'

Ivy paused to clear a lump from her throat before going on, 'I had no choice but to move back in with me mam and dad. Then, as if Him upstairs hadn't given us enough grief for the time being, two weeks after my Cyril died me dad keels over on his allotment. Dead before he hit the ground. Doctor said it was natural causes. His heart stopped, just like that, with no warning. He was only forty-four and never had a day's illness in his life. So there was me and me mam, both widows in the space of two weeks.

'I'd had to give up my job at the bakery by then because of my condition, and Mam's part-time wages from her cleaning job weren't enough to keep us. She was heartbroken when she had to give up the tenancy of the house she and me dad had lived in since they'd got married. It was where I was born, and we had to leave it and move to this area, into this . . .'

She paused and looked around, and Cam knew by the look on her face that this place was a big comedown from their previous home. 'Mam's had to take on more work to keep us all. We just about get by, as long as we watch every penny. Me and Mam have both forgotten what butter tastes like.'

Cam could say the same herself. In fact, it was probable that she and Ann weren't that much better off than Ivy and her mother, but she decided not to interrupt the other woman's story. 'I shouldn't grumble, though, things could be a lot worse,' Ivy was saying. 'I just wish I could contribute more and ease Mam's load, but with the baby there's only outwork I could do, and there's not much of that going these days. And whenever I have found a place where there's some, as soon as I tell them where I live, I'm sent packing because of the bad reputation these streets have got, no matter that not all of us would think nothing of stealing the shoes off a child and spending the proceeds down the local pub.'

Cam was well aware that the only reason she had secured the outwork she had was because of Ann's connections at her place of work.

A look of horror was clouding Ivy's face as she exclaimed, 'Oh, Cam, I'm so sorry. Here's me telling you I understand how upsetting it is for you to talk about losing your husband, and I've been reminding you of it by telling you how I lost mine.'

Ivy wasn't the only one feeling mortified. So was Cam. The woman before her was genuinely grieving for a dead husband, and showing real sympathy towards Cam's supposed grief too.

Ivy went over to finish making the tea, bringing the pot to the table along with two enamel mugs. Then a thought obviously struck her and she said worriedly, 'We've no sugar. No money to buy any until Mam next gets paid. I hope . . .'

'I can take it with or without,' Cam politely interjected, despite the fact that tea without sugar was like drinking poison to her. The tea that was poured was as weak as dishwater and it was obvious to Cam that the leaves they had were being eked out too until Ivy's mother next got paid.

While they drank their tea, Ivy told Cam that she had an eighteen-month-old son, called Cyril after his deceased father. He was a placid child who'd never caused his mother a moment of bother . . . unlike Rose who let Cam know she was around from the moment she woke until she dropped off to sleep. Ivy led the conversation, chattering non-stop about the trials and tribulations of raising a child without the support of a husband. Cam was relieved to have her mind diverted from her upset earlier on seeing Adrian, although it was still very much fresh in her mind.

When it was time for Cam to take her leave, Ivy asked if she could take a peek at Rose. Prepared for the usual shocked expression which many people did not try to hide when they first clapped eyes on her, Cam was pleasantly surprised when all Ivy said was, 'Oh, she's a tiny little thing, isn't she? My Cyril made two of her at her age. What a weight he was to carry around! I was so thankful when he started to walk and I didn't have to carry him any more.'

Cam hadn't met Ivy under the best of circumstances but, regardless, was glad that she had. It would be nice to have someone to walk to the shops with or drop in on for a cuppa, and vice versa.

Back home, mindful not to wake Rose, Cam stealthily parked the pram in the corridor downstairs, opened the door leading up to the flat, then gently lifted the sleeping child out of her pram and began to make her way up.

As she did the sound of voices reached her as the flat door was slightly ajar. Ann and Brian were home. They had been going to the cinema, or so Cam had understood. Obviously, considering the time, they hadn't enjoyed the film and had left early. As she neared the top, it struck her that Ann and Brian weren't just talking, they were having an argument. Cam stopped abruptly, gaping in shock as just what was being said became audible to her.

Brian was saying, 'You keep telling me to have patience, Ann. But how much patience is a man supposed to have? It's been nine months now and there's no sign yet of Cam making any move to start managing on her own. All I'm saying is that if she knew you'd put a halt to us getting married just so you could see her on her feet, then she'd make the effort to start living on her own. That's all.'

Ann erupted, 'And I told you, Cam is never to know we shelved our wedding plans! She'd be absolutely mortified. She's been through enough without needing to find out that.'

'But if you don't start encouraging her to go it alone, then she's bound to be thinking that you're happy to go on with these living arrangements until God knows when. You could at least suggest her finding someone who'd have Rose while she went out to work full-time. And before you say it, I know jobs aren't exactly growing on trees at the moment, but it's not like Cam hasn't got good credentials so she'll stand a better chance of getting something than others will.

'Look, Ann, I just want us to be together. I want to share my bed with you each night, wake up with you in the morning, for us be planning to have our own kids. Now I'm out of my apprenticeship and my firm is paying me properly for my skills, I can afford to rent us a little house of our own. It's not like we'd be living with my folks like we first planned to, before Cam found herself in a predicament and you felt obliged to help her.'

'Obliged? I've never felt obliged to help Cam. She's my friend . . . my best friend. I consider her my family, you know that. She's not an obligation, Brian.'

'I'm sorry, that came out wrong. I know Cam's no burden to you, but you've already done far more for her than some blood relatives would.'

'And I'll continue to do what I can until the time comes when she doesn't need my help.' There was a pause then before Ann added: 'I explained to you when I first decided to do this that I'd understand if you couldn't stand by me while I see it through. I'll just have to hope you're still free when this is over . . . and still want me.'

Brian blurted, 'Of course I'll be free! There's no other woman who'd suit me like you do, Ann. I love you more than life itself . . . how many times have I told you that? You know I'll continue to stand by you while you see Cam through this. Doesn't mean to say I have to like it, though.'

Ann's voice was tender and sincere when she responded, 'I love you too, Brian, couldn't imagine my life without you. You know I want to get married as much as you do . . . to be with you all the time. But I just can't be until I know Cam can manage on her own, I just can't.' She gave a heavy sigh. 'Look, I will touch on the subject of her finding someone to mind Rose while she goes out to work full-time.' She sighed again. 'Mind you, finding someone willing to mind Rose could be tough. I feel so sorry for Cam. Was it not enough to be lumbered with raising a child she didn't want? And then for that child to look like . . . well, as unkind as it is, I speak the truth . . . a goblin, and as yet with no sign of her looks improving any. And she's such a difficult child . . . so demanding and disagreeable most of her waking hours. I've yet to see Rose smile. And Cam is right – the way she looks at you, it's as if she hates you. She's only a baby. Can't possibly know what she's doing, can she? Yet it's as if she's purposely making it hard for anyone to like her. As though she doesn't want them to. It's like she was born with a grudge against life. Cam thinks herself wicked for not being able to feel for her like a mother should for her own child. In all honesty, if I was in her shoes I'd be having the same trouble, although I'd never tell her that and hurt her feelings. I just pray . . .'

The rest of what Ann said was lost to Cam. What she had over-heard already had absolutely horrified her. Not what had been said about Rose. Any other mother would have been outraged to have heard her child being described as Ann just had hers, but Cam could not dispute a word of it. No matter how much attention she received, how many things were done to try and please her, Rose was disagree-able and bad-tempered for the majority of her waking hours. Seemingly it was her sole purpose to make the life of the woman who had given birth to her as fraught as possible. And she wasn't a pretty child . . . did have an impish look about her. What was mortifying to Cam was the revelation that Ann had put her marriage to Brian on hold in order to prevent her friend from landing up in the workhouse. Cam's own love for Ann would have had her laying down her life in order to save her friend's, but to have Ann's sacrifice revealed to her in this way left her feeling very emotional. And what a sensitive and caring man Brian was, to be standing by Ann while she did what she was for her friend, even though he did not like having to wait to make her his wife. If she hadn't happened to overhear Ann's and Brian's conversation tonight, would Cam ever have found out what her friend had done for her?

Common sense should have alerted her at the time. Who in their right mind would have voluntarily left comfortable lodgings with an amenable landlady in order to move into a crumbling hovel in what was probably the most deprived area in the city? But at the time Cam had been too consumed by her own affairs to see the reason for Ann's actions. Since then Ann had given her no reason to believe she wasn't happy with their living arrangements. But now she was aware of the truth, Cam could not allow her to continue to make such a monumental sacrifice on a friend's behalf.

Rose stirred in her arms, reminding Cam she needed to put her down in her cot before she risked waking her and then having the devil's own job getting her off to sleep again. She must not upset Ann by giving her any inkling of what she had overheard. Taking a deep breath, Cam straightened herself and continued the rest of the way up the stairs, to push open the door with her shoulder and enter, purposely looking surprised to see Ann and Brian home.

In a whisper she said to them, 'You're home early from the cinema. Weren't you enjoying the film?' Without waiting for a response, she continued, 'Rose wouldn't settle so I took her out in the pram for a walk, to see if that'd do the trick. Thankfully it did. I'd better put her down before she wakes.'

She went off to the bedroom to tend to Rose and when she returned there was no sign of Brian.

Ann told her as she handed her a mug of tea, 'Brian said cheerio. There's a big job on in the garage tomorrow so he's decided to get an early night and turn up for work in advance to get a start on it.' Then she looked quizzically at her friend. 'What's wrong, Cam?'

Was Ann wondering if she had overheard what she and Brian had said and probing Cam to find out? Or was it that Cam couldn't hide the fact that she was upset? She purposely looked puzzled and gave a nonchalant shrug. 'Nothing's wrong,' she lied. 'Oh, apart from the fact I'm worried how I'm going to make up the time I lost when I took Rose out.'

Ann was still looking at her questioningly. 'Camella Rogers, I know you better than I know myself and something is bothering you. Something more than being behind with your work.'

Cam gave a heavy sigh. 'I should know by now that your beady eyes miss nothing. You're right, I am upset. I was trying to forget what I saw but . . .'

'Saw! What did you see?' Ann demanded.

Cam gave another heavy sigh. 'Not a *what*, Ann, but a *who*. Adrian.' She paused for a moment to let Ann digest what she had been told before going on, 'I didn't realise I'd walked so far, trying to get Rose off to sleep, until I found myself opposite the theatre on Belgrave Road. Adrian was paying for tickets for himself and a woman. She was very pretty. They looked so happy together.' Cam's bottom lip trembled and tears glinted in her eyes. 'It's one thing to wonder if he's met someone else, but to have it confirmed and see them getting on so well together . . .'

Ann laid a gentle hand on her arm. 'I'm so sorry, Cam.'

'I suppose it was bound to happen one day, that I would see him. Leicester isn't that big a city. As much as I've tried not to, I do think about him sometimes and wonder how he is. But actually seeing him has brought it all back. How much I cared for him. I loved him so much, Ann. He was the one I was supposed to be with, I just know he was, before that . . . *man* . . . gave me no choice but to end it with him. It kills me to think that Adrian thinks I finished with him because I didn't feel that way about him. I shouldn't begrudge him being happy with someone else, but I do, Ann. It's breaking my heart to think that that woman I saw him with, he'll be waiting for at the end of the aisle. She'll have his children, when it should have been me. I don't suppose he gives me a thought now.'

It distressed Ann greatly to see her friend so upset. 'Oh, love, come on. For all you know, that woman you saw him with is his sister.'

'Adrian hasn't got a sister. And anyway, you don't act the way he was with a sister.' She shot Ann a wan smile. 'I know you want to say something to make me feel better, but there's nothing you can that will. I know I'll go to my grave mourning the loss of Adrian and that's something I'll just have to live with. Now, I need to get cracking on my work or it won't be done when Mr Abbott calls for it, and then he'll be giving my job to someone else.'

'I'll give you a hand, and that way you can catch up with the time you've lost and not have to stay up all night.'

Cam threw her arms around her friend and gave her a bear hug. 'I bless the day I met you. I dread to think what would have happened to me if I hadn't you as my friend.'

Thinking of the number of cakes Cam had bought that Ann had eaten when they used to meet each other in town on a Saturday afternoon and end up in a cafe, money allowing, Ann laughed. 'Well, you'd have been fatter for a start, eating all those cakes I saved you from!'

She helped Cam with the majority of the remainder of her work, leaving her with just a small amount to finish off in the morning. Much later Cam lay in bed, her friend snoring softly beside her, going over all she'd overheard Ann and Brian saying and wondering how she could possibly ever repay Ann for the sacrifice she had made. She could go partway towards it, though, by managing to fend for herself so that Ann was free to marry Brian. As tired as she was, Cam's mind was too busy working on this problem to allow her the luxury of sleep.

As Brian had said, she needed to get herself a job that paid enough to support her and Rose. In this recession it was not going to be easy, but finding someone who was willing to care for her wilful child and put up with her ways was going to be a worse difficulty. There must be a woman somewhere who would welcome a few shillings a week to mind Rose . . . the sort not to let a strong-willed baby get the better of her. Then suddenly a woman Cam already knew, who would certainly welcome the chance to earn some money, sprang to mind. First thing in the morning Cam would pay her a visit and put her proposition to her.

CHAPTER SIXTEEN

Next day, as soon as Leonard Abbott had collected the outwork order and left another for collection in two days, Cam put Rose in the pram and set off to see Ivy, hoping she hadn't gone out so she could put her idea to her and get her reaction as soon as possible. Rose had been particularly trying that morning, nothing seeming to please her. She was crawling now, and despite the toys Cam had managed to acquire for her from the junk shop, would only be content when she had installed herself in the middle of her mother's work in progress on the floor and dismantled the piles of inspected socks Cam had left ready to be banded into dozens. In desperation, she had barricaded Rose behind the sofa, armchair and the two kitchen chairs, leaving her a good space to move around in with her toys and left her to it, shutting her ears to the howls of displeasure in order to finish off her work.

As she journeyed the short distance to Ivy's home, Cam was relieved that it was too early and too cold, it being mid-December, for the local women to be gossiping on doorsteps. Despite having lived in this street for nine months, she and Ann were still viewed by the majority of the other residents with suspicion, made to feel they didn't belong. Amongst them, no doubt, was the culprit who had stolen their belongings when they had first arrived. It was deeply galling to Cam to think that this person was laughing at them behind their backs.

Ivy was surprised to see who her caller was at just before nine o'clock that morning, and intrigued when Cam told her there was a reason why she had dropped by so early. The young woman eagerly ushered her inside. A blond-haired, very handsome little boy was playing with a selection of old toys on a threadbare clippy rug in front of the antiquated range. The child was obviously Ivy's son, Cyril. Rose, who had been tetchily grumbling since being put in the pram and taken out in the cold, was now scowling and watching the other child intently. It was very rare for something to capture her attention like this, and Cam prayed it continued long enough for her to have the peace to relay her idea to Ivy, and also for her new friend not to witness just how bad-natured Rose usually was . . .

She refused the cup of tea Ivy offered. When they were sitting opposite each other at the kitchen table, Cam began, 'Yesterday you said you'd do anything to be able to earn some money?'

'And I would,' Ivy answered. Her eyes lit up eagerly. 'Do you know someone who wants something I can do while I'm looking after Cyril?'

Cam nodded. 'Yes. Me. I really need to go out to work so I can earn more money, but to do that I need someone to mind Rose.'

Ivy blurted, 'But I could do that!'

Cam smiled. 'That's what I was hoping you'd say. Trouble is, I don't know how much I could afford to pay you until I get a job and learn how much I'll be earning. I promise you, though, that I would pay you what I could reasonably afford, nothing less.'

'Anything would be a Godsend to me and my mam at the moment, Cam.'

'Well, if I got a job, on top of the money I gave you for minding Rose, I could possibly give you the opportunity of earning your-self a bit more. I don't suppose the man I get the outwork from will care if I farm out half of it as long as it gets done, but to be on the safe side we'd best keep the arrangement to ourselves.'

Ivy's eagerness mounted. 'I'll cut my tongue out if that's what it takes! What would it involve?'

'Trimming, inspecting and pairing socks, then banding them into dozens. That's the outwork I do. It's hard work, laborious, and the pay is terrible. To be honest, I can't wait for the day when I can afford to give up doing it, but at the end of the day needs must. Even should I get a full-time job, it would be stupid of me to give up my outwork until I was absolutely positive I could manage on what wage I get, but with working full-time I wouldn't be able to complete the orders on my own. I thought, if you were interested, we could split the work and the pay between us?'

'Oh, yes, I'm willing to do that,' cried Ivy in delight. 'Cam, you don't know what a difference earning a bit of money will make to our lives. I don't know how to thank you.'

'Well, I do need to get myself a job first, and who knows how long that will take me in these times?' Cam looked bothered then. 'There is something else I need to make you aware of, though, before we go ahead with this.'

Ivy looked worried. 'Oh?'

Cam took a deep breath. 'It's Rose.'

Ivy looked puzzled. 'What about her?'

'Well, she can be . . . difficult. She's not an easy child.'

Ivy turned her head to look over at Rose, sitting in her pram, still entranced by the sight of Cyril playing contentedly with his toys. She turned back to address Cam. 'She doesn't seem much trouble to me. Little angel, sitting there watching my Cyril.'

Cam looked over at them both. Maybe being in the company of another child would have a calming effect on Rose. Hopefully. 'Well, I just need you to know that she can be very demanding.'

'You should see how demanding my Cyril is when he wants his dinner and it's not ready. He can scream the house down!'

Cam doubted if he was as loud and frenzied as Rose when something wasn't suiting her.

'I'm sure me and Rose will get on fine,' Ivy said with conviction. She then asked eagerly, 'How soon do you plan to start looking for a job? If you've nothing else on and you want to make a start this morning, I can watch her for you. I won't expect any payment until you get set on.'

Well, the sooner Cam did start her search, the sooner she'd be able to free Ann to marry Brian, and Ivy and her family's lives would be helped by the improvement in their finances.

Outside in the street, Cam stood still for a moment to take stock. She hadn't given a thought to just where she would start looking for a job as she hadn't thought past approaching Ivy, to ask her to consider the proposition. She didn't want to have to travel too far, but knew that she'd have to get out of this deprived area to get something decent. The busy thoroughfare of Humberstone Road was only a twenty-minute or so walk away and there were many merchants who operated their business from there. That was where Cam would begin her search.

Her route took her through a short narrow jitty which brought her out in the middle of Humberstone Road. She stood for a moment, looking up and down, wondering whether to turn right or left.

She turned right, and had barely put one foot in front of the other when the sound of a loud commotion coming from a yard she was just about to pass, brought her to a halt. The sign above the double gates told her it was a carpenter's premises, owned by a William Gates & Son. To Cam's surprise two young men came tearing out of the yard and raced off down the road. They were closely followed by an extremely worried-looking, middle-aged woman, who was still struggling to put on her coat while she ran. Only yards behind her was a youngish man – in his thirties, probably – who stopped just outside the gate and shook his fist angrily at the fleeing woman.

'You bloody thief!' he yelled after her. 'I trusted you . . . paid you well for looking after my paperwork . . . and *this* is how you've been treating me behind my back! If I ever see any of your faces around here again, I'll . . . I'll . . . Huh!' With that he turned and stormed back inside the yard.

Cam stared after him blindly, her heart racing. Had she just witnessed what she thought she had? The owner of this yard had obviously caught someone thieving . . . well, he'd need someone else to work there now, wouldn't he?

Eighteen months ago Cam had been in the wrong place at the wrong time. Could it be that she was now ideally situated to find what she sought? There was only one way to find out.

She followed the man inside the yard.

The walls were lined with stacks of wood of varying sizes and qualities; some planks were in a rough state, some planed ready for use. There were also panes of glass and the rest of the yard was littered with carpentry tools. A handcart stood loaded with three window frames and a tool bag. Just inside the gate stood another small handcart that held a bulky sacking bag and several lengths of wood. There were two brick buildings visible. The doors to both stood open. The smaller of the two was obviously a store as Cam could see stacks of tins holding paint, glue, putty, and wooden trays fixed to the walls holding nails and screws. An open box on the floor had an array of small tools spilling out of it, and other tools were scattered over the floor too. The larger building was obviously the office as there was a sign on the door spelling out *Enquiries*. There was no sign of the man so Cam assumed he must be in the office.

Weaving her way through the clutter, she went over to the door, tapped on it and entered.

Over by the far wall was a desk that held an Imperial typewriter and Bakelite telephone. By the side of it stood two filing cabinets on top of which were several overstuffed files. The man she'd seen sat over at a table beneath a window so grimy hardly any light was filtering through it. On the heavily marked table stood a bottle of milk, blue bag of sugar, packet of tea, several chipped enamel mugs, a brown tea pot and a Primus stove with a kettle on it that started to whistle loudly.

On hearing her tap on the door, the man turned the gas off under the kettle and looked over at his visitor enquiringly. 'What can I do for you?' he asked.

Cam took a deep breath. 'Well . . . actually, I'm hoping it's what I can do for you.'

He frowned. 'Eh?'

Straight to the point, she said, 'I was just passing when I witnessed what happened just now. I assume you'll be looking for replacements. I'm looking for a job so I'd be very interested in replacing the woman who did your office work.'

Jonah Gates was about six foot tall. His rippling muscles announced the fact that he did manual work. He was ruggedly handsome with a thick thatch of dark, almost black, hair. Leaning back against the table, he folded his arms and looked straight at her. 'If you were privy to what happened, you'll know that the woman who just ran out of here worked for us. For the past five years, in fact. We thought she was as honest as the day she was born, but she was fleecing us. Thankfully I just discovered what was going on before she got away with any more than she already has. How do I know I could trust you to be left on your own while I'm out on jobs, and not be up to 'ote untoward?'

Cam told him, 'My own word that I'm honest, and I've a reference from my last job. I could also get you testimonials from people who know me and will vouch for me.'

Jonah pulled a face. 'Our last employee had glowing references and several testimonials – it turns out now none of them was worth the paper they were written on.'

'Well, with due respect, just because you'd had one bad experience doesn't mean it's fair to assume everyone is a thief and a blackguard.'

The telephone shrilled.

Due to her training with the GPO, it was second nature for Cam to answer a ringing telephone. It kicked in now, the fact it wasn't her place to answer this particular telephone completely escaping her.

'Good morning,' she said. There was only the slightest of pauses while the name of the firm she'd spotted outside flashed to mind and she continued, 'William Gates and Son. How may I be of assistance?' Cam's tone was welcoming but efficient. As she listened to the caller, her eyes searched around the desk for a piece of paper and a pencil, which she found. She started to write a note. She was so engrossed in the telephone call she did not realise that Jonah Gates was watching her, astounded. 'I will certainly pass this message on to Mr Gates as soon as possible, Mrs Garson. Thank you for calling.'

Cam replaced the receiver, put down the pencil, then walked over to hand the piece of paper with the message on to Jonah Gates. Still dumbstruck, he accepted it. 'Mrs Garson is accepting the quote you gave her yesterday to reframe and replace her back door, and wishes you to do the job as soon as possible. She's asked you to telephone her with a date and time. I have written her number down for you.' It then struck Cam just what she had done. Mortified, she blurted out, 'Oh . . . oh, I'm so sorry! It's just that I've been trained never to leave a telephone ringing and . . .'

'Well, whoever trained you certainly did a good job,' he cut in. 'Mrs Norman never answered it so efficiently and politely all the time she worked here. Who did train you?'

'The GPO. I was a senior telephonist by the time I left.'

He was looking at her with interest now. 'And why did you leave?'

Cam stared back at him blankly. She was desperately hoping to land a job from this man. There was no telling how long it would take her to find another when hundreds of people were applying for one vacancy. But as long as she was qualified to do the work and did it well, earned what he paid her, was it really any of his business to know what lay behind her having to give up her job at the GPO? She was already telling one whopping lie about her fictitious dead husband . . . did another really matter? So Cam told him, 'My mother was very ill and needed constant care. I'm an only child so it was up to me to do it. I looked after her until she died.'

Jonah looked genuinely concerned to hear that. 'I am sorry for your loss. My mother died when I was young, and my father a month ago. I looked after him while he was ill. Thank God Father isn't alive now to learn what Mrs Norman got up to. It would have broken his heart; he was a very trusting man.'

Curiosity got the better of Cam and she asked, 'Just how was Mrs Norman fleecing you?'

Jonah flashed her a look as though to say, What business is that of yours? But then obviously decided it didn't make any difference if she knew or not. 'It wasn't exactly she who was fleecing me, but she was definitely guilty of turning a blind eye to those who were. When the recession bit, Mrs Norman's two sons both lost jobs with a local factory whose orders dried up. They started doing handyman work to make ends meet while they tried to get set on in another place. She told me so herself. What I didn't know was that they were helping themselves to the materials they needed from my supplies when I was out on jobs.

'My father had taken ill, so Mrs Norman took over all the ordering and making sure we never ran out of anything. After his death it was a relief for me not to have that burden as I was then running the business single-handed. I saw no reason not to let her carry on. Thankfully, I forgot to pick up a quantity of flat-head screws for a job I had on this morning, and had to come back for them unexpectedly. That's how I discovered what was going on. I caught them loading a cart with what they needed for a job they'd landed. If they think they're getting that cart back, then they've another thing coming! Though I doubt the cost of it would go anywhere near repaying what they've had off me. I would eventually have twigged we seemed to be spending more than necessary on materials when I got around to doing the yearly tally of the books, but I would probably have put it down to some jack-the-lads coming over the wall, not my own staff. I'll never take my eye off the ball again, though. Taught me a valuable lesson this has.'

Jonah took a look at his wrist watch. 'I should be somewhere. My customer isn't going to be happy I'm late. Some firms are struggling for work, even going under due to this dratted recession, but thankfully for the likes of me, people still have to find the cash for repairs to their homes.'

Cam's disappointment was unmistakable. 'Oh, but what about the job? You will be needing someone, won't you? I don't live far away . . . I could come back.' Not that she would ever tell him just where she lived, that area having such a bad reputation. 'Please, won't you just give me a try?' she implored.

Scratching the back of his neck, Jonah looked at her. He did need someone, and urgently, as there was no telling how much work he'd miss out on if there was no one here to answer the telephone or deal with anyone who came in personally. And as soon as word got round he'd a vacancy, hordes of desperate people would be descending on him, begging to be given a chance at the job. And when was he going to have time to wade through them all and pick out the best candidate, when he was supposed to be out dealing with his customers' needs? This young woman had certainly proved to him that she was adept at answering the telephone in the proper manner, so why should he doubt she was capable of handling the rest of the clerical work just as efficiently? To have gained the role of supervisor with the likes of the GPO she must have impressed them with her abilities.

He had been so consumed by anger at his employee's betrayal of his trust that he had not as yet taken a proper look at the young woman. Thoughtfully, he did so now. Her clothes were shabby but they were clean and presentable, and he could tell she had a good figure underneath her coat. She was certainly attractive, to his mind with a look of the actress Janet Gaynor about her. He certainly liked what he was seeing. He found himself wondering if she had a boyfriend . . . His last girlfriend had dropped him when all his spare time was taken up by caring for his sick father. She hadn't been prepared to wait for him. It would be nice to have some female company again. Maybe this young woman before him could be the one. It would be good as well to have someone nearer his own age, bringing more vitality to the office. Mrs Norman had been very set in her ways, didn't like change or welcome new ideas about how to run the office. She'd had a limited sense of humour, certainly hadn't appreciated his jokes or been the type to play an innocent prank on, whereas this young woman seemed more on his wavelength.

Jonah smiled at her. 'All right, I'll take a risk on you. But I want to see your reference from the GPO. How soon can you start?'

A short while later Ivy was staring at Cam, confounded. 'You've got a job already?'

Cam nodded. 'Just happened to be in the right place at the right time. How lucky for me was that?' She told Ivy all about the job and what she would be doing and said that her new boss seemed like a fair man. She then concluded, 'But, of course, that depends on whether you still want to go ahead with minding Rose after this morning?'

Ivy was adamant. 'Yes, yes, 'course I do. I can't deny that she started to get grizzly and grumpy about twenty minutes after you left, but she had her rag dolly to play with and there was nothing wrong with her so I just got on with what I was doing and left her to it. She's certainly got a good pair of lungs on her, I'll give her that. But then, she isn't used to me and Cyril yet. Give her time. She'll be fine once she is.' Ivy clapped her hands in delight then. 'Oh, I can't wait to tell me mam this good news. Can't wait to lift some of the worry from her.'

And next Cam had Ann to tell of this turn of events.

She waited until she had settled Rose in her cot for the night so there'd be no interruption. And she must be very careful how she did break this news. The last thing she wanted was for her friend to realise her generosity had been discovered. Ann had been so careful to spare her feelings. She must be the same towards her friend.

From what she had overheard the previous evening, she knew the news Ann was longing to hear. It served to show Cam that her welfare was still top priority with Ann, above even her own happiness, when with a worried look on her face, Ann said, 'But you've never mentioned you were looking for a full-time job. Are you sure you're ready . . . can you cope with working full-time as well as caring for Rose?'

'I'm as ready as I'll ever be, Ann. With how things are jobwise, I wasn't sure how long it would take me to get one. I know you said at the time that us sharing with you was doing you a favour as you didn't want to live on your own, but it's really not been fair you've had to shoulder most of the bills, except for the bit I've contributed from my outwork.'

'Well, I would have had to do that anyway, had you turned down my offer, as I wouldn't have had anyone else share with me. So it was no skin off my nose.'

'Well, now I can properly pay my way, I'll feel better for doing that.' Cam took a deep breath. 'The last thing I want to do is hurt your feelings, Ann, but I feel I'm ready to get a place of my own now that I can afford to. I need to make a permanent home for Rose.'

'Oh, yes, well, of course you do . . . and I understand that.'

'I'm so glad you do, Ann. But then, I knew you would. It'll have to be around here, for me to be able to afford the rent.'

Ann was looking at her thoughtfully. 'Well, maybe you could take this place on.' She took a deep breath, her eyes lighting up excitedly. 'This is really a coincidence. I was going to tell you when you'd finished telling me your news, but . . . well . . . Brian's asked me to marry him!'

Ann would never have guessed that Cam already knew this. She gave a whoop of delight. 'Oh, Ann, at long last! I was beginning to think he was never going to.'

'Well, now he's made his mind up, Brian wants us to get married soon as . . . but I told him I was in no rush as I was happy with our living arrangements. Now you tell me you're ready to get a place of your own, though, well . . . it seems daft you having to find another place, especially as we've done such a lot to make this one better. Another flat will only be in the same state this was in at first. Why hand it on to other tenants who'll get the benefit, or that crook of an agent who'll only put up the rent? When I leave to marry Brian, you can carry on living here. Do you think you can put up with me for a while longer?'

They were sitting side by side on the sofa. Cam gave her her answer by throwing herself on Ann, hugging her tightly. The thought of losing the day-to-day support of her friend terrified her witless but their living arrangements couldn't have gone on forever, however much Cam wanted them to. Despite the way Ann professed herself happy living with Rose and Cam, she herself found Rose's temperament hard to cope with so it must grate on her friend. This had always bothered Cam, so at least she wouldn't have to worry about it any longer. And they'd still see each other, as often as possible. When they did, hopefully at those times Rose's mood would be a good one. Cam could live in hope anyway.

CHAPTER SEVENTEEN

Cam shut the door to Ivy's house behind her and stepped off jauntily down the street towards her place of work. She had been in her full-time job for a year now and had more than proved her worth to Jonah Gates, so much so he had broken his promise to himself never to trust another employee to handle and monitor the ordering of the stock and had handed it over to Cam to take care of. She was also now doing basic accounts. To her absolute delight, yesterday he had told her he was giving her a pay rise. This had come as a real shock to her, considering most other workers were having to do without a rise for the foreseeable future or else being told their job was gone while the country was still in the grip of the recession.

Cam wasn't blind. She was well aware that her boss liked her more than a boss usually did an employee. Cam was flattered, she liked him too, he had many good qualities ... although no one would ever match up to Adrian in her eyes. Had things in her own life been different, she would have liked the chance to get to know Jonah better and see where the relationship went. She had never encouraged him, though, and never intended to. She knew that it was unlikely any decent man would want to pursue a relationship with her when he discovered she was in fact an unmarried mother, no matter how that had come about. Besides, there was also the fact that if a relationship didn't work out between them, she could lose her vital job.

The shock pay rise had made her wonder whether she could afford to move herself and Rose out of Sun Street to a better area. Cam planned to check out the rents being asked for small terrace houses during her dinner break today. She didn't plan a move far away; could still use Ivy for her minding services. Besides, she knew the young woman was dependent on the money she earned for looking after Rose, and it gave Cam much pleasure to know that what she paid was making such a difference to other people's lives. For Cam, though, this extra in her pay packet could see the end to her need to supplement her wages with outwork, which often took up four hours a night. She used the proceeds to pay for Rose's care. Maybe she wouldn't need to now?

The arrangement with Ivy minding Rose had gone far better than Cam had expected. Not once had Ivy complained that she'd had a bad day with Rose and regretted her decision to mind her, as Cam had dreaded would happen. This state of affairs remained a mystery to her, though. At twenty-one months now, Rose's wilful, demanding and bad-tempered ways had not lessened one iota when things did not suit her, which was the majority of the time. The only conclusion that Cam could reach was that Ivy had a way with children. There were times, when Rose was being a particular handful, that Cam wished she could hand her over entirely to Ivy and pay her to take sole charge, especially since she had lost the day-to-day support of Ann who had many times previously stepped in when Rose was having one of her tantrums and Cam herself was at breaking point.

It had taken her a good while to get used to not having Ann by her side, and not just in a supportive way. She missed having her to talk to in the evenings, especially the times when she hadn't been seeing Brian and would help Cam with her outwork. While they were working, the pair of them would put the world to rights as well as listening to and advising each other on any problems or worries they had. Ann, though, was revelling in her new role as Brian's wife, and was extremely happy. In Cam's opinion, no one deserved that more than her friend after what she had done. Cam had tried to come up with a way to repay her, but when it came down to it, the only way she felt she could was to keep herself and Rose out of the workhouse, which was why Ann had made her generous sacrifice in the first place.

Ann and Brian's wedding, which had taken place on a frosty February morning two months after Ann had told Cam about the proposal, had been a very small affair, all done on a shoestring as neither of them had any savings to speak of, having each in their own way been a benefactor to Cam. The majority of the twenty guests had come from Brian's side, Ann having only Cam as family plus her old landlady, Mrs Middleton. Ann had made her own wedding dress with material bought from the market and her accessories had been second-hand or borrowed. Brian had looked handsome in a second-hand suit.

The food for the reception had been simple fare, just enough to go around, but it had all tasted delicious. Brian's boss had kindly donated a barrel of beer for the men, and three bottles of sherry and three of port for the women. Music had come from a borrowed gramophone along with several recordings by Mario Lanza, whom neither Ann nor Brian could stand but it was better than no music at all.

Just before the wedding, they had managed to find a small terrace house at an affordable rent around the corner from Brian's parents. It had been lived in for over fifty years by a very old lady who had recently died so was in great need of a good clear out, fresh paint on the dingy walls and repairs to the woodwork. But in comparison to the state of the flat in Sun Street when Cam and Ann had first moved in, the tiny house was a palace. With donations from family, friends and neighbours, they soon had enough furniture, pots and pans to give them a start.

Listening to them both say their vows, seeing the love they felt for each other brimming in their eyes, had brought a choking lump to Cam's throat. Try as she might, she couldn't help but wonder if maybe by now she and Adrian would have been promising to love, honour and obey each other, had she not decided to take that route to meet him down by the canal that fateful night.

Rose, though, didn't allow her to stay in church for the whole of the service. Before the vicar was a third of the way towards pronouncing the pair man and wife, she had decided she'd had enough and howled her displeasure. There was nothing Cam could do to quieten her, so she'd had no choice but to take her child outside until the service was over. It was the same at the reception held in Brian's parents' terrace house. After only half an hour of

Cam enjoying the celebrations, Rose started to get restless, then to start grizzling, and nothing Cam or any of the other guests could do was able to appease her. Cam had had no choice but to leave in order that Rose's temper tantrum did not ruin the party, but not before she had overheard two women speaking.

One was saying to the other, 'According to Ann, her friend had not long been married after a whirlwind romance when her husband had an accident. Killed instantly, apparently. Poor girl, as if she's not suffering enough, widowed so young, but to have to cope with such a difficult child as well . . .'

'Mmm,' mouthed the other. 'She's not the type to be fought over by us women for a hold of, is she? She's not an attractive child at all.'

'Not at all she's not, and considering how pretty her mother is . . . Must take after her father. Some pretty women are attracted to ugly men, ain't they? He must have had money.'

'She doesn't look to me like she's been left any, considering them old clothes she's wearing.'

'Must have been love then 'cos I can't think of any other reason why a pretty thing like her would marry an ugly man. Well, the kid's looks might improve as she gets older . . . ugly duckling into a swan . . . but if her moody ways don't, she's gonna have a tough time of it with the other kids at school. Do you remember Mabel Turnbull's youngest? Just like Ann's friend's kiddie when he was that age, and you remember what happened to him . . .'

Cam didn't want to know what happened to Mabel Turnbull's youngest. She had enough to worry about already. She didn't want her daughter becoming an outcast. Cam might not have proper motherly feelings for Rose, but she did care about her and wanted her to have a happy and fulfilling life, and she would do her utmost to bring that about.

This morning as she made her way to work she felt privileged that, for the first time since she had commenced her employment with him, Jonah had asked her if she would open up for business as he was going to go straight from home to finish off a job that he hadn't managed to get done the day before. Jonah had given her a spare set of keys so she could let herself in. He was usually at the yard by seven thirty in the morning to prepare his tools for work that day and load them on the cart, ready to depart as soon as Cam arrived at eight. Customers in need of Jonah's services would sometimes call in at the yard on their way to work to consult him over it. Not wanting Jonah to miss out on any possible revenue, Cam meant to arrive there at seven thirty herself. Ivy, the previous evening, had agreed to take Rose earlier that day.

Cam had just turned the corner of Sun Street when she stopped abruptly as a thought struck her. Last evening, when she had got home, Rose would give her no peace to cook the dinner. She was pulling at Cam's skirt, yelling to be fed. In desperation, Cam had put her back in her pram and delved into her handbag for the keys to the flat, having put them in there when she had let herself in. Rose loved playing with keys. Too late, Cam had realised it was the yard keys, not the flat keys, she was in possession of. Cam was loath to swap them over as they were certainly doing what had been intended; Rose seeming fascinated by the jangling sound the keys made when she shook them. Knowing her daughter, though, Cam suspected this situation wouldn't last long. She took advantage of what time she'd got by rushing back into the kitchen to finish off the corned beef and potato pie she was in the process of preparing, meaning to return the yard keys to her handbag when Rose tired of playing with them. Only now she realised she had forgotten to do that as she'd been so busy getting Rose to eat her dinner and then into bed before tackling her household tasks and the pile of outwork she needed to do before she could even consider going to bed herself. The keys, therefore, were still in the pram.

Cross with herself for this oversight, she spun on her heel and retraced her steps to Ivy's, mindful she would have to run to work now if she intended to have the yard open for business at seven thirty.

Arriving back at Ivy's rotting, ill-fitting front door, she was aware after a year of coming and going that the wood swelled in winter, making it difficult to open, so after first tapping on it, Cam then put her shoulder against it and gave it a shove. Thankfully the door burst open and she tumbled inside, which she found very funny. She was laughing as she announced, 'It's only me, Ivy. I forgot to pick up the yard keys from Rose's pram when I left. I've had to come back for them.'

She could see Cyril sitting on a chair at the table, spooning porridge from a bowl to his mouth with only a margin of success. At least half of it was dripping off to fall on the bib he was wearing. Ivy was standing close by the table, preparing a baby bottle of milk. For Rose, Cam assumed, as her child had had her breakfast. It must be to give to her as soon as she let it be known she was peckish for her mid-morning snack. Cam was confused, though. She couldn't understand why Ivy was staring back at her with such a look of guilt on her face. She was performing a normal everyday task so why was she acting like she had been caught doing something she shouldn't be? It was then that Cam noticed what Ivy was holding in her hand over the bottle of milk. It was an eyelet dropper. Then her eyes fell on another bottle close to Rose's milk bottle. It was of plain glass and half-full of clear-looking liquid.

Going across to join Ivy at the table, frowning quizzically, Cam asked her, 'What are you putting in Rose's bottle of milk?' Then she realised there was no sign in the room of Rose or her pram but Cam could hear her crying. The sound was coming from outside in the yard. 'Why is Rose out there?' she asked, bewildered. Without waiting for an answer, Cam spun on her heel and ran the short distance to the back door, wrenching it open. As she did, Rose's muted wails became audible. It was still dark that early-winter morning and Cam could just about make out the outline of the pram with Rose inside it, her arms waving wildly, over by the crumbling boundary wall. Cam dashed over to her. Rose had a habit of howling and wailing at will but it was very clear to Cam this was no tantrum Rose was having, but that she was very upset. Making soothing noises, she grabbed hold of the pram handle and wheeled it back into the house, where she lifted Rose out and held the hysterical child close. For once Rose clung on to Cam, burying her head in her neck as if terrified of letting her go.

Ivy now sat hunched on a chair at the table, cradling her head in her hands, sobbing uncontrollably. Cam demanded, 'Why had you put Rose outside in this bitter weather?' When there was no immediate response, she cried, 'Ivy, will you answer me?'

The young woman reluctantly lifted her head and, with the bottom of her threadbare apron, wiped away the river of snot pouring down her wet face. She then blubbered, 'As usual, Rose started playing up as soon as you left this morning. She was after Cyril's breakfast. Wouldn't stop shouting out: "Me want. Me want." I said to her, "But your mummy told me you'd had your breakfast, and you only want it because it's Cyril's." I know this as she's done it before, then, when I've relented and given her something, she's just chucked it. She didn't really want it 'cos she was hungry, she wanted it 'cos Cyril had got what she hadn't. And I can't afford to waste food! When she realised I wasn't going to give in to her demand this morning, she started a temper tantrum. I just wanted a few minutes' peace, to see that Cyril ate his breakfast and have my own, so I put her outside. I was about to fetch her in as you came back, honest I was.'

Cyril, who up until then had been fully engaged in eating his porridge, lifted his head to look quizzically at his mother and said, 'But, Mammy, you never fetch Rose in 'til it's her dinnertime. Then, soon as she's finished, you put her out again.' He looked at Cam and said in all innocence, 'I don't like Rose. She's got a funny face, and all she does is scream 'cos she wants what I'm playing wiv all the time.'

Cam stared at the little boy, struggling to digest what he'd just said.

Ivy was scolding him, 'Oh, Cyril, don't tell such fibs. I only put Rose outside sometimes when she's having a paddy, 'til she calms down.'

Cam looked at her with narrowed eyes and said darkly, 'Cyril is too young to make up what he's just said.' She then accused Ivy: 'It's not your son who's the liar, it's you, isn't it? You've always told me when I've asked that Rose has been a perfect little angel for you. I even thought you'd got this magic way with her that I hadn't got. I realise now why she's not been causing you any bother . . . for most of the day she's out in the yard. You were lying to me! You weren't about to fetch her in when I returned.

'Now I know why she created every morning as soon as we got here. Not because she was just playing up but because she knew what was in store for her until I came back to pick her up. And all the time I went happily off to work, thinking she was playing with you and Cyril, just like you told me she was.'

Cam's eyes fell on the clear glass bottle on the table, then flashed to the eyelet dropper Ivy still held poised over Rose's bottle of milk. 'And you haven't told me yet just what you were about to put in her bottle when I came in.' When Ivy stared back at her wildly Cam demanded, 'What is it, Ivy? And I want the truth.'

She gulped, the look of guilt returning to her face, and then cried frenziedly, 'I wasn't lying! I was just about to fetch her in when you returned as it's so cold outside and I couldn't risk her catching pneumonia. I've *never* left her outside when it's really cold . . . or raining . . . and I only give her a drop of this stuff when I've no choice but to have her inside with us. It calms her down so she's easier for me to cope with.'

Cam's brows knotted in bewilderment. 'And just what is this stuff that calms her down so?'

Ivy shrugged. 'I don't know.'

Rose was merely whimpering now, but still clinging to her mother. Hitching the baby higher on her hip, Cam reached down and picked up the bottle. There seemed to be nothing on it to indicate just what the colourless liquid inside actually was. Then she saw moulded letters in the glass running down the side: *Laudanum.* Cam gasped and stared at Ivy in horror. 'Do you know what this is?'

She shrugged again. 'Me mam got it. She told me she used to give it to me when I was a kid, when I was teething or fretful. She ordered me to put no more than the tiniest of drops in some milk for Rose when she wouldn't be pacified by anything else. Said it would do the trick. And it did.'

Cam erupted, 'Ivy, what you've been giving Rose is laudanum. It's a dangerous drug. People become dependent on it. It can kill, if you take too much at one time. I've seen what it can do, 'specially to children. I was raised in an orphanage. When I was about ten, two little children, one just a baby, the other under two, were brought in. Their mother had been found dead from an overdose of this stuff. She'd been dead at least a couple of days before she was found, and those poor children were discovered in their cots with no food or water, caked in their own muck, and both in a right state, crying and shaking.

'Mrs Cummings just couldn't get them to settle until it struck her that the mother had been giving them laudanum and they were both suffering from withdrawal symptoms. With the help of the doctor she managed to wean them both off it. Mrs Cummings told us older kids what was going on with the new arrivals, because she needed to give them constant care and was relying on us older girls to help Mr Cummings, but she also wanted us to be warned about medicines like laudanum and how dangerous they could be.'

Ivy was gawping at her, shocked. 'I didn't know it could be so dangerous. Honest, Cam, I didn't.'

She snapped back incredulously, 'Oh, come on, you're not stupid, Ivy. The fact that your mother warned you not to give Rose any more than a tiny drop must have made you realise it was dangerous or why else would she give you that warning?' Just then Rose, seemingly recovered from her trauma, started to wriggle in Cam's arms. It was apparent she wanted to be put down on the floor. When her preoc-cupied mother didn't seem to notice, she let out a high-pitched squeal. Not at all in the mood for her nonsense, Cam went over to the pram and plonked her down in it. Totally ignoring the howls of protest, she returned to continue where she had left off. 'Has this way of looking after Rose been going on all the time you've had her, Ivy?'

Head hanging in shame, she nodded. 'I know you warned me Rose could be hard work, but I never dreamed just how hard. And she's got this way of looking . . . glaring daggers at you like she's . . . well, to me it's like she's warning me – dare to cross her and I'd better beware. After only a couple of days of having her, I was dreading you turning up with her in the morning and desperate for the time you came back to pick her up. But I needed the money you pay me. That few bob every week makes such a difference to us. It was then that I came up with the idea to put her outside when she started her antics, and teach her that every time she did start, that's what would happen. But she didn't seem to learn. As soon as I brought her in again, she would start up her demands.'

Cam had to admit Rose was hard to please and there had been numerous times when she herself had been reduced to putting her

in her cot in her bedroom and shutting the door until that particular tantrum was spent. But to leave her outside on her own virtually
all day . . . and to drug her to keep her quiet when the weather was
too bad to keep her outside!

Ivy was going on, 'I'd keep checking on her through the window,
to make sure she was all right, and bring her inside for her dinner.
And then I'd bring her back in again just before you were due home.
I hated the days when the weather was too bad to put her outside
. . . the stuff I gave her kept her quiet for a few hours, but I still
had to cope with her when it wore off. I didn't dare tell you I was
finding her a nightmare to look after. I was too frightened you'd
find someone else who could handle her better or that you'd give
up working. Either way I'd lose me job.'

Cam said icily, 'Well, you certainly have lost it now.'

At Cam's announcement, Ivy's face turned ashen. She jumped up
from her chair, begging, 'Oh, please, give me another chance! I
promise I'll never give Rose that stuff again or keep her outside. I'll
not let her tantrums get on my nerves. Cam, please, please, give me
another chance.'

Cam stared at her in disbelief. Did this woman really think that
she would leave Rose with her for another moment, having just
found out how she was coping with her?

She responded, 'I'll settle what I owe you at the end of the week.'

With that she grabbed hold of the pram handle and left, to Ivy's
cries of: 'Please, Cam, please . . . I beg you, please, change your mind.
Oh, and what about the outwork? You will still share it with me?'

Outside in the street, Cam found that she was shaking. For a
moment she pulled the pram to a halt and rested her back against
a wall, taking deep breaths to calm herself down. Thank God she
had left the yard keys in the pram last night or she dreaded to think
for how much longer Rose would have suffered those long periods
of isolation in the yard or been drugged to make her manageable.

It was then that the severity of her situation hit Cam. She needed
to find a new child minder for Rose, and quickly. A stalwart type
of woman, a no-nonsense sort, who wouldn't let a strong-willed
child get the better of her. But where did she begin to look for such
a person? During the time she had been working for Jonah Gates,

Cam had come to know several shopkeepers and their assistants in the area, along with some of the locals who regularly came into the yard wanting work done, and now she felt positive each of them would know of at least one woman who minded children. Or the local shops would have advertisements from women offering this service. Hopefully, amongst them was just the type of woman Cam was after.

But what did she do with Rose today? She couldn't take the day off without getting permission from her boss after giving him a good excuse. Then she remembered that Jonah was finishing off the job from yesterday and had intimated to her that it would probably take him all day. He wouldn't be back at the yard at all. A plan began to form in Cam's mind. She would take Rose with her to the yard and stay there until after nine. Those who might pop in needing a quote for a job on their way to work would all have come in by then. Cam would then leave a note on the door, stating she had gone out on an errand, and be back later. Hopefully she would have the deed done by dinnertime at the latest. With a bit of luck, the new child minder would start her duties that afternoon. She would be honest with Jonah when he returned, say that she'd taken time off to attend to an important appointment, and would just have to suffer the loss of pay and his possible annoyance that she'd left the yard unattended.

A great sense of sadness then came over her. She couldn't continue to be on friendly terms with Ivy after what she had discovered today. What a convincing liar she had proved herself to be! And how unforgivable of her it was to have treated a defenceless child so cruelly in order not to lose the money that child brought her. Cam didn't feel she could even remain on speaking terms with anyone who could stoop to such a level. Regardless, though, she would miss the times they had spent together, and the comfort of knowing that there was someone in her street she could turn to if the need arose. But then, thanks to her pay rise, she was soon going to be leaving Sun Street for pastures new. She'd make new friends then. After the events of this morning, and considering most of the other residents hereabouts had not exactly gone out of their way to make her or Ann feel welcome, that time couldn't come quick enough for Cam.

CHAPTER EIGHTEEN

As Cam made her way to the yard, about half a mile away, in the back garden of a well-maintained palisade Edwardian terrace house owned by a bank manager, Jonah Gates swore angrily under his breath and rubbed his thumb where the hammer had forcibly struck it. He then looked in dismay at the split piece of fascia wood he'd been nailing into place on the new back doorframe he was in the process of finishing off. He'd cut and planed that piece of wood especially for this particular doorframe and its spoiling meant he would have to return to the yard to make a replacement before he could finish here.

The customer who had commissioned him to do this job was a new one, and Jonah had already broken his promise to have the job completed by the end of yesterday due to several silly mistakes he had made. Now this latest one was going to put the job back even further. He'd be lucky if the customer didn't demand a discount, let alone never use him again or recommend his services to his neighbours and friends.

Jonah was normally so conscientious, allowing no distraction to take his mind off the high standard of workmanship upon which his father had built the firm's reputation. But, despite himself, he could not manage to free his mind from a particular matter that, for the last three days and nights, had been causing frequent lapses of concentration and actual loss of sleep.

After a year of humming and hawing, three evenings ago he had finally decided to ask Cam if she would like to have dinner with him, praying that this lovely woman who had stolen his heart would consider the invitation worth accepting. So far he hadn't managed to find the right moment to suggest the outing.

Something had stirred within him that first morning Cam had come into the yard to apply for the job. He had at the time been shocked by the discovery of the previous woman's dishonesty and still very much in mourning for the loss of his beloved father. He had definitely not been in the frame of mind to be seeking romance But, as the weeks had gone by and he had grown to know his new employee better, the spark of interest stirring within him had fully ignited. Now he had found himself wanting to be in her company all the time, thinking constantly of her when she wasn't there and willing the hour to arrive when she would be again. The fact that this attractive, intelligent young woman was not already married, nor even had a boyfriend, was a source of some bewilderment to Jonah. He only prayed that wouldn't alter before he found the courage to approach her.

Cam had given him every reason to believe that she liked him in return: always looking pleased to see him, offering to make him cups of tea, interested in how his day had gone and what plans he had for that evening or the weekend, laughing at his silly jokes, showing pleasure when he returned from a job having paid a visit to the baker's first, to buy a sticky bun for her.

He had meant to approach her yesterday but nervousness over this made him unable to concentrate on his work. Late back at the yard, he'd found Cam clearly awaiting his return only so that she could take her leave. It was apparent to him she was in a hurry to be somewhere else. He hoped it wasn't to get herself ready for a date with a man. Another sleepless night had resulted.

Jonah had hardly been back on this job an hour and already he was making mistakes. He had no choice now but to return to the yard and make a replacement fascia board. Then a thought struck him. Maybe this mistake could work in his favour. Hopefully Cam would be on her own now, no customers in the office wanting to settle an outstanding bill or giving the details of a job that wanted doing. He'd finally get his opportunity to ask her out, then, when he returned, he'd be looking forward to his first date with her and able to focus all his attention on the job.

Meanwhile, back at the yard, Cam was extremely anxious to get on with finding a minder for Rose. No one had come in since she had opened up, which Cam was relieved about as she wasn't faced with having to excuse away the presence of a child, which could get back to Jonah. It was now nearly nine. She felt it would be safe to lock up temporarily after pinning a notice to the door, asking any caller to return.

Much to Cam's relief, Rose had only a few minutes before accepting the fact that she could protest as much as she liked, her mother was not going to get her out of the pram to toddle freely around. There was too much danger she would come to harm here, with all the carpentry paraphernalia that was lying around. She had dozed off, her hour or so of screaming having worn her out. Hopefully she would stay asleep and give Cam the peace to find a suitable minder for her.

Cam was sitting at her desk, putting the finishing touches to the note, when she heard hob-nailed boots clattering across the cobbles in the yard and then the very last person she'd wanted to see arrived.

Having built himself up to fever pitch on his way back to the yard, Jonah beamed his delight at finding her alone. He couldn't understand, though, why Cam was looking so horrified to see him when normally she would have been jumping up to mash him a cup of tea while informing him of any enquiries made during his absence.

It was at that moment Rose made a whimpering noise as she stirred in her sleep.

At the sound, Jonah automatically turned his head in the direction and gawped in surprise to see a dilapidated coach pram by the table holding the tea-making equipment, a sleeping infant inside it. He turned back to face Cam and said laughingly, 'Some women would forget their heads if they weren't fixed on! One left a dog here once and it was hours before she realised and came back for it ... but not before it'd eaten the pork pie I'd just fetched from the baker's for my lunch!'

Cam still stared at him frozenly for several long moments, her mind whirling frantically as she tried to work out the best way to deal with this situation and still hopefully keep her job. She could explain Rose away with the old excuse that the child was her sister's. Say she'd been taken ill and had no one to care for her baby meantime as her husband worked away. Or Rose could be her landlady's child in the same situation ...

But Cam's conscience pricked her. She wasn't a natural liar, and the chances of her making a slip in future and betraying herself were high. Jonah Gates had been a good boss to her. It was one thing being economical with the truth in order to get a job, but blantantly lying was another. Cam knew it was time for her to come clean and pray that her boss would be understanding. He was a thoroughly decent man and she felt sure that, once he knew her reasons for not coming clean in the beginning, he would be forgiving. Apart from keeping her unmarried mother status to herself, she had otherwise proved to be a trustworthy and reliable employee

Cam took a deep breath and quietly said, 'No forgetful customer left her baby behind. The child belongs to me.'

It was his turn to stare frozenly at her. A few moments went by before he asked, with a hopeful tone in his voice, 'It's a family member's that you're looking after, is it?' Although he had learned from her over the course of time that she had no family.

Heart hammering now, Cam whispered back, 'No. The baby is mine. I had no choice but to bring her with me to work. I found out this morning that her minder was mistreating her.'

Jonah's whole world was shattering around him. He was having difficulty accepting what he was being told. 'But you can't have a child! You're not married ... otherwise that would make you ... make you ...'

'A fallen woman? A slut?' Cam finished for him. 'I'm neither of those,' she said with conviction.

'Then you've lied to me and you *are* married! But what's your reason for calling yourself Miss when you're a Mrs?' he demanded.

'I've never lied to you, and I'm not married. You never asked if I had children when you interviewed me, and to my mind having a baby makes no difference to how well I can do the job. I must have done it well, you've never complained. In fact, you've just given me a pay rise.'

Jonah couldn't argue with her about that. In fact, he couldn't wish for a more conscientious and efficient clerk overseeing his office. But Cam's ability to do the job was not what was at issue. He was appalled to discover that he had fallen in love with a woman who didn't actually exist. Now his hopes and dreams for their future together lay in tatters. He realised why she'd been in such a hurry to be off last night: not to get ready for a date with a man but so as not to be late collecting her child. He ran his hand through his hair, remembering with a sense of despair all the numerous hours he had spent imagining what his life would be like with Cam by his side as his wife. How nervous he'd been of taking the first step and asking her out.

'You should have had the decency to tell me you had a child,' he reproved her in icy tones.

'I didn't like keeping it from you, but I couldn't take the risk of your not wanting to employ an unmarried mother when I desperately needed the job. Would you still have given me it had I told you everything?'

Jonah couldn't answer that. He would certainly have had to consider how his customers would react if they found out he was employing a woman with a child born out of wedlock, especially the religious ones who viewed such women as the scum of the earth. He would risk losing their custom, and any more they might have put his way. His father had worked his guts out to build up the business to pass on to Jonah . . . would he have put all that in jeopardy just to give this woman a job? And he most definitely wouldn't have considered her as marriageable, not a slut who obviously had so little respect for herself and such low morals that she'd let a man have his way with her before making an honest woman of her.

Then the reason why she had not told him hit Jonah like a bullet between the eyes. 'You used your charms to make me fall in love with you, didn't you? Saw me as a potential father for your bastard? When were you going to tell me about it . . . or were you going to wait until after the wedding? Break it to me on our honeymoon . . .'

Cam was outraged he could think so little of her. 'I never had any such plan! How dare you insinuate that I had?'

Despite the rage that was building within him for what she'd done to him, Jonah did actually believe her. Regardless, to his mind she must have been aware of his feelings for her and had done nothing but lead him on. That was unforgivable. He looked her right in the eye and demanded, 'All right, if that wasn't your aim, why did you not come clean when you must have known I was falling in love with you? All you did was lead me on.'

Cam gnawed her bottom lip. She *had* known he had feelings for her, much more than those of a boss for an employee, but his admitting it went as deep as love came as a shock to Cam. She had thought that, by holding him at arm's length and making sure she never acted towards him in any other but a friendly fashion, she'd convey that he was wasting his time. Instead he had seen this friendliness as her leading him on. She implored him, 'But I have *never* led you on. All I have ever been is friendly.'

He hissed at her, 'Just being friendly? Fussing around me when I was in the yard, making me cups of tea, smiling at me all the time, always asking me what I had planned for the evening or weekend, noticing if I wore a new shirt . . . I could go on. If you view acting like that as just being friendly, then I'd like to see how you behave with a man you're *more* than interested in.'

She insisted, 'But I *was* only being friendly. I'm sorry you saw it as more than that.'

He snarled back, 'Nowhere near as sorry as I am.' Then he narrowed his eyes at her. 'Just go – and take your brat with you.'

Cam deeply hoped this didn't mean what she feared it did. 'You want me to take the rest of the day off and come back tomorrow?' she asked tentatively.

He looked at her as though she was stupid. 'What? No, I don't want you to come back tomorrow. I can't bear to look at you! I just want to forget you ever existed. Well, in fact, the woman I thought you were doesn't, does she?' He thrust his hand into his pocket and pulled out three pound notes, far more than he owed her but he was on the verge of breaking down and wanted her to go before that happened. He pushed the money into her hand, telling her, 'Make sure you take everything of yours with you. I don't want you to have any excuse to come back. Hurry up about it and then get out!'

The scorn in his eyes made Cam shrink under its ferocity. He was leaving her in no doubt that it would be futile to try and salvage her job. She quickly gathered her belongings, pulled on her coat and grabbed the pram handle. Just before she left, she looked across at Jonah, standing with his back to her. She wanted to say she was sorry that she had brought about such hurt for him when her only intention had been to secure herself a job in order to care for her child. But she could tell by his rigid stance that when he had told her to make haste and leave and never darken his door again, he had meant it.

Cam made her way home in a daze, fighting to come to terms with what had just happened and the significance of it. Had she not been so consumed by what had transpired she would have been amazed to realise that Rose had slept through the whole angry exchange and was still asleep. She would have been very grateful for that small mercy, as in her state of mind Cam would not have been able to cope with one of her daughter's bad moods.

Back in the flat, and sitting on the sofa, Cam remained totally oblivious to the now wakeful Rose's intermittent outbursts of temper as she desperately tried to grab hold of her mother's set of keys, poking just over the edge of the table. She wanted to play with them but they were well out of her reach. Cam was desperately trying to accept the fact that her life had changed so drastically in only a matter of hours.

The events of this morning, though, had taught her a painful lesson. Never again would she be anything other than honest about her personal status with any prospective employer, regardless of the fact that she risked not being accepted for the job. She could never have foreseen at the time, though, how her new employer would come to feel about her. But the fact that her actions had resulted in such hurt to a kind and generous man, to the extent that she dreaded their paths ever crossing again, was something it would take her a long time to forgive herself for. Cam just hoped he'd find another woman soon so that his suffering at her hands was short-lived.

She sighed heavily as the weight of her own problems pressed down on her. It wasn't going to be at all easy to find another job. Times had been difficult enough when Jonah had taken her on. A year later the recession was biting even deeper, and there were even fewer jobs going now than there had been. Thanks to the three pounds he had given her, she could manage to pay the rent and feed Rose and herself for three weeks, possibly four if she was extremely frugal and no expensive emergencies arose meantime. But if she had not found a job by then . . .

Out of the corner of her eye she caught sight of Rose. A short while ago she'd conceded defeat over not getting the keys off the table and had now discovered her mother's knitting bag, shoved down the side of the armchair where Cam had thought it safe to leave it. A determined Rose, though, had managed to pull out the moth-eaten tapestry bag, undo the top and pull out the pair of knitting needles on which was the front of a jumper that the child was now pulling off the needles and unravelling. Rose must have sensed she was being observed and flashed a glance over at her mother before returning to concentrate on what she was doing. But the look Rose had shot her made Cam stare over at her, dumbstruck. Surely she had misinterpreted it? Rose was far too young to be aware that what she was doing was wrong, her mind not yet developed enough for her positively to enjoy the fact that she was undoing all her mother's hard work and causing her more.

Then, before she could stop it, a surge of resentment for the child reared up in Cam again. With Ann's help she had managed to bury it for a while, telling herself it was in no way Rose's fault she had been conceived or that her mother had been left with no choice but to raise her alone. Now, the return of that old resentment taking all sense and reason from her, Cam shot to her feet, dashed over to Rose and snatched the knitting needles and what was left of the front of the jumper off her. She slapped her small hands hard and bellowed harshly, 'You naughty girl! You know very well you shouldn't be doing that. You're only doing it to cause me more work, for the sheer devilment of . . .'

She was stopped short by the sight of Rose's pixie-like face puckering and tears of distress beginning to fall. Guilt swamped Cam then. What kind of woman was she, to take her worries out in such a way on a small child, unable to defend itself? Scooping up her baby, she hugged her. 'I'm so sorry, Rose, I'm so sorry. I didn't mean to shout at you like that or slap you. Please forgive me.'

The words were hardly out of Cam's mouth before she felt a painful thump on the side of her face. Stunned, she shot a look at Rose, to see her glaring darkly back. Cam was about to scold the child for hitting her, but then felt that in the circumstances she was justified in doing to her mother what had been done to her. She was hardly leading by example, was she, teaching her daughter to meet violence this way? Rose was now fighting to be put back on the floor, which Cam did. Immediately the child grabbed the knitting needles and proceeded to finish off what she had started. Cam was far too dispirited and ashamed of her behaviour towards her to retaliate again. She made her way back to the table, sinking down on a chair and letting her worries consume her again.

She felt a great need to go and see Ann when she got home from work, just to have the luxury of someone to spill out all her problems and worries to. But then, knowing Ann, she would drop everything to try and help her best friend sort out her problems, to the point of making huge sacrifices herself. Hadn't she already done enough of that for Cam in the past? And Ann had her own problems to deal with. She thought she might be pregnant. Although both she and Brian wanted to have a family, they weren't in a good financial position right now, or even for the foreseeable future if Ann had to give up work to care for a child, as the garage Brian worked for had had to cut back their four mechanics' hours. No, Cam had to sort out her present problems by herself.

She realised that Rose was very quiet and looked around to see what she was up to. She had unravelled all of the knitting and was sitting surrounded by the tangled mess she had created, fully immersed in emptying the rest of the odds and ends that were inside the tapestry bag on to the carpet. Still, what she was doing was keeping her occupied and saving Cam the job of contending with her, so that was fine by her.

As she turned her head away Cam's eyes fell on the pile of outwork she had yet to do. The bags were to be collected the next evening. Since she had started going out to work during the day, Leonard Abbott had agreed to swap around his house calls and make his collections and drop-offs of work to her in the early-evening instead of mid-morning. Leonard Abbott was a kindly, middle-aged man who valued his good workers and did his best to keep them, unlike the other rogue 'putter-outters', who treated their workers as if they were owed a favour for putting work their way, and thought nothing of cheating them by skimming off the top of their earnings.

Cam had been worried that Leonard Abbott might finish with her when she had landed her full-time job, but instead he had told her that she could have as many jobs as she liked as far as he was concerned, so long as she still got her orders from him done on time and to the standard expected. In light of recent events, Cam was thankful Ivy had already brought round her share of this particular order. Her mother helped her do it and so she always had her quota finished in half the time it took Cam to do hers.

Then a thought struck her. Since they had made their deal, Cam's financial situation had changed. Her outwork was at the moment her only source of income until she found another job and therefore she wasn't in any position to be splitting it with anyone. She would write a note to Ivy explaining this to her. She would also enclose the child-minding money Ivy was due, and push it under the door. That way she would be ending their arrangement for a perfectly valid reason and it need not be perceived by Ivy as Cam's way of taking revenge on her.

She realised that her only way of earning a living until she secured a full-time job was staring her in the face. It would also alleviate her need for a minder for Rose in the meantime, and save her the cost. The idea did not appeal to Cam one bit as she had been willing the day to come when she could give up the outwork, but at the moment she would be stupid not to pursue this course.

A few weeks ago, when Leonard Abbott had called on her, Cam as usual politely offered him a cup of tea while they conducted their business. This evening he didn't seem in such a hurry to be on his way as he normally did, and actually sat down to drink his tea with her. As they chatted, the subject turned to the recession and how detrimentally it was affecting so many people. Not him, though, Leonard had told her. The recession was proving a blessing to him financially. He wasn't exactly making a killing, but he was certainly making more money than he was before it had taken hold. The reason was, he had explained, that the factories he dealt with, looking at ways to cut their overheads, had realised it was far more cost-effective for them not only to put out the overflow of work to outworkers, but the whole of the work that didn't actually need to be handled in a factory environment as well. As a result the demands made on him by factory owners for these services had sky rocketed.

This did not come without its headaches for Leonard, though. Outworkers came and went, depending on their circumstances. Cam didn't need to ask why as she knew only too well that the work was laborious and badly paid, and long hours had to be worked to make any decent wage. For Leonard this meant he was constantly having to vet and take on new workers and just pray that they were as conscientious as they professed to be. Else he got into trouble for handing back work to the factory that was sub-standard, and didn't get paid for it. If it happened too often, he risked losing his contract with them. Therefore he did his best not to lose the good outworkers he unearthed and treated them with respect, always remembering that if it weren't for them he wouldn't have a business.

Cam had never given him reason to fault her work in all the time she had worked for him. If she asked for more, as much as she could handle, in fact, he would more than likely jump at the offer. He was due to call tomorrow evening. She would put her request to him then. In the meantime, she supposed it was in her best interests to complete the work she had in hand.

It gave her absolutely no comfort to have come up with this way to supplement her income until something better presented itself; in fact, the prospect filled her with dread. It wasn't the mind-numbing work that bothered her, or the prospect of working an eighty-hour week to make the same amount of money that she was making now. She could live with the sleep loss, too. But spending her days in virtual isolation, with her only human contact being Rose who wasn't yet properly talking, only babbling a few words . . . that would be hard indeed.

CHAPTER NINETEEN

1946

Cam heaved a tired sigh as she blew her sore nose before popping two aspirin into her mouth and swallowing them back with a drink of water. After three days the dreadful head cold she was suffering from was really getting her down, but nowhere near as much as her fifteen-year-old daughter was.

She sighed wearily again, rested her throbbing head back against a cushion and closed her eyes. Was it really only fifteen years she had been struggling to raise her difficult child? It felt like a thousand to Cam. She had lost count of how many times she had sobbed herself to sleep after something Rose had done or said with her acid tongue. She had lost count of the number of times she had wished that, after all, she had left her as a baby on the doorstep of the children's home and saved herself all the subsequent stress and heartache. She often wondered how she had got through the last fifteen years and was still sane enough now to tell the tale.

After Jonah had dismissed her, a better way for Cam to earn a living than labouring away over her outwork never came along. For the next couple of years even the most menial jobs were scarce, most of them only part-time and the pay offered criminally low. Employers knew lower-class working people were so desperate for wages, they could get away with it.

But, thankfully, Leonard Abbott was more than willing to keep Cam supplied with as much work as she could handle, and so her prison sentence had begun. Cam remained incarcerated inside her home all day, labouring hard to keep up with her quotas and make sure she had enough money coming in for them to survive on. She was constantly tired, and constantly having to remind herself that it was not Rose who was to blame for her miserable, arduous existence, especially when she had had a particularly bad day with her, which was frequently.

Ann had been extremely distressed to learn of the events that had resulted in Cam's losing her precious job at the carpenter's yard, and of just what she was having to do to keep a roof over her own and her child's head. Regardless of how permanently tired and drained her friend was, though, at least Cam was managing to survive when so many others were going to the wall. Ann was lucky herself still to have her job, although her hours had been cut, the same as Brian's, and they themselves were only just managing to get through. She had been disappointed to learn that she wasn't after all expecting a baby, though in reality it was a blessing as they could never have coped financially. Ann wouldn't have wanted any child of hers to end up with only rags on its back, no shoes on its feet, and, for the majority of the time, no food in its belly.

Although she couldn't help Cam financially, she did try to help her out as much as she could by taking Rose off her hands, at least once a fortnight for a couple of hours, to give her a break. No matter where Ann took Rose, though, or how hard she tried to entertain her, the child never seemed to be enjoying herself, always with that disagreeable scowl on her face. These excursions were never pleasurable to Ann, but she continued with them out of her deep regard for the contrary child's mother.

There was one thing that happened to bring a margin of joy to Cam in her otherwise arduous existence. A couple of months after Jonah had dismissed her, Ann burst into the flat with wonderful news to tell her. She had heard of a little two up, two down terrace house, only a couple of streets away from where she and Brian lived, that had become available due to present tenants being evicted for rent arrears. The state of the house was not that much better than the flat had been when they had first moved in, but Brian was willing to do what he could to make it more habitable. More importantly, the rent on the house was the same as Cam was paying here and the landlord was willing to give her first refusal.

At long last Cam was being given the chance to leave this miserable street where the majority of the locals did their best to make her feel like an outcast and she could not leave her back door open without fear of being robbed. At last it would be safe for Rose to play out, with children whose language wasn't peppered with vile expletives they'd picked up from their parents. What Cam couldn't understand, though, was why even if the house wasn't in a good state of repair, the landlord wasn't asking the couple of shillings more a week he could have demanded for a property in that street. Ann, however, had told her not to question why, just accept her own good fortune. So Cam did.

She wasn't to discover the real reason why until many years later. In Ann's desire to help Cam in any way they could, she had badgered Brian to approach the landlord and put a proposition to him. In exchange for his letting their friend have the house for six shillings and sixpence a week, Brian and his wife would clear the house of the mounds of rubbish the last tenants had left there and do what repairs were necessary, even giving all the rooms a coat of emulsion which Brian could get cheap from a friend who worked in the paint trade, saving the landlord the cost of paying out before he could rent it again. And Brian was willing to maintain the landlord's car, and those of his two sons, at cost price only while Cam lived in the house. The landlord knew a good deal when it was offered him. He jumped at it.

It was a huge relief to Cam when the time came for Rose to go to school. For six hours a day, five days a week, she would be able to get on with her work uninterrupted, and as a result not have to work so long into the night. Rose would need to be at least seven before Cam could consider looking for a full-time job. Then, hopefully, she would be sensible enough to be trusted to let herself into the house and remain there after school until Cam came home, although she knew of children as young as five who were being given this responsibility. She just prayed Leonard could keep her supplied with outwork until then.

It had become apparent to Cam that, even from a young age, Rose did not take kindly to being told what to do, so she should not really have been surprised by the fact that her daughter hadn't been at school for an hour before Cam herself was fetched by an older child who said she was wanted. Running all the way there, out of breath when she arrived, she was acutely embarrassed to find her daughter lying on the floor near the teacher's desk, arms and legs flailing, screaming blue murder while the young teacher whose class she'd been assigned to looked helplessly on. It transpired that Rose had decided she did not want to sit at the desk the teacher had allocated her, next to a pretty little blond-haired girl, or at any other desk the desperate teacher had tried her with. She had decided she didn't like school and would keep up her temper tantrum until she was taken home.

Before she had even got into the classroom she had disobeyed a teacher by refusing to line up with the other children, so the teacher had manhandled her into the line and received a kick for her trouble. The other children in the queue had all started sniggering then and this made Rose's temper flare up even more. So she pulled the hair of the one in front of her and kicked the shins of the one behind, making them both cry. When the teacher demanded a reason for what she had done, Rose just shrugged nonchalantly.

Knowing her daughter did not posses a better nature to appeal to, and as humiliating as it was for her, Cam had no choice but to drag the frenzied child out of the classroom and into the cloakroom where she picked her up and plonked her down on a bench. She told Rose in no uncertain terms that she was no different from any other child and had no choice but to go to school. She had better do as she was told there or the school had a way of dealing with naughty children, which Cam felt sure Rose wouldn't like.

Rose was to find out just how her school punished badly behaved children, but not before she'd caused her poor teacher several more headaches. Before the week was out, it was decided that Rose was going to be assigned to a different teacher. Miss Gertrude Wilberforce was a formidable, humourless, sixty-four-year-old spinster who certainly wasn't going to allow a disobedient, wilful five year old get the better of her. She put a desk for Rose in the corner of the classroom, as far away from the other children under her charge as was possible, and when the stubborn girl still persisted in causing mayhem by refusing to do any work, Miss Wilberforce introduced her to the way the school dealt with disobedience by administering several extremely painful sharp raps on her hand with a ruler, warning her that if she refused again to do what she was told, next time it would hurt even more.

Cam had never resorted to using physical punishment on Rose for any of her misdemeanours, despite the many times Ann had advised her that a good spanking on her bare bottom would go a long way to get Rose to think twice before she played up. But Cam just could not bring herself to do it. Miss Wilberforce had no such scruples. Rose had not liked one bit her way of imposing school rules, or the humiliation of her punishment being carried out in front of the class. The fact that they had enjoyed seeing her suffer was an affront to Rose. Regardless, she hadn't allowed them or Miss Wilberforce the satisfaction of letting it be known the blows from the ruler had really hurt her. She didn't, though, ever want a repetition of it, and was intelligent enough to know that to avoid this, she would have to do as she was told while at school.

Under the strict regime of Miss Wilberforce, Rose learned her three Rs and produced a reasonable standard of work. Aware that the senior school dealt with errant pupils in the same way as the junior school did, but using a thin cane that would prove ever more painful than the ruler, Rose behaved herself there too.

But she didn't let her mother off so easily. Having to keep control of herself during school hours or face the painful consequences put Rose under a terrible strain, which she gave went to as soon as she was out of the school gates. To Cam the door always seemed to be being knocked on by mothers of children Rose had had an altercation with on her way to or from school, giving Cam the humiliating task of apologising on her daughter's behalf and smoothing matters over. Rose would always vehemently profess herself innocent of anything she was accused of.

It grieved Cam greatly that her daughter had no friends, was never invited to any birthday parties or to play with other children in their homes. Despite her trying to encourage Rose to go outside and play with the other children in the street, she flatly refused, telling Cam she didn't like them. She preferred to stay indoors where she amused herself mostly by reading books. Cam knew that other children too could be cruel. She worried that Rose preferred her own company rather than suffering the hurt of being ridiculed, because she wasn't exactly the most attractive girl. But then, it was Cam's opinion, and also Ann's, that personality played as big a part in whether someone was liked or not. It could be that Rose's disagreeable and argumentative temperament was the real reason other children didn't want to be associated with her.

On numerous occasions Cam tried her utmost to talk to her daughter about how her behaviour was affecting her, how she would never make any friends if she carried on acting the way she was, but always Rose's response was to give a nonchalant shrug and say she didn't care.

Like everyone else in Great Britain, Cam had been dismayed by the announcement that her country was at war. In September 1939 she didn't face the prospect of waving her man off to fight and face possible death, no other family members either, although she did perceive Brian as her family and wept along with Ann on the railway station platform when he went off to join the REME where his mechanical skills were in great demand. Like the rest of those who stayed back home, Cam had been deeply concerned by the fact that many of the men would not return. Wives would be left husbandless, children fatherless, mothers mourning their sons, sisters their brothers, before the final bullet was fired, the last bomb dropped. But without their sacrifices Hitler would have got his way and be dictating how Britain and the other countries he was trying to conquer were governed. Along with everyone else, Cam was prepared to do her bit to make sure that he didn't.

The war had come as a blessing in disguise, in fact, as she joined the army of other women filling the vacancies left by servicemen. At long last Cam was able to wave goodbye to long hours spent working in virtual isolation at home, and instead tackle the far more rewarding work of operating a busy switchboard. She ran it along with another woman of her own age, in the offices of a large hosiery company that had swapped producing clothes to suit the pockets of the middle classes for manufacturing uniforms for the air force and the army. Even more of a blessing was the fact that she was paid twenty-two shillings a week more for her far less arduous fifty-hour week than she had been for labouring for ninety hours over her outwork.

That extra money in her wages meant that Cam could afford a little more coal on the fire on icy nights, butter on their bread as well as jam, meat or fish three times a week, even a poke of sweets twice-weekly for Rose plus a bar of chocolate on a Saturday night for Cam herself. She was also able gradually to turf out her own and Rose's shabby old clothes and replace them from a second-hand shop that dealt with better quality items. She was able to put sixpence away in the Post Office each week, to build up a little nest egg for Rose in the future, and over time replaced the moth-eaten, shabby furniture that had come with the flat for more comfortable modern pieces. The only trouble was that soon it didn't matter that Cam had the money to buy luxuries as there was nothing in the shops for her to spend the extra money on. Regardless, when the war ended and rationing was lifted, Cam had a nice nest egg of her own of over £200, to do with as she pleased, something that at one time would have seemed an impossible dream.

Six months after VE Day, with the war in the Far East looking set to end any day now, Cam celebrated as enthusiastically as everyone else – especially with Ann over the safe return of Brian. But that was not the only thing that had come to an end. So had Rose's school days. It was time for her to start making her own way in the world.

Over the years Cam had never given up her fight to feel for her daughter as a mother should, but those feeling just would not come. She had always striven very hard, though, never to let Rose sense this and tried her best to nurture her as any loving mother would their child, though there had been many times when she had wondered if she could go on. Life for her in general had been one long struggle, but it would not have proved so purgatorial if Rose herself had been just a little more agreeable.

Cam opened her eyes and looked across at her daughter who was lolling in an armchair, her nose, as always, in a book, the romantic sort where the smouldering-eyed, devastatingly handsome and rich hero fought to win the heart of the stunningly beautiful but desti-tute heroine, who was usually a lowly nursemaid or governess in the clutches of the villain of the story.

The longed-for transformation from ugly duckling to beautiful swan had not happened in Rose's case. She had not lost her pixie look, with her large domed forehead and hooked nose, but at least her chin wasn't quite so fiercely pointed now, having rounded off. She was uninterested in having her mass of carrot-red corkscrew curls cut and styled to soften her features but always wore them in a tangled mop, cutting them herself when the mood took her. Her skin was no longer quite so translucent but was still very pale, almost colourless, and her small grey eyes always had a hard glint sparking in them. She was small, under five foot, and painfully thin, stick-like legs slightly bowed. Despite every effort she'd made Cam could not get her daughter to take any interest in wearing the type of clothes that would make the best of her slight frame, the girl always dressing the way she liked in shapeless skirts and baggy jumpers. Her temperament hadn't mellowed at all. She was still as surly and obnoxious as she'd always been, not making any effort whatsoever to endear herself to anyone. Cam had yet to learn what her daughter would look like if she smiled.

She was pinning her hopes on a personality transformation when Rose embarked on the journey into adulthood by leaving school and starting work. To get on in the workplace, she needed to get on with her colleagues and superiors. Hopefully she was sharp enough to work that out for herself. And Cam hoped that Rose would find herself becoming caught up with her fellow workers' interests outside work, too; would realise how dull the life she had created for herself actually was and want to be part of a wider circle. She did not care what profession Rose chose to go into as long as she enjoyed what she was doing. As matters stood, though, it didn't look like Rose was even going to settle into a job, let alone have her eyes opened to what sort of life she could make for herself.

In the six months since she had left school she had only had one job, as a trainee shop assistant for Lee's department store, and then only stayed in it for a fortnight, telling Cam that she didn't like it. Since then she had been for many interviews but not landed any of the jobs, and Cam had a strong feeling she had purposely put off all the prospective employers. Rose did not want to go to work. Why should she when her mother was keeping her?

Cam had asked her several times in the last hour if she would run an errand for her, but her requests had fallen on deaf ears. She would like to think that this was only because Rose was so engrossed in her book she hadn't heard her, but she knew that the girl was bone idle. In the past Cam had only managed to get her to help by warning her that she would take her books off her should she continue to refuse. Now she was older, though, that ploy no longer worked as Rose hid her books and that was the only thing Cam could think of to blackmail her over. Rose did nothing unless there was something in it for herself.

Ann had advised Cam to warn her daughter that she wasn't prepared to keep her any longer now she had left school. If she wasn't prepared to earn money to pay her board then she would be thrown out. Cam, though, couldn't bring herself to do that, but had stopped giving Rose any spending money. Trouble was, though, because Rose did not socialise like most girls of her age, her personal needs were nowhere near as great as theirs would be. She didn't have a constant need for new clothes and shoes and money to go out with. All she spent money on was books, and if she hadn't the money to buy any she would get them from the library.

Before she resorted to doing something she really didn't want to, Cam decided to make one last attempt to get her daughter to help her voluntarily.

Taking a deep breath, she began, 'Rose, I really would appreciate . . .'

She got no further. The girl's head jerked up and, shooting Cam her usual dark glare, she snapped, 'For God's sake, Mother, if there was a competition for nagging you'd win hands down. You can see I'm busy. I don't know why you can't run your own errand. It's not like you're doing anything yourself, is it?'

Cam flinched at the disrespectful way her daughter spoke to her, but there was no point in wasting her time chiding her for it as she knew Rose would take absolutely no notice. 'You can see I'm not well,' she replied.

'You've a bit of a cold! Hardly at death's door. If Ann so badly wants to borrow your fur wrap for the wedding reception she's off to tonight, why can't she come and fetch it herself or send one of the children?' A wicked glint sparked in Rose's eye when she added, 'Oh, I forgot, she can't, can she? She hasn't got any kids 'cos she's barren.'

Cam gawped at her in horror. 'Oh, Rose, do you have to be so nasty? Ann and Brian desperately wanted children, and the fact they haven't any isn't their fault.'

'I'm not being nasty, I'm speaking the truth. Anyway, I don't know why she would want to be seen dead in that moth-eaten old thing.'

The wrap hadn't been new when Cam had bought it, but it definitely wasn't moth-eaten. It was, in fact, in excellent condition, and she'd been lucky to get it at the price she had. But Cam was too physically drained from her cold to be drawn into a discussion over it with Rose. 'I promised Ann I'd take it round for her this afternoon, only I didn't realise at the time that I was going to go down with this awful cold. I have no way of letting her know and that's why I'm asking you to take it, please.'

Cam sighed. It was obvious to her that Rose was determined she wasn't going to do this errand for her, not without a bribe anyway. She hadn't the energy to fight. 'I'll give you threepence to get yourself a book, if you'll take the wrap to Ann.'

Rose was pretending to be engrossed in her book again but a malicious smirk of satisfaction curled her lip. She had prepared herself to use all her wiles to get her mother to resort to bribery. Cam giving in so easily must mean she really was ill. Not that that made any difference to the girl.

Rose had known from a very young age that her behaviour greatly upset her mother, but felt no sympathy for her. The knowledge gave her the power to achieve whatever she wanted. She only had to cause a fuss and keep on doing so and she got what she wanted, time after time.

There was something that bothered Rose, though. It was when she had realised that she wasn't at all the pretty girl her mother had led her to believe she was, by constantly telling her, 'What a beautiful girl you look now' when she had dressed her or brushed her hair. She had realised then that the looks she received from others were not of admiration for her cleverness, but pity for her plain face. Even in her pram no one cooed and clucked over her like they did over other children; no two women ever vied with each other to pick her up and hold her on their knee. Rose felt a deep bitterness and resentment within her for the cruel way life had treated her. The only way her own nature allowed her to deal with this was by acting like she didn't care what people thought of her, and lashing out nastily or acting vindictively against anyone who dared openly mock or even show her any pity.

Rose, though, did not consider that her own spiteful, obnoxious, nasty-tongued ways had any bearing on the reason why people steered clear of her, wanted nothing to do with her any more than they absolutely had to; that no boys, no matter how unattractive they were themselves, ever looked in her direction. She was convinced that it was only the body she was trapped inside that caused her alienation from others.

And she resented her mother especially because Cam was pretty and Rose didn't consider it at all fair that she herself wasn't. And since Cam was pretty then Rose's father must have been the ugly one. So Rose blamed her mother for marrying an ugly man and not giving a thought to the children they might have. She consequently displayed her bitterness towards her mother at every opportunity she could.

Up until only last week she had been convinced she would die a spinster; that the only way she was ever going to experience romance was through her books. But a story she'd read showed her there was a way she could achieve a relationship for herself and have people treat her with reverence. Rose began to read the novel under the impression it was the usual rags to riches saga, but the heroine in this story was different. She wasn't pretty but in fact very plain-featured, some of the other characters even referring to her as ugly. Unlike the impoverished heroines in Rose's other books, this one was heiress to a vast fortune. Her dilemma lay in not knowing which of the handsome suitors claiming her hand in marriage did in fact love her for herself, as they professed, and which were only after her money. This got Rose thinking that if she were wealthy then at least she might stand a chance of getting herself a man even if it was only by the lure of her money. And what wouldn't she give, to be able to parade her wealth and her man before all those around her, showing them how wrong they had been to write her off. And she'd never give them a penny of her money either, no matter how desperate they were.

But how did a person like herself, from a lowly background, acquire the substantial amount it would take for her to attain the life she craved? She had no rich relatives who might die and leave their wealth to her. And even if she saved up every penny of the wage she could earn in a factory, shop or office, the amount would go nowhere near to helping her fulfil her dreams. The task seemed an impossible one but Rose was secretly determined to find a way to acquire riches. She had realised through reading novels just what she needed in her own life; hopefully another story would point her in the direction of how to secure it for herself. Meantime she was quite content to carry on as she was.

'Make it a tanner and I'll go,' she said to her mother, who was still waiting for her response to the bribe.

Not having the energy to battle with her, Cam sighed and reached down to pick up her handbag.

CHAPTER TWENTY

Rose was wearing her usual scowl as she made her way to the Williams' back door. She did not like her mother's best friend or her husband, and she knew that neither of them liked her. On many occasions they, especially Ann, had had to restrain themselves from giving her a hard slap for her vileness towards her mother in their presence, but they always held themselves in check from respect for Cam. That hadn't stopped Ann constantly telling Rose to stop treating her mother so disrespectfully in their presence – as if she had any right to interfere. With this in mind, purely out of spite and for the pleasure it gave her, on her way here Rose had found a muddy puddle and splashed the wrap in it before putting it back in the brown carrier for Ann to discover later when she came to put it on.

Arriving at the back door, she found it ajar and pushed it open, calling out, 'You there, Ann?'

It gave her a lot of pleasure to be addressing her mother's friend by her Christian name, as she knew it was considered very disrespectful of her, but long ago she had defied her mother by refusing to call her aunt. Mum might consider Ann family but Rose certainly didn't, and she wasn't going to call her Mrs Williams either as Ann didn't show her a similar courtesy by addressing her as Miss Rogers.

When she received no reply to her call, Rose pushed the door wider and entered.

There was no one in the kitchen so she went to the door leading into the back room and poked her head around it. That was empty too. She knew Brian sometimes had a nap on a Saturday afternoon after finishing work for the weekend at one o'clock, so that might have been where he was. Maybe Ann was out shopping. Rose was about to leave the carrier with the muddy wrap inside it on the kitchen table when she noticed Ann's handbag standing there. She wouldn't go shopping without her handbag . . . Maybe she was upstairs with her husband, having a nap in view of the hectic night ahead of them at the wedding reception, and had forgotten to shut the back door when they'd gone up. Rose again made to leave the carrier on the table when the lure of what was inside Ann's handbag became too much for her to ignore.

She had never felt any guilt as a child about helping herself to a few coppers, or even some silver, out of her mother's purse and spending it on sweets on her way home from school. She was very careful never to arrive home with any evidence on her in case her mother should discover money missing and challenge her. Rose had been well aware that her mother already gave her all that she could, and definitely could not spare the money she stole, but it made no difference. Despite the fact that Cam never actually caught her in the act, she did eventually become wise as to where her missing money was going and even to this day her handbag was never out of her sight. Until now Rose had never stolen off anyone else, but with the handbag before her, and no Ann in sight to catch her rummaging through it, temptation beckoned.

Putting the carrier bag on the table, she unclipped the handbag and opened it wide. A brown envelope, with the edges of several ten-shilling and pound notes poking out of the top, immediately caught her attention. Rose picked it up. It was bulky, telling her there were coins as well as notes inside. She flicked a finger across the notes, doing a quick calculation in her head as she did so. Her eyes gleamed. She was holding at least five pounds in her hand. She wondered how Ann had come to have such a substantial amount of money on her.

Then suddenly she didn't care what the answer was. Ann didn't own this money any longer, *she* did. And her mother's friend had only herself to blame for its loss as she shouldn't have left it lying around for anyone to take. Rose would make damned sure she hid it where no one could find it. This money was to be the start of her get wealthy fund. It might be a while before she found another opportunity to

196

steal more to add to it, but at least she could comfort herself with the fact that she had made a start on bringing her plan to fruition. No one had seen her come in here and she'd make sure no one saw her leave. When Ann discovered the envelope missing, she could never cast suspicion in Rose's direction. She would go to the bookshop now and return later with the wrap as if for the first time.

Thoughts of a hurried getaway filling her mind, Rose made to snatch back the carrier bag and simultaneously put the envelope in her skirt pocket, adding to the sixpence she'd already fleeced her mother out of, when she froze. Sensing another presence, she looked across to the door and saw Ann staring over at her, an expression of utter disbelief on her face at what she was witnessing. She was holding an empty Jeyes toilet roll in her hand. It was obvious she'd just returned from a visit to the outside lavatory, a possibility Rose hadn't considered.

She did no more than drop the envelope back inside the handbag and say matter-of factly, 'Mam asked me to bring the wrap round that she promised you. I was just leaving it for you on the table.'

Ann's voice was accusing. 'And helping yourself to the Christmas money I collected this morning off the neighbours, while you were at it?'

Rose's permanent scowl deepened with a show of indignation. 'How dare you accuse me of stealing? I was doing no such thing,' she insisted.

'Why, you bare-faced liar!' Ann erupted. 'I saw you with my own eyes.'

The girl responded nonchalantly, 'Well, you must need glasses then. You never saw me doing anything of the sort.'

'There's nothing wrong with my eyes. I know what I saw, Rose, and that was you about to put an envelope full of money into your pocket as I came in. I don't know what *you* call it, but that's stealing in *my* book.' Ann's lips tightened. 'This is too serious for me to turn a blind eye to.'

Rose snorted, 'Apart from the fact you've no proof you saw me doing anything, what do you propose to do? Give me a slap on the wrist?'

Ann fought to keep control of her temper, something she was

practised at since Rose had tried it so often. 'I've a duty to tell your mother, and advise her I think you should be reported to the police. They might make you think twice before you're ever again tempted to take what isn't yours.'

Rose laughed mockingly. 'My mother will never report me to the police! She can't even bring herself to raise her hand to me when I've more than earned a good pasting by what I've done. The worst she's ever done is put me to bed with no dinner, and that was for cutting off the plaits of a girl at school 'cos I caught her pulling a face at me. She's far too soft is my mother. I reckon it's because deep down she's riddled with guilt for what she's put me through.'

Ann looked astounded. 'What *she's* put you through? I can't for a minute imagine what you mean by that remark. Your mother's been no less than a saint, putting up with your antics and nasty ways from the minute you were born.' She shook her head reprovingly.

'Had I known just what hell you were going to put her through, I would definitely have persuaded her . . .' She suddenly clamped her mouth shut, realising just what she was about to divulge. Cam had always been adamant Rose was not to know her origins until her mother felt she was ready to cope with the knowledge.

Rose was frowning now. 'Persuaded her to do what?'

'Nothing,' Ann snapped back dismissively. She wagged a warning finger at Rose. 'Now you listen here, madam, you haven't even shown a trace of guilt for what I caught you doing. You weren't just about to steal off me before I thankfully stopped you, but forty odd women in this street who've been saving for Christmas. They all worked hard for that money, most of them going without to put a bit past for the holiday and buy their kiddies a little present, so I hope you feel proud of yourself, trying to steal off people who hardly have a pot to piss in? Not to mention the fact that, had you got away with this, I would have been left to replace it, being's it was in my safekeeping when it went missing. I'm not prepared to turn a blind eye to this, even for your mother's sake.

'Now you get your backside out of here. And, I'm warning you, never come back again unless I invite you. Be sure to tell your mother to be expecting a visit from me as soon as I've done a couple of things, and if you've got any gumption about you at all, you'll tell her just why I'm coming. Meantime you can stew, wondering what will be decided about you. Now . . . get out.'

An hour and a half later, Cam was blowing her nose and dabbing her streaming eyes as she tried to summon the energy to prepare the evening meal, not that she was hungry but she still needed to make something hot for Rose. Her daughter came in with two books in her hands and plonked herself down in the armchair she had vacated earlier.

Cam ignored the fact that her daughter made no effort to greet her, this was not unusual, but said to her, 'Did you deliver the wrap to Ann all right?'

Rose shot a look at her as though she was stupid. 'Well, what do you think I did with it?' she said in a sarcastic voice.

Cam sighed. 'I was only enquiring if you got there and back all right, Rose, that's all. Is Ann all excited about the do she's going to tonight?'

By now the girl had her book open and was reading the last few pages. She gave a nonchalant shrug. 'I never saw her, she was out.'

'Oh, but you did leave the wrap where she could find it?'

Rose lifted her head and snapped crossly, 'No, I hid it! For God's sake, I left it on the kitchen table. Unless she's gone blind, she can't miss that when she gets back. Now will you just shut your prattling so I can finish this book and make a start on one of my new ones?'

'How dare you speak to your mother like that, you nasty-mouthed little madam?'

At the sound of the furious voice, Cam turned her head in astonishment to see Ann standing framed in the doorway. She had known her friend for thirty of her thirty-four years and never before had she seen her look so incensed. Ann's face was screwed up and red with anger, her fists clenched tightly by her sides. She was visibly shaking with temper. The hair that she'd had styled earlier that day especially for her night out was wind-swept from her hurry to get here and she was still wearing her pinafore. Ann never left the house wearing her apron.

Cam demanded, 'Ann, whatever is the matter?'

But Ann didn't hear her. All her attention seemed to be fixed on

Rose, curled up in her armchair, seemingly unsurprised by her sudden appearance or the state she was in.

'Well, you've really surpassed yourself this time, lady,' Ann hurled at the girl. 'How could you do what you have to Brian, after all he's done for you?'

Eyes darting from one of them to the other, Cam piped up, 'Could one of you tell me what's going on?'

Her question went unanswered.

Rose scoffed, 'He's never done anything for me. I owe him nothing. Or you either, come to that. All you've ever done is try and tell me what to do, when you've no right to.'

Ann shrieked, 'What? Now you listen here, lady. If it weren't for me and Brian, you would've been raised in the workhouse. When you were born, your mother had nowhere to live and hardly any money. Me and Brian put off our wedding and I left my lovely lodgings, to move into the most Godawful flat in probably the worst area of Leicester, the only place your mam and I could afford that'd let us have a baby. I did that so you'd both have somewhere to live and I could help your mam take care for you until she could manage on her own. The day after we moved in, some kind neighbour stole all the household stuff and the pram your mother had bought, using the bit of savings she'd got, and if it hadn't been for Brian using what he'd put aside for our wedding, and getting his family and neighbours to chip in to replace the stuff that was stolen, we wouldn't have been able to carry on living there.

'And I'll tell you something else . . . if life wasn't a hard enough struggle for us there, trying to manage on my wages and the bit your mam made from her outwork, *you* made our lives hell. You were the most bad-tempered, difficult child. Sometimes I dreaded coming home from work because hardly a night went by you didn't have a paddy, for no apparent reason. Do you know, I swear blind that even at a young age there was something in you that realised the upset you were causing us and got enjoyment from it.'

Wiping her running nose, an utterly bewildered Cam again demanded, 'Ann . . . Rose . . . will one of you tell me what's going on?'

She was ignored as Ann's tirade continued. 'When your mother told us she was able to manage on her own, I moved out to marry

Brian but we still helped out as much as we could by taking you off her hands for a while so she could have some peace. She worked day and night so she could earn enough money to keep a roof over your head and food in your belly. I knew she'd never take any money off us to help ease her money worries, but I'd share food with her when I could, telling her I'd got too much and didn't want to waste it.

'It was Brian who heard about a little house that was going. It wasn't up to much, but far better than the flat and in a nicer area. To get it for you both, we did a deal with the landlord. In exchange for a low rent, the same as your mam was paying for the flat, we'd give it a spruce up after the state the last tenants had left it in and, for all the time you both lived there, Brian would mend his car and his two sons' at cost-price. For nine years he did that until your mam went out to work and was earning enough to take this better house you're in now. So how dare you say me and Brian have never done anything for you?' She paused then and shot a wild-eyed look at Cam, blurting out, 'I'm sorry, love, I never meant you to find out any of that, but Rose needs to know that what she's lyingly accused Brian of is despicable, considering—'

Astonished, Cam erupted, 'Rose has told lies about Brian?' She then demanded, 'What have you done, Rose?'

'I'll tell you what she's done—'

As quick as lightning Rose was out of her chair and cutting Ann short by screaming at the top of her voice, 'He did do to me exactly what I told the police! He did, he did! When I got to their house to take the wrap, the back door was open and I didn't know whether either Ann or Brian was in. I was in a hurry to get to the bookshop so I went in to leave the carrier on the table. I was just about to leave when Brian came in. He was looking at me funny, and next thing I knew he had his hands on my . . . my breasts, and I was trying to push him off, and that's when Ann came in and caught him doing what he was to me.

'He shot off quick enough, but she had me round the throat, threatening me that if I told anyone about this she would make up something bad enough to have me thrown in jail . . . like she'd caught me stealing off her or something like that . . . and that I was only making it up about her husband doing what he did to me to black-mail them into not reporting me for stealing. But it's them that's lying, honest it is, and I couldn't let him just get away with—'

The hard smack across her face which Rose received from Ann stopped her dead and sent her reeling back into the armchair. So forceful was the blow that for several long seconds she saw stars.

Cam was so dazed by trying to make sense of Rose's garbled tale that she had not responded to it. But Ann's ferocious physical attack on her daughter shook her out of her confusion. 'Ann, for God's sake! What on earth are you doing, hitting Rose...'

Her friend spun to face her, crying out, 'If I wasn't risking a murder charge, I'd do more than hit her – I'd strangle the life out of the little liar!' Then she spun back to face Rose and spat furiously, 'Your nasty little scheme to get the heat taken off you has backfired. Thought you were being very clever coming up with that idea, didn't you? Well, madam, not nearly clever enough. My Brian is a wonderful man but a magician he's certainly not. He can't appear in two places at the same time. If you'd been clever enough, you'd have made sure he was at home at the time you say he was before you falsely accused him. But he wasn't home, see? He was at Filbert Street, watching the match, and all four of the cronies he was with will swear on oath to it. The police don't take kindly to anyone who tries to get someone into trouble on a trumped-up charge, especially such a serious one as you tried to get Brian on, so you're in serious trouble yourself. You can expect the police to call on you very shortly.'

Still slumped in the chair, her face smarting painfully and displaying a vivid red handprint, Rose glared back at her, a defiant glint in her eyes.

Looking absolutely horrified, Cam told her, 'I can't understand why you would make up such a terrible lie about Brian, Rose. Why did you? Why, Rose... why?'

The girl stared back at her blankly.

An enraged Ann shouted, 'Answer your mother when she asks you a question! And have the gumption, for once in your life, to be honest and tell her just *why* you cooked up this lie.'

With a sneer of indifference on her face and a couldn't-care-less tone in her voice, Rose spoke up. 'Well, she was threatening to go to the police and lie about something she was accusing me of doing. Why shouldn't I accuse them of doing something to me . . . see how they liked it? I tried to tell her I found the envelope with the money in it on the floor and was just putting it back in her handbag, but she wouldn't believe me. Accused me of trying to steal it . . .'

Ann erupted then. 'Oh, my God, why can't you just for once tell the truth, girl? I caught you about to put that envelope in your skirt pocket, and the only place you could have got it from was out of my handbag. That was where I put it safely after tallying the money with what was written in the collections book. I take it all in to the Post Office first thing Monday morning. I've got a witness who'll say I put it in my handbag as Mrs Tiller from next-door was with me at the time. She'd popped in to check we were all still walking to the wedding reception together later. She left to go back next-door and I walked her down the yard and paid a visit to the privy. Now, lie your way out of that!'

Cam's thoughts were torment to her. She didn't want to believe that Ann had caught her daughter stealing, but at the same time knew that Ann had never lied to her in all the years they'd been friends. In a mortified voice she said to Rose, 'Why were you so desperate for money that you'd resort to stealing from Ann?'

Her eyes narrowed, Rose cried, 'Because I needed it.'

Cam looked confused. 'But what for? Why didn't you ask me if you were that desperate for something?'

Rose tutted disdainfully. 'Because I need more than the paltry tanner you give me now and again. I need lots of money, to get myself a better life than the hell I live in now, that's why.'

Cam gawped at her. 'What! I don't understand what you mean.'

'No, nor do I,' Ann roared. 'What's wrong with your life?'

'What's right with it?' Rose cut in. 'It's not fair that my mother's pretty and I'm not. Why couldn't I have taken after her instead of my father?' She stamped her foot in temper. 'It's not fair I took after him! It's not fair, not fair . . .' Then she furiously attacked her mother. 'Why did you pick him to be my father when you could have had anyone you wanted? Because you settled for him, you sentenced me to a life of Purgatory.'

Cam gasped in horror, 'Oh, Rose . . .'

But her words were drowned out by Ann erupting, 'You stupid child, your mother isn't to blame for the way you look. If anyone is to blame it's Mother Nature. She put you together. So you're not the prettiest girl in the world. There's a lot you could do to make yourself more attractive, but you don't even try.'

Rose snorted, 'Know someone who'll give me a new face and body, do you?'

Ann shook her head at her and snapped, 'You could smile more instead of glowering all the time, that would make an improvement. You could get your hair cut in a far more flattering style. And look at the clothes you wear. You dress like an old woman, not a young girl of fifteen. You aren't stupid. You know you could make more of yourself, and don't tell me your mother hasn't tried her best to get you to because I've been here when she has. It's my opinion you haven't made any effort because then you wouldn't have such a good reason for wallowing in self-pity. Tell me I'm wrong in saying that?'

She waited for Rose to answer her but, when all she got was an icy glare, continued, 'It's not surprising you've no friends. That's got nothing to do with your looks. You've no friends because of the way you treat people. Someone has only to be looking in your direction, not even at you, and you're attacking them with your vile tongue . . . and them with not a clue why. You've no one to blame for your miserable life but yourself. You could start making yourself a bit happier by being nicer to people. Whatever excuse you feel you've got for your behaviour, you absolutely cannot take what doesn't belong to you or to cover it up by accusing someone of a terrible thing. You deserved to be punished for that. You're not stupid. You know right from wrong, Rose.'

'Well, send me to jail, see if I care, but think before you do . . . it's my mother who's going to suffer, being stared at and talked about behind her back for having a thief for a daughter. Still, at least it might give her some idea what I've had to suffer all my life, being taunted and whispered about because of how I look.' She glared at Cam. 'And didn't you think for a minute that you were actually making it worse for me, constantly telling me I was pretty? The fact you had to keep saying it made me even more aware that I wasn't. I hate you for that.' Then she yelled at Ann: 'And if you think for a minute I'm sorry for trying to steal off you, I'm not. Just sorry you caught me.'

Ann screeched, 'Why, you nasty piece of work! You don't deserve your mother. In fact, it's about time you knew . . .'

Cam gasped in horror, realising just what Ann was about to divulge. 'Ann, no!' she cried.

Rose shouted at her, 'It's about time I knew what?'

Cam cried back, 'She was going to tell you that your father would be turning in his grave if he could see the way his daughter is turning out. Now get upstairs so I can talk to Ann about what's best to do with you. But I tell you, Rose, things are going to change around her from now on. Upstairs, I said.'

Her mother had never stood so firm with her before and this shocked Rose. Without further ado she stormed from the room, slamming the door behind her.

Ann's heart was pounding and she was shaking so hard she was having difficulty keeping her balance. She suddenly became aware that Cam had gone very quiet and turned her head to see her slumped on the sofa, head in hands, sobbing her heart out.

Ann took several deep breaths in an effort to calm herself, then went to her friend. 'Cam, I know I went too far but I couldn't stop myself,' she said remorsefully.

Cam sniffed and dried her eyes with her handkerchief. 'I can't blame you, Ann. What she tried to do was despicable. She needed to hear those home truths you told her. I know I've allowed her to get away with her bad behaviour for too long, but the trouble is I'm no match for her. In future I've got to find a way to be or I dread what she'll try and get away with next. Hopefully she'll be up in her bedroom, thinking on what's been said and taking a good long look at herself. I've always been aware she resented the fact she wasn't born pretty, but I never realised she blamed me for it. I used to keep telling her she was pretty in the hope that she would believe she was. You know . . . if my mother says, then it is. But one thing I do know is that I can never tell her how she came to be born. She's bitter enough about herself as it is. Finding out she was the result of a rape and not even wanted by me in the first place . . . well, I fear that would just tip her over the edge.'

Ann nodded. 'Thank God you stopped me from blurting it out when you did.'

Cam sighed in despair. 'I can't believe she actually tried to steal from you or what she did then to put a stop to you reporting her. I never would have thought her capable of such behaviour. I'm so ashamed, Ann, I . . .'

'*You've* nothing to be ashamed of. You've brought that girl up to know right from wrong. She knew what she was doing, and was aware of the consequences should she be caught.' Ann looked thoughtfully at Cam for several long moments before she added, 'We've always been honest with each other, and I have to be now. I used to think Rose had a big chip on her shoulder that she'd hopefully grow out of one day. But after what she got up to today, without showing one bit of shame, well, it's my opinion you've got a bad 'un on your hands. Maybe she's inherited more from her father than just her looks.'

Cam looked at her quizzically. 'What do you mean?'

'Well, maybe she inherited his mental traits too. He can't possibly be a respectable member of the community . . . not considering what he did to you, can he?' Ann paused for a moment before she went on, 'But also it's my belief that some people are born with a grudge against life. It's like something bad happened to them in a previous existence and they begin another while still angry about that. Rose wasn't a happy baby at all, was she? Never content, whatever you did for her, and she couldn't have been aware then that she wasn't as pretty as other babies so that can't have been the cause. I did wonder if, as a child, she sensed you didn't have the usual maternal feelings for her and that's why she's like she is . . . well, if your mother can't love you, who can? But then, I know for a fact that there's many a woman who doesn't have motherly feelings for their baby, for one reason or another, so you're not on your own.

'Eunice Grantly . . . you remember her? She lived two doors up from me and Brian when we were in Watson Street . . . she could hardly bear to look at her last three kids. After she'd had five she hadn't wanted any more, but Mother Nature saw to it that she did. She resented those kids with a passion, was quite open to me about that, and it really upset me to be thinking that those poor kids had a mother who didn't want them and I'd have done anything to have a child to love when it just never happened for me. But, after all, those kids grew up as happy and good-natured as their five elder brothers and sisters.

'Besides, after we had that chat when Rose was only a day old, and you began to play the game of pretending to be looking after your sister's child, you've been as good a mother to her as anyone could have been. So, Cam, I can only reach the conclusion that Rose was born with a kink in her nature. It wouldn't have mattered if she were the most beautiful child in the world, born into the wealthiest of families and wanting for nothing, she would still have been discontented, found something wrong with her life, to give her an excuse to lash out at everyone around her.'

Cam was looking at her friend thoughtfully. It seemed a far-fetched explanation for Rose's behaviour, but it certainly was better than anything Cam herself could come up with. She heaved a deep sigh and said, 'What am I going to do about her, Ann?'

'It's not for you to do anything. You already do all you can for Rose. It's her that needs to look at herself and change her ways.'

A thought struck Cam then and she said, 'I know we can't let Rose get away with what she tried to do today, but the thought that she could end up in jail . . .'

Ann sighed. 'I suppose everyone deserves a second chance, even Rose. Brian doesn't know of her accusation against him yet as he wasn't home from the match when the police called. What he doesn't know won't hurt him. I still believe Rose should be brought to book for what she tried to get away with, if nothing else to make her think twice before she tries 'ote like this again, but for your sake, I'll tell the police we've decided not to press charges.

'Luckily it was Bill Brown who came from the station to see me about Rose's claim. He's known us for years . . . often pops in for a cuppa and a quick chat when he's on the beat in our area. Before I'd even told him that Brian couldn't possibly have done what Rose said he had, Bill told me himself that he didn't for a minute believe it. But should Rose dare do anything against us again, anything at all, I *will* press charges and personally lock the cell door after her!'

Meanwhile, upstairs in her room, Rose was sitting on her bed, seething with anger. Life really had it in for her. Why had Ann not been another couple of minutes in the toilet instead of coming out when she did? Then Rose would have been well away with her booty in her pocket. And why hadn't her ploy to get back at them by accusing Brian not worked out? Now that fat cow was threatening her with jail! It wasn't fair.

Panic rose within her at the thought that she could end up in prison. The descriptions she'd read of what life was like inside the walls there had filled Rose with dread. If any of the other prisoners decided to make her the butt of their jokes, she wouldn't be able to retaliate as easily as she did now. Those hard-faced witches wouldn't stand for a tongue-lashing from Rose. And there was the fact that you were made to work in prison, doing mind-numbing menial jobs like sewing mail bags or working in the laundry room for long hours. And you only got a couple of coppers a week for your labour, hardly enough to buy a bar of soap. She wasn't even sure she would be allowed to read her books inside.

She couldn't go to prison, she just couldn't. There must be a way to get herself out of this. Her mind searched and searched, and then a memory stirred. Rose had made her mother so angry once . . . she had done so many things over the years she couldn't remember exactly what . . . but the end result was that she had been ordered to bed and not allowed to read for an hour before she put the light off. Had even had her book taken off her so she couldn't. Rose hadn't been willing to accept that, so in defiance had run off and hidden herself in the coal shed. It had been icy cold and frightening, but she was determined not to come out until her mother agreed to change her mind. Her ploy had worked. By the time Cam had found her, she was so frantic she had relented on the punishment and had given Rose her book back.

There was no reason why this ploy wouldn't work again. Rose

would only pretend to leave home. Her mother would be so frantic and worried that she would agree to put it all behind them and beg Ann to do likewise. Her mother had always been a sucker for Rose's lies so there was no reason to believe she wouldn't fall for this one too. For her plan to work she would need to hide somewhere her mother would easily find her, though.

Rose jumped up from the bed and began to gather her belongings together.

Meanwhile, on hearing Ann say she wouldn't take matters any further and was prepared to give Rose a second chance, Cam was giving her friend's hand a squeeze by way of telling her how grateful she was for her generosity towards Rose, which in truth was undeserved. She thought she heard a sound then and said to Ann, 'Was that the front door I heard?'

Ann was lost in her own thoughts, hoping vehemently for Cam's sake that Rose was giving some serious thought to reforming herself. But she had a dreadful feeling that the girl had no intention of doing any such thing after her parting shot before she'd stormed off upstairs. Instead she was probably planning somehow to worm her way out of the situation and emerge unscathed. 'Eh? Oh, I never heard anything, love.'

Cam gave her ear a rub. 'Must be this cold affecting my hearing.' She made to lift herself off the sofa, saying to Ann, 'I will just go up and check on her.'

Cam may not love her daughter the way a mother should but she certainly cared about her welfare, Ann thought. Whether Rose deserved such caring was debatable after all the nasty things she had said and done today. Ann put a hand on Cam's arm. 'I'll go, in case she hasn't calmed down and decides to lash out. You've had enough of her nasty tongue for one day. Then I'll make you a cup of tea.'

Cam was so emotionally exhausted and physically drained she doubted if at this moment she would get up the stairs anyway. 'Thank you.' Then a memory stirred. 'Oh, but don't you need to be home, getting ready for your night out?'

Ann managed a chuckle. 'These days it takes me less than ten minutes to slip my clothes and shoes on and put on a bit of lipstick. Not like when we were young, eh? Then it took us all afternoon to get ready for a night out.'

She left Cam to go upstairs and check on Rose for her.

Ann's mention of days past made Cam's thoughts drift back to a time when she was carefree, believing that she had a happy future ahead of her. At this moment those days seemed like a hundred years ago instead of the fifteen they actually were. A sudden vision of her old landlady, the prim and austere Miss Peters, sprang to mind and Cam wondered if she was still ruling the lives of her young lodgers. Or if, in fact, she was still alive. Cam hadn't known her age when she had lived with her, but she had seemed ancient at the time. She thought of her old job at the telephone exchange and wondered if the friends she had made were still working there or had moved on by now? Then a vision of Jonah rose in her mind. She hoped he'd found someone who suited him and they were happy together. It hurt Cam to know that he would always think badly of her, but she could never have divulged the truth of how she'd come to be an unmarried mother to him, so she just had to bear this.

Without warning, the vision of Jonah changed to one of Adrian and, as low as she was feeling, she couldn't stop a further swamp of sadness from engulfing her. Thankfully she was brought back to the present by the return of Ann. Cam looked over at her enquiringly. 'How is Rose?'

'She's gone, Cam.'

'Gone?'

Ann nodded. 'Packed all her stuff. It was the door you heard as she left.'

Cam's face clouded over. 'Oh, but where would she go, Ann? She's no money that I know of. No friends to turn to. It's not safe for a girl of her age . . .' She made to rise. 'I'd best go after her.'

Ann stopped her. 'And where will you start looking? As you said, she's no friends to turn to so she could be anywhere. Don't worry about Rose's safety, Cam. One of her glares is enough to wither the toughest criminal and send him scarpering. We both know that.

We've been on the receiving end of them often enough. She'll be home when she's cold and hungry, mark my words!'

Despite her worry for her daughter, Cam knew Ann was right.

'Once she realises her plan has failed and that it's freezing cold, she'll be home. Now you sit there and stop worrying. I'll make you that cuppa.'

CHAPTER TWENTY-ONE

B ut Rose did not come home that night.

Twelve months later, Cam had still not heard a word from her. None of the locals had seen or heard anything either. It was even more upsetting that not one of them seemed at all bothered by Rose's disappearance. No one offered to help her search for the girl, and that made Cam realise just how unpopular her daughter had made herself to the people they lived amongst. She herself hadn't been able to sleep a wink that first night, listening out for Rose to come home, and first thing the next morning had reported the disappearance to the police. They had checked all the hospitals. No one of Rose's description had been brought in, so at least Cam knew she hadn't done anything stupid to herself or been attacked. Her mind had been put to rest on that score. The police had circulated her description around the other stations in the city, but all these months later no sign had yet been seen of Rose. It was as if she'd disappeared off the face of the earth.

Not happy with leaving it to the police to find her, for over three months after she'd run away, Cam had traipsed the streets, on the look out for her, every spare minute she had. But with no luck whatsoever. Her worry for Rose's whereabouts prevented her from sleeping properly and loss of appetite caused her to lose weight. This would have carried on indefinitely had not a worried Ann given her a good talking to, warning Cam that she'd kill herself if she continued like this and then Rose wouldn't have a mother to come home to when she decided to. But had Cam ever wondered if, after Rose had received a few home truths, it had resulted in her miraculously taking a long, hard look at herself? Maybe she had got herself a job and was paying her own way; didn't want to come back until she could show her mother what great strides she had made to better herself? Cam so hoped that was the truth of why her daughter had kept her distance, but it did not stop her from automatically keeping an eye out for the girl wherever she went.

There was one benefit that had come about from her daughter's absconding, although Cam felt guilty about admitting it to herself: at least she no longer had to deal with Rose's continual bad moods and cutting tongue, the loathsome way in which she always looked at her mother. It was such a relief.

When Rose had reached an age where it was safe for Cam to leave her to her own devices for a couple of hours, Ann and she had resumed their Saturday afternoon trip to town together and, as they had done as teenagers, in the middle of doing their shopping they would take a break for tea and cake in a cafe, to catch up with each other's news. They usually took it in turns to call for each other and then catch the bus together. But today Cam was going into town earlier than they normally did as it was Ann's birthday in a few days and Cam wanted to look for a little something for her. She couldn't very well do that if Ann was with her, so had arranged to meet her in their usual cafe for tea and cake at three o'clock.

Cam was in Woolworth's, at the counter that sold costume jewellery, and couldn't make up her mind between a very pretty brooch and a compact case. The assistant, a po-faced, middle-aged woman, was becoming very frustrated with her, but Cam would not be rushed. Her friend was special to her and she wanted to be sure that Ann would be thrilled with the present she gave her. She was just about to settle for the compact case when a commotion coming from over by the entrance resounded through the store. Everyone there, including Cam and the sour-faced assistant, looked over to see what was going on. It appeared that a woman and her two young children had been caught shoplifting.

But it was not the shoplifters who caused Cam's breath to freeze in her body, her heart to pound madly. It was the curly red head of the person just departing through one of the double entrance doors where the shoplifters had been apprehended by two assistants. That red head was Rose's, Cam knew it was. To the utter shock of the miserable assistant, without a word of explanation, she thrust the two items back at her then ran off in pursuit.

Outside, the busy shopping street of Gallowtree Gate was thronged with people. Cam did her best to catch sight of Rose again. There was no sign of her, no sign of anyone with red hair. But she couldn't just have disappeared . . . Rose had been only seconds ahead. Cam's heart was hammering more painfully now, panic rushing through her. This was her first sighting of her daughter in a year and she couldn't let it slip away from her. She jumped up and down, trying to see over the heads of the milling crowd. Then, suddenly, quite a distance away from her, she caught a glimpse of carrot-red hair bobbing up and down. It was obvious the girl was running away: Cam kicked up her heels and followed, dodging around the pedestrians blocking her way.

Past the Clock Tower she raced, as fast as she was able in Rose's wake, and on down the length of Churchgate, still weaving between the passers by, calling out her daughter's name. But, for all she tried, Cam just could not seem to close the gap. By now her lungs were on fire and her legs so tired they were in danger of collapsing beneath her, but sheer determination to see her daughter kept her going.

Just as she was beginning to give up hope of ever catching up with her, to Cam's great relief through a gap in the crowd she caught a glimpse of red curly hair. It was no longer bobbing up and down. It seemed that Rose was stationary now. Praying that whatever had caught her attention continued to do so, Cam tried her best to put on an extra spurt. Her prayer seemed to be being answered as the crowds were thinning now and she had an almost complete view of Rose in the distance. She had her back to Cam but appeared to be in conversation with another woman. The woman was facing Cam and appeared to be laughing. Cam hoped that Rose was building herself a good life, like Ann had suggested. She had never seen anyone laughing at something her daughter had said to them before, only look hurt or upset.

She was within a few yards of Rose and it did strike Cam that, by now, considering how loud she was shouting, Rose must have heard her name being called, but it seemed not. Then that was forgotten as she saw the two women part company and Rose kick up her heels and run off again. Cam had the advantage, though, as she was already up to speed. Before Rose got into her stride, Cam was upon her. She flung out one arm to grab the back of the girl's coat, pulling her to a halt. Rose swung around to face her assailant, exclaiming, 'What the hell . . .'

Cam, gasping for breath, bent double to rest her hands above her knees, wheezing, 'Give . . . me . . . a . . . minute . . . to . . . catch . . . my . . . breath . . . love.' Having taken several deep ones she straightened up, and immediately she settled her eyes on Rose, realised just why the girl hadn't stopped in response to her calls. This young girl wasn't Rose. She was taller for a start, and bigger-built, and she had milky-coloured skin and a fetching smattering of freckles across her nose. The only similarity she had to Rose was that they had the same curly red hair, but whereas Rose's was very fine this young woman's was thick and lustrous. A great wave of embarrassment engulfed Cam, mingled with a huge sense of disappointment that she hadn't found her daughter after all.

The young girl was looking back at her quizzically. Finding her voice, Cam said apologetically, 'I'm so very sorry. I thought . . . well, that you were someone else.'

The girl gave a smile which lit up her pretty face. 'Oh, that's all right, we all make mistakes. Please excuse me but I'm in a hurry to catch a bus.'

Cam watched her as she scooted off towards the bus station, then with a heavy heart began to retrace her steps to Woolworth's. She was conscious she had used up a lot of time with her fruitless chase and it was nearly time to meet Ann. She hadn't bought her present yet so she'd better get a move on if she didn't want to keep her friend waiting.

Back at the Clock Tower, Cam was waiting at the kerb to cross the busy road in order to head back up Gallowtree Gate where the store she was after was situated. The traffic was nose to tail with no gaps in between to cross the road without the risk of being knocked over, so she had no choice but to wait patiently. Quite a crowd had gathered around her, all of them waiting for a break in the traffic to cross the road. Cam saw her chance, between a coal cart and a Corporation bus, and prepared herself for a mad dash.

But just as her opportunity came and she was about to step out, a woman at the side of her elbowed her out of her way and, along with several other people, ran through the gap and across the road. Before Cam had had time to recover her balance her chance had gone, the bus was pulling to a halt in front of her and passengers were alighting.

Next thing she knew she found herself amidst a large crowd of people pushing to get on. It was apparent to her that, once the passengers had all got off, unless she fought free pretty smartly she would be herded on to the bus along with the waiting crowd.

It wasn't in Cam's nature to barge her way rudely past anyone, like that woman had just done to her, so she turned to the person squashed to the side of her to ask them politely to move aside so she could get through. It was a man, much taller than she was. As they were so close, looking him in the eye would have caused a crick in Cam's neck, so it was his coat lapels that she addressed. 'Excuse me, please, I'd like to get through.'

He genially responded, 'Yes, of . . .' To Cam's bewilderment the words died in his throat then and she sensed him staring down at her. Bewildered, she tilted back her head and, as her eyes met his, knew just why his words had given out. She gave a little gasp and everything else melted into the background. All she was aware of was the man whose eyes she was looking into. The awkward, boyishly good-looking young man that she had fallen in love with all those years ago had gone. In his place was a very handsome, self-assured man. Under his light-coloured trenchcoat he was dressed casually in grey Oxford bags, shirt and V-neck jumper; he wore a Homburg hat at a jaunty angle on his neatly cut dark hair. Cam's heart was pounding so painfully she felt sure he would hear it. Before she could stop them, all the old feelings for him that she had carefully locked away flooded back to overwhelm her.

It was Adrian who spoke first. 'Hello, Cam. Well, this is a surprise. How are you?'

Her insides were turning somersaults. She knew he was waiting for her to respond to him, but feared that if she opened her mouth an incoherent babble would come out and then he would think her a raving idiot. Taking several deep breaths, and praying that her fears did not come true, she managed to say, 'Hello, Adrian. I'm fine, thank you. And you?'

'I'm very well too.' An awkward silence fell between them. Cam was searching for something to say and could tell that Adrian was too. Again it was he who spoke first.

'So . . . er . . . how is your aunt then? Well, I understood she was elderly so I expect she won't be around now. It was fifteen years ago you went off to look after her, wasn't it?'

Cam looked at him, puzzled. Adrian knew she was an orphan. She hadn't got an aunt. Then it hit her to whom he was referring. The fictitious aunt that she'd made up by way of an excuse to cover up her pregnancy. He'd obviously heard this through gossip at the GPO when she didn't turn up on the Monday after ending their relationship. She was surprised he knew exactly how many years ago it had all happened, though. She didn't like continuing the lie to him but the alternative was even less appealing. 'My aunt, yes . . . she passed away a few years back.'

Adrian said sincerely, 'Oh, I'm sorry to hear that, especially as I know she was the last relative you had and that you'd only just found out about her existence. Well, according to what I heard anyway.' Yet another awkward silence fell between them and Cam was very aware that Adrian seemed to be deliberating over something. Finally he came out with it.

'Look, I don't wish to embarrass or upset you by raking up the past, but there's something that's bothered me since we parted. While I have the opportunity, I'd like to clear it up. It's that night you ended things between us. Well, I know I was rather wet behind the ears in those days but I was absolutely shell-shocked when you dropped your bombshell on me. When you were telling me it was over between us, I could hear what you were saying but I got the impression you didn't really mean it, not deep down. I could tell by the way you couldn't look at me and . . . well, just the whole way you were.

'After you'd left I sat there for ages, mulling it over, and decided to catch you on Monday and speak to you about it . . . well, I was hoping you'd have changed your mind. Anyway, when you didn't come into work the following week, and I heard you'd left and why,

I got to wondering if the real reason you'd finished with me was because . . . well, it wasn't like we were engaged or anything . . . so maybe you did it because you didn't feel you could ask me to wait for you, as you had no idea how long you'd be gone. Was that how it was, Cam, or have I got it wrong?'

She had known she had hurt him terribly at the time, but it was shocking for her to learn that after all these years it was still enough of an issue for him to want answers to his questions. She hadn't been wrong. He had loved her as deeply as she had him. Given the chance, it would have led to their marrying and spending the rest of their lives together. She sighed heavily and told him, in all honesty, 'Yes, you were right, Adrian. I really didn't want our relationship to end but I felt it was the fairest thing to do. I'm so sorry I hurt you.'

'You did, Cam. You broke my heart, if you want the truth. But it was a long time ago and I know now that you thought you were doing the right thing.' He planted a smile on his face and said breezily, 'So, happily married with children now, are you?'

'Er . . . no. No, I never married.' On hearing this, his face clouded over with a mixture of shock and surprise and something else that Cam couldn't fathom. 'What about you?' she asked him.

'Oh, I married. Veronica. We were very happy together. We have two children. Harry is eleven and Harriet . . . Hattie . . . is nine.'

A brief stab of pain shot through Cam. Children that should have been hers. She did her best to sound pleased for Adrian. 'I'm so glad for you.' Then something he had said struck her. 'You said *we were* happy together?'

A fleeting look of sadness crossed his face. 'Veronica died three years ago. She had cancer.'

Cam was quite genuine when she exclaimed, 'Oh, Adrian, I am so sorry to hear that.'

'Oi, either of you two want the bus? Only we're setting off now.'

They both automatically looked over at the conductor, hanging on the platform pole addressing them.

'Yes, actually, I do,' Adrian called to him. He told Cam, 'I have to get back as a neighbour is keeping an eye on the kids for me while I pop into town to get some shopping. I told her I wouldn't be back later than three-thirty.' He looked at Cam for a moment again, seeming to be deliberating something in his mind before telling her, 'It's . . . er . . . really been good to see you again, Cam. You take care of yourself.'

'And you, Adrian,' she told him.

She watched him hurry off towards the bus and thought her heart would break in two. Part of her so wished she hadn't encountered him today. It had raked up old feelings she knew would be hard to suppress again, but at least she knew that he wasn't carrying bad memories of her now. She had put his mind at rest that she hadn't after all finished their relationship because he meant nothing to her, but because she'd had no choice. Giving a heavy sigh, Cam made to turn and continue on her way when to her surprise she saw Adrian change his mind about getting on the bus and heard him say to the conductor, 'Please hold the bus for a couple of seconds.' Then he hurried over to her and nervously began: 'Er . . . do you . . . would you . . . er . . . what I'm trying to ask is . . . well, would you like to have a drink or a meal with me, for old times' sake? I'd really like it if you would, Cam. Tonight, if you're free? I can get a babysitter.'

There was such a hopeful look on his face. Her heart was leaping in her chest. The answer was out of her mouth before she had time to think of the possible consequences. 'Oh, I'd love to, Adrian.' Oh, God, she hoped she hadn't come across as too eager.

He looked delighted by her acceptance. 'Here, at eight?'

Smiling, Cam nodded her agreement.

'Oh, finally! I was ready to give up on you. The coffee I got you is cold by now and I was just about to eat the cream bun I bought you. You did say three and now it's twenty-past. I hope you've a good excuse for leaving me sitting on my own like a twit!' As Cam eased herself into the chair opposite her at the cafe table, Ann noticed the state of her friend and said, 'I can't decide whether you're upset or excited about something, but it's one or the other.'

'Well, it's both actually, Ann. I've had rather an eventful time for the last hour or so.'

She looked intrigued. 'Oh? I hope it's something to do with my birthday present. Upset because you couldn't afford the solid gold bracelet you knew I would have just adored, but excited because you know I'll still love what you have got me? Are you going to eat that cake or not?'

Cam tutted as she pushed the plate away. 'I can't remember the last time I ate a cake in here. For some reason or other, you always end up having it.'

'Well, you have got a figure to worry about keeping slim whereas I've never had one to be worried over.' Without any shame, Ann picked up the cake and took a big bite. Then, through the mouthful, she asked, 'What did you get me for my birthday?'

'If I told you now it wouldn't be a surprise, would it? Actually, I haven't got you anything yet,' Cam admitted.

Ann's face fell. 'Oh! So what's been so eventful this last hour then, if it wasn't anything to do with buying my present?'

'Well, I was in the process of doing so when I got sidetracked. You see . . .' She told Ann of her chase across town after a girl she'd thought was Rose, only to find out she had been mistaken.

When Cam had finished Ann leaned over and took her hand, giving it an affectionate squeeze. 'I'm so sorry, love. It must have been awful.'

'It was. Thankfully the young lady was very nice about it.'

'Rose will surface one day, Cam, when she's ready to. All you can do meantime is get on with your own life.'

Cam knew this advice was sound. She picked up her cup of coffee and took a sip. She grimaced. Ann was right, it was cold. Cam liked her tea or coffee piping hot so couldn't drink it. She got up, saying, 'I'm going to get myself a fresh coffee. Would you like another?'

Ann said she would, and by the time Cam returned to the table with their drinks she was desperate to tell her friend her other news. Ann got in first.

'Well, what you've just told me obviously upset you, so now I want to know what happened to excite you?'

Cam stirred sugar into her coffee from the container on the table and took a sip before she began, 'I bumped into an old friend. I was waiting to cross the road and he was standing next to me.'

Ann looked at her quizzically. 'He?'

Cam nodded. 'It was Adrian. To cut a long story short, his wife died a couple of years ago so he's on his own now. I've agreed to meet him tonight for a meal.'

It was very rare that Ann was struck speechless, but the news Cam had told her had certainly taken the wind from her sails. With a delighted grin on her face, she exclaimed, 'Well, fate has finally seen to it that you two are being given another chance.'

'Oh, hardly, Ann. If we did start seeing each other again then I'd have to tell him how Rose came about, and a respectable man like him isn't going to want to be with a woman with such a sordid past, no matter how much he loved me once. I'm just worried that, by agreeing to meet him, I'm going to end up hurting him again. It was plain to me he still has feelings for me, even after all these years.'

'And you've never lost yours for him, so don't forget the hurt this could bring you too,' Ann warned her. She then folded her well-padded arms and rested them before her on the table. 'You're jumping the gun somewhat in my view, Cam. It's a long time since you've had a date with a man. In fact, the last time you did it was with Adrian himself, the night you finished with him. Fate has brought you both together again. Why don't you just look forward to a night out with him and no further than that? If he likes being with you enough to ask to see you again, and you want to see him, that's the time to start worrying about coming clean with him. Anyway, you've agreed to meet him now so it wouldn't be fair of you not to turn up.'

Cam looked at her for a moment before saying, 'You're right, Ann. It wouldn't be fair of me to leave him waiting just because I'm worried about something I may never have to say. He probably won't want to see me again.' Then her face lit up excitedly. 'Oh, I've no idea what to wear . . .'

A warm glow filled Ann. It had been a long time since Cam had had anything to be excited about. In fact, not since she had discovered she was pregnant, more than sixteen years ago. It was good to see that expression on her face again.

CHAPTER TWENTY-TWO

For the umpteenth time in the last twenty minutes Cam lifted her eyes to look at the clock ticking merrily away on the tiled mantelpiece. Only three minutes had passed since the last time she had looked. She had never known time pass so slowly. Each passing minute seemed like thirty to her.

By the time she and Ann had finished discussing what Cam would wear it was getting on for four. Ann had told her to forget accompanying her around town to get the rest of her shopping, and get herself home instead so she had plenty of time to get ready for her date. Consumed with thoughts of wanting to look her best Cam had not argued, completely forgetting she hadn't yet purchased Ann's birthday present. If Ann had remembered, she hadn't said anything.

By the time she'd arrived home it had been too late for Cam to light the fire under the copper in the outhouse to heat water for a wash in the tin bath. It took a good couple of hours for it to heat so instead she had given herself a good scrub down at the sink in the kitchen. She usually wore her hair in a tidy, fashionable forties roll, but tonight had decided to wear it loose in waves around her face and shoulders. Ann said she looked like Rita Hayworth when she styled it like this.

Then she set about deciding what to wear. Not that she had much to choose from. The war might have been over for six months but strict rationing of luxury goods still prevented the buying of new clothes, unless you were very wealthy or had blackmarket contacts, which Cam wasn't and didn't. Decent second-hand clothes were also hard to come by now. With everyone having to make do and mend for the last six years, it meant they'd had no choice but to hang on to their clothes until they were beyond repair. It really came down to a choice between a dark green tailored dress modelled on a style they had seen Joan Crawford wear in the film *Mildred Pierce* or a two-piece suit in navy blue with a straight skirt and short-sleeved fitted jacket.

After much deliberation Cam settled on the dress, and hoped Adrian wouldn't notice she wasn't wearing any stockings as she hadn't got any without ladders. That afternoon she had intended to scour the market but today's events had prevented her. Neither had she any makeup left except for just the tiniest bit of lipstick, which she had to get out of the container with the aid of the end of a matchstick. She had been saving it for a special occasion and couldn't think of a better one than this, so on it went along with several pinches to her cheeks to bring colour to them.

Having checked herself several times in the mirror, and knowing there was nothing else she could do to improve her appearance, Cam put on her shoes and coat ready to leave to catch the bus. But she realised she was far too early so took them off again and settled down in an armchair to thumb through a tattered three-year-old copy of *Harper's Bazaar*. She had actually read it from cover to cover several times before, not that she noticed anything that was on the page as by now her nerves were jangling in anticipation. She couldn't stop her eyes from straying to the clock, willing the time of departure to come.

Cam was just about to get up and check her appearance again in the mirror, in an effort to while away another minute, when she heard the back door open and shut, and smiled to herself. It would be Ann, popping in to give her some moral support on her way to the pub with Brian, something they did most Saturday nights. Since her financial position had improved several years ago, Cam had taken to accompanying them and had intended to tonight until she got a better offer. They didn't usually go this early, though.

She placed a warm smile on her face, ready to greet her friend.

But it quickly faded, to be replaced by a look of utter shock.

Cam stared at her unexpected visitor for several moments before her brain accepted who it was she was seeing. 'Rose!' she uttered. 'Oh, Rose, you've come home at last.'

A sly smile played on her daughter's lips. 'You can forget that.

I've just come to bring you a present. But it can wait. I expect you'd like to know what I've been up to since I last saw you?'

As she took off her coat, flinging it over the back of a dining-chair, and made her way over to the sofa to sit down and cross her legs, Cam gawped in astonishment at what her daughter was wearing. Rose had run away that early-evening a year ago looking what she was: a young girl of fifteen. Now she could be mistaken for eighteen at least. She had put on weight and her previously slight figure was now curvy. She had breasts, an ample amount of cleavage showing over the top of her low-cut red blouse. The black skirt she wore hugged her hips and finished just above her knees. She was wearing black silk stockings with seams up the back and, despite everything running through her mind, Cam wondered just how she had managed to acquire those scarce items. The clothes she wore might be gaudy, but were definitely expensive. And it was a fur coat, albeit second-hand but very expensive when new, that she had taken off and casually thrown over a dining-chair when she had first arrived.

Her youthful face was plastered in makeup. She wore swathes of blue eye shadow, her lashes were blackened, lips painted a bright red. The hair that she used to wear in a tangled mop, in an effort to hide her face, was now piled on top of her head, curly tendrils framing her jaw – a style that was far too grown up for a girl of sixteen. Just what type of people was Rose mixing with if they encouraged her to dress like this? And how was she getting the sort of money to afford the clothes she was wearing and silk stockings too? No wonder the police had not found her. She looked nothing like the description Cam had furnished them with.

While her mother had been appraising her, Rose herself had been staring back with an amused smile on her lips. 'Well, you can't say I'm not making the best of myself now, can you, Mother?'

Cam looked at her aghast. 'Oh, Rose, have you taken a good look at yourself in the mirror? You could be mistaken for . . . well, for . . .'

'A prostitute?'

Cam swallowed uncomfortably. 'I hate to say it but, yes, Rose, you could.'

She grinned and said proudly, 'Then I've achieved the look I intended to.'

Cam gawped at her in astonishment. 'What are you telling me, Rose?' she uttered, terrified of hearing the answer she suspected her daughter was about to give her.

Rose sneered at her, 'Need me to spell it out for you, Mother? And I thought you were an intelligent woman. I told you I was going to find a way to make myself a lot of money and get the life I wanted. Though it never would have entered my head that someone who looks like me would be so popular with certain men.' While Cam looked on, horrified, Rose unclipped her handbag and extracted a packet of cigarettes. She took one out and lit it with a gold lighter, blowing a plume of smoke in the air. She fixed her mortified mother with her eyes and said harshly, 'That night I ran away from home, I waited and waited for you to come and find me, but you never did.'

'But I had no idea where to start looking for you! You had no friends for me to contact. You never went out except to the book-shop. I had no choice but to wait for you to come home of your own accord, Rose.'

She snorted, eyeing Cam with disgust. 'Don't lie to me, Mother. You knew I had no money and nowhere to go, and you knew I couldn't come home because I'd be frightened that the police could be waiting to throw me into jail. You never came to look for me because it was your chance to be rid of me, wasn't it? I bet deep down you'd always resented having an ugly daughter. Couldn't wait to get me off your hands. Wanted to be free to find a man to replace my father. Well, not many men want to take on someone else's kid ... and especially one who looked like I did.'

Cam was staring at her, appalled. 'Rose, none of this is true and you know it. I . . .'

She harshly interjected, 'No, I don't. You never came to find me so that's the only conclusion I could come to. I wondered if you ever had in fact cared for me, or merely suffered having me around because you had no choice. Anyway, it was about eleven o'clock before I finally admitted to myself that you'd abandoned me. I didn't know what to do but I realised I had to find shelter for the night unless I wanted to freeze to death. With no money to pay for anywhere a shop doorway seemed my only option, but I daren't risk staying around here in case the local bobby might be on the look out for me. So I walked into town. Mrs Monks found me huddled in a doorway.'

Rose took another long draw from her cigarette and then threw the stub into the fire. 'Thankfully for me, she'd decided to take a stroll out that night or I dread to think what would have become of me. She offered to take me home with her. She was like my guardian angel. I almost leaped on her with gratitude. The house she took me to was huge, set back off the road with its own driveway. It had big double-bayed windows and steps leading up to the front. It had four floors . . . it was so impressive. But when she took me inside . . . I had never imagined a place could be so grand. The carpet on the floors was so thick your feet sank into it. All the walls were papered, and even I know expensive wallpaper when I see it. And as for the furniture, it puts the shabby stuff in here to shame.'

Cam was shrinking inside. Her daughter was describing a high-class brothel. Her so-called guardian angel Mrs Monks was obviously the Madam who ran it, maybe even owned it. Cam suspected that she had not been taking a leisurely stroll that night she had come across Rose, but been on the look out for likely candidates to work in her establishment.

Rose was going on, 'Mrs Monks took me into her office and had a maid bring in a tray of tea. It was the best tea I'd ever tasted, not like the cheap leaves you buy. While I was drinking it, she asked me how I'd come to be where she'd found me. So I told her how my mother had thrown me out without any money or anywhere to go. That I was in her way because I wasn't pretty, and now I was fifteen she saw me as old enough to fend for myself. She asked me what my plans were. I told her I hadn't got any. I supposed I had no choice but to get any job I could and hope the pay was enough for me to live on. She said that if I was interested, she could offer me a job paying far more than I'd ever earn in a factory, even when I was fully skilled, and that it came with accommodation. Of course I was interested.

'I was shocked at first when she told me just what the job entailed, but then, what did I really care when this was my big opportunity to make the sort of money I could only ever dream of otherwise?

I was a bit concerned, though, as I thought it was only good-looking women men went after. Mrs Monks told me that she catered for all tastes and that I would be surprised how attractive some men would find me. To hear that . . . when I hadn't thought it was even possible! And they do, Mother. My clients all tell me how beautiful I am to them, and make me feel special. Several have bought me jewellery. Mrs Monks told me that I would be nervous the first time but that she and all the other girls would give me whatever moral support I needed. So I thought, Why not? I had no one to answer to but myself. I could do whatever I pleased. Thanks to your actions in throwing me out.'

Cam shut her eyes and tried her best to close her mind also. It was horrible to learn how her daughter had been earning her living. She seemed to have no shame about letting men do whatever they wished with her, in exchange for the money she'd receive. She could tell Rose was enjoying seeing how much she was upsetting her. It was her way of paying Cam back for not running after her. Rose had always had a spiteful and vindictive streak, but Cam had never before realised how low she'd sink to wreak revenge for what she saw as a wrong against her.

She was going on, 'Of course, Mrs Monks needs to take her cut of her girls' earnings for providing them with such a lavish place to work, as well as some towards our accommodation . . . which, by the way, is in a lovely house nearby where I have a really nice room . . . and what she does with the rest is give us a few pounds to spend as we like and then the rest she saves up for us so that, when we decide to leave her employ, we have money to set ourselves up with. I don't intend to leave until I've made at least a thousand pounds. With a thousand behind me . . . well, people aren't going to see a poor ugly woman any more, are they, but a woman of substance who deserves their respect? But I intend to make lots more money thanks to that first thousand pounds. I'm going to open my own establishment. What do you think of that, eh, Mother? A year ago the most I could have hoped for was a job in a factory. Now I'm on my way to becoming a successful, wealthy businesswoman.'

Cam didn't like the sound of this. Her gut feeling was telling her the woman Rose was seeing as her guardian angel had no intention of handing over the money she was supposed to be saving up for her protégée. But would Rose listen to her concern and, if nothing else, get proof that Mrs Monks was indeed putting this money aside? Cam needed to try at least.

'Rose, I don't think that—'

She eyed her mother coldly. 'Your opinion stopped mattering the night you showed just how much you cared for me. To be honest, it wouldn't have bothered me if I never saw you again. You belong in the past, to which I've no intention of ever returning.' She smiled. 'So now I can see you're wondering why I'm here, apart from giving myself the great pleasure of letting you know that your daughter sells her body for sex.' She added sardonically, 'Don't forget to sound proud when people enquire how I'm getting on. And, Mother, you were always berating me for being a liar so I expect you to be strictly honest. Now where was I . . . oh, yes.

'A few months ago, I found myself with a problem. Actually it was Mrs Monks who told me I had one as I hadn't a clue why I was being sick in the morning and feeling out of sorts, because you never told me about anything like that. Mrs Monks assured me, though, that it was a hazard of the job and it had happened to many of the girls who have worked for her, some of them several times. She has a doctor in her pay . . . well, actually, he's a client and they have an arrangement . . . and she could arrange for him to get rid of my little problem for me.'

Cam was gawping at her in utter shock. 'You mean, you were pregnant!'

'Well done, Mother, that's exactly what I was. Mrs Monks said I could always have the kid if I didn't want to have it aborted. If I was Catholic, for instance, and it was against my religion to take a life. She had an arrangement with a woman who would take care of disposing of it.'

Cam strongly suspected that Mrs Monks received a cut from the fee that the grateful new parents paid over in exchange for a baby they couldn't conceive themselves.

Rose was continuing, 'I asked her to arrange for a visit to the doctor.'

She paused long enough to take another cigarette out of her packet and light it, drawing deep on the smoke. Then she took up where she'd left off. 'The night before my appointment, I got to thinking. There was my mother, happily carrying on with her life, more than likely not giving me a second thought or feeling any guilt for what could have happened to me if I hadn't been saved by Mrs Monks. That didn't seem fair to me. Not fair at all.' Rose leaned forward and smiled widely at Cam. 'But then it struck me that I had the perfect way to make sure you were never for a minute allowed to forget either me or what you did to me. Well, for at least the next fifteen years . . . until you decide it's old enough to fend for itself and kick it out like you did me. I never had the abortion. All the time I was carrying it, I prayed and prayed that it took after me in looks. It arrived yesterday, finally, and I looked at it just long enough to see if my prayers had been answered. They had. It's the image of me. There is some justice in this world after all.'

She pulled back her sleeve and glanced at her watch, then uncrossed her legs, picked up her handbag, stood up and smoothed down her skirt, saying, 'Having a kid has got its benefits. It's done wonders for my figure. Anyway, I've a taxi waiting. I've stayed longer than I told him I would. I really shouldn't be here, should be resting to get over the birth as quickly as I can so as to get back to work and earning money. But I didn't want it around any longer than I had to. Besides, I couldn't wait to give you my surprise and see your face. If you've got to tell it anything about me, tell it I'm dead. I don't want it looking for me when it's older.' Rose was putting on her coat now and heading for the door. 'You won't see me again, so goodbye, Mother. Oh, goodness, I nearly forgot. It's in the coal house. Didn't want to bring it in when I arrived and spoil my surprise.'

Cam was still trying to digest the news that her sixteen-year-old daughter had had a baby, so what she had just been told wasn't really registering. Then suddenly it did, like an arrow piercing her. Panic-stricken, she jumped up and rushed over to Rose, grabbing her arm, crying out, 'Just a minute, Rose. Are you telling me you're leaving your baby for me to raise?'

She snapped, 'Have you not been listening to me?'

Cam frenziedly cried, 'But . . . but . . . you can't do this! It's your baby, it needs you. Look, Rose, please come home and I'll help you look after it. Think about that, please. And what about its father? Surely he . . .'

'You really are stupid, Mother. I told you, I only went through with having it because it was such a good way to make you pay for what you did to me . . . now and for a long, long time to come. And just why would I want to bring up a kid I didn't want in the first place, was going to get rid of until I saw I had good use for it? I haven't a clue who its father is anyway.' She shook her arm free from her mother's grip. 'Now get your hands off me,' she said nastily, as though Cam's touch was repugnant to her. Without another word, she left.

Cam's mind was numb, completely refusing to process any of what Rose had been saying. Her body was rigid as she sat ramrod-straight in a chair at the table, hands clasped in her lap, staring into space. She did not hear the back door open and was unaware that someone had come in. She didn't hear Ann speak to her until she repeated what she had said, jolting Cam out of her trance-like state.

She looked at Ann blindly for a moment before she said distractedly, 'Oh, it's you.'

Confused, she replied, 'Yes, and it's you who's still sitting here. Why is that when you should be in town, enjoying yourself with Adrian? I couldn't believe it when I saw your lights on while I was passing with Brian on our way to the pub. He's gone on ahead but I had to come and find out why you're still here. So why are you, Cam?'

Cam stared at her blankly for several moments before she said absent-mindedly, 'Oh, yes, I was supposed to be meeting Adrian, wasn't I? I'd forgotten about that.'

Ann's mouth dropped open in astonishment. 'You forgot? But . . .' She stopped dead, it hitting her then that just where Cam's mind was she had no idea but it wasn't in this room. And she had never seen her look so . . . haunted. Cam had had a shock. A huge one. Ann's mind raced, worrying about what it could be. The only thing that would affect her this badly would be something to do with her daughter.

Ann dashed across to the table, pulled out the chair next to her friend and sat down, demanding, 'It's Rose, isn't it, love? Is she in trouble . . . is that it? Oh, she hasn't had an accident, has she?' Then her own face paled alarmingly. Her friend was far too upset for it just to be that. 'Oh, Cam, she's not . . . she's not . . .' Ann couldn't bring herself to say the word 'dead'.

Cam turned her head to look at her. A lone tear glistened in her eye then rolled down her cheek. More followed, then her whole body started to shake and a flood of heart-wrenching sobs ensued.

Cam's obvious pain was distressing for Ann to witness. Her arms flew around her, to gather her in. Stroking her hair, she uttered, 'I'm so sorry, love. So, so sorry. How did it happen? Was it an accident?'

It was a while before Cam could answer. In a whisper she said, 'Rose . . . isn't dead, Ann.'

She wasn't? So what could possibly have happened to cause her friend such grief? 'What is it that upset you so much then?' urged Ann.

Cam pulled away from her embrace to wipe her face on her handkerchief and blow her nose. 'It's . . . Oh, Ann, I can't bear it, I really can't! It's . . . it's the way Rose is earning her living. She's . . . she's . . .' Her bottom lip started to tremble again. She opened her mouth and tried to force the words out but they would not come.

'She's what, Cam? What?' demanded Ann.

She swallowed hard and blurted, 'Selling her body.'

It took several long seconds for the significance of what Cam had said to sink in. Ann then stared back at her in absolute horror. 'She's *what*? Who told you this? They must have it wrong.'

Cam shook her head. 'She told me herself, Ann.'

'Rose has been to see you?'

She nodded. 'About seven o'clock she turned up. I got the shock of my life as she was the last person I was expecting. You should have seen what she was wearing, Ann, and all the makeup she had on her face! She said she'd come to bring me a present but insisted I listen first to all the sordid details of what she's been doing since she left.'

Ann cried, aghast, 'Good God, she's sixteen and she's put herself on the streets! Has she no respect for herself?'

'She seems very proud of what she's doing. And she's not on the streets, Ann, but works for a high-class establishment, so she says. Told me a Mrs Monks . . . her guardian angel Rose calls her . . . approached her the night I abandoned her and asked if she wanted a job.'

Ann's expression was bewildered. 'The night you abandoned her?'

'She's insisting I did because I never went to look for her when she ran off. I tried to tell her that we hadn't any idea where she could have gone so didn't know where to start looking, but Rose wouldn't listen to me. She said I'd known she wouldn't come back because she'd be terrified of the police so I obviously saw it as my opportunity to get rid of her and get on with my life, without having the burden of her. Find myself a new man . . .'

'But how does Rose know you never went to look for her that night?' Then the truth dawned and Ann exclaimed, 'Why, the little madam! So that was her game.' Her temper rose and she blurted out, 'That night she hadn't left home at all! She was waiting some-where close by so you'd find her. Hoping that you'd be so frantic and worried about her by the time you did that you'd forgive and forget. She'd played that trick before, I remember, when she was younger, and obviously thought it would work for her again. So now she's blaming you because you didn't go looking for her. Making that her excuse for choosing the life she has.'

Cam shuddered, sniffed hard, and through a renewed flood of tears, said, 'No, she's not, Ann. She's saying she has me to thank. Says if I hadn't abandoned her, she never would have met Mrs Monks and got this opportunity to make her fortune. According to Rose, she's very much in demand among the sort of men who patronise Mrs Monks' establishment. Rose reckons she's going to continue working for her until she's earned enough to open her own place.'

Ann sighed heavily, raking a hand through her hair. 'I know she's your daughter, Cam, but that girl has never been civil to anyone in her life so it defies belief that she can find it within herself to be pleasant to her . . . um . . . clients. But does she seriously think that being rich is going to bring her respect and people flocking to be associated with her . . . men falling at her feet, begging her to marry them? Does she think she's going to be happy, knowing people are only wanting to be with her as they're hoping she'll be generous with her money, and once they realise she's not, they'll be off. Rich or poor, unless she accepts that it's her manner she needs to sort out then eventually she's going to end up a lonely, sad woman.'

Ann's face screwed up then as a memory stirred. 'You said she came to bring you a present? Well, I hope you chucked it back at her, knowing just how she got the money to pay for it. And I'm surprised she has bought you a present myself. As soon as she was old enough to know what she was doing, she purposely forgot whenever it was your birthday before, as she knew how upset you'd be. As for Christmas, well, she'd always get you something she knew very well you wouldn't like, just to be spiteful. Like that lavender soap and talc that last Christmas when she knew very well the smell of lavender gives you a blinding headache.'

Cam wiped her face. 'Her present to me isn't one you'd buy in a shop.' She lowered her head, wringing her hands in despair. 'Her present to me was her baby to look after.'

Ann's hand was pressed to her mouth. 'Rose has had a baby?' she uttered, stunned.

'Apparently it's a hazard of the job, getting pregnant, and the *kindly* Mrs Monks usually arranges for an abortion with a proper medical doctor. For those who don't agree with that, for religious or other reasons, she can arrange for the child to be adopted. I suspect she gets a cut of the fee paid by the prospective parents. Rose was going to have it taken away until she saw this as a good way to pay me back, by giving it to me to look after. She said while she was carrying it, she prayed every night the child would resemble her when it was born. And she said she'd got her wish.' Her face contorting in agony, Cam added, 'She instructed me to tell the child that she's dead as she doesn't want it looking for her when it's older.'

Ann was struck completely speechless by this further revelation. It was several minutes before she finally said, 'I . . . I just can't believe that even Rose would bring a child into the world as a way to get back at her mother. She's definitely got a screw loose. In fact, I'd go so far as to say she's unhinged.' Then Ann mused, 'It's that poor little mite I feel sorry for. I hope to God it never finds out how it came to be born, let alone what kind of a mother it's got.'

Cam sighed, 'I'll do my best for it.'

Ann looked taken aback. 'What do you mean, *you'll do your best for it*? You never let her walk away and leave the child with you!'

'I couldn't stop her, Ann. I begged her to come home, said I'd help her look after it, but she just laughed at me for even suggesting it.'

Ann cried, 'But this isn't fair! You've already raised one child you didn't want. Fifteen years of hell you went through as a result of that madam's ways. You've just got your life back . . . another chance with Adrian, to be happy with him . . .'

At the mention of Adrian a look of horror filled Cam's face and she exclaimed, 'Oh, Ann. What is he going to be thinking of me for not turning up? I don't even know where he lives. So I can't visit and tell him I didn't purposely let him down.' Then her shoulders sagged in despair. 'But even if I did know where he lived and went to apologise, I couldn't lie to him, Ann, say I fell ill or something, because if we did continue seeing each other the truth would eventually come out. It was bad enough me worrying how he would react to the fact that I'd really ended our relationship all those years ago because I'd been raped and was having an illegitimate baby. How could I tell him that my baby is now earning her living as a prostitute and has had an illegitimate child of her own, which she's given to me to raise to pay me back for the wrongs she thinks I've done her?'

Her face crumpled in sorrow. 'It looks as if I'm going to be made to pay forever for that one mistake I made all those years ago, doesn't it? Oh, Ann, why didn't I stop and think before I walked down that unlit path?' Cam put her elbows on the table and rested her head despairingly in her hands. 'I don't want to raise another child. The thought fills me with dread. But unless Rose has a change of heart, whether I want to or not, I have no choice. If it does look like Rose as she says it does then no one is going to want to give it a home, for the same reason they wouldn't take her. For the same reason I couldn't leave Rose on the steps of an orphanage, I can't leave this child either. I'd never live with myself, worrying if it was being mistreated.'

Ann fervently prayed that the child did not take after its mother in more ways than its looks. Cam probably faced another fifteen years of hell raising it. But it seemed she was stuck with this child through her daughter's utter selfishness, and as her friend Ann would do her best to help out as much as she could.

'So, what have we got then, a boy or a girl?' she asked.

Still distracted by the news of the dangers Rose faced every day, Cam murmured, 'I don't know.' Then a memory stirred within her and she exclaimed, 'Oh, God, what kind of woman am I? The poor child is still in the outhouse where Rose said she'd left it.'

She jumped up from her chair and rushed off, returning moments later carrying a basket which she put on the table.

Ann stood up and they both looked into it. The blanket the child was wrapped in obscured its face. Ann gave Cam a look as if to say, It's you that should be the one to lift the baby out, it's your grandchild. Cam took a deep breath, then reached into the basket and took out the bundle inside. Ann followed her as she went over to the sofa with it and placed it down gently. She carefully eased back the blanket to reveal its face. Both she and Ann gasped then.

'My God, Rose wasn't exaggerating. That baby is her double,' exclaimed Ann.

For Cam it was as if the last fifteen years had not happened and she was back in the home for fallen women, looking down at the daughter she'd never wanted to raise.

Ann meanwhile was taking a peek inside the child's nappy and brought Cam out of her déjà-vu moment by declaring, 'It's a girl, Cam.'

Her heart sank. She had been hoping it would be a boy. Boys weren't supposed to be pretty and wouldn't be teased so much by other kids for their lack of attractiveness.

Just then the child's eyes opened and she looked straight into those of her grandmother. Then she did something that Cam had never seen Rose do, unless it was maliciously. She smiled.

Her eyes were benign. This smile was different from that caused by wind. All Cam's instincts told her that the child was giving her a message, and that message was: *Hello, Grandma, I'm pleased to meet you.* She then gasped in shock as something happened to her that she had never known with Rose. Her whole body was filled with a feeling of inexplicable love, so overwhelming it took her breath away.

CHAPTER TWENTY-THREE

1961

Sitting at her dressing-table, brushing her hair, Cam turned her head at the sound of the door opening and smiled affectionately as her fifteen-year-old granddaughter entered the bedroom.

Lindy made a great show of appraising her grandmother, who was wearing a simple emerald green boat-necked shift dress which hugged her still shapely figure, then smiled back. 'You look the bee's knees in your new dress, Nan,' she said in all sincerity. 'Auntie Ann is so clever with her sewing machine.' Then she added jokingly, 'You sure you've not got a bloke you're after down the pub?'

Over the years there had been several men who had made it clear to Cam that they were very interested in her, but since her ill-fated last meeting with him, when her buried feelings had re-emerged and proved to be as strong as they had been on the night she had ended their relationship, Cam knew her heart would always belong to Adrian. A relationship with any other man would not be fair on him as she would never be able to give herself completely to him.

She chuckled, 'I'm a bit long in the tooth to be thinking of romance, love.'

Lindy scoffed, 'Nan, you're forty-nine . . . not exactly a step away from your coffin! Irene's dad fancies you something rotten. I've seen the way he ogles you and goes all tongue-tied whenever he comes face to face with you. He's not a bad-looking man for his age, he's got a good job as a foreman and Irene's mam has been dead five years now, so it's not like he's still in mourning and the locals would talk. Why don't you just go out with him and see how you get on?'

'Because I'm happy as I am, Lindy.' To change the subject Cam asked her, 'Why are you in your baby doll pyjamas and not dressed up for going out with your friends as usual on a Saturday night? Didn't you tell me there was a new skiffle group playing at the coffee bar that you wanted to check out?'

Lindy sat down on Cam's bed, placing the book she was carrying to one side of her, and said, 'I was all set to go, but you know what it's like, Nan. Sometimes you just want a night in, to cuddle up in a chair with a good book. That's what I fancy doing tonight.'

Her granddaughter's words swept Cam involuntarily back sixteen years, as a vision of Lindy's mother rose up before her. She could see Rose sitting in the armchair by the fireplace, engrossed in whatever book she was reading at the time. Like her mother, Lindy loved to lose herself in a good book, but unlike her mother she wasn't obsessed with reading and neither was it her only pastime. Lindy might have inherited her mother's looks and build – although she was a couple of inches taller than Rose at five foot two – as well as her wild red curls, but that was where the similarities ended.

Any worries Cam had had that she faced years of strife in raising Rose's daughter had swiftly been dispelled. From that first heart-melting smile Lindy had given her, a powerful bond had formed between Cam and her granddaughter. That first night she would have remained staring down at the child, completely absorbed in wonderment at the feelings she was experiencing for her, had it not been for Ann reminding her that the baby would need feeding soon and Cam wouldn't be able to oblige, so somewhere or other they had to get hold of some National Dried Milk to feed her on. As it was a Saturday night no chemist was open, and Ann volunteered to contact neighbours with young babies themselves to scrounge some until the shops opened on Monday, along with a few other essentials . . . like nappies and a change of clothes.

Cam was not prepared to lie about the child's sudden appearance and cover for the fact that her sixteen-year-old daughter had had a baby which she had left in her mother's care. She was prepared for a backlash and consequently surprised and gratified that, apart from the odd look and whisper behind her back from the more prudish sort, nothing was said to her and she heard no malicious gossip via others. It was Ann's opinion that was because of how much the locals liked and respected Cam herself. Secretly, though, Ann suspected that it was a source of wonderment to the locals just how the dislikeable, bad-tempered Rose had managed to be pleasant long enough to get a man to be intimate with her!

Just where the name Belinda had come from Cam did not know, but it was the first that sprang to her mind when Ann asked her what she was going to name the baby. It was a pretty name, and Cam wanted a pretty name to go with the child's lovely smile. Right from that first night Belinda, or Lindy as she became affectionately known, proved to be a contented child. When she woke for a feed or from a dirty nappy, she would just give a little cry, alerting them to the fact that she needed attention. Never once did she give out an ear-shattering, frenzied scream like her mother had done. When she was not sleeping she would lie happily in her cot, in Cam's arms, or on the rug, gurgling contentedly to herself. No friendly females had ever dared poke their head into the pram when Cam had been out and about with Rose, for fear of the scowls and screams they would provoke from her. But with Lindy the locals would go out of their way to stick their heads inside the pram, just to witness her infectious smile and hear her giggles in response to their attention.

Finding a minder for her granddaughter while she went to work had been a huge cause of concern to Cam that first night. She needed to find someone to take her from the following Monday as company rules meant no time off would be given to any employee unless it was to attend the funeral of a close relative or you were on your own death bed. To Cam's great relief a neighbour a few doors down, a capable, likeable young woman with three very young children herself and who Cam knew would welcome the opportunity of earning a few shillings to help eke out her husband's meagre wage, readily agreed when Cam approached her with a proposition to give it a try. Their arrangement was to last for nine years until Lindy was old enough to be responsible for herself before Cam came home from work.

Any fear that Cam had had that Lindy's looks could hold her back from making friends proved to be unfounded. Lindy was so pleasant and fun to have around that she was able to pick and choose for herself who she wanted as her friends. Cam had lost count over the years of the number of times she could not find room to sit in her own house for the number of friends who had come to call on Lindy. On leaving school at fourteen and a half, she had won over interviewers with her likeable personality and been offered every job she had gone after, so was able to chose which one she felt would give her the best prospects. She had settled for a job as an office junior with a firm of solicitors and was attending night school to learn shorthand and typing.

Unlike her mother, who'd done her best to enhance her unattractiveness by wearing shapeless dull-coloured clothes, Lindy did her best to make the most of herself, although Cam knew she did secretly wish she been blessed with a little more meat on her hips and bigger breasts, against what she termed her 'two fried eggs'. Apart from work, when she dressed smartly in a skirt and blouse, for casual wear she leaned towards the beatnik style of the day, choosing slacks and big jumpers or fitted Capri pants and a blouse, but when she went rock and roll dancing with her friends she resembled the pictures Cam had seen in magazines of the American Bobbysoxers in her bright-coloured, full-skirted shirtwaister dresses, with layers of net underskirting underneath. She was a good dancer and never without a male clamouring to partner her. On starting work, the first item she had saved for was a record player so that she could listen in her bedroom to the latest disc she had bought. One of her walls was covered with pictures of the likes of Cliff Richard and the Shadows, Billy Fury, Adam Faith, Elvis Presley, John Leyton, Del Shannon and Eden Kane, and Cam had often spotted her as she had passed the bedroom using a hairbrush as a pretend mic and miming to Helen Shapiro or Connie Francis in the mirror.

Lindy had come into the world facing the same disadvantages as her mother had, but whereas Rose, through her own choice, had wallowed in self-pity and used her lack of looks as a means of venting her anger against the world, Lindy had accepted what she had been given, made the best of it, and had had a happy and fulfilling childhood.

Now she was building herself a promising future. For Cam her fifteen years spent raising Rose had proved miserable and problematic, whereas her fifteen years of raising Lindy had brought her nothing but joy, which she hoped was going to continue for a few more years yet before the girl left home to marry.

Cam tried her best not to think of Rose. Not that she wanted to forget about her daughter, dispel her from her life, but it was unbearable for her to picture just how she was making her living. Cam knew that men might display respect and regard towards women in Rose's chosen profession while these women were satisfying their needs, but outside of that time they were perceived by their clients as the lowest of the low. Men they knew very well would pass them in the street without a second glance. As Cam hadn't heard a word from or of Rose since the night she had presented her with Lindy, she could only presume the girl was still continuing with her plan to make a good deal of money from her employment with Mrs Monks or else had actually done so by now and was the owner of her own establishment. Cam just hoped she was happy and that the life that she had chosen for herself had brought her fulfilment.

Cam had always been aware that a time would come when Lindy would want to know why she lived with her grandmother and not her own mother and father, like her friends all did. She had been four when she had asked. By this time Cam had decided that Rose was never going to regret giving up her child and come back to reclaim her. Lindy was a happy and well-adjusted little girl, so Cam decided to do as Rose had instructed her and tell her that her mother and father had both died in an accident when she had been very tiny. Not quite understanding what death meant at the time, Lindy had thrown her arms around Cam and said that she was glad as she liked living with her nan and didn't ever want to leave. To cover the fact that they shared the same surname, when Lindy queried this Cam was going to tell her that it was pure coincidence her father had had the same surname as her mother.

Cam was shaken out of her memories of the past by Lindy jumping off her bed and announcing, 'I've got a fancy for some chocolate. I'm going to get dressed again and fetch some from the corner shop. Do you need anything while I'm there, Nan?'

Cam shook her head. 'No, thanks, love.' She took a quick glance at her bedside clock and grimaced when she saw the time. 'Oh, goodness, I'd best be off myself as June will be waiting outside for me and Ann already at the pub, saving our seats, wondering where we've got to.' Then she laughed. 'Every Saturday, June proclaims that it's her night for a win. Must be getting on for twenty years now since she joined us at bingo and she's never won so much as a line. Mind you, apart from winning one line, neither Ann nor I have won anything, so I do hope that tonight one of us will win. Keep your fingers crossed for us, love.' Then an old fear overcame her and she said, 'Oh, Lindy, please don't go the back way to the shop down the jitty . . . it's dark and you never know who might be lurking.'

Lindy had no idea why her grandmother always warned her strongly not to travel down any route on a dark night or she might have taken more heed. Going the back way through the jitty was so much quicker than taking the main street. She just said, 'Enjoy yourself, Nan. And when you come in, I'll make us a cup of cocoa and, hopefully, we'll be celebrating your win at long last.'

With that she went happily off to her bedroom to throw on some clothes for her visit to the shop.

Minutes later, as Lindy left by the back door, Cam left by the front, totally unaware that across the road, hidden in the dark shadows of an entry, someone was watching her departure with great interest.

CHAPTER TWENTY-FOUR

As soon as Cam had disappeared around the corner of the street, the figure in the shadows of the entry emerged and made its way towards the entrance to the jitty that led around the back of the houses. Keeping to the shadows, they opened the gate leading into the Rogers' small yard. Slipping inside, the intruder stole across to the back door, taking hold of the knob and smiling as it freely turned and the door opened. It seemed that no one round here locked their doors still, which saved the trouble of having to break in. Inside the kitchen, the trespasser shut the back door behind them, then made their way into the back room and stopped for a moment to take a look around.

Rose had never intended to be in this room again after walking out of it fifteen years ago. That had been the moment when she had pushed all memories of her past life into a box in her mind and locked the lid on it. It was only thanks to yesterday's events that she had been forced to revisit her past. But as soon as she had got what she had come for she'd be off again, locking away the past and the people associated with it and concentrating only on her future. As she looked around, it felt to Rose as if she was in a shabby dolls' house compared to the size of the place she had been working in for the last fifteen years. The same went for her lovely room in the house she had shared with the other girls.

Anger welled up in her as the events of the previous night came flooding back to mind. Fifteen years she had worked for that woman, and not once during that time had she ever had any reason to doubt that Mrs Monks was anything other than a kind and caring employer who had her employees' best interests at heart. Last night Rose had discovered, to her cost, that her employer was nothing of the kind. She only acted benevolently towards her workers while they were contributing towards her profits. As soon as that started to change she showed her true colours.

After five years of working for Mrs Monks, calculating that she must have more than enough saved for what she intended, Rose had gone to see her to tell her that she was leaving her employ and wanted what money was due to her. She couldn't wait to start up her own business and be revered like Mrs Monks was by employees and clients alike. She was rolling in money, always dressed in the latest Paris fashions and dripping with jewellery, with a large chauffeur-driven car to ride around in. Throughout her time in Mrs Monks' house Rose had watched closely to see how the woman ran her operation and had perfected her ideas of just how she wanted her own establishment to be; how she would furnish it, what sort of girls she would have working for her, and how she would operate it.

When Rose had divulged these to her boss after five years in the job, to her shock Mrs Monks' kindly eyes turned to steel. She had told Rose it was she herself who decided when a girl would leave her employ. And she wasn't ready to let Rose go yet; she was far too valuable to her. Rose had her own list of regular clients who would be most disappointed should she leave, and could possibly go elsewhere if Mrs Monks was unable to replace her quickly with another girl who could satisfy these particular clients, the way Rose herself did. Of course, if she insisted on leaving, then Mrs Monks would keep what money she was due to recompense her for her loss of future earnings.

Rose was left in no doubt that she was trapped until Mrs Monks decided she was no longer bringing in the kind of money she expected each of her girls to earn for her. There was nothing she could do about it unless she was willing to turn her back on the money she was due, without which she could kiss goodbye to the kind of future she'd planned to make for herself.

So she stayed on, and another ten years passed. What Rose had at first perceived as an exciting and glamorous profession, she now loathed. She was mortally sick of being pawed about by perverted men, several of whom had left her scarred after they had been rough with her, but thankfully she'd managed to avoid ending up needing the sort of medical attention she knew a number of other girls had when their clients had got carried away. Mrs Monks would have these girls whisked away to be taken care of in a private facility, and then paid off in order to protect the guilty client – a prominent businessman or highly respectable member of society, as all Mrs Monks' clients were. It was rumoured that more than one of those girls had actually died from their injuries. Rose was now desperate to leave the more depraved side of the business to others and be the one running the show and raking in the profits.

Over the last few weeks it hadn't escaped her notice that Mrs Monks had gradually been replacing the older girls like herself with much younger ones. As she was now over thirty, it was apparent to Rose that her list of regular clients was dwindling due to their veering towards the fresh new girls. It was only a matter of time before she was given her marching orders, she knew.

Last night she had finally been called into the office. Mrs Monks wanted a chat with her. Rose wasn't stupid. She knew just what it was about, but would not let Mrs Monks witness how pleased she was that she was finally being released. After being kept waiting for over an hour Rose was joined in the office, not by Mrs Monks herself but by two of the burly henchmen she employed to keep order. Before Rose knew what was happening, one man had grabbed her by her throat and pulled her out of the chair she was sitting on. He pushed his brutish face into hers and told her that her time here was over, warning her in no uncertain terms that if she ever dared show her face around these parts again she would end up the same way that several other obstinate girls had: in the mortuary. Next thing she knew Rose was being frogmarched off the premises by the back way, the other henchman following behind with her case of belongings which had been packed unknown to her while she had been waiting in the office.

As she had been pushed out of the back gate, her case of belongings thrown out after her, she had frenziedly asked about the money she was owed by Mrs Monks and when she would get it. The men's response had been to laugh at her harshly as the gate had been slammed shut on her and she heard several bolts being shot.

She had been numb with shock, powerless to move, barely able to comprehend that as each week had passed over the last fifteen years Mrs Monks had been lining her own pockets with Rose's money – and there was absolutely nothing she could do about it. Not unless she wanted to risk ending up dead.

So wretched did she feel, she couldn't remember picking up her case and walking to Victoria Park or sitting down on a bench there until she became aware of pounding footsteps and looked up to see a scruffy young boy of about sixteen years old, who didn't look like he'd had a wash for weeks, arriving at a bench a little distance away and plonking himself down on it, panting heavily. He had something in his hand which he opened up. Rose saw it was a wallet. She watched as he proceeded to count the money inside. It was obvious to her that the boy had pickpocketed the wallet and was counting his spoils. He sensed someone watching him and his head jerked up. He stared at her blindly for a moment, it being apparent he hadn't noticed her when he had first arrived. He hurriedly stuffed the wallet in the pocket of his worn jacket, jumped up from the bench and ran off.

Rose's thoughts returned to the question of what she was going to do for money now.

Her eyes caught sight of the suitcase by her feet and her shoulders slumped despairingly. Inside that case was all she had to show for her fifteen years of hard labour for the double-crossing Mrs Monks. Then, like a bolt of lightning, a thought struck her and her spirits lifted. She did still have something to show for her years of effort ... the jewellery bestowed on her by gratified clients. At first she had been thrilled to receive the gifts, but after a while the novelty had worn off and she just chucked whatever she received along with the rest in a box, only wearing a few of her favourite pieces. She wasn't actually sure just how many valuables she had accumulated but it was all good quality stuff, from reputable jewellers, some of the pieces encrusted with precious stones. Surely collectively it would fetch a good sum. Maybe not the thousand pounds she had wanted behind her, but a few hundred at least. She could do a lot with that towards setting herself up.

Bending, she tipped over her case and slid the catches. When she saw how little was actually inside, Rose scowled darkly. Only a fraction of the clothes she possessed had been packed, and no shoes; neither had the sable coat she'd bought only a few weeks ago from the furriers on London Road, nor her extensive array of toiletries and perfumes. Then her heart started to race as panic reared within her. Had her jewellery box been packed? Frantically she rummaged around. It was not until she had tipped everything out of the case and there was still no sign of the box that she admitted to herself that not only had Mrs Monks been helping herself to her earnings, she had also helped herself to anything of value Rose owned before she had had her turfed out. With murder in her heart for the woman who had given her such hopes for a lucrative future for herself, only to take them away so cruelly when Rose was no longer of use to her, she rammed everything back in the case and slammed shut the lid. Despite that thug's threats to her life, one day she was determined to find a way to get even with that woman.

She was startled by a slurred male voice asking her, ''Ow much then, love?'

Rose looked up to see a shabby, drunken, middle-aged man swaying before her. She scowled darkly at him and hissed, 'You couldn't afford me. Are you too drunk to see that I'm not your common or garden street woman? I wouldn't let the likes of you kiss my feet . . . let alone anything else.'

Through bleary eyes, he stared at her for a moment before he snorted, 'My God, but you're ugly. Forget what I asked yer. I ain't that desperate.'

With that, he stumbled off, laughing.

The encounter only served to remind Rose that unless she found another establishment that catered for the kind of clientele Mrs Monks had, she would have to find another way to make herself the kind of money she needed. She wasn't fussy what she did, from burglary to blackmail. Thankfully for her, she had learned many new tricks from the other girls about how they had made themselves lucrative livings before Mrs Monks had employed them. It was just a matter of copying what she felt was the least risky caper: the one that would bring her the best reward in the shortest time.

And she'd better decide quick and start carrying out her plan because the thirty shillings she had in her purse wouldn't get her far. It would just about cover some cheap lodgings and food for a week. How she now regretted squandering the pocket money Mrs Monks had handed her each week Had she known then what she did now, saving even half of that over fifteen years would have amassed a nice tidy sum for her that would have got her off to the start she wanted. But, oblivious, she had wasted most of it on the extensive wardrobe of clothes that she had quickly tired of and continually replaced, drawers full of underwear, dozens of pairs of shoes – some of them never worn, quality makeup, expensive toiletries and perfumes, ornaments and soft furnishings to make her room in the shared house more individual. She had got such a thrill out of patronising expensive shops, witnessing the sneering looks the snobby assistants had shot her when she first entered, then the way their attitudes completely changed towards her when she let it be known she had money to spend. They'd respectfully call her 'madam' then, and pull out chairs for her to sit on while they attended to her. Rose was used to that sort of treatment now and she was damned if she was going to return to any shabbier way of life. If only she had some savings . . .

The word danced in her mind's eye, like a large neon sign. She *did* have savings. Not much, granted, but better than nothing.

When her mother's financial situation had improved with her wartime salary, she had opened a Post Office savings account for Rose, putting whatever she could afford into it each week, telling the girl that when it was time for her to go to work she could draw out what was saved in order to kit herself out with work clothes and anything else she needed to look smart for her job. Rose reckoned there could be a good £5 in that savings book now. Used sparingly, it could keep her for the couple of weeks it would take her to come up with a way to make her start-up fund. She knew her mother well enough to realise that she would not have cashed those savings in as they were for her daughter, not her, and the money would still be left intact for Rose's return. Well, she would return home tomorrow . . . but only for as long as it took to get her savings book. And while she was there, she might as well have a look round for anything else worth a few bob that she could pawn.

It was Saturday tomorrow. Hopefully her mother's habits hadn't changed and she'd be out at the pub with that busybody friend of hers and her husband. Rose would have her chance then to break into the house, and plenty of time to root out what she was after.

Now, safely undetected inside the back room of her old home, having had a quick look round and found nothing she felt was worth more than a few pennies, Rose made her way upstairs to her mother's room in search of a bigger prize.

Rose knew that all women kept anything of value in their dressing-table drawers, so on entering the room she immediately made her way over to these. Cam's was the kind of dressing-table that had three drawers to each side of it, and Rose found what she was after in the second drawer down on the left-hand side. Much to her delight, there was not just one Post Office savings book, but three. As she opened one after the other to check the balances her heart leaped higher and higher. The balances of the three books combined amounted to nearly £240. Considering that the average factory wage for a man was £4 a week, or less even in this year of 1961, this was a small fortune for the likes of her mother to have saved up. But then, her mother had always told Rose that if she took care of the pennies, the pounds would soon mount, and it seemed she had followed her own teaching – to Rose's benefit. The amount still wasn't enough for what she needed to set herself up with, but it would keep her more in the style to which she was accustomed than the few pounds she'd thought she was getting.

She put the savings books in her coat pocket and, after looking through her mother's jewellery box and finding nothing of any worth to her amongst the cheap Woolworth's costume jewellery, was about to leave when her eyes fell on a book on her mother's bed. Rose hadn't read a book for a long time as her love of reading in her spare time had been replaced by a love of browsing the shops and revelling in the attention she received there. Well, now she hadn't the money to shop, so while she was making her plans, this book might help her while away some time in her lodgings. She walked over to the bed to pick it up.

Meanwhile, downstairs, Lindy had just arrived home by the back room and was taking off her coat when she stopped short hearing footsteps crossing her grandmother's bedroom. She felt her heart start to thump. Panic reared within her. There was an intruder in the house! They were being burgled! She wondered what she should do. She thought she could run around to fetch Arthur Evans from next-door to tackle the burglar, but then she realised it was Saturday and all the men in the street would be propping up their favourite bar, including Arthur. The local bobby could be in any street on his beat. The burglar would be long gone, along with their possessions, by the time she found him and brought him back. There was nothing for it but for Lindy herself to confront the trespasser. It would be wise to arm herself in case they turned violent on being caught in the act so she dashed across to the fireplace to grab up the poker.

Meanwhile, back in Cam's bedroom, Rose was frowning in disgust at the book in her hand: *Oliver Twist* by Charles Dickens. She had read it as a child and, if her memory served her right, this was the very same copy, one of a set of five, which her mother had bought her. Not the sort of story that Rose had come to enjoy when she had reached her teens and discovered romance novels, with their handsome heroes and pretty heroines. She would go into her old bedroom and see if her mother had kept any of those.

She was about to throw the book back where she had found it when the door flew open and a young woman bounded in, brandishing a poker and crying out, 'Got yer!'

The two of them then stared at one another agog.

CHAPTER TWENTY-FIVE

L indy had been expecting a man to accost her, not a woman. And certainly not a woman who looked so very familiar to her, though she couldn't for the life of her think why as she knew they had never met before.

Rose felt as if she was looking in the mirror at a younger version of herself, apart from the fact that this girl was taller than she was and wasn't concealing her slim figure under baggy, shapeless clothes or her unattractive face behind a mop of hair, like Rose used to do. Who was she? Then it hit her. Of course she knew who this was! It hadn't struck her at first because she hadn't given the girl a second thought from the moment she had walked out of this house fifteen years ago. So this was the child she herself had borne. Rose couldn't think of her as her daughter as she felt no connection to her at all, had absolutely no feelings whatsoever for her. But she had certainly got her wish: the girl took after her in looks. So much so that her mother must have been constantly reminded of her appalling treatment of Rose while raising her offspring.

Lindy found her voice again. Waving the poker menacingly, she demanded, 'Who are you? And what are you doing in my grandmother's bedroom?'

Rose answered her matter-of-factly. 'Fetching something that belongs to me.'

Lindy glanced at the book in her hand and seemed deeply puzzled. 'My book? You broke in here for that?'

Rose answered sardonically, 'Actually, it isn't your book, it's mine, not that it's . . .' Her voice suddenly trailed off. She'd been about to say it was none of the girl's business what she had come back for, but as she opened her mouth to do so she had an idea. And it was all thanks to the book she was holding in her hand. Rose immediately lapsed deep into thought as her idea started to take root.

Lindy was meanwhile staring at her in confusion. 'What do you mean, it isn't my book but yours?'

Rose flashed a dark glance at her. 'Shut up while I'm thinking!'

Lindy gawped. 'What?'

'You heard. Keep quiet.'

Lindy couldn't believe this woman had ordered her to shut up, considering she had broken into her grandmother is house. She was struck speechless by her gall.

Rose's money-making plan was already formulated, thanks to Charles Dickens and Mrs Monks, but she just wanted a moment's peace to go over it and tweak it here and there. Make sure that nothing could be traced back to her if the law got wind of what was going on. It was such a good plan . . . she knew it could work! She envisaged it would take her a couple of weeks to find and take up the rent on the two properties she'd need, and also find the type of youngsters she was after to work for her. Ones like the youth she'd seen in the park last night, checking what he'd procured for himself by his light fingers. But her most important employee would be a housekeeper who'd look after the workers and be made a scapegoat of should the law get wind of what was going on before Rose had made enough money for her needs and had closed the operation down. She needed someone she could manipulate; someone who would do her bidding without question. And now she had the perfect candidate in mind.

All she had to do was manoeuvre this girl into joining her. She lifted her head and looked at Lindy. She was young and impressionable. The story Rose was about to tell her should do the trick.

The fact that she was about to destroy a young girl's whole world to further her own selfish aims was of no consequence to Rose.

Taking a deep breath, she plastered a look of deep apology on her face. Wringing her hands in a distraught way, she said, 'I'm so sorry I snapped at you. You see, I've been planning this moment for such a long time that, when it came to it, I got cold feet . . . worried how you'd react to me. I wasn't sure what you knew about me . . . what she'd told you. I was waiting across the street for her to go out, hoping she still did on a Saturday night, then just praying that I caught you or I'd have to come back again and again until I did. You've caught me just having a last look around my old home before I left. When I told you I was here to fetch something that belonged to me . . . well, that's you, you see?'

Lindy was looking utterly bewildered, her mind fighting to make sense of what was being said to her. The arm still holding the poker aloft was slowly lowered and she mouthed, 'Me? But what have you got to do with me?'

Rose planted a look of deep sorrow on her face. 'Haven't you realised by now? I'm your mother.'

'What!' the girl exclaimed, shocked. She then shook her head vehemently. 'I don't know who you are but you're not my mother. She's dead.'

Rose gasped and forced tears to her eyes by thinking of all the money Mrs Monks had fleeced her out of. 'She told you that? How could she be so cruel? I am your mother, please believe me.' She leaped over and grabbed Lindy's arm, pulling her in front of Cam's dressing-table mirror. 'You only have to look at us to see I am. We're the image of each other.'

It was Lindy's turn to gasp. Now she realised why this woman had seemed so familiar to her when she had first set eyes on her. She couldn't deny their strong likeness to one other. She shook herself free from Rose's grasp on her arm and walked over to the bed, sinking down on it, trying to digest what she had just been told. Still having difficulty, she looked across at the woman claiming to be her mother, and asked, 'If you are my mother then why has it been Nan who's raised me and not you? Why did she tell me you were dead . . . you and my father in an accident when I was tiny? Why has it taken you fifteen years to come back for me?'

The despicable lies tripped unashamedly off Rose's tongue. 'I was sixteen when I had you – in no position to raise you without Mother's help and she wouldn't entertain the idea, no matter how much I begged her. The only way I could avoid your being adopted or put in an orphanage was to blackmail her into taking you herself, but even then she still insisted she would only do it if I agreed to her terms.

Said she couldn't face the shame of anyone knowing her granddaughter was illegitimate.'

Lindy's face paled and she stared at her aghast. 'I'm illegitimate! My father never died in an accident? You weren't married to him?'

Rose shook her head.

Lindy was mortified by this shocking news about herself and for several moments tried her hardest to digest it, but she couldn't because the grandmother that she knew and loved was definitely not the person this woman was describing. Lindy looked across at her and exclaimed with conviction, 'But my nan would never treat anyone like you're saying she did you. She's never been bothered what the neighbours think. You're lying about her . . . you've got to be.'

'Your grandmother is not the woman you think she is. She's cold-hearted and callous. Maybe you've never done anything to show her up before the neighbours so you've never seen this side of her. Until I got pregnant with you, I thought she was a lovely woman and that I couldn't have wished for a better mother. What a shock I got when I discovered the truth!' Rose stepped across to the bed. She sat down and patted the top of it so Lindy would join her. 'Look, Jessica . . .'

The girl blurted, 'Why did you call me Jessica? My name is Belinda . . . everyone calls me Lindy for short.'

Rose planted a look of deep hurt on her face and cried, 'She changed your name! Was she determined to take away everything from me? She knew I wanted to name you Jessica. You need to know the whole story and then you'll see the kind of woman your grandmother *really* is.

'You came about because I was out with my group of friends one Saturday night. We were down the park, just chatting and having a lark. Then this lad I'd never seen before joined us. He sat next to me on a bench and told me he had recently moved into the area with his family. We just chatted. I told him about the youth club that we all went to on a Thursday night, and about my job as an office junior in a local factory. I didn't realise until afterwards that he never actually told me anything about himself at all. Anyway, before I knew it, it was time for me to go home. By now all the others had gone in and it was just me and the lad left.

'He looked upset when I told him I had to go and asked me to stay a little longer as he liked being with me. I'd never had a lad show interest in me like that before . . . I tried not to let it bother me but I knew lads didn't really find me attractive and it was the prettier ones they went after, so I was very flattered by his attention.' She paused and looked at Lindy knowingly. 'I expect you understand exactly how it was for me . . . you looking like me? I'd resigned myself to the fact I'd never have a boyfriend. I expect you have too.'

Lindy opened her mouth to tell Rose that she had eyes. Although Nan was always telling her she was pretty, she knew she hadn't been blessed in the looks department but had certainly not resigned herself to never having a boyfriend as in fact she'd had several already. But she never got the chance as Rose was already continuing.

'The lad then pulled a bottle out of his pocket . . . sherry it was . . . and asked if I wanted a drink. Said it would warm me up as it was getting chilly by then. I'd never had an alcoholic drink before except for a small glass of egg nog at Christmas, but, stupid as it was of me, I didn't want him to think I was childish so I took the bottle off him and had a mouthful. It was horrid and burned the back of my throat, but I never let on. I did like the feel of the warm glow inside me, though, and I didn't feel quite so awkward or on edge. I had a couple more swallows after that, thinking it wouldn't hurt. When he kissed me . . . well, I'd never been kissed before and for me it was like fireworks were going off in my head. Next thing I knew we were in the bushes and he was standing up, doing up his trousers, telling me he had to get home or he risked a thick ear off his dad if he was late. Then he was gone.

'I realised I didn't even know his name. Mother had always told me I wasn't to let a boy touch me anywhere intimate until I was married. I felt deeply ashamed of what I'd done. I decided not to tell anyone and forget about it, hope I never saw him again.

'I was naive in those days, but I did know that your monthly stopped when you were pregnant. When I hadn't had my monthly curse for two months, I plucked up the courage to tell Mother. I expected her to be upset, tell me how stupid I'd been . . . of course I did, I was only fifteen after all . . . but when she'd calmed down, I thought she would put her arms around me and tell me that she would stand by me. I wasn't expecting to see such rage at my news. She called me a slut and a whore, amongst other things, and told me that she wasn't going to allow me to bring shame on her. I wasn't to mention a word of my condition to anyone, ever. She was going to arrange for me to go into a home for unmarried mothers to have my baby, and they would arrange to have it adopted. To cover my absence up, she was going to tell anyone who asked that I was with a relative who needed help after having twins. After the baby was born I was to come back here and carry on as if nothing had happened.

'I was fifteen and, if I'm honest, I didn't want to be a mother then so I was glad my own mother was taking control. Within days I was in the home. It was run by nuns and there were strict rules to abide by, but it wasn't too bad. Most of the other girls in there in my position were friendly enough.

'Trouble was, though, that when I started to feel you moving inside me, I started to love you. By the time you were due to be born, I just couldn't bear the thought of parting with you and made plans to escape the home with you before they handed you over to the parents they'd found for you. I found out through one of the nuns what would happen when I gave birth. She told me that because I was underage it was my mother who would have to sign the papers agreeing to the baby's adoption. As soon as my baby was born, Mother would be sent for and so would the people who were going to take it. Meanwhile they would leave me with my baby so I could say goodbye to it. That would be my only chance to slip out with you.'

Rose paused momentarily, pretending to draw breath but in reality taking a quick look at the young girl's face so she could tell whether her tissue of lies was being accepted. To Rose's gratification, there was no look of scepticism. So far so good, she thought.

'I was very friendly with one of the other girls and took her into my confidence. She agreed to help me. As soon as I knew I was in labour, before I even summoned the nuns, I would let her know. When I was taken down to the labour room, she would slip into my room and pack up my belongings. The nuns knew we were friends so wouldn't think it odd that ... er ... Mabel would be wanting regular updates on how I was getting on. Even if it was during the night, she would make them believe she couldn't sleep because she was anxious about me. As soon as the nuns left me alone to say goodbye to my baby, she would slip my suitcase to me, I would get dressed and sneak off with you out of the back way, down by the laundry room. I just had to hope that I managed to get out of the grounds before it was discovered I was gone. Our plan worked a treat. I was very wobbly and weak but I found the strength because I just couldn't bear to be parted from you. You were my child and I loved you and I wasn't going to let you go.

'I had nowhere to go but home and prayed that once I was there I could persuade Mother to change her mind and let me keep you. I was so nervous waiting for her to come back from her wasted trip to the unmarried mothers' home. I knew she'd be annoyed with me for what I'd done, and cross about having to face the neighbours. I hadn't expected her flatly to refuse me a home or any help. I begged and pleaded with her to let me keep you. She absolutely refused, wouldn't budge. She told me to put my coat back on, that she was taking me straight back to the nuns to hand you over for adoption. Apparently she'd been promised a pay off from the new parents. She had a basket to conceal the baby in, in case any neighbours were lurking outside.

'I couldn't believe she was willing to give her own granddaughter away sooner than face some idle gossip. But I was not willing to give you up until I'd tried all I could. I told her that if she didn't let me keep you, I would make sure all the locals knew what she'd made me do. And not just that . . . the fact that she had sold her granddaughter for money. I told her I'd like to see her live *that* down. She knew I meant what I said. That I would do it. She said the only way she would agree not to insist I had you adopted was if I gave you up to her. She said she would come up with some way to excuse you to the locals and save her face, but I was never to darken her door again for any reason but live the other side of town so we never bumped into each other. If I dared show my face, she would call the police and say she'd found me robbing the place and have me slung in jail. It was up to me. If I loved you as much as I said I did, then I would agree to that.'

Rose paused and heaved a theatrical sigh, conjuring a look of deep sorrow on to her face. 'The thought of never seeing you again was unbearable to me, but her offer was at least better than me worrying if your adoptive parents were treating you well and if you were happy with them. So I had no choice but to agree to her terms. She told me to leave then. I told her I had no money and would she give me some, just so I could get myself some lodgings and to tide me over while I got a job and my first pay packet? She laughed at me. Was I seriously asking her for money when she had stuff to buy for a baby she'd never asked for and a roof to keep over its head until it was old enough to fend for itself? I remembered my savings then. Mother had always encouraged me to save, and from any errands or babysitting I did for the neighbours I'd always put half the money in my Post Office savings account. I had nearly three pounds in it. Mother said I wasn't having it as she would need that for the baby too.

'So she sent me packing without a penny in my pocket and wouldn't even let me give you one last kiss or a cuddle. If it hadn't been for old Molly, out walking her dog and coming across me crying my heart out on a park bench, I'd have starved or frozen to death. She offered to take me home and, bless the old dear, let me stay there until I found a job and could afford to get myself lodgings. I don't know what I would have done without her. The last fifteen years have been so hard for me, especially at Christmas and on your birthday. I never married. I did have a couple of chances, but I couldn't have any more children as I felt that would be betraying you.' Rose lowered her head, again wringing her hands. 'I feel so awful . . . terrible . . . to be telling you this about your grandmother, but was it not awful of her to let you believe your mother was dead? I'd have done anything to be allowed to raise you only I wasn't . . . and all because of her fear of being looked down on by the locals. It's not right of her to have denied me my child and you of knowing your mother, is it?'

A mortified Lindy, her eyes tear-filled, was shaking her head in incredulity. 'I can't believe Nan lied to me about you being dead . . . and my father too. But how could she force you to abandon your baby . . . me . . . like she did? That was so cruel of her. How could she make you leave the house, knowing you'd no money? Anything could have happened to you.'

Rose inwardly smiled to herself. This stupid young girl had believed everything she had said. She wasn't quite finished blackening her grandmother to her yet, though. She just had to make absolutely sure Lindy was well and truly sucked in. She said softly, 'I was always worried about . . . well, whether she hit you?'

Lindy looked at her, puzzled. 'Hit me? Nan has never lifted a finger to me so why would you worry about her doing that?'

Rose made a great display of looking mortally relieved to hear this. 'Thank God! You obviously didn't give her any reason to. I'll always carry the scars from her attacks on me.' To prove her point, she pulled up the sleeve of her blouse and showed Lindy a deep scar on the top of her arm that had actually been caused when a client had tied her to the bed post too tightly. The rope had cut into her skin and turned it septic. After giving Lindy a long look, Rose pulled down her sleeve, telling her, 'Mother did it with the poker. The same one you're holding, in fact.'

Lindy gazed at her in horror, clamping her hand to her mouth, shocked by this revelation. The poker dropped out of her hand, to land with a heavy thud on the floor.

Rose went on, 'Twice Mother attacked me. The first time was when I told her I was pregnant. After calling me what she did, she seemed to lose control of herself and started lashing out at me with her fists. Then she took up the poker and starting hitting me with it. The second time was when I came back here with you, the day you were born, to beg her to let me keep you.'

Lindy's eyes were darting wildly. If anyone else had told her this story about her grandmother she would never have believed it, but the woman before her wasn't just anyone, she was her own mother, the woman her grandmother had told her was dead. And if she had doubted her grandmother was capable of physically attacking anyone, her mother had just proved it by showing her the damage that had been inflicted on her. Lindy frenziedly cried, 'I hate Nan for what she's done to you . . . to me! I *hate* her. How am I expected to continue living with her, knowing what I do about her now?'

Rose grabbed her hand. 'That's just it . . . you don't have to. You don't ever have to see her again. I've never before been in a position to be able to offer you a home, but I've had this amazing bit of luck. Remember that old lady I said first took me in when Mother abandoned me that night? Well, I always kept in touch with her after I'd moved on. She died last week and has left me some money. It was a shock to me, I can tell you, I never thought she had two ha'pennies to rub together, but it just shows how wrong you can be about people. Anyway, the money meant that at last I could offer you a home with me. It wasn't a fortune, but enough to build us a new future on.

'As a start, I plan to get a lodging house. It won't be up to much and not in the best of areas, but it'll be comfortable and clean. There are always people crying out for good lodgings. If we both live as cheaply as we can and do all the work so we don't need to pay any staff, we can save up most of the profits and then, when we've enough, put it towards getting another lodging house. Before long we'll have our own string of houses and will be living in luxury on the proceeds.'

Lindy was looking at her, wide-eyed. 'You really came back for me? You really want me with you?'

'There's nothing I want more. It's what I've dreamed of since the day *she* took you off me and kicked me out.'

Lindy threw her arms around her and hugged her fiercely. 'Oh, Mum, Mum!' she uttered, over and over.

Rose had to force herself to respond.

Finally Lindy released her and said, 'I've got some money. I want you to have my savings towards setting up the lodging house.'

I've already got your savings, or I will have when I go to the Post Office with your book on Monday, along with the two others, Rose thought maliciously. What she said was, 'Go and pack your stuff and we'll be ready to face Mother with the news we have to tell her as soon as she comes in.'

Rose smiled to herself as Lindy jumped up and rushed out of the room. She rubbed her hands together. She'd got her scapegoat!

While they waited for Cam to return, Rose continued to enthuse to Lindy about her plans for their future; about all the things they were going to do together now they were reunited. She was careful to keep up the façade of a mother delighted to have got back the beloved child she'd had taken off her through no fault of her own.

Cam had had a really enjoyable night at bingo, although, once again, neither June nor Ann nor she had won anything. However, she was looking forward to getting home and telling Lindy all about it over a cup of hot milky cocoa. She was feeling just a little tiddly after her three bottles of light ale, and was giggling to herself over something Ann had said when she arrived in the kitchen and called out, 'It's only me, love.'

In the process of taking off her coat she walked a little unsteadily into the back room, ready to address her granddaughter whom she was expecting to find curled up in the armchair, either reading her book or watching a programme on the black-and-white television, but she stopped in her tracks to stare, dumbstruck, at the person standing with their back to the fireplace. 'Rose!' she uttered. To her confusion, she then took in the fact that Rose was holding the poker in her hand and that Lindy was standing beside her, throwing Cam a look of loathing. By her feet was a suitcase and a couple of carrier bags which looked like they'd all her belongings inside them.

Before Cam could get her thoughts in order, Rose waved the poker at her and spat nastily, 'Don't dare think of setting about me or my daughter or I'll use this on you, the same as you used it on me. And don't waste your time trying to make out I'm a liar as I've shown *my daughter* just one of the scars I was left with after you attacked me.'

Astounded by such an outrageous accusation, Cam erupted, 'Oh, Rose, I have never . . .'

She was cut short by Lindy angrily crying out, 'How could you hit my mother like you did – and when she was pregnant? And how could you lie to me for all these years, telling me my mother was dead? You lied about my father too. You're not the woman I thought you were at all. You're cruel! I don't know how you sleep at night. I hate you,' she shouted.

Cam's face drained of colour as she implored her, 'But your mother told me . . .'

Rose erupted then. 'There's no point in trying to lie your way out of this. I've told her everything. She knows all about how you gave me no choice but to leave her with you and never darken your door again for fear you'd have her adopted. She doesn't want anything more to do with you. I had no way of looking after her before, but now I have and she's coming to live with me. She's my daughter and there's nothing *you* can do about it.' She turned to look at Lindy. 'I can't bear to stay with this woman any longer. Come on, let's go.'

'I want my savings book,' Lindy demanded.

Rose ordered Cam, 'Hurry up and get it, we've a bus to catch.'

Cam cried beseechingly, 'Lindy, please listen . . .'

Rose menacingly waved the poker at her. 'I said, hurry up and fetch it.'

Shaking like a leaf, Cam ran from the room and up the stairs. The thoughts were all jumbled inside her mind. She just couldn't think straight. She rummaged through the drawer she kept the savings book in and thought she was going mad because she couldn't find it. But she knew she had put it back there after depositing some money last Saturday on behalf of Lindy. And it wasn't just that book that wasn't there; neither was her own savings book or Rose's either. Cam rummaged in her other drawers but they yielded nothing.

She returned downstairs. 'I'm sorry, Lindy, I've mislaid your savings book.'

As she addressed her granddaughter, out of the corner of her eye she saw a hint of a smile twitch at the corners of Rose's lips and knew then why she couldn't find the books. Rose had got them.

Lindy was snarling at her, 'Well, you'd better find it, because it's *my* money and we need every penny of it to put towards our new business, don't we, Mum? I'll be back for it.'

It took Rose a long second to realise who Lindy was calling 'Mum'. 'Yes . . . yes, we do,' she said hurriedly, and gave Lindy a nudge to make her pick up her belongings.

Cam's heart was thumping madly. As Lindy walked past her towards the door, she grabbed her arm and begged, 'Please, just hear me out before you go. Please, Lindy . . . please?'

The girl cried harshly at her, 'Get your hands off me!'

At her tone, Cam released her hold on her as if she was letting go of a hot coal. Helpless, she watched as Lindy walked out of the door followed closely by her mother. Just before Rose walked out of the back door, she turned her head and shot Cam a look of pure triumph.

Ann, dressed in her nightclothes, metal curlers in her hair and a brown hairnet covering them, was just about to make her way up the stairs to join Brian when she almost jumped out of her skin. There was a hammering at the front door and a frenzied voice was calling out, 'Ann? Ann, I need to speak to you. Ann, Ann!'

It was Cam. Ann had only left her half an hour ago and, apart from being a little tiddly, she was fine then. Feeling puzzled as to what could have happened, she hurried over to the front door, took the snib off the lock and yanked it open. An hysterical Cam almost fell inside but was just stopped by Ann catching hold of her.

'Good God, gel, what's ado?' she demanded as she shut the door.

Wild-eyed, Cam opened her mouth. To Ann, what came out was a frenzied, incoherent babble. She grabbed hold of Cam's arms and gave her a good shake, ordering, 'Take a breath, for God's sake. Calm down . . . I can't make out a word you're saying.' She then proceeded to haul her friend along the corridor and into the kitchen. After pulling a chair out for her, Ann sat herself down on the chair opposite and ordered her friend, 'Right. Now, tell me what's going on, in words I can understand.'

A while later, a grave-faced Ann leaned over and placed her hand on Cam's. She looked into her friend's harrowed, tear-streaked face. 'Look, love, I've no idea either what Rose's motive would be for suddenly wanting to be a mother to her daughter or why she had to blacken your name with such terrible lies to get Lindy to go off with her. If she has taken your savings books, like you suspect she has, then she's not changed any for the better during these last fifteen years.

'As to this business Lindy told you they were going to go into together, well, I certainly do appreciate why you're worried in light of the one Rose has been involved in. Still, if that's what Rose has in mind, give Lindy some credit, Cam. She's a bright girl with a good head on her shoulders. No matter how much Rose has suckered her into believing that she wants to make up for all the time she's been denied motherhood, Lindy wouldn't knowingly get involved in anything she didn't consider right. You know as well as I do that it's not in Rose to be nicey-nicey for long. Sooner rather than later she's going to let her smoke-screen slip and then Lindy will see her for what she is and be straight back with you, where she belongs.'

Cam sniffed miserably and wiped her eyes on her sodden hankerchief. She hoped Ann was right.

'Meantime, love, there's nothing you can do but get on with your own life.' Ann got up then and tightened the faded pink candlewick dressing gown around her full figure. 'I'm going to make you a cuppa and put a dollop of whisky in it, then you're going up to sleep the night in our spare room. And I'm not taking no for an answer.'

CHAPTER TWENTY-SIX

Rose's perseverance had finally paid off. For three days she had been closely watching a group of lads in town as they had gone about their business. She felt sure they would admirably suit her purpose. Twice she had lost them as she had followed after them in the hope they would lead her to their headquarters where she planned to tackle them with her proposition, but the third attempt was to prove successful.

She watched them now from the wall she was secreted behind, as, having first checked around to make sure they were not being followed, they picked their way over potentially dangerous mounds of building rubble to get to a crumbling, derelict warehouse. They pulled aside a piece of rusting corrugated-iron sheeting and disappeared through the hole in a wall it was hiding.

In her quest to bring her plan to fruition Rose was willing to risk life and limb. After first making certain no one was watching her, she followed after them.

Having pulled the corrugated iron back over the hole she had climbed through, she found herself in a dark dirty corridor, the floor strewn with rubble. There were stairs to the front of her, leading up to the floors above and down to the basement level. She stood still for a moment and listened. She could just make out the very faint murmur of voices. They appeared to be coming from below. Rose went over to the basement stairs and trod softly down them, not wanting to alert anyone to her presence until she was ready to announce herself.

At the bottom of the stairs she again found herself in a corridor leading into the distance. There were many rooms off it: old store-rooms, she assumed. The air was pungent with the smells of damp and decay along with candle and cigarette smoke. There was not much light down here, it was very gloomy in fact, and Rose was thankful it wasn't dark outside or she would have had a job seeing anything. The voices were clearer now and they appeared to be coming from a room near the end. She could see the flicker of candlelight on the floor outside the open door.

She arrived at the room she was aiming for and took a deep breath to ready herself. The success of the meeting she was about to have was paramount to her putting the last stage of her plan into place.

Finding the right property to suit her purpose had been much easier than she had dared hope. The morning after she had taken Lindy back to her hotel room with her, telling the girl she was off on a quick errand and to amuse herself while she was gone, Rose set out early to visit three different Post Offices and collect the cash out of the three savings books to which she had helped herself. Then she visited local estate agents. She found what she was after at the third agent she called on. It was a hundred-year-old, flat-fronted, four-storey property, in reasonable repair, sandwiched between a factory and a row of shops in the rundown area of Highfield, on the outskirts of town. The ground floor had a reasonable-sized living-room with cast-iron fireplace, dining-room, and kitchen with an old-fashioned range. On the first floor were one large bedroom, one smaller one, and a bathroom; the next two floors each had two bedrooms; and in the attic were servants' quarters of a small boxroom and bathroom. Rose planned to pack as many single beds into the sleeping quarters as possible: sixteen in total. That should bring her in the best possible return.

The radiators were heated by a coal-fired boiler situated in the cellar. The rundown premises had been for sale for over two years and the owner was at the stage where he thought he would never sell what he was now perceiving as a white elephant. Rose did not want to buy the house, she didn't plan to be in this particular business for longer than six months, so she persuaded the agent to ask the owner if she could rent it for that long, with a view to buying it later if her business were successful. The owner readily agreed, glad to be making some money out of the place at last. The expected rent was relayed to Rose who knocked a pound a week off it and said that was all she was prepared to pay. A deal was struck. She signed the contract using the name Belinda Rogers.

On arriving back at the hotel room, she excitedly told Lindy that their business together had just got off the ground as she had happened to be passing an estate agent's and in their window had seen advertised the ideal premises for their business, which she'd wasted no time in securing for them. Telling Lindy that she herself would take on the task of getting the building ready for occupation, she then despatched the excited girl on a mission to trawl the second-hand shops for sixteen single cast-iron bed frames, the same number of mattresses and sets of bedding, plus all the other things they would need to run the lodging house – but not without first priming her how to haggle with the pawnbroker for the lowest price he would take, especially if she was buying several items at the same place. Rose then got a taxi back to Highfields and, by looking in shop windows, found two local women to blitz the building from top to bottom and an odd job man to do a quick cosmetic tidy up on the place: resticking peeling wallpaper, emulsioning over what wasn't repairable and cleaning out and firing up the boiler.

The whole operation from start to finish took just over a week and a half to complete, much to Rose's delight. Leaving Lindy making beds and hanging up cheap curtains, she had then set off in search of the sort of lodgers she was after . . . the ones she now hoped she had found.

Rose stepped inside the room. A vile smell of body odour hit her from a number of shabby and grubby-looking young males. Doing a quick scan around, she calculated there were about fourteen to sixteen of them, which was just the number she was after to fill her rooms and make the maximum amount of money. Their ages ranged between fifteen and seventeen. They were lolling on several dirty-looking flock mattresses and threadbare blankets. All but one of them were smoking roll-up cigarettes. Several candles sitting on jam-jar lids lit the room with a flickering light. Empty beer bottles and chip wrappers were strewn about. Beyond the other smells, the room stank of unwashed bodies and dirty clothes. Immediately she entered, heads turned and eyes stared at her in alarm.

The oldest of the boys, whose drunken slut of a mother would unkindly have described the tiny woman who'd just come in as having a face like a money sucking a sour lemon, shouted over to her, 'Who the fuck are you?'

Rose smiled at him and said casually, 'Don't worry, I'm not from the authorities. I might just turn out to be your guardian angel.'

He gave her a funny look. 'We don't need no guardian angel. We're doing all right by ourselves. Now fuck off!'

'Yeah, that's right, Bernie, tell her to clear off. She's no right to be coming in our gaff wi'out us asking 'er,' piped up another boy.

Rose pulled a disdainful face as she glanced around and said sardonically, 'Yes, it certainly looks like you're doing all right for yourselves. When was the last time you all had a proper hot meal?'

She was eyed with suspicion. 'You one of them do-gooders from the church, here to try and save us?'

Rose shook her head. 'I've never been to church in my life.'

'So why should you be bothered whether we're all eating proper or not?' the lad called Bernie demanded.

'Maybe I just am.'

Another boy piped up, 'Well, yer'll be the bloody first. No one gives a toss about the likes of us. If one of us lay dying in the gutter, people'd just step over.'

'Well, if you look like scum, people will treat you like it.'

'Oi, who are you calling scum?' another boy blasted her.

Rose ignored him. 'So when was the last time you had a proper meal?' she asked again.

Intrigued now as to why this woman was here, Bernie told her, 'We shared four pies between us to have with our chips yesterday.'

'So things really aren't that good for you, in your line of work?'

He challenged her, 'What d'yer mean, our line of work?'

Rose looked knowingly at them all in turn before she said, 'The only type of work that's open to homeless boys like you. No one will give you a proper job when you've no fixed abode and look like you all do. Don't deny you're a gang of opportunist thieves . . . pickpockets. Only you hardly make enough to feed yourselves regular, do you? I'll tell you why. Because you look what you are. Immediately people spot you, they're on their guard in case you're going to try and rob them ... ready to shout blue murder for help should you attempt anything. It's my guess the police know you all by sight and are constantly watching out for you, and you're always having to watch out for them to make sure the coast is clear before you risk robbing a target.

'Now, if you all smartened yourselves up, made yourselves look the part of respectable young men, people wouldn't suspect you before you even had a chance to target them. The police wouldn't recognise you all spruced up either. If you asked an old lady if you could help her across the road, looking like you all do now, so you could rob her bag off her, she'd give you short change. But with you dressed smart, she wouldn't think for a minute that such polite, respectable young men, kindly offering to help her, were out to rob her, would she? A housewife wouldn't hesitate to allow two of you to enter her house and use her facilities when one of you got caught short, or whatever other excuse you used to get inside her house. And while one of you chatted to the woman, it wouldn't cross her mind that the nice young man upstairs wasn't using her facilities at all but was in her bedroom, helping himself to her valuables and any cash lying around.

'There are a few more scams I could tell you about, if you're interested. But you could get away with all sorts you can't currently, under a respectable cover, and just think of the money you could make yourselves against the paltry amount you do now.'

All the boys were staring at her, spellbound.

Bernie shot at her, 'I can't work out what your game is. Why are you here, bothering to tell us all this? You can see yer wasting yer time. We ain't got the money to smarten ourselves up with and work these other scams to better ourselves.'

Rose smiled widely at them all. 'What if I was to give you the money to buy yourselves the clothes you need? What if I was to offer you a nice place to stay, a comfy bed to sleep in, a hot meal cooked for you every night, and washing facilities so you can keep yourselves clean and smart-looking? Plus a blind eye turned as to how you make your money ...'

They were all staring at her, stupefied.

One of the boys murmured, 'I can't remember the last time I slept in a proper bed.'

Another said, 'I can't remember when I last had a bath.'

Suspiciously, Bernie asked, 'I ain't that stupid as to think you're some missionary come to save us, so what's in it for you?'

'Well, for the first week, while you get yourselves properly organised, nothing. But after that, ten pound a week from each of you?'

Bernie nearly choked. 'What? But that's a bloody fortune.'

'Oh, come on, boys. You could easily make three times that amount each a week, maybe more, if you put your minds to it. Do you want to live like this for the rest of your lives, never knowing where your next meal is coming from and with the police constantly on your backs, keeping an eye out for you to put a foot wrong so they can have you? You're going to have to find another hide out very soon as it's my guess the bulldozers will be in to flatten this place in the not-too-distant future. I'm giving you all a chance to get yourselves out of the gutter. But if you don't want to accept, there're other gangs knocking around that'd jump at the chance I'm offering.'

She could see that Bernie was mulling it over.

One of the boys said to him, 'I wanna do this, Bernie. I don't wanna live like this any more. I wanna car and nice clothes . . . get meself a decent bird. No decent bird looks at me, looking like I do.'

'Yeah, so do I,' voiced others.

Bernie looked at Rose. 'Okay, yer on.'

She smiled. 'Right, well, I'll meet you all tomorrow morning at ten, at the bottom of Wharf Street. We'll go shopping, then you're all off to the public baths to get yourselves scrubbed and changed, and then you can move in. But there are a few house rules. If one of you breaks any of them then you're all out. Is that clear?'

They all nodded.

'Good. During the week, you're all up, dressed and out by eight at the latest. Well, if you're playing the part of a respectable working young man, you've got to act like one. You don't come back until six. You don't leave any evidence of your activities lying around in your rooms for the housekeeper to come across. There'll be a chest of drawers each provided for you, to put your stuff in while you go about hocking it. As far as the housekeeper is concerned, you've all got legitimate jobs. Keep it that way.' She addressed Bernie then. 'On a Friday night, you're to put everyone's ten pounds in an envelope, seal it and give it to the housekeeper. Have we got ourselves a deal?'

They all nodded eagerly.

Back at the lodging house, Rose joined Lindy in one of the bedrooms where she was in the process of making up a bed. For the last three days, while her mother had been out as she had told Lindy putting up advertisements in shop windows and doing other things to drum up trade, Lindy had kept herself more than busy getting the rooms shipshape and ready for occupancy. She had also paid two futile visits to her grandmother in search of her bank book. Each night she had joined her mother, back in the small temporary flat Rose had rented for them while they got the house ready, feeling fit to drop. But as her mother had told her, it would all be worth it when the money started rolling in and they could start to look for their next lodging house.

'Do you think you'll have all the rooms ready as we've lodgers moving in tomorrow afternoon?' Rose asked.

Lindy looked stunned. 'You've managed to drum up some trade already then?'

'Well, what do you think I've been doing while I've been out . . . browsing the shops?' Rose snapped back. Then it struck her she was supposed to be playing the part of a loving mother, and hurriedly added, 'Sorry, love, I've had a tiring day. But then I expect you have, too, doing all this by yourself. I was hoping not to be out for so long and to come back and give you a hand, but things took longer than I thought.'

Lindy smiled at her. 'I've just got this room to finish off, then it's all done. I've put all the stuff away in the kitchen, and all the towels and extra bedding away in the cupboard in the bathroom. Oh, and I just need to make up the new beds in our room in the attic and then that's ready for us to move in to.'

'Ah, well, I need to speak to you about that . . . I've had a bit of a blow today . . . well, quite a big one actually. I found out that I can't charge each lodger as much as I thought I could so we're not going to make the profit each week that I was hoping. It means getting our next place will take us at lot longer.'

'Oh, Mum, I don't mind if it takes us much longer to get our string of lodging houses. The most important thing is that we're in it together, getting to know each other and making up for all our lost time.'

Maybe to you, not me, Rose thought. She said, 'When I got my windfall from that old dear and it gave me the chance to invite you to come and live with me, I made up my mind I was going to use it to give us both a good life – and that doesn't mean us living in cramped attic rooms in a lodging house for any longer than we have to. I want us to have the money to go on long holidays abroad together, or on shopping trips to London . . . and I want to do all that before I'm too old or I lose you when you get married. So I've decided that I can make up the shortfall and keep us on track by getting a job while you run this place. Well, actually, I've already got one. To start Monday.'

Lindy looked aghast. 'Me . . . run this place on my own!'

Rose tutted. 'It will practically run itself. A clean around once a week, change half the beds one week, which you wash and get dried over at the launderette, and the other half the next. Cook a simple meal every night, and wash up afterwards. It's just toast and cereal for breakfast, so hardly anything to do there. It's me that'll have the hard work, labouring over a machine all day.'

Lindy supposed, when her mother put it like that, there didn't seem much to object to.

'It's not for long . . . about six months, I reckon, at the most. Then we can get a woman in to run this place for us . . . some poor hard-up widow would jump at the chance of getting a living in job, while we get cracking setting up our next place. Now, about us moving into the attic room together – I'm going to stay on in the flat. Stupid, I know, but I get claustrophobic and that is a very small room for two of us to be knocking around in. And I don't like to tell you this because you're asleep so don't know what you're doing, but you're very restless and keep me awake most of the night. I'm not getting much sleep . . .'

Lindy exclaimed, mortified, 'Oh, Mother, I'm so sorry.'

'Well, if I'm to work hard and make as much money as I can

from my job, then I need to get my sleep. In the next lodging house we get, we'll make sure there is proper accommodation for the two of us. You could actually move in here tonight, couldn't you, and be all ready to welcome the lodgers when they arrive tomorrow?' Rose never gave Lindy a chance to make any response but continued, 'I won't hold you up any longer. I've a couple more things to do.'

Lindy was feeling nervous when Rose left. She hoped she was capable of running this place by herself, like her mother seemed to think she'd be, but then she would just have to be if her mother was working all the hours she could to enable them to get the money together for their next house. She was also dismayed that they wouldn't be living together for the foreseeable future as she'd been so looking forward to getting to know her mother properly. They hadn't really had time for talking, being so busy getting this place ready to open for business as soon as possible, but Lindy did appreciate her mother's reason for wanting to keep the flat on and felt terrible that her own restlessness had kept Rose awake. She was perturbed, though, that her mother hadn't asked her anything about herself yet, virtually all their talk being about the opening of the lodging house, but then she supposed Rose was so determined she was going to provide a good future for them both that it was all she could think of at the moment.

Well, Lindy wanted her mother to know that she was equally as committed and would do whatever it took to make it all work. If that meant running this place on her own for a while, she would work her guts out to do so.

CHAPTER TWENTY-SEVEN

It was Saturday afternoon and Cam was hurrying up Churchgate so as not to be late meeting Ann in the cafe in the market-place at two thirty. It had been two months since Rose had woven her web of lies about herself to Lindy and taken her away with her, though what motive she'd had for doing so Cam could only wonder.

Cam had discovered Lindy had not gone back to her job since the night she had left. The solicitor's office had got in touch and asked what had happened to her. She hadn't been in for a week, and had left no word as to why, they said. Cam had had to tell them that the girl had unexpectedly gone to live with her mother, and had apologised that they had received no proper notice from her. As she had given up her job, Cam could only assume that mother and daughter had indeed gone into some sort of business together as Lindy had told her they were planning to. It couldn't be the sort that Cam had first worried it might be either. As Ann had pointed out, Lindy would never involve herself in anything so distasteful, no matter how much she wanted to please her newfound mother. The fact that the girl was now under the impression that Cam was an absolute monster distressed her, but even should she come face to face with Lindy again, how could she tell her of her mother's lies and blacken Rose in her eyes, now that they were at last building a relationship together?

This did not stop Cam from trying to catch sight of Lindy, just to see for herself that she was doing all right. She had been a mother to her for fifteen years, loved her as much as if she'd given birth to her herself, and couldn't just stifle her maternal feelings because Lindy was no longer living with her. Every Saturday since Rose had reclaimed her, Cam had got up early so she could arrive

277

in the town at nine and wander round and round, hoping that she'd catch sight of Lindy doing her shopping. Up to now her search had proved futile, but there was always next week.

That was what she had been doing this morning, but again with no luck. Mindful of her arrangement to meet Ann as usual for tea and cake and for them then to continue around town together, she was waiting behind a crowd of shoppers at the Clock Tower for a break in the heavy traffic so she could cross the road. A bus came around the corner and pulled up right in front of her. Before Cam could do anything about it, she and a few other shoppers waiting to cross had become caught up in the surge of passengers wanting to get on the bus immediately all those alighting had got off.

A strong feeling of déjà-vu came over Cam but, with her need to extricate herself from the crowd before she was herded along with them on to the bus, she hadn't time to work out why she was feeling she'd been in this position before. She turned around and began to request the person immediately behind her if they'd be so kind as to move aside so she could get past, when she found herself looking at a pair of lapels and automatically glanced up to make eye contact . . . and as she did so, gasped in shock.

The sound made the man in the overcoat look down at her automatically. He then exclaimed 'Oh!' when he saw who she was.

Cam knew then why she had experienced that feeling of déjà-vu a few moments ago. Fifteen years before she had come into contact with Adrian the first time through exactly the same series of events. And here he was again.

He had always been handsome in her eyes and the intervening years had done nothing to lessen that. His dark hair was greying at the temples and several age lines were etched into the corners of his eyes and mouth, but these signs of maturity only served to make him look distinguished. As ever he was smartly dressed. He was obviously going home after doing some shopping as he was carrying a bag laden with groceries. Without Cam being able to resist, all her old feelings for him were reawakened.

It was Adrian who found his voice first. Stiltedly, he said, 'Hello, Cam.'

She managed to smile at him. How could she explain that she

had not ignored their date, but had in fact been prevented from attending by Rose turning up with Lindy? His tone of voice now did not speak of joy to meet her again. She felt an overwhelming need to give him some sort of explanation for letting him down that night, hating the thought that he was thinking so badly of her. She could tell him she had fallen unexpectedly ill and didn't know how to get in touch with him. 'Adrian . . . that night . . .'

'Don't worry about it,' he interjected dismissively, in the same stilted tone. 'I appreciate that I put you on the spot that day and you didn't really want to meet me but didn't like to say. Anyway, you wanted to get by,' he said, as he stood aside to let her pass.

Although he was brushing it aside, his whole manner told Cam that her non-appearance that night had devastated him. She didn't think she was assuming too much by believing that he had been hoping to rekindle their relationship that night. She just couldn't walk away and leave the man she loved so much thinking she didn't care enough about him to turn up on a simple date. Nor did she wish to lie, just to make herself look better in his eyes. She owed Adrian the truth as to why she had let him down that night. Not only that, but the real reason why she had finished their relationship all those years ago.

Cam took a deep breath. 'Adrian, I *was* so much looking forward to meeting you that night, but something came up that stopped me. Would you please allow me to explain to you the reason? Not here, though. Could we go somewhere we can't be overheard?' He was looking at her stern-faced. She could tell he couldn't understand why she would want to unburden herself to him. She explained, 'It's just that what I have to tell you is very personal.'

He was frowning in bewilderment and she could tell that his mind was whirling, trying to fathom just what could be so personal to her that she didn't wish others to be privy to it. But he was too much of a gentleman to ask her before she was ready to impart it.

Without a word, with his free hand Adrian cupped her elbow then steered her through the crowd waiting to get on the bus. Silently Cam accompanied him as he took her all the way down Churchgate and over the road to St Margaret's. Sitting on a bench in the deserted churchyard, his bag of shopping by his feet, he turned to face her expectantly.

She couldn't look at him; didn't want to witness the expression in his eyes when she told him of the rape on the night of their first date and her subsequent pregnancy, which was the real reason way she has finished their relationship. She was afraid she would see a look of disgust on his face; that he would see her as defiled. Neither could she look at him when she told him that she had never been able to muster any maternal feelings for the child she had borne, worried that he might see her as cold and unnatural. And she still couldn't look at him when she told him of the reason why she had not turned up for their date that night fifteen years ago: because her daughter had unexpectedly turned up to present her with a granddaughter to care for, as a way of paying her back for the great wrongs she felt her mother had done her.

And as she had told him so much, Cam felt she might as well tell him everything. Still with her head bowed and hands clasped tightly in her lap, she relayed to him the events of the night two months ago when she had come home to be confronted by Rose and Lindy, and the despicable lies her daughter had told in order to cajole the girl away.

When she had finished, Cam said softly, 'Well, at least you know the real truth of why I ended our relationship thirty years ago, and why I let you down when we arranged to meet last time, and it wasn't because I didn't care for you.'

She lapsed into silence then and waited for a response from him.

And waited.

After what felt like an age to her Cam felt him stand up, heard the rustle as he picked up his bag of shopping, and then his footsteps as he strode away down the gravel path. A lone tear rolled down her cheek. His reaction told her that he couldn't even bear to speak to her after hearing all he had. Couldn't bring himself to be associated with someone with such a sordid past.

Then, to her confusion, she heard hurrying footsteps approaching, and as she turned her head to see who was coming she saw Adrian sit down beside her again. It was apparent to her he'd been crying. Before she could say anything to him, his arms were around her, he had pulled her to him and was hugging her tightly, saying her name over and over. 'Oh, Cam! Cam...' Finally he released her. With his face wreathed in remorse, he told her, 'I'm so sorry I walked away from you, but hearing what you've been through I felt so helpless, I didn't know what to say. I can't begin to imagine what your life has been like.' A look of anger filled his face then and he said harshly, 'I hope that man rots in hell for what he did to you . . . to both of us, in fact. He robbed us of our future together.'

Cam sighed heavily. 'Yes, he did. But then you met your wife and were happy with her.'

'Yes, I did. I was very happy with Veronica, but I never quite forgot you. You had a special something Veronica didn't have. It was as if, deep down, I just couldn't shake off the feeling I was with the wrong person. I never let Veronica know that . . . she didn't deserve to think anything other than that I was totally in love with her. I understand now, though, why you never married. When you told me you hadn't the last time we met, I couldn't understand why a woman like you hadn't. But it makes sense to me now.' He grabbed Cam and pulled her to him again, holding her as if he was afraid to let her go. Finally he released her, to look at her searchingly for a moment before, to her bewilderment, he fetched a small notebook out of his pocket along with a pen, and asked, 'What is your address?'

'My address? Why?'

'Just so I know where to come and collect you, to take you out for dinner tonight. This time I'm not taking any chances.'

Cam was sitting at her kitchen table nursing a cup of tea later that afternoon when Ann arrived and immediately enquired: 'So . . . how is she then?

Cam had been lost in her own thoughts, still having difficulty accepting that nothing she had told Adrian had lessened her in his eyes, and that she was being given yet another chance. Ann's arrival and words jerked her out of her introspection. 'Sorry? How is who?'

As she sat down at the table opposite her friend, Ann shot her an accusing look. 'Lindy. Well, you've seen her . . . been with her . . . that must be why you never turned up to meet me in the cafe.'

'Oh, no, another wasted search,' Cam told her.

Ann's face screwed up in reproach. 'Well, it had better be a good excuse you've got for standing me up, leaving me looking a right greedy guts with two coffees and three cakes in front of me!'

Ann's joy then at hearing the excuse Cam gave her for not turning up was readily apparent. 'Oh, Cam, it's about bloody time fate was kind to you! What time is Adrian calling for you?'

'Seven thirty.'

She scraped back her chair and stood up. 'Right, I won't be long. About an hour it'll take me to give Brian his dinner, then get myself ready for the pub tonight. I'll be back after that.' She saw the look on Cam's face and added resolutely, 'Well, if you think I'm going to let anything stop you from going out with Adrian tonight, you've got another think coming. I don't care if Lindy comes back, the Queen herself calls in for a cuppa, or World War Three breaks out ... I shall be here to deal with it. I'm not risking this chance of being with Adrian being scuppered for you again.'

CHAPTER TWENTY-EIGHT

Weighed down by heavy shopping bags, Lindy was making her way towards the bus stop to go back to the lodging house after a trip into town. Her mother had made it sound a breeze, running the place by herself, but in truth it was damned hard work. Apart from everything else she had to do, shopping alone for the amount of food needed to provide a meal, even a basic one, for sixteen ravenous young men every night, was no easy task. She had not received any complaints yet, though, about what she dished up for them, and no food had ever been left on any plate. They may be polite and smart-looking young men but their table manners left a lot to be desired, in her opinion, and she did wonder what sort of homes they all came from.

She had not thought to enquire from her mother just how many lodgers she would be welcoming on that first day of business, but hadn't expected sixteen of them to descend on her, surprisingly all of around the same age, give or take a couple of years, and none seemingly having any other personal belongings than the clothes they stood up in. When she had mentioned these facts to her mother, Rose had just shrugged and said it was of no consequence to them what age the lodgers were or what they possessed or didn't, just that they paid over their dues every week for their board and keep. Lindy supposed that was right. But she did get the feeling that all the young men were on their guard in front of her, and it was noticeable to her that should she arrive in a room when going about her business and find any of them talking with each other, they would immediately stop and just smile politely at her until she had done what she came to and gone on her way. Maybe they felt they were showing respect for her by not ignoring her and carrying on talking when she unexpectedly arrived on the scene.

Lindy was aware that one of them, Bernie, was developing a fancy for her, by the way his eyes lingered on her whenever their paths crossed. He was a good-looking young man and she certainly would consider going out with him, should he ask her. All the lodgers did seem conscientious, and not one of them had missed going to work in the three months or so they had been lodging in the house. They were all washed, dressed and breakfasted, out on the dot of eight in the morning, and all arrived back on the dot of six, just as she was putting their dinner on the table. What they did for a living she had no idea, and her mother had made it clear that it wasn't her place to pry into their lodgers' private lives. Not wanting to go against her, Lindy was left feeling curious. But whatever they were doing, they seemed to be well paid as, since they had arrived with just what they stood up in, all of them had expanded their wardrobes, acquired a wrist watch and other personal things, and most nights went out.

She was very relieved that her mother appeared pleased with her efforts. When she called in each Friday evening after Lindy had cleared away the meal to collect the lodger's money, she was always keen to make a good impression on her, wanting Rose to like her, so she'd never come to regret defying her own mother and coming back for her child. Lindy just wished that her mother wasn't working such long hours, as nowadays they saw very little of one another.

Part of Lindy felt sad that her grandmother couldn't participate in the prosperous future she was helping her mother to build for them; the grandmother she had known her to be that is, not the monster she had found out Cam actually was. She missed that lovely grandmother, the one who had made her feel so safe and secure and so loved while she was growing up, but would never be able to forgive her for keeping herself and her mother apart. Lindy did, though, feel terrible remorse and shame for attacking her grandmother for failing to surrender her savings book. She had never raised her hand to anyone before. It had been so out of character but she had been so angry with her for refusing to give up her bank book and so cross about the lies her grandmother had told her about her birth, and for the way she had physically abused Rose, that she hadn't been able to stop herself.

Lindy wondered just what excuse her grandmother had come up with to save her face before the neighbours when they'd asked where the girl was. Her mother had persuaded her not to serve out her notice at work as she was desperate for them to start building their future together. And, as her mother had pointed out, Cam was always so hell-bent on keeping her respectability in others' eyes that she would have come up with something plausible.

The town wasn't too busy that morning and so Lindy was saved from having to weave her way through crowds with her heavy bags. As she made her way down Humberstone Gate to catch her bus, she noticed a smartly dressed businessman, carrying a briefcase, coming her way. Following a short distance behind were two young men whose attention seemed to be focused on the smart man ahead, as if they were keen not to lose sight of him. But what was really catching Lindy's attention was that the young men in question were two of her lodgers. She wondered what they were both doing, walking through town when they should be at work. They were probably on their lunch hours. But then it struck her that it was only eleven o'clock so it was too early. Maybe the two of them worked together and the smart businessman was their boss and they were accompanying him to a business meeting or to visit a client. Out of respect for him they were following behind, and of course they didn't want to lose sight of him in case they missed the meeting and got into trouble.

Seeing the arrival of her bus at the stop further down the street sent the incident from Lindy's mind. She quickened her pace to catch it.

As Lindy was making her way back to the lodging house, laden with shopping, Rose was sitting at the kitchen table in her small rented flat, rubbing her hands in glee and giving out cackles of hysteria at the balance showing on the A5 book she had bought to keep her accounts in. Now and again during the week, she would take the book out of the drawer where she kept it, just to look at the balance and feel the thrill of knowing her clever plan was bearing such fruit.

After fourteen weeks of the lodging house being in business, and considering she had been very generous and allowed the lodgers their first week free while they organised themselves, the balance was now showing at £1,755. Of course, she'd have had more had she not had to pay out the £25 a week running costs, which included the couple of pounds she handed Lindy each week, the girl being under the illusion that the rest of her wage was being put towards their next property.

Rose's gamble on that particular gang of homeless boys had paid off. They had all seized on the opportunity of bettering themselves which she had offered them and not once to date had she failed to receive her full dues. She had learned a lot from the pillow talk of some of her less scrupulous clients and also the other girls she'd worked with, some of whom had criminal pasts. No scam could run forever, though. It was only a matter of time before some smart arse twigged something was not right and started to investigate. Not that Rose was worried because nothing could be traced back to her, but she had now decided that £1,000 was not enough. She wanted £3,000 at least before she made her departure. She just hoped these lads kept themselves away from the eyes of the police for another three months or so. Rose wasn't stupid. She had not banked the cash, not wanting any suspicious teller to question why a woman of her sort would be regularly depositing £135 a week, but stored it in a cash tin at the back of the drawer in the bureau where she kept everything else pertaining to her scheme. She didn't consider that folly on her part. No one would consider the likes of her worth burgling, considering the nondescript flat she lived in, in a rundown area, and the cheap way she dressed.

All this lazing around while her money built up was giving her time to really consider her future. After much deliberation she was no longer prepared to plough it all into the setting up of a high-class brothel, working the same long hours as Mrs Monks had while overseeing her operation, always aware that the law could descend should her influential clients fail to protect her and then she'd be facing a jail sentence for her illicit operation. Instead Rose was going to play it safe and buy several profitable legitimate businesses, which between them would give her enough money to base her lifestyle on.

Why should she herself work when she could get others to do it for her, and then sit back and enjoy the profits?

With this in mind she had been scouring the *Mercury*'s Businesses For Sale columns, just to get a feel of what was on offer and what sort of prices were expected. And she'd made another decision. She wasn't going to remain in Leicester but would relocate to Nottingham so that she was saved the possible embarrassment of coming face to face with one of her old clients, as the majority had moved in the social group Rose aimed to associate with. She had read that Nottingham was prospering even more markedly than Leicester after the war, which meant there was more to be made there by Rose.

After this interim time spent lying low and playing the part of a meek factory worker in front of her gullible daughter, Rose felt she deserved a treat, so was going to take a few pounds out of her savings, and next Wednesday would catch the train to Nottingham and have a look around the place. She'd visit a couple of agents to get a feel for how many going concerns she would be able to buy with the money she had made from the lodging house, and would also buy herself a couple of outfits of the type a wealthy businesswoman would be expected to choose.

Giggling childishly to herself as she closed her ledger and returned it to the drawer in the old-fashioned bureau that had come with the flat, along with a copy of the rental agreement for the lodging house in Lindy's name. Rose gave a yawn. All this planning for her future was very tiring. She would have a nap.

That night at just before eight, having finished her chores, Lindy was up in her attic room, slumped tiredly in front of the television, when a knock came on her door. Her accommodation was out of bounds to the lodgers so her hopes soared that this was her mother come to pay her a visit. In anticipation of at long last spending some proper time with her, Lindy jumped up and went to answer the door.

She was taken aback to find Bernie standing awkwardly outside.

'I know I ain't supposed to be up here but . . . well . . . it's hard to catch you on yer own with all the others around.'

'And why would you want to do that?' Lindy asked him, as if she wasn't intelligent enough to have guessed.

'Well, I've had me eye on you since I came here.' Which surprised him as she wasn't the type of girl he normally went for. The pretty sort. This girl was very plain. In fact, some might even call her ugly. As ugly, you could say, as the woman who'd offered them this opportunity to better themselves. It was apparent the girl was very closely related to her, but neither he nor the other lads had dared ask for fear the woman would pull the plug on their living here. She had made it quite clear they weren't to associate themselves with the housekeeper any more than was necessary. But there was something about this girl that drew Bernie to her, a quality of warmth that intrigued him and made him want to get to know her better, and as long as he never discussed his way of earning money with her then he wasn't breaking any of the rules, was he? 'I wondered if you fancied going out?' he said to her.

Lindy looked at him for a moment, not wanting to make it easy for him. 'Where in particular?'

'Wherever you fancy. We could go for a few drinks first, then a meal and dancing after, if you want.'

An expensive night out, she thought. 'Well, I could maybe find my share for a couple of drinks, but that's about it.'

He looked offended. 'You're expecting to go Dutch? If I ask a gel out, I expect to pay.' By way of showing her he could, and in his need to impress her, he pulled a wad of notes out of his inside pocket and flashed them at her. 'I've got money.'

Lindy gawped at him. 'Where did you get money like that from? You must have about twenty pounds there!'

He froze. God, how *did* he explain how a lad of his age had this kind of money to squander? He said the first thing he could think of. 'Oh . . . er . . . I won it on a bet.'

'But you're only about seventeen. You're not old enough to bet.'

'A bloke at work put it on for me. So, do you fancy a night out then?'

Lindy did. She missed her friends, and all the things they'd done together. She'd had no social life at all since she'd been reunited with her mother as they'd both been so busy. She was too tired tonight, though, and by the time she got herself ready half the night would be gone. Besides, she didn't want to come across to Bernie as too keen so she said, 'I'm not doing anything Saturday night.'

He grinned. 'Saturday night it is then.'

CHAPTER TWENTY-NINE

The following Wednesday morning, Lindy had just finished cleaning the bathroom, her most hated chore. It was a job that should only need doing weekly if all her lodgers left the room as they had found it, but they didn't. By the time they'd all used it night and morning the room looked like a bomb had hit it, and the sink and bath were both caked in dirty soap scum. And did her lodgers not think to hang a wet towel up to dry? Leaving it dumped on the floor wasn't going to help.

Lindy then made her way to one of the first-floor bedrooms. Wednesday was bed-changing day for half the rooms. She would strip the beds, bundle up the dirty linen, take it all across the road where the kind old lady who ran the launderette would wash and dry it for her for a couple of shillings, ready for Lindy to collect four hours later, and then have the beds re-made before the lodgers returned from work. Considering the state they all left the bathroom and communal rooms in after they'd used them, they kept their own rooms surprisingly tidy. No personal items were left out by anyone, but were all put away in the small bedside chests of drawers they'd been provided with. They hung their expanding wardrobes up on coat hangers from the picture rails around the walls, having allotted themselves a certain amount of space each.

As she began to strip the first bed Lindy started humming to herself. She was feeling excited as it was her birthday next week, and for the first time ever she would receive a card from her mother and maybe a little something, too, considering they were living as frugally as they could at the moment. She had pushed aside any thought that she wouldn't for the first time ever receive a present from her grandmother, as that was too painful to think about. She was also excited because she was going out again with Bernie tonight and was looking forward to it. He had really shown her a good time last Saturday night. It had been quite embarrassing really when she had met up with him down in the hallway at seven thirty. The lodgers who hadn't already gone out themselves had all nudged and winked at each other when they had left together, to which Bernie had commented that they were only jealous because he had got in first with Lindy.

They had caught the bus into town and gone for a couple of drinks at the White Hart Hotel on Humberstone Gate, then on for a meal at the kind of restaurant where the *maître d'* had first discreetly taken Bernie aside to check that the likes of him, with his pronounced Leicester accent and considering his age, could actually pay the bill. Satisfied he could when Bernie showed him his wad of cash, the man had then personally shown them to their table. The meal had been delicious and Lindy dared not think what it had cost, but Bernie seemed to be spending his winnings like there was plenty more where they came from. As it was his money to spend it wasn't for Lindy to comment. They had then gone on to the Palais-de-danse, and had rock-and-rolled the rest of the night away to the Dallas Boys. Bernie had certainly proved to be good company. He was a very self-assured person and had taken it for granted that Lindy would agree to go out with him again.

She wasn't expecting a repetition of Saturday night's entertainment as she doubted he would have had much change left from his winnings, so maybe they'd have a quiet drink in a local pub, one that had a juke box so they could listen to the latest hits while they enjoyed each other's company. Her mother hadn't told her that she wasn't to go out socially with any of the lodgers, just that it was not her place to pry into their personal lives.

As she bent down to gather a pile of dirty linen off the floor, out of the corner of her eye she caught sight of something under the bed. It was a wallet. Obviously Frank, whose bed it lay under, had not realised he'd dropped it. Lindy worried he wouldn't discover he hadn't got it on him until he went to pay for his lunch. She supposed he could always borrow some money off a work colleague and give it back tomorrow. She got down on her hands and knees to reach under the bed and retrieve it. Having got it, she made to stand up and as she did so momentarily lost her balance. She reached out to put her hand on the bed, to steady herself, and in the process dropped the wallet on the floor, where it flapped open.

She bent to pick it up and her attention was caught by a photograph inserted into a pocket that had a clear front to it. It was of a family group: a man, woman and three children. She wondered if this was Frank's family. But then she realised that the man and woman in the photograph were far too young to be the parents of a seventeen-year-old boy. Then she spotted a matching clear pocket on the other side of the wallet. That had inserted into it a card showing the name and address of the owner. It wasn't Frank's name, and neither was the address that of the lodging house. Lindy stared at it for a moment, wondering what Frank was doing with someone else's wallet under his bed. Then she realised he must have bought it from a second-hand shop and not removed the former owner's details yet. Her mother had instilled in her that she must at all times respect their lodgers' privacy and she shouldn't really be poking around in their drawers, but regardless she felt she should put the wallet in one of Frank's for safekeeping.

She opened up the drawer and made to slip the wallet in when what was inside registered with her and she gasped with shock. The drawer was filled with a jumble of items that seemed to have been carelessly thrown there, but amongst them all were several wrist watches, pieces of jewellery, another couple of wallets, a money clip holding several one-pound and ten-shilling notes, a lot of loose silver coins, several expensive-looking rolled gold cigarette lighters, and a pile of what looked like pawn tickets and receipts from second-hand shops.

Wide-eyed, Lindy stared down at it all, her thought whirling. What was a young working man doing with costly items like these? On the wage Frank could expect at his age, he'd not have enough left, after he'd paid his dues and had several nights out, to buy such expensive things, surely. Curiously she opened the other two drawers and found only what she would expect to find in a young man's possession: a couple of pairs of underpants, socks and vests; a shaving brush and razor; and a used bar of soap in a plastic dish with several hairs embedded in it.

Her eyes then lifted and she looked at the suits hanging from the picture rail. Whether they were new when bought or second-hand she couldn't say, but they were made from decent quality material and there was also a leather jacket of the kind James Dean wore in the film *Rebel Without a Cause*. Frank's wages would hardly buy him clothes of this quality either. She then looked at the other two lodgers' clothes. They, too, seemed to her to be above the price range she would expect working men of their age to be able to afford.

Lindy was beginning to feel that all was not right here. She went over to one of the other sets of drawers and opened the top one. It held the same sort of items as Frank's, but not so many, and the two other drawers merely underclothes and other personal items. She then went over to the third lodger's chest of drawers which repeated the pattern. Lindy went around all the lodgers' rooms then, noting the quality of the clothes hanging up and finding that each chest of drawers held items that would reap a reasonable sum if sold, along with a good amount of cash.

Deeply bothered now by her findings, she returned to Frank's room and sank down on his bed to think things over. Could there be a plausible explanation for how the lodgers had come by these goods that she just wasn't seeing? But to her mind there was only one way young men of her lodgers' ilk could come by such items.

A vision of Bernie came to mind, flashing his wad of cash on Saturday night. His winnings from a bet, he had told her, but certainly the way he was spending it had seemed to imply there was more where that came from. Was that because there was? Then Lindy remembered the incident that had happened a couple of weeks back. It had seemed unimportant to her at the time but was now taking on an entirely different significance. Had the two lodgers she had seen then not been out with their boss on a way to a meeting but in fact sizing up the man as a potential victim, for them to rob as soon as the right moment presented itself? It then struck her why they all stopped talking if she happened to arrive unexpectedly in a room where any of them were in conversation. Was that not out of politeness towards her, as she had thought, but because they did not want her to overhear anything they were saying?

God forbid, but had her mother innocently taken in a criminal gang as lodgers? Lindy did sincerely hope she was wrong as she liked all of them individually, especially Bernie. But should her suspicions prove to be correct, then sooner or later the police would be alerted to their lodgers' activities and that would lead them back here to the lodging house. Then not only were they all going to end up in jail, but her mother too could be perceived to be harbouring criminals and end up serving a prison sentence.

Lindy's heart raced frantically. She must inform Rose of her suspicions as soon as possible. She would be waiting for her when she returned from work this evening. She had planned on making shepherd's pie for the lodgers' evening meal, so would just leave a note for them, telling them she'd had to go out on an urgent errand and to help themselves to their meal from the huge enamel dish keeping hot in the oven.

Rose alighted from the train at 5.15 and made her way to the taxi rank. She had spent a marvellous day, getting a feel for the city she was going to relocate to and browsing around its shops, looking at all the things she would soon be able to afford to buy for herself. She had actually bought a new coat and dress from Selfridges department store where the affluent ladies of the city shopped. She had also called in to several estate agencies and told them that she was looking to buy three or four profitable going concerns. She gave them her address so they could send her details of any that matched her requirements. She then lunched in a smart little bistro and had a glass of wine with her smoked salmon salad, and certainly enjoyed the attentive care she received from the very handsome waiter, who assumed that because she was dining in such an upmarket establishment she was a woman of substance. It was now several hours since she had eaten, though, and she was hungry again. Rose thought it would be a good way to end her day to treat herself to a meal at the Grand Hotel.

As her mother was selecting her choice of food from the à la carte menu in the elegant Grand Hotel restaurant, a highly anxious Lindy sat on the stairs leading up to her flat in a freezing cold hall, waiting for her to come home.

She jumped up to look expectantly down at the front door as it opened, but then slumped back on seeing it wasn't her mother but the middle-aged widow woman who lived in the flat below hers.

As she approached the door to her own flat, the woman spotted Lindy sitting on the stairs and recognised her as having lived upstairs with her mother for a couple of weeks . . . Well, she guessed they were mother and daughter as they looked so alike. The woman said to her, 'Oh, hello, me duck. Not seen you for a while. Anyway, what are you sitting there for? You look perished to me.'

'I'm waiting for my mother to get home from work, only she's later than she normally is so she must be working late.'

The woman frowned in bewilderment. 'Your mother doesn't go to work, dear. I hear her during the day, moving around. What made you think she did? She went out today, though, all dressed up. I know because I heard the front door open and shut, and looked out of me window.'

Lindy just looked at her. She was too worried about what she had on her mind to argue the toss about whether or not her mother went to work. The early-Victorian villa had been converted into four separate one-bedroomed flats by the owner a few years back. This woman was obviously getting her mother confused with one of the other flat-dwellers who didn't go out to work.

The woman asked her, 'Want to come in and wait in my flat for yer mam to come home? I could mash you a cuppa?'

Lindy hadn't it in her at the moment to engage in small talk so politely refused. 'Thanks for your offer, but my mum shouldn't be much longer now.'

'All right, love. Oh, but why don't yer let yerself in and wait for her in her flat? She's your mother so I can't see her minding. Last tenant left a spare key on the lintel over her door in case she ever locked herself out. Unless your mother found it, I bet it's still there.'

Lindy jumped up. 'Oh, thanks, I'll check.' Hopefully it was still there and she could have the kettle boiling for when her mother came in. She'd need a cup of tea to soothe her, considering what Lindy had to tell her, and it would be warmer than waiting out here.

To her relief she put her hand on the key almost immediately and let herself in to the flat. Apart from the few pieces of shabby dated furniture that were included in the rental price there was nothing here by way of adornment and the whole place seemed cold and uninviting. But then, Lindy couldn't blame her mother for not wanting to make it more homely. She only intended to live here for another few months, until they'd acquired enough from her job and the profits from the lodging house to buy and set up their next property.

Lindy went into the tiny kitchen, checked the kettle for water and put it on the stove, lighting the gas jet underneath using a match from the box her mother kept on a shelf. Leaving it to boil, she went back into the living-room and sat herself down in an uncomfortable armchair. She could have put the television on while she waited for her mother to show, but was in no mood for watching it.

Time ticked by and the kettle started to whistle. She got up to turn the gas jet down to its lowest and removed the whistle from the spout, to keep the water at its boiled temperature. She then returned to the living-room to resume her seat.

By the time the tin clock on the 1950s-style tiled fireplace showed seven thirty, Lindy had conceded that her mother must have been offered more overtime and accepted it. But she had been at work since six that morning and had worked a twelve-hour shift. She must be exhausted. This just made Lindy even more determined to do all she could towards building a good future for them both. She then felt guilty that the hours she worked running the lodging house, although it was hard work and laborious for someone with an active brain like hers, were nowhere near as many as her mother seemed to be putting in. What time Rose would get home tonight depended on how many hours' overtime she had agreed to work. Lindy could still be sitting here after midnight.

She had work of her own to do back at the lodging house. Even though she had her suspicions over the way their lodgers earned their living, it didn't mean she could neglect her duties. She would return and tackle them, and come back later to check if her mother had returned. But she could meanwhile leave her a note, telling Rose she needed to speak to her on a very urgent matter.

Lindy looked around for something to write her note with. Where would her mother keep such items? Of course. In the old-fashioned bureau. She opened the door that when pulled down served as a writing table and looked inside. It was very dusty, and apart from a couple of spider's webs there was only an old envelope inside. She could use the back of it for her note. There was nothing to write with, though. She shut the door and then pulled open the first of the two drawers below.

This drawer held several items and Lindy immediately spotted what she was seeking poking out of the top of an A5-sized notebook. Beside the notebook was a Post Office savings book which she assumed was where her mother put their money each week for safe-keeping. Lying on the other side of the notebook were a couple of sheets of paper, stapled together and covered with type-written words. The quick glance Lindy gave it revealed it to be a legal document. Then she realised it would be something to do with the purchase of the lodging house. At the very back of the drawer was a metal cash tin without a key in the lock where she assumed her mother kept the profits from the lodging house when she gave them to her every Friday night, until she could get to the Post Office to deposit them when her long shifts allowed her the time.

As she made to pick up the A5 book and take out the biro inside, it nudged the savings book and displayed the fact that there were another two beneath it. Lindy looked at them for a moment, wondering why her mother would need three separate Post Office savings accounts. Then the name of the account holder displayed clearly on the front of the top book struck her. Camella Rogers. Why did her mother have a Post Office account in her own mother's name? Curiously Lindy picked it up ... and it was then that she saw the name on the account book beneath it. Belinda Rogers. Why would her mother have an account in *her* name? She picked that book up too. Then she saw the name of the holder of the third account book. Rose Rogers. So her mother had opened an account in her own name, and one each for Lindy and Cam? But why would she do that?

Lindy's eyes then fell on the official-looking document and she took in what the bold heading on it read: *Rental Agreement for* ...

Then it stated the address of the lodging house. But her mother had led her to believe she had bought the lodging house, using the majority of her windfall, so why had she a rental agreement for it? Lindy put the three savings books back in the drawer and picked up the rental agreement to cast her eyes over it. It was a lease for six months and, when she came to the line stating the name of the lessee, she frowned in bewilderment. It was her own name. But she hadn't signed any documents agreeing to take on the rental of the lodging house. The signature wasn't anything like hers.

Her mind began to search for a plausible explanation of all she had found, but she couldn't think of one.

Lindy put the rental agreement back in the drawer and again picked up the three savings books. The one on the top was the one her mother had opened in Lindy's name. Then she suddenly went cold. This was no new book but in fact her old account book, the one her grandmother had given her years ago, to encourage her to save. Lindy recognised the mark on the front cover that she had made herself. Her heart began to thump. No wonder her grandmother couldn't find the book when she had demanded it. Rose must have had it all along.

A feeling of dread began to mount inside her when she opened her book and saw that, apart from a couple of shillings, the balance of the £30 she'd had in here had been withdrawn. She then opened the book in her grandmother's name and saw that all but a few shillings of Cam's painfully saved £200 had been withdrawn too. The book in her mother's own name, showing its last deposit over fifteen years ago, had also had the balance withdrawn but for couple of shillings.

Lindy's heart was thudding and she was beginning to feel sick. She realised now just where her mother had received her windfall to set up the lodging business – and it wasn't from a bequest left to her by an old lady who had befriended her years ago.

She then stared blindly at the A5 notebook with the biro wedged inside it. She was terrified of what it might reveal to her. But she knew she must investigate if she was going to get to the bottom of the mystery. Taking several deep breaths, she pulled out the biro and opened the book. For several minutes Lindy tried to make sense of the entries. There were thirteen in all. On one side of the page was a list of dates. The first was for roughly thirteen weeks ago, if she had calculated correctly. Entered next to each of the dates was the same figure of £160. Next to that was a minus mark and beside that the figure of £25. The last entry was for the previous Friday and Lindy gasped when she saw the amount of the running total: £1,755. An absolute fortune to Lindy whose weekly wage before she had left her job to join her mother had been £3.2s.6d.

But what did these figures in the book represent?

Then a thought struck her. Was her mother keeping a record of her wages every week? No, that couldn't be what these figures represented. No matter if she worked twenty-four hours a day, seven days a week, she would not make that kind of money in a year from her job as a machinist in a factory. She might do, though, if she *owned* the factory. Lindy kept looking up and down the figures until slowly the only plausible explanation of what they represented dawned on her. Each date recorded was a Friday. Each Friday, when Lindy's mother called at the lodging house after work, Lindy handed her the sealed envelope given her by Bernie, containing all the lodgers' dues that he'd collected from them. To make up a total of £160 her mother must be charging each of her sixteen lodgers £10 a week. Considering normal lodging houses charged about fifty shillings a week this was an extortionate amount of money. But for her lodgers to be earning the kind of money to afford to meet these extortionate rates, at their age and given their obvious working-class backgrounds, Rose must have known when she accepted them that they were earning money illegally as not even a bank manager earned £10 a week. The minus £25 figure must be the weekly running costs. This meant her mother was making £135 a week in profit, far in excess of what Lindy had been led to believe. Was it all stashed away in the locked tin at the back of the drawer?

But that didn't explain why Rose had taken the rental of the lodging house out in her daughter's name, not her own . . .

Then suddenly all the pieces of the jigsaw came together and Lindy saw the whole picture.

Her mother was providing a safe house for a criminal gang to operate from and they were paying her handsomely to turn a blind eye to their illicit activities. But it was apparent to Lindy that her mother hadn't liked the idea of herself being incriminated if this came to the attention of the police. So she had needed a scapegoat, and who better than the long-lost daughter she'd recently reunited herself with? Lindy had trusted her and believed that together they were building a prosperous future. That woman tonight had been right, though. Her mother didn't go out to labour the long hours she professed to, it was just a ploy to keep up the pretence that she was putting in as much effort as Lindy. She didn't need to go to work, did she? Not with all the money she was making for herself each week with her clever scheme.

What kind of mother could put her own daughter in such a terrible position, one that could have dire consequences for her, purely to protect herself while she lined her own pockets? And who would tell such diabolical lies to get her daughter on her side? Because Lindy was sure now that Rose's tale of Cam's cruelty had been a complete fabrication. Only a cold-hearted, selfish, greedy woman, who had no maternal feelings whatsoever for her own daughter.

A great fear rose up in Lindy then. What if the police had already got wind that a criminal gang were living in her lodging house? What if they were already making investigations, and it was only a matter of time before she herself was hauled off to jail? She vehemently prayed this wasn't the case and that she had time to get herself out of this situation before it all came crashing down around her. But how did she manage that? She had no idea. Then it came to her. There was only one person she could turn to for help. In her mistaken trust in her mother she had treated that person badly but, regardless, Lindy knew without a doubt that she would be forgiven and helped in her time of need. Cam would take her back.

Putting everything exactly where she had found it so as not to alert Rose that she was on to her, Lindy fled from the flat.

CHAPTER THIRTY

Cam was looking through a pattern book that Ann had brought round for her so she could choose a new dress for herself, but she wasn't seeing the array of possible outfits, only the face of her beloved granddaughter. It was Lindy's birthday in a few days, and for the first time in her life Cam would not be writing a card for her or scouring the shops for a gift; she wouldn't be making a celebration sponge cake for her and watching her laughingly blow out the candles.

She knew she should be happy that Rose had found it within herself to want to be a mother to her daughter. Given the length of time they had been reunited now, Cam could only assume that they were getting on well and making a future together. She was glad of this, but sad too that it had to be at the cost of her losing her beloved granddaughter.

By rights Cam should be feeling happy about the rest of her life. She and Adrian had only been seeing each other for two weeks, but already he had asked her to marry him – and as soon as possible. He was unwilling to waste any more time now that he had found her again. Cam had been over the moon at his proposal, the only thing to mar her delight was the fact that she couldn't share her wonderful news with Lindy. Adrian had wasted no time in immediately introducing her to his two grown-up children, both with families of their own, and they had expressed their delight at the prospect of having Cam as a stepmother – and step-grandmother to their children. Adrian had arranged a family get together, along with a few carefully chosen close friends, for a week on Saturday, to celebrate their engagement. That was why Cam was in need of a new outfit to wear, something special, and she couldn't think of a better person to make it for her than her very special friend. In truth, Ann herself had insisted she should.

Sitting opposite her at the table, Ann urged, 'You must have seen something that's taken your fancy in that book. You've been studying it for the last hour.' Knowing Cam as well as she did, Ann knew her mind was not fully on the task, but that she was thinking of Lindy. It would be her birthday in a few days' time and that would be on her grandmother's mind. There was nothing that Ann felt she could say to ease her hurt over this, only time would do that, so she felt it best not to bring up the subject.

'Well, I quite like this one,' Cam told her, turning the book around for Ann to get a good view of the smart shift dress and waist-length matching jacket she was pointing at.

Ann smiled in approval. 'You'll look smashing in that. In linen . . . a soft raspberry pink, I think.'

Cam nodded.

Ann took the pattern book off her and put it aside to take with her when she left. Then she leaned her arms on the table and smiled dreamily, saying, 'Like a fairy tale, you and Adrian are. So romantic. He's like a dog with two tails and you—'

She was interrupted by the door bursting open. They both jumped and turned their head to see who had entered.

Before Cam or Ann had time to register just who the new arrival was, a frenzied Lindy had launched herself across the room and into her grandmother's arms, hugging her fiercely and blubbering, 'Oh, Nan! Nan . . . I think I could be in such terrible trouble and I don't know what to do about it! I don't deserve it after the way I treated you, but you will help me, won't you? Please say you will!'

Instinctively Cam knew that whatever trouble Lindy was in, her mother lay behind it.

So did Ann.

They both knew that they were about to discover the real reason Rose had wanted her daughter to go and live with her – and it wasn't because she'd found it within herself to be a mother to her at long last.

After first calming Lindy, they sat her down between them on the sofa and listened while she told them of the terrible situation she feared her mother had got her into, under the pretext that she was building a future for them both.

Lindy was sobbing her heart out by the time she was finished, but both Cam and Ann felt only relief. Rose had not put Lindy to work in her old business, but it seemed likely that she had left Mrs Monks virtually penniless, as Cam had always feared she would. In her lust for money and the lifestyle it would bring, she had not hesitated to cheat, lie and steal – not giving a damn that her new plan to make a fortune could destroy her innocent daughter's life.

But Cam was not about to let her profit at Lindy's expense.

CHAPTER THIRTY-ONE

After spending such an enjoyable day, tasting just a little of what her life was going to be like all the time very soon, Rose was in her bedroom, about to get ready for a good night's sleep, when the sound of the front door opening and shutting reached her ears. It couldn't be Lindy as she didn't have a key to the flat. In fact, so far as Rose was aware, no one else but she had. She must have been hearing things. Then to her shock she heard a familiar voice call out, 'Have you got a moment, Rose? I'd really like to speak to you.'

She gasped. That was her mother's voice! So she *had* heard the door opening and shutting after all. But what was Cam doing here? How had she found out where Rose lived? How had she let herself in?

Rose went to find out. If she was shocked to discover that her mother wasn't alone, she did not show it but matter-of-factly said, 'I could have you both arrested for breaking and entering.'

'We didn't. We used a key, courtesy of your predecessor leaving it on the lintel outside in case she ever accidentally locked herself out,' Ann told her.

Rose scowled in bewilderment as to how they could know that when she didn't herself. But before she could enquire her mother was speaking.

'We came to tell you that you'll no longer be making any money from your lodging house. As from half an hour ago there are no lodgers there. We sent them all packing with the threat that the police were on their way. I've never seen lads move so quickly to gather up their belongings. First thing tomorrow the agents who handled the rental agreement will rip it up when they learn of their own negligence in leasing it to an under-age girl of sixteen. That contract isn't worth the paper it was written on.' Then Cam's eyes narrowed in contempt. 'I can't believe even you would sink so low as to place your own daughter in such a position. Her whole future could have been ruined, just so you could satisfy your greed. Thankfully for Lindy, she sussed out what you were up to before it was too late.'

Rose was furious. She had not bargained on her daughter being so astute; had been more worried that it would be her uneducated lodgers who would be the ones to bring the scheme to an end by slipping up and alerting the police. But she gave a nonchalant shrug. 'Well, there's no harm done then. You can take her home with you. I've no use for her any more.' In a couldn't-care-less tone of voice, she added, 'I would have liked my plan to have carried on for a while longer, but as it is I've made enough from it to give me a good start towards the future I deserve.'

'You're referring to this, I suppose,' Ann piped up, having opened her capacious handbag. Allowing Rose a glimpse of what she had secreted inside, she snapped it shut again.

As it registered with her just what Ann had showed her, Rose's face first turned ashen then darkened thunderously. She menacingly bellowed, 'You give me that back! It's all mine.'

'No, it's not,' Cam told her. 'Not a penny of it. Rightfully it belongs to the people your lodgers stole it from. It would be impossible to arrange for all the victims to get their belongings back, but I can at least make sure the money made from their misery is put to good use. There must be some sort of organisation for helping criminals mend their ways that would be delighted to receive an anonymous donation to help them continue the good work. Unlike you, who was bent on encouraging young men to cause misery to innocent people just to line your own pockets.'

Cam had often before witnessed Rose in a fury, but she had never seen her appear quite so enraged. Shaking uncontrollably, she screamed, 'I've already been robbed of one chance to get what I want after fifteen years' hard work. I'm not about to let your rob me of this one!' She launched herself at Ann in an attempt to grab her handbag off her, but forgot that the other woman was twice her size and not about to let her get away with what she was attempting. Ann put up one beefy arm and shoved her away.

Rose stumbled and fell to the floor. She stared wildly up at Ann then her mother. Her mind was thrashing for a way to turn this situation back in her favour, but her mother had well and truly put a stop to her plans. As matters stood, she had no means to better herself nor to fund any other plan she might come up with. Then suddenly all she could see was a red mist whirling before her eyes and she could hear someone screaming hysterically.

What she didn't realise, in her torment, was that the horrendous screams were in fact coming from her.

CHAPTER THIRTY-TWO

Cam looked through the glass screen into the room beyond and watched Rose having a conversation with herself. She was amazed to see her daughter actually laughing and joking with her imaginary friends.

The night Ann and she had gone to inform Rose that they had put a stop to her scheme, an ambulance had to be sent for as she wouldn't stop screaming and throwing herself around the room. They had both feared for her safety. Rose was committed to a psychiatric ward. The doctor there had informed Cam that it was his opinion her daughter had been tipped over the edge after learning something that her brain couldn't accept. She had now taken herself off into an imaginary world where she was able to achieve what had obviously been denied her in the real world.

Cam knew just what it was that Rose had failed to achieve, but for Lindy's sake she didn't want it to get out. It did, though, give her much comfort to know that her daughter was at long last happy in the world she had created for herself, as she had never been happy in the real one. There was nothing Cam could do for her now. All her care was directed at the girl Rose had almost sacrificed in her attempt to become rich.

It was four weeks since Rose had been committed and Lindy was making good progress towards coming to terms with her mother's true nature and accepting that she had not been capable of loving herself, let alone anyone else. Cam only hoped that the love she showered on the girl would go a long way to making up for the lack of a mother's love.

311

Lindy's remorse and shame at the way she had treated her grand-mother had been apparent and it had taken Cam a while to convince Lindy that she bore no grudges. In fact, she was just relieved to have Lindy back with her again and for Lindy to know that Cam was not guilty of the things Rose had accused her of.

Cam felt a presence by her side and turned to see that Ann had joined her. She had instinctively known that her friend had not been looking forward to seeing her daughter in such a place as this and had insisted on coming along to support her, as she always had done in Cam's times of need.

Ann observed Rose through the window for a moment and patted Cam's arm before saying. 'I never thought I'd see her smile. It does my heart good to witness it at last. Her face looks so different without that permanent scowl on it. I'd even go as far as to say she looks . . . well, pretty.' She then turned to look at Cam. 'Rose proved to be nothing but a worry and a heartache to you, from the minute she was born. You never asked to have the burden of her. I know this is not the way you would have wished, but you've been relieved of that burden now. You know that she's happy with herself at last, when you'd lost hope she ever could be. Now you're back where you should have been thirty years ago, before that man committed his vile act against you and left you with this legacy. You're about to marry the love of your life, and you, Adrian and Lindy are going to become the happy family you had lost hope of ever having.'

Cam took her hand and squeezed it affectionately. 'If I hadn't had you for a friend, Ann, I wouldn't have got through the last thirty years and have such a good future to look forward to. I owe you so much.'

She squeezed Cam's hand in return. 'Well, it did help me at the time to know that if the roles had been reversed you would have done exactly the same for me.'

'Actually, there is a way I hope to be able to repay you. Ann, I'd like you to give me away at my wedding.'

Her friend had tears glinting in her eyes now. 'You mean that? You actually want me to give you away?'

'I would be so honoured if you would. You've been beside me

all the other times I've needed your support, why break the habit of a lifetime?'

The tears in Ann's eyes were not just at Cam's wonderful gesture, they were also at the fact that, at long last, she knew without doubt that her friend, in future, was not going to need the kind of help she had given her in the past.